JUICY GHOSTS

BY RUDY RUCKER

Transreal Books

Hardback ISBN: 978-1-940948-48-5
Paperback ISBN: 978-1-940948-54-6
Ebook ISBN: 978-1-940948-50-8

The cover art is *Invaders*, by Rudy Rucker.
Versions of three chapters appeared as short stories.
"Treadle's Inauguration" in *Big Echo*, October, 2019,
as "Juicy Ghost."
"The Mean Carrot" in *Big Echo*, March, 2020.
"Mary Mary" in *Isaac Asimov's SF*, March, 2021.

Transreal Books
Los Gatos, California
www.transrealbooks.com

CONTENTS

THE MEAN CARROT

"Hi, I'm Molly. Do I know you?"

I hit him with my smile and widen my eyes. I touch him on his cheek. He's weathered, but handsome, in a costume-party way, and with a beard. He's far from being a Californian. A Euro tech bro? Quiet, watchful, and with a feral quality, like a dog with no master.

"Now known," says he. "I'll message you a link to my lifebox. You may research how awesome is Anselm Saarikoski of Copenhagen. Product designer for the Finn Junkers. I'm sending you my link. Well known in cool circles. Junker is an old word that means young noble. We're not noble by family tree, but by—extreme excellence."

The soft plastic uvvy phone on the back of my neck twitches. Anselm has sent me a link to his cloud-based lifebox—the kind of personal database we used to call a home page. The word *lifebox* carries with it the buzzy hope that, as tech moves forward, we might someday have immortal online souls.

Digital souls are a type of project that the Finn Junkers might work on. I know about them, and I'm now remembering that I've vaguely heard of Anselm too. I'll tell him some of this in a minute. But for the moment, I'll go for mystery. I sway to the music, faintly smiling, watching him. Setting the hook.

He wears sandals with socks, and he has a really large duffle bag at his feet. Like for a musical instrument. Or maybe it's a suitcase, and he's in the process of changing apartments.

The party is in a concrete yard behind a one-story wood house off Judah Street in San Francisco. So many parties I've been to this year, so many high hopes, so many nulls. Ross Treadle is crushing our country's soul. Him and this Top Party, and their big-money backers, the Citadel Club. We have an informal countermovement—we're called the freals, and there's a lot of us—but somehow I'm losing hope. While I've been partying, summer ended and the leaves fell.

The chirpy, thuddy music feels heartbreaking, the way it mixes with the traffic's hoarse roar, the beeping of drones, the ecstatic mad-house shrieks of unseen brain zappers, and the tragic sense that the U.S. is done. Like I'm in a bummer movie about a spoiled world. But it's not a movie. It's my life, the only life I'll ever have.

I'm still dancing, still looking at Anselm, kind of wishing I could feed him the full scope of my thoughts, without even using words. Send him my feelings, my dreams, and my sense of what it's like in this corner of the world. In short, I wish I had full teep—which is short for telepathy. My research group is working on it.

My roommate Leeta Patel and I are friends with the host, Qumar, who throws a cash-bar networking party every Wednesday. Qumar is a deal-maker, a freal, a biotech investor, and to some extent an artist. His person-sized kritters creep around—where a kritter is any kind of gene-tweaked, wetware-engineered organism.

I see a traditional eyeball with wings, a rolling scroll of Sanskrit writing, President Ross Treadle as a rotting zombie, and a kritter like an avenging angel. The party is a typical scene for me—soiled, hip, and despairing—a lure for the outsiders we scam.

"I work for One Wow," I tell Anselm, sending him my lifebox link. "A wetware engineer."

"I know," Anselm now tells me. "I've been hoping to meet precisely you. That's why I appear at this particular party. I positioned myself—and you came to the bait."

"Greetings, brother," I say, recognizing a kindred spirit. "So you know that One Wow is testing kritters for full teep—with emotions included. Our current test product is called stumble. Makes you feel gooood." I cock my head and look playful. Running a come-on routine—even though Anselm's far from being a rube off the street. "Want a dose?"

"Accelerated intimacy protocols," remarks Anslem.

"This party is that kind of scene," I say. "Net and get. Know and show. We feel like we're running out of time. What with the Treadle election coming up."

"I am ear," says the bearded Anselm. I'm not sure if this is bad English, or if he's being poetic.

"What things do you like?" I ask, by way of getting to know him. Talking is more fun than scanning his lifebox site.

Anselm makes a gesture that takes in the motley guests, the shabby bungalows, and the nanopercenter city beyond. He gives a gentle smile. "I grew up in Finland. And there, to feel good, we go to a wooden sauna house. We sweat, whack ourselves with birch switches, jump in the lake. Tingly."

"How might we translate that into a San Francisco experience for you?" I ask.

"A naked hug with you?" he suggests. "If I dare dream. Is this rude?"

"It's not rude, but it's unlikely. We're talking about you beta-testing a high-end teep product. And I don't have sex with men. But, yes, I want to know you. Spill some more of your soul, reindeer man."

"I'm here all this week with my Mean Carrot. Sniffing out the top players in the biotech teep race. Especially your crowd at One Wow. I'm also making inquiries about the weaponized teep research at the Top Party lab. It's in a hardened bunker beneath their headquarters. Odd that those right-wingers have their national headquarters in San Francisco, isn't it?"

"They did it to get in our face," I say. "Also a couple of tech tycoons went darkside. They helped found the Top

Party's giga-donor group: the Citadel Club. What's in that Top Party bunker lab anyway?"

"Word is, they have a tank with six human brains linked together. Old school mad science. Six Top Party brains? Why not consult a gaggle of gabbling geese? They have a biocomputing mass like a cow liver as well, using it to emulate a mausoleum for top-ranking Top Party lifebox minds." Anselm shrugs. "Many leads, lots of talk, piles of bullshit. I am lonely. The zero in the one. Vibrate your voice to me, kind Molly Santos."

"Who says I'm kind? You gonna test my new teep fungus with me or not?"

Right about now Anselm's floppy duffel bag crawls onto my foot. I squawk and hop away. One end of the bag is tightly packed, but the end near me is almost empty. Something writhes beneath the synthetic cloth.

"What's in there?" I ask.

"He is a narrow orange cone, five feet long, with a twisting tip, and green leaves at his plump end." Anselm chuckles, amused by himself. "He is not a reptile." He gives me a quizzical, expectant look. There's something *off* about this guy. That semi-autistic hacker vibe, but odder. The man has been *around*.

"I'm supposed to play Twenty Questions?" I ask.

"You have adequate information already. Reprocess."

"Oh! He's that Mean Carrot you talked about?"

Gravely Anselm nods. "He is a prototype grown by Gee Willikers for Finn Junkers. Gee is an old friend of mine, and some of Gee's wetware is also being used by your One Wow. Huffy and the gossip molecule. I'm sure you know this."

"You're in with Gee!" I exclaim. "I should have realized. Yes, we were indeed testing Gee's huffy mold. And then I redesigned it to get stumble for One Wow. Stumble uses the same gossip molecule that Gee used with huffy. But stumble is cleaner. Huffy nearly killed my friend Leeta. That's her over there."

"I know Leeta," says Anselm. "Gee and I met her when she came to Copenhagen spring." Anselm is shaping up as very interesting.

Right about then, the Mean Carrot humps up against my shin, and pulses against me like a rutting dog, although he's still inside the bag. The material is damp. It's too much.

"I don't have to take this from you," I snap. "We're done."

I turn away and signal for Leeta. She and I watch each other's backs when we're recruiting. She's working a prospect across the courtyard. I'll go join her.

Anselm's face crumples like a child's. He kicks the Mean Carrot's bag so hard that he hurts his toe, which is no surprise, given that he's wearing those guh-roovy sandals. He stands on one foot, holding his toe and moaning like a cartoon character. I burst out laughing.

"Do use me for your stumble test!" Anselm begs. Are those tears in his eyes? Even though he's a player, he's coming on like the biggest goob I ever met. Like he's a cartoon. Gingerly he puts his weight on his foot. Raises his forearms with his hands dangling down like puppy paws.

"Please, *Maammo*? I need to learn how you mutated the huffy mold into the stumble tree-ear mushroom. I admire your craft, Molly. Like you, we Finn Junkers are on the road from peep to teep."

"Peep?" I ask.

"That's what Gee Willikers and I call lo-fi uvvy-style telepathy," says Anselm. "Belittling it. Peep is a weak sound made by a newly hatched chick. Full teep will voice our thoughts with the resonance of roosters."

Uvvies, just as they are, have already driven smartphones out of business. Uvvies are soft lumps of intelligent computational piezoplastic. An uvvy uses quantum vortex fields to probe into the user's brain, reading and writing info.

When I place an uvvy call to you, the uvvy on my neck analyzes the words or images in my brain, encodes the info as brainwaves, and sends the brainwaves to your uvvy. In turn, your uvvy extracts the info from the brainwaves, and then uses its quantum vortex fields to put the info into *your* brain. Very smooth, very seamless. The brainwaves travel via ultraweak wireless.

At the risk of boring the shit out of you, I'll say a word about ultraweak wireless. It's quite distinct from the wireless signals that were used for old-school smartphones. The giggle is that *ultraweak* wireless is in fact much *stronger*. It's not a standard electromagnetic-wave-type signal at all. Ultraweak wireless uses new physics. It wriggles out of our workaday four-dimensional spacetime continuum, out into the raw Hilbert space of quantum mechanics, and wings wildly through those lofty caverns, unfettered by mundane niggling factors such as distance or signal power. You teep someone via ultraweak wireless, and, baby, you're *there*. And even so feeble an organ as a human brain has the *oomph* to power it.

So this is all very cool. But transferring actual emotions is beyond the abilities of uvvies. And that's the next step.

"We want more than video phone calls in our heads," I say, agreeing with Anselm. "More than sending my subvocal speech to your auditory nerves. More than sending the images I see."

"Hi-res teep will be when we're sharing our emotions," agrees Anselm. "True teep means being *understood*. That's what Gee's gossip molecules are for. They let you exchange neurochemicals, right? And the chemicals are triggers for emotions."

This guy is right on the beam. "Do you have a car?" I ask. His duffel bag is motionless. The Mean Carrot is on his best behavior.

"I approximately have a car," says Anselm. "Where would we go?"

"To my apartment, like I've been talking about. South of Market. I share it with Leeta. With the lank black hair? Kind of gawky? She's recruiting a volunteer, too. The four of us will have a research encounter. Stumble teep, right? No birch branch beatings. And, Anselm, you leave that skeevy

Mean Carrot outside our apartment—or I'll goddamn well chop him into disks."

"One cannot so easily damage the mighty Mean Carrot of Anselm Saarikoski and Gee Willikers," goes Anselm. "This carrot is highly robust. He can function as a valet, an enforcer, or, if need be, an emergency medical tech. But, fine, I accept that the Mean Carrot waits in the street. I'll leave my valuables with him."

"Oh, now you don't trust me?"

"I make no judgments. I anticipate outcomes. Once you and I are in the apartment, you place a curl of stumble fungus against my skull. I have a *grand mal* seizure, or no—" He closely studies my face, as if reading my thoughts. "No, I fall into a state of paralysis. I savor the sweets of teep. A golden moment of neurochemical intimacy with you, my charming Molly, with our brains in molecular resonance. And then—perhaps I awaken in the street, naked and bruised." He shoots me a stern look. "Mark you this: the Mean Carrot will resolve all contested issues."

"Quite the man of the world, aren't we?"

"I am Finnish," says Anselm. "Our tongue resembles the Hungarian language and the speech of the Sami, who live high above the Arctic circle. I sing birds from non-existent trees. Like every Finn, I deserve to have my biography written." Pleased with his speech, he smooths his beard.

"Let's go."

I flip Leeta a thumbs-up. We work with Chex Chapster, a fellow contractor for One Wow. He's like an aide. He lurks in our apartment, eating takeout, processing video feeds, uploading data to One Wow. He's obsessed with the stock market, and he's always reading the *Wall Street Journal*. He wears a crewcut and a tie and a crumpled charcoal suit. He feels he's retro and ironic. And he likes me, although not in a sexual way. Not Chex.

It might appear that One Wow pays Leeta and me to party. But we're scientists doing hands-on research. Well, I'm the scientist. Leeta is more like an embedded project manager.

Initially I imagined that luring and doping our subjects would be exciting, in a transgressive way. But it's dull. Thankfully we don't have sexual intercourse with our victims. Some of them might *think* we do—but that's an illusion.

During a session, Leeta, our test subjects, and I share true teep. Not only do we converse and share images as with the uvvy, but we also swap emotions and over-all body sensations. Making that work is a matter of exchanging neurochemicals. And that's where the gossip molecules come in.

Aside from all this, I have a personal issue. The stumbles get me high. They don't hit everyone that way, but for me it's a problem. I'm hooked. I frikkin *live* for my stumble sessions. I can't go on this way. But I do.

As we leave the party, Qumar is near the exit, dancing with a dragon-shaped kritter. I uvvy Qumar a payment, and usher Anselm outside. Turns out that Anselm's "approximately a car" is, oh wow, a big sleigh with tufted leather bench seats and giant curly runners. Like something a horse would pull. It's black. And it's alive.

I'm delighted. "For real?"

"Thanks to my excellent taste in product design, the Finn Junkers are fielding a surreal bagatelle of prototypes. Including the Mean Carrot and this Happy Sleigh. Her name is Vixen." Anselm slings the bagged Mean Carrot into the back seat. "Vixen's runners can act as a magnetic drive." Anselm beams at me. "Tonight she emulates a pirate streetcar. Help me align Vixen on the rails, and then I raise the pantograph."

"What's that supposed to mean?"

"The pantograph is the trolley pole that drinks the electricity that Vixen enjoys to eat. And Vixen lifts herself above the rails."

"Aren't the real trolleys mad at you?"

"In Copenhagen, yes, Gee and I get in trouble for our Happy Sleigh. She's not allowed on the rails. She's all right on any land or water, but she like rails. And thus far in San Francisco nobody says boo. You people—so loose, so rich, so high. You *like* to see a Happy Sleigh trolley, yes? And now you and I ride her."

"Ooo," I exclaim. Is this bearded Finn the one to cure my raging stumble habit? The one to guide Leeta and me to commercial teep? I raise my voice another octave. "Where's your sack, Santa?"

Anselm smiles and pats the bag with the Mean Carrot. Vixen's runners wriggle, and she scoots onto the tracks of the Judah line. I hop into the comfy front seat and snuggle against a wooly blanket, like Lara in *Dr. Zhivago*. Anselm flips up the paradiddle or hockey stick or whatever he calls it. A gratifyingly huge spark explodes. I catch a summer-storm whiff of ozone.

"On Vixen!" cries Anselm. We rise a tiny bit into the air. I peer over the edge. Fronds of mini-sparks shower from the runners to the rails. And before we can start, here comes Leeta and her date, tumbling out of the house, with Leeta whooping and tossing her hair. She and her victim pile into our sled's back seat, and we glide down Judah Street toward town.

Leeta was born in Bangalore, but her family moved here when she was young. She matured into a full-on California geek, complete with four years in the undergrad biotech management program at UC Berkeley. For reasons she doesn't care to share, she got expelled without a degree, which may be why she has this highly transactional job with One Wow. Leeta is normally staid, even dull, but she can vamp with the best of them when it suits her needs.

"I'm Loftus," says Leeta's catch of the day. He looks like a cowhand instead of like a techie. Solidly built, talks with a drawl, strides with a strut, and even wears a frikkin cowboy hat. All kinds of people are in town for the biotech goldrush.

"I'm a little spooked about this here stumble stuff," Loftus continues. "I don't want to go and lose my mind. Gonna need my mind come morning."

"You'll be okay by lunch time," I tell Loftus. "Just remember to scrape off the stumble crust when you get up. It grows tiny filaments into your brain. Technically known as hyphae. In the morning, they'll be dead like the stumble. But the scraping helps. Take a hot shower, drink a bunch of coffee, and you'll be good to go."

"Don't alarm our boy with your stumblebum tips," says the oblivious Leeta. "All he needs to know is that he's about to party San Francisco style. The One Wow research lab is fun!"

"I'd still like to know more about what stumble does," presses Loftus.

As always, I have to wonder if our test subject is an industrial spy. I'll lay some info on him and see if he lights up. I was a teaching assistant when I was a grad student at UC Santa Cruz.

"A stumble is a rind of fungus that takes up residence on the side of your head," I tell Loftus. "The stumble has smooth, slightly sticky flesh. It grows filaments or hyphae through the pores of your skull, and it tunes in on your brain activities, accessing a rich sample of your mental life. And it uses gossip molecules to send and receive emotions."

Loftus chuckles vapidly. It's not clear which parts of the explanation he does or does not understand.

"The stumble broadcasts signals, using your skull as an ultraweak wireless antenna," I conclude.

"Why?" say Loftus.

"What the fuck are you trying to ask me?" I say.

"What's in it for the stumble crust?" says Loftus.

"The stumble wants to have, virtual sex with stumble fungi on other people's heads," says Leeta. "And to swap gene codes with them. A standard reproduction move. Once your stumble has jiggered its genes, it puffs out fresh spores. And then it dies. And on its way out, it tells its tendrils in your head to die too. All in a night's work."

The city lights stream past.

"Score," says Loftus. "I'm all set. On my way to get zonked with Anselm Saarikoski."

"How do you know my last name?" says Anselm.

"Hell, I heard Leeta say it," Loftus easily responds. "She was talking about you at the party. Said you was a big deal."

"You remember me too, eh, Leeta?" says Anselm. "You made quite an impression on Gee Willikers and me in Copenhagen."

"Gee was supposed to offer me a job," says Leeta. "As you very well know. But he didn't follow through. And look what a cruddy gig I have now."

"We'll talk tomorrow," promises Anselm. "We'll work something out."

"I bet," says Leeta, letting her irritation show. "And what's this stupid bulky bag under my feet? It's wriggling! Can't we ever find *normal* test-subjects, Molly? I mean, here we are with cowboy and a Finnish con man."

"That's my bodyguard in the bag," goes Anselm. "Or, in another sense, he's my colleague. Undo the zipper, Leeta. Let my friend out."

So Leeta frees the Mean Carrot, and right away the carrot squirms heavily onto Leeta's lap and reaches over to Loftus, and knocks Loftus's hat into the street, and wraps his tip around his Loftus's neck, and feels all over the increasingly annoyed man's craggy face, the carrot tickling Loftus's nostrils with root hairs. Loftus doesn't like this at all. He's yelling so hard that cords in his neck are standing out, and I'm giggling like mad. For once I'm having fun.

"Down boy," Anselm says to Loftus.

"That was a damn good hat," gripes Loftus. "It was a Stetson."

"I'll pay you back," says Leeta, keeping him on the hook. "Remind me later."

The Mean Carrot worms into the front seat and gets in between the Finn and me. The carrot is ringed by wrinkles seamed with dirt. The annular grooves form eye slits, a nose bump, and a mouth. He doesn't actually look all that mean. Serious and thoughtful is more like it—if a giant carrot can be deemed thoughtful. He's as big as a thirteen-year-old kid, with no arms or legs. On top, his ragged green leaves flutter in the chill October air. His tip twitches on the floor by our feet.

"Hey thar, Mean Carrot," say I, talking like Loftus. The carrot's flesh is hard as mahogany. I'm starting to feel giddy because, addict that I am, I'm heavily previsualizing tonight's stumble trip.

The Mean Carrot studies me, twists around, looks at Leeta, and emits a thin wolf whistle.

"No," says Anselm, as if answering the Mean Carrot. "That's not appropriate, Mean Carrot. Molly Santos and Leeta Patel aren't what you think they are." He turns to me. "Forgive the carrot's rudeness."

"We're high priests of biotech," calls out Leeta from the back. "Same as Anselm and Gee. Abandon all hope, Loftus." She lets out a wild burst of laughter. Back to playing the flirt. Leading Loftus down the garden path. She's had too much to drink. Leeta really can't hold her alcohol.

"I'm game for anything," says Loftus.

"The man is suspiciously meek," I say. "Do we trust him?"

"He better not be from the Ross Treadle campaign!" Leeta shouts. She thumps Loftus on the top of his head, maybe not all that hard, but Loftus is taken aback. "No false moves," Leeta adds, wagging a finger. "We're freal terrorists, you ought to know."

"Thanks a *lot* for saying we're terrorists," I tell Leeta. I turn my attention to Loftus. "She's wasted, man. We're harmless. Science Barbie and *Biz* Babe. So don't got ratting us out to your fellow pigs at the Top Party."

"I ain't no damn Treadler," says Loftus. "So take it easy, you two nuts."

"I'm lost in dreams," says Anselm, making his voice thin and reedy. "I hope only that my stumble trip includes visions of Molly's beaming face." He gives me a veiled look. "I am like the hobo who gets a cup of coffee in return for his blood. A beggar on your threshold. Hoping for a simple act of human goodness."

"Stumble sex is very, very abstract," I primly tell Anselm. "It's neurochemicals from gossip molecules."

"Yes, yes, I know," says Anselm. "I helped Gee Willikers orchestrate the open source release of the ribbon diagrams for huffy fungus and the gossip molecules."

"I've always wondered why Gee gives away things that valuable," I say. "Is he stupid, or what?"

"He does it to make a better world for us all," says Anselm, looking wise with his beard.

"Hah!" puts in Leeta. "I bet Gee is planning for a bigger project down the line. He's crowdsourcing development work from the rest of us."

"Fancy talk," says Loftus, wanting to get back in the conversation. "I like you guys. I'm still in on tonight's action, right?"

"Oh, sure," says Leeta. "Molly and I get a finder's fee for each test subject we bag."

"Deep teep with Loftus will be revealing," says Anselm. "He's not the kind of person one often meets."

Our streetcar tracks swerve left, and we're tooling up Market Street amid seething crowds with knots of rioters: Increasingly anxious backers of Sudah Mareek, violent Treadle stooges, hardcore freals with shock batons, cops trying the keep the peace, and provocateurs with spasmo-darts. Amidst the chaos, ball walkers wend their way, delivering food and drink. Two-legged, armless kritters with big, hollow heads.

Today is Wednesday, October 27, and the Presidential election is in six days, on Tuesday, November 2. We've had the fascist, narcissistic, heartless Ross Treadle as President for nearly eight years, and he's looking to claim a third term at behest of his donors, the Citadel Club.

Congress and the courts have made the third-term option legal. It's not clear if Treadle's rival, Sudah Mareek, is going to be able to beat him, nor is it clear if she'll be allowed to take office if she *does* win the vote. Leeta and I hope our new high-end version of teep might somehow help block Treadle, but the clock is ticking fast.

Some of the rioters point at us on the sled, like they're trying to figure out if we're pro-Treadle or pro-freal. I raise my palm and do a beauty-queen wave.

"I hope we're near your flat," says Anselm. "Ugly America. The Treadlers—their faces are so doughy and askew. What's happened to you people? How did you sink so low?"

Hard to answer that. "Turn at Fifth Street," is all I say. "Our place is two blocks in."

Loftus wants to talk to Anselm about Vixen. "I think I caught some teep of you telling Molly Santos here that a Happy Sleigh can run without rails?"

Anselm glares at him. "You planning to pirate the design?"

"Open for offers," says Loftus. "I get around."

"Do you happen to know anything about the Top Party's plans for the Treadle campaign?" asks Anselm, getting right down to it. "I'm hearing chatter about a brain-control virus called Treadle Disease. It's in the prototype stage. A physical virus. Like a germ. Are you in on that?"

"You got the wrong guy," protests Loftus. "I'm a tourist from the farm. So lighten up on me or I'll kick your moth-erfucking ass."

"A thug *and* a spy," snarls Anselm.

"All I want is a seat at the table," says Loftus, shaking his head. He strikes a pose of a beefy innocence. "I'm curious to see what you fellers have."

"If you think teep with Loftus will be *revealing*, don't push him away," I tell Anselm. "It's boring when men spar and roar. Let's get on with the session."

My body is telling me it's stumble time.

Anselm veers off the trolley tracks, and Vixen the Happy Sleigh slides two blocks to an alley off Fifth, moving on her own power. Rippling her runners, helping us along. When we arrive, the Mean Carrot sounds a shrill, wavering note.

"Agreed," Anselm says to the carrot. "You'll guard the sled. And you hurry into Molly's apartment if I whistle for you." He takes out his phone and wallet. The Mean Carrot opens a crack in his side. Anselm stuffs his valuables in there. He glances at Loftus. "You want to stash anything?"

"I'm good," says Loftus. "I can take care of myself."

Fat chance. Loftus thinks he can hold his own against me, Anselm, the Mean Carrot, and *Leeta Patel*? Leeta is ruthless.

The alley winos and brain-stimmers assess the sleigh and admire her curved runners. Anselm gives them some cash, and the bleary posse settles into Vixen's cushioned seats with the Mean Carrot. The big carrot doesn't faze them. So much crazy shit in our lives these days. You take it as it comes.

The apartment is on the third floor of a wood frame rooming house next to the alley. Chex Chapster holds the lease, but it's One Wow who pays the rent. The place really *is* a lab, in that we lure in subjects, test psychoactive biotech on them, and tweak the wetware as we go along. These aren't public double-blind studies; these are skunk works runs. Some products will be withdrawn entirely, some will be distributed via the black market, and some will undertake the rigorous FDA path to legal distribution.

Before I joined the group in June, Leeta was researching that nasty huffy mold. Both huffy and stumble use the gossip molecules that Gee Willikers invented. The gossip molecules allow clients to send templates of their current brain chemicals to each other.

The difference between huffy and stumble is that huffy grows entirely inside your head. You inhale huffy spores to get it started. In the tradition of pioneering health researchers who test new meds on themselves, Leeta snorted huffy spores every day for a week. She was that eager to make a breakthrough—and to move to a higher-level job.

Do keep in mind that, following standard wetware engineering protocol, we develop an antidote or removal drug for each of the biological add-ons that we design. So Leeta was in possession of a huffy scrubber chemical. Therefore, self-testing seemed safe enough.

During each session, the huffy spores would grow a short-lived mold colony in her brain, and the mold would essentially mimic the behavior of an uvvy—and more than that, it was exchanging templates for mood chemicals with other users. During each session, the huffy colonies would complete virtual breeding cycles via the web, and they'd end by puffing new spores out of Leeta's nose. At this point the mold would die. And to be on the safe side, Leeta would inhale a dose of the huffy scrubber.

But Leeta failed to take into account that the *spores* didn't die. Some of them made their way down into her lungs—where they furtively settled in long-term. She developed thick, ropy, growths in her chest. A type of pneumonia, quite resistant to the huffy scrubber. Leeta started having frantic coughing fits, with hard, icky crusts of huffy flying out of her mouth and skittering across the floor. She required two weeks of intravenous huffy-scrubber drip in a private clinic. One Wow gave her a fat cash settlement.

Leeta used her money to spend April and May in Copenhagen, doing her best to break into the cool biotech scene around the Finn Junkers. In particular she wanted to get something going with Gee Willikers, who was visiting with the Junkers. Finally she met him at a party. According to Leeta, Gee said he'd get her a job with the Finn Junkers. The next day, Leeta couldn't find Gee, and the Junkers, including Anselm, weren't up to speed on Gee's informal offer—if he'd really made one—and Leeta's Danish visa was about to expire.

And on top of that, One Wow suddenly offered to double Leeta's salary, and they promised her full autonomy over her team, and a hot new wetware engineer on her staff, said hot engineer being me.

So, start of June, Leeta came back to working at the One Wow apartment lab in San Francisco. And I began there too. The first thing I did for Leeta was to port the huffy teep gene to a tree-ear shelf-mushroom fungus that we ended up calling stumble. We picked the name because the first time we stuck these little mushrooms onto our temples, I got so high I kept falling down. It makes your arms and legs be stiff like wood. Like a mannequin.

I know it's insane for us to be doing self-experimentation—especially after Leeta's fungal pneumonia—but that's how it is on the experimental teep scene. How else would we know how well the stuff works? I engineered a stumble scrubber reagent of course. And the stumble's centralized tree-ear morphology makes it easier to control.

You have no idea how good stumble feels to me by now. It gives me this heavy, mythic sense of life, partly due to the teep, but also thanks to an alkaloid that's in stumbles. Yah, mon. I'm Eve in Eden, Einstein in Zurich, a gull in the sky. In nature, parasites like stumble survive better if they give their users a good buzz. Makes it worth the host's while! And, by the way, Leeta hardly notices the stumble high. Like I say, she's staid.

When Leeta and I get to our apartment with Anselm and Loftus, Chex Chapster opens the door for us. He's cute in his wrinkled suit, and he has the big smile he gets when he sees me.

"Let the mad revels begin," Chex intones. "Welcome to our lair, gents."

As usual Chex is holding his paper copy of the *Wall Street Journal*, open to the stock listings, covered with the tiny hand-written annotations he makes. Where does he even *get* a paper newspaper? Well, he grows it in a bioprint tank. Talk about compulsive. Not that I'm one to point the finger.

"Is today's stumble ripe?" is the first thing I ask.

"In the Petri dishes," goes Chex. He leads us into the kitchen.

A pair of flat glass dishes are set out on the counter, each of them with a layer of gel, each of them inhabited by two or three meaty curls of shelf fungus. Little double-scroll shapes, glossy and leathery, with fuzzy tendrils where they touch the gel. Fresh grown from the stumble spores that Leeta and I hatched last night. The crazy thing about my addiction is that I use my body to grow my supply. A loony loop.

"I'd like to ask Chex about this stuff," says Loftus. "One on one. Not sure I believe what you three con artists are telling me."

"Go for it," Leeta tells Loftus, not really interested. "You and Chex go into the living-room."

So those two are out of the picture for a minute. Leeta and I have our attention on the big fish. On Anselm.

"You ready?" I ask him.

"Indeed," says Anselm. "I'm eager to experience the advances you two have made." He smooths his beard, then presses a curl of stumble to his temple. Fiddles with it for a minute till it settles in. Somewhere in the cloud, One Wow credits me with my finder's fee bonus.

Anselm staggers, and his eyes glaze over. His arms and legs stiffen. He gropes robotically for the kitchen counter lest he fall down. I usher him to a couch in the living-room, then shoo Chex and Loftus back into the kitchen.

"Me next," says Loftus, squaring his shoulders.

Quick to close the deal, Leeta slaps a stumble slug onto Loftus's forehead, accidentally on purpose clawing the guy's skin with her crimson-nail-polished fingernails. Lady Dracula. Then she fits on her own little stumble tree-ear.

"We're getting closer," Leeta says to me before she fades. "Let's show Anselm how good we are."

And then her limbs grow rigid too. In full zombie mode, Loftus and Leeta stomp into the living-room and flop down on the couches.

I take another minute, picking out the plumpest, shiniest stumble curl of them all. I'm savoring this moment of maximum drug-lust. It's the most alive I'll feel all day.

"A word with you?" puts in Chex, doing his cold-war-spy routine.

"What."

"Loftus is an intelligence op." Chex lays his finger along his aquiline beak. "The nose knows."

"We kind of suspected that," I tell him. "But for now we'll let it ride."

"There's something worse," says Chex. "It's not just who Loftus works for. It's who works for *him*."

"What's your point?" I ask, getting impatient. It's time for my damn fix.

"Loftus has suborned me," says Chex. "Covertly crossed my palm with silver. Or with greasy bills."

"Yadda yadda," I say. "Screw the details. Just make sure Leeta and I are safe. Be the hero."

"I'm always on your side," says Chex. "And…Molly?"

"What?"

"You're too good for One Wow. You need to quit."

"Not today."

I position the damp scrap of my stumble fungus on the skin behind my ear. It tingles. My muscles turn sluggish—and I start feeling really good. I stagger into the living-room and drop onto a couch. I'm so far from having sex with Anselm that I hardly notice I'm next to him. We four sit there for a long time, three of us on the one couch, with Leeta stretched out on the other.

In her last moments of vestigial awareness, Leeta has assumed a dramatic pose, leaning back against the cushions with the back of one hand against her forehead. She isn't conventionally beautiful, but she works every possible angle she has. She's a purposeful flirt—like how a Venus flytrap is a flower.

My trip begins; the hours pass. I don't exactly *see* when I'm in deep teep stumblebum mode. But it *feels* like a dark summer night with blinking fireflies. Or like I'm in a sleeper car on a midnight train, and I know there's other passengers in the other trains. Clickety-clack, lights moving past the window.

I love this part, calm and relaxed, riding my stumble like I'm a dead princess on an altar. My thoughts are middle-of-the-night smooth, with nothing to stress about, and nothing to do but breathe. Chilling amid my happy neurons.

The lights around me are the minds of other people on stumble trips. One Wow runs five of these underground test labs. There's at least twenty people in teepspace with me. They're in the Mission, and in Oakland, Pacifica and Santa Cruz. We're all aware of each other. And thanks to the gossip molecules in our brains, our moods ping-pong among us. Our gossip molecules act as biotech assemblers, enhancing the neurochemicals of our peers' emotions.

And, to quote the eloquent Loftus: *Why?* Because our stumbles need to exchange gene codes. It bugs me that a fungus is using our noble telepathy for—*fucking*. So low, so crass.

To make it more galling, the accuracy of the stumble signals isn't what it needs to be, if we're ever use the stuff for practical communication. At this point the voice quality of an uvvy call is much better. I haven't yet finalized the wetware design for stumbles—that's what these test runs are all about.

Regarding teep communication via stumble, I tend to hear several lines of dialog at once—even when I'm only teeping with one person. The things a person leaves unsaid—the teep channel transmits those things too. As well as the voices, there's smells and tingles mixed in, plus clouds of images, and looming sensations of full-body presence.

On top of that, my gossip molecules are continually readjusting my neurochemicals, which jiggles my moods. It can be hard to fit together into a coherent sense of who I'm teeping with, or whether it's more than one person. We contain multitudes.

By four or five in the morning, it's like I'm looking at a crazy shared bulletin board in a college dorm, with random cartoon voices reading the scraps. I stop drifting and bear down. I filter out the offsite minds, and focus on Leeta, Anselm, and Loftus.

Leeta is, as per usual, preoccupied with some kind of business plan.

Loftus is mum—keeping his cards close to his wild-west yee-haw vest.

As for Anselm—here's his jovial voice in my head. "You rang, madame?"

Very clear signal. Seems like during the night, Anselm has tuned his stumble output into razor-sharp hi-fi teep. I've been trying and trying to get into this mode. And frikkin Anselm is already there. He's using stumble teep like the super-uvvy-plus-plus that it's supposed to be.

I feel the shimmer of Anselm's inner self; I taste the shadings of his soul. The guy is too much. An ascended master of interactive product design.

"Is it thou, Hamlet?" I message Anselm, maintaining my cool by going Shakespearean on his ass. I see my words as lilies on the drowned Ophelia's breast. And, yep, that's me floating supine on the glassy brook. Oh, *sigh*. "How dost thou teep so cogently, good sir?"

"I parasitize the parasite," says Anselm. "My signals ride astride my stumble's low, coarse sex codes. They are my steeds. Thus elevated, I chime out my thoughts and moods."

"How opportune that our fungi twine virtual phalli, find nuptial bliss, and birth their bastard codes," I say. "Pray teach me, Anselm, to hone my teep. I would ape thy eloquence, but I wit not how."

"She that hath ear horn, let her hear on," ripostes Anselm. "Loosen all constraints. Pour forth your stream of self—yea unto the fluttering flutes and sad oboes of doom. Forget not to enrich your chat with links to your lifebox and to mine. Context is all, my dear."

I do as told and—*zounds*! "We are as one," I tell Anselm.

"See me see you," says he, passing me a stored image of myself dancing at Qumar's party. He has a crush on me? That's nice, but, as I told him, I don't do men.

"What news of vile Loftus?" I ask. "Canst scry within his knobby, stolid skull?" All I'm getting from Loftus is a low grumble, interspersed with hoarse cheering as if for some asshole sports game. Loftus's thoughts and emotions, if not actively cloaked, are so utterly alien to me as to elude comprehension. But Anselm reads him like a book.

"Loftus has paid Chex to squash his stumble," says Anselm dropping the Shakespeare routine. "I think Chex wanted to warn you. But you didn't give him time. You wanted your fix. It's stupid to get addicted to products you research, Molly." He flashes an image of animated rule-book with skinny arms and legs. The tome wears glasses. It wags an elderly finger.

I respond with a three-level utterance: "Go to Hell." / "I long to heal." / "Tell more of Loftus."

"Loftus will mash the main bodies of our tree-ear stumbles against our heads," says Anselm. "He'll do it so abruptly that the stumbles don't shut down their hyphae tendrils. Presumably the unleashed hyphae will multiply with no control. And Loftus's employer wonders if the hyphae levels might plateau, and give us persistent teep."

"I mislike this. I do dread it exceedingly."

"Loftus will do worse," continues Anselm. "Indeed it seems he's targeting me. But for your sake, I'm glad I came. You don't have a proper supply of stumble scrubber. Sloppy addict that you've become. And putting scrubber fluid into your brain—you'd have little luck with that. Especially when you're high."

I'm stung by his rebukes—but I act snotty just the same. "I only hope your hysterical auguries are ill-founded."

"*Snap out of it!*" blasts Anselm. "You're likely to *die!* Why oh why do you and Leeta run unsupervised tests on yourselves? That's for noobs and stoners. Trust me now. I'll get you two into the Finn Junkers. You can play with the pros."

It doesn't take me long to decide. "I say yea."

We need this guy. I don't have much confidence in Chex's powers to defend us when Loftus goes ape. I try and alert Leeta, teeping her some mental images of exploding sky-rockets. But for the moment, she's way down in her stumble's metabolism, trying to pinpoint the cause of her tree-ear's bad audio.

Anselm teeps a trumpet blast and an image of the golden horn.

"Arise!" he cries "Chex has squashed Loftus's stumble slug! But his tendrils are still teeping. Low thoughts like lumpy yellow dog-vomit in a pungent cloud of stink. Here he comes and—*ack!*"

Something crude rams against me. My vision of teep-space contracts to a point—then explodes in a flash. Loftus has mashed the main body of the stumble fungus on the side of my head. A smear of pain. But my hyphae tendrils pulse on undisturbed. I toss and shudder, on the verge of a seizure. *Keep it together, Molly.*

I blink twice—and reenter the workaday world. I touch the wet remains of my own stumble behind my ear. The night is done. It's dawn.

All knees and elbows, Loftus is wrestling with Anselm. Loftus's stumble is a smear beside the scratch on his forehead. And Anselm's squashed stumble is like a road-rash scrape on the side of his head. Loftus is holding a little black thorn. Like he wants to stab it into Anselm.

All three of us still have teep. I can see into Anselm's and Loftus's minds; I can taste their brain chemicals; I hear their neurons' inner songs. I can teep Leeta as well. She's slumped on her couch with her stumble still intact, seemingly asleep, but not really.

"Stay away from Loftus," Chex warns me aloud. He stands in the door between the kitchen and the living-room. But that's all he's doing.

"You were supposed to protect me," I yell.

He shrugs. "You're doing okay. Anselm's the one in trouble. Loftus's people want to kidnap him."

"Not if I can help it," I say.

I lean over the grappling pair of men and pound my elbow into the back of Loftus's neck—just so. I know my pressure points. This isn't nearly so brutal a beatdown as I'd like to lay on Loftus, but it's enough. He collapses and lies still.

With pleasure I deep-teep the flexing geometry of Anselm's limbs as he gains his feet.

"Dear friend," say I. There's a dot of blood on Anselm's neck, and a black dot in the middle. Shit. Loftus shoved in the thorn.

Anselm senses my unspoken questions. But all he says is, "My lady."

The next act of our play begins.

Solemn in his beard, Anselm produces a tiny silver whistle and blows it very hard. I don't hear the sound. But I know who he's calling. The Mean Carrot.

Around now Loftus surges from the floor like a breaching humpback whale. He has some ridiculous plastic handcuffs he wants to put on Anselm. We take off running, with Loftus behind us.

It's like a cartoon, especially with Anselm in his sandals. Loftus chases us around the living-room, down the hall to my bedroom, through my bedroom to the kitchen, across the kitchen into Leeta's room, then back into the living-room. Just to be that much more of a prick, Loftus squashes Leeta's stumble as he passes.

Leeta was ready for this. She leaps at Loftus, head-butting the burly man's midriff. Loftus gasps and staggers back. Chex darts over, and with a finicky, precise hook of his well-shod foot, he yanks Loftus's right leg out from under him. Loftus hits the floor with the back of his head—an enormous, rebounding bonk—and for the second time in five minutes, he's out cold. Chex scoots back to the kitchen door and plays the innocent bystander—just in case Loftus wins.

Anselm turns gleeful, like a puppet-show elf, hopping up and down, chanting a kind of nursery rhyme: "Garden gnome, garden gnome, beware the frightful garden gnome!" Anselm says this over and over, merrily skipping about. He doesn't seem to care about that thorn in his neck.

Loftus is blank, and Anselm is into his chant, but I'm getting good teep off Leeta, channeled by our undead stumble hyphae. I see nested shells of light around Leeta, and I see a hidden thong of stumble hyphae between the hemispheres of her brain. It's a moment of calm for us two, a deep level of intimacy.

Our conversation goes beyond words, and into glyphs, thought blocks, body sensations, memories—and moods.

Each of us knows how the other one feels—we know it all the way down. And meanwhile we're teeping about—what? New careers, and finding better paths to commercial, emotion-compliant teep, and—lest we forget—saving our nation from that foul and insane criminal, President Ross Treadle. Oh, and the meaning of life.

Somehow we become captivated with the silly phrase: *Love is All You Knead.* It's something that one of us saw somewhere—on a sign, or on a cook's apron—a corny joke beneath notice. But at this moment we feel a need to think about it.

Why? Well, one reason that Leeta and I get along is that we're both rather low on the empathy spectrum. Like I said before, Science Barbie and Biz Babe. Stone cold loners. But here our full-meltdown psychic union. *Love is All You Knead*—we can dig that. And wow, here comes a companion phrase—*Everything Is Kneadable.* Yes. The twinned phrases are the final answer. Meaning? If I could only open my heart, I wouldn't need stumble stim to help me feel good. Check. I snap back into an awareness of the room.

Loftus is coming back to life. For sure I'm not feeling any empathy for *that* guy. Meanwhile someone is heavily thumping up our apartment-building's stairs.

"Time to go," I tell Anselm, nodding my head toward the living-room window.

"*Joo.*" Finnish for yes.

I teep for Leeta to come, but she has a different strategy. She'll exit the living-room and lurk in the bedroom, out of sight.

The apartment door splinters. It's the Mean Carrot! The tough-guy vegetable curls his pointy end beneath himself and raises his thick end like a giant's fist, ready to smite. Loftus darts for cover in the kitchen.

By now Anselm and I are out the window and on the fire escape above the alley. Anselm's sleigh Vixen is down there in a poodle, puddle, patch of early morning sunlight. The winos have cleared out. Anselm and I scurry down the fire escape. The Mean Carrot follows us, in a festive mood, squealing as he toboggans down the metal steps.

Loftus crawls out onto the fire escape too, very angry. He leans over the railing and waves a rail-gun pistol that's like a fat, shiny, L-shaped candy-bar. So typical for that kind of man.

"I need to take Anselm to Boom Consumer Metrics for tests!" His voice is all deep and pompous and official. "Don't make me use force."

Despite Loftus's teep, he's lost track of Leeta. A type-two error. In full attack mode, she rampages out the living-room window and shoves Loftus so hard that he somersaults over the railing, and falls toward the street, thrashing and screaming the whole way.

Keep in mind that at this moment, Leeta, Anselm, Loftus, and I are in telepathic contact with each other. So this is very intense. A reality that's gnarlier than a hallucination.

Loftus lands—dammit—on one of Vixen's cushioned seats, which is lucky for him, and he lands on his upper back, even luckier. Like a stunt-man. He's still clutching his dick-substitute pistol. I sample the stew of greed and anger in his head. Aggro numb-nuts that he is, he still imagines he's going to take charge.

"Drive this sled to the Top Party bunker lab!" he orders Anselm. "I'm taking you in."

Just then Loftus's teep signal goes bonkers, I mean *way* over the top, and something very nasty begins. The out-of-control mass of stumble hyphae inside Loftus's brain is generating a crop of fruiting bodies. More tree ears. Lots of them. The shrooms wriggle out of his ears, burst in a slimy bouquet from his mouth, flute from his nostrils, and form fringes around the edges of his eyes. His eyeballs glaze over, turn gray, and burst into twin clouds of spores. Loftus keels over—off the sled and onto the pavement.

"Yuk," say I.

Not done yet, the stumble colony's growth goes hyper-exponential. A few seconds later Loftus's body is an indecipherable patch of street crud. A flattened log of sinew, like the corpse of a dog well-ripened on a country road, and repeatedly run over by cars, rife with rot and fungi.

"That's a stumble design flaw I meant to discuss with you," says Anselm, all poker-faced.

"We're fucked," I groan.

"No, no," says Anselm, "Gee and I have a fix. Hey, Mean Carrot! Synthesize and deploy the stumble scrubber. Quick!"

And, yes, we're healed by the great, orange vegetable himself. Thudding and throbbing, he rushes from Anselm, to me, and then up the fire escape to Leeta. The Mean Carrot twirls his bristly, stumble-scrubber-dampened tip into our nostrils, down our throats, around our ears and—most important of all—he darts his wet root hairs through the porous stumble-site wounds on our heads and into the recesses of our skulls, and thus he expunges every percolating stumble hyphae remnant from our bods.

We three are well. Our teep is gone. Leeta skips down the fire escape with her arms held wide. She's singing the theme song of a Bollywood musical that she loves. Chex comes downstairs too. The four of us hold hands and dance in a circle—with the noble Mean Carrot at the center. Anselm leads us in chanting his pet line over and over again.

"Garden gnome, garden gnome, beware the frightful garden gnome!"

Our harmonizing voices reverberate in the narrow lane. On each cycle, we make the last word longer, deeper, and more resonant. Eventually we collapse, gasping for breath and giggling.

"Take me to Copenhagen?" I ask Anselm.

"*Joo*," says he.

"Can Leeta and Chex come?" I ask.

"Why not?" goes Anselm. "We'll form a research pod within the Finn Junkers. You'll like it. Copenhagen is where it is at. The Freetown Christiana zone?"

"I loved it when was there," puts in Leeta, reminding Anselm. "With Gee Willikers."

"Gee will see you soon," says Anselm, a twinkle in his eye.

"Me, I'm staying on in San Francisco," says Chex. "This apartment is too good to give up. I have my own wide and vibrant circle of friends, you know."

"But, Chex," I say. "One Wow is going to be pissed about tonight. And Loftus's people might come back. Whoever they are. Boom Consumer Metrics?"

"No hits on that from the search nets," says Anselm. "A nonce name. Probably a Top Party front."

"I'm hanging in here till my One Wow stock options vest," continues Chex. "They're all I have. It's not like I'm a bad-ass hacker-genius-girl like you, Molly."

He gives me a courtly peck on the cheek, and scoops Loftus's shiny pistol from the ground, ignoring Loftus's gross remains. Miming one of his world-weary-secret-agent salutes, Chex heads into our apartment building.

An unusually tall ball walker strides past the alley's entrance, as if on an errand. Probably carrying something in her hollow head. I'm slightly worried she might have been sent here to mix with our scene, but she doesn't even glance our way.

It's time to get out of here. Leeta and I have plans of our own—we had some ideas during our minute of pure deep teep in the living-room.

But now the Mean Carrot interrupts my thoughts by piping a questioning tone.

"Of course," Anselm tells the carrot. He turns to me. "You're supposed to punch the Mean Carrot, Molly. Pound that guy as hard as you hit Loftus."

The Mean Carrot stands beside me, resting on his curled tip. He stands as high as my shoulder. His wrinkles are bent into what he means to be a smile. He nods encouragingly. So I thump him in the middle of what you might call his forehead. I hear a tiny *crack*.

The carrot whistles, egging me on.

"Do it furiously!" goes Anselm. "As if you were hammering blindly on a locked door! Use both fists."

So I wail on the Mean Carrot, drumming high and low, not letting up. The cracking noise builds—like the sound of a lake's ice breaking up. As a climax, I let the carrot have it with an elbow to his crucial node. *Whomp.* The orange flesh splits and falls to pieces on the ground.

A wizened figure stands where the Mean Carrot had been. A shrunken, prune-wrinkled man who's been nestled inside the intrepid vegetable all along.

"Presenting Gee Willikers!" cries Anselm with a hoarse gust of laughter.

"Water," says Gee, very faint and husky.

Anselm finds a hose and plays a stream over the shriveled man. He plumps up—and he has a lot of plumping-up to do. Especially his arms and legs. Strange as it seems, the long bones of his arms and legs had been temporarily shorter.

In five minutes, the guy is his own right size—nearly six feet tall. He's a pale male programmer with long hair and thoughtful eyes, quite at ease amid the broken chunks of carrot.

He smirks at me. "Yes, I'm Gee Willikers."

I hold out my hand. "Molly Santos."

Leeta sashays over.

"Nice move" she says. "Glad to see you, Gee." By now we're totally distracted from our worries about needing to rush off.

"Likewise," says Gee. "In Copenhagen I said I wanted to hire you, but first I wanted to see you in action. It took me a while, but here I am. You might say this—" Gee's gesture takes in the Happy Sleigh, the shattered carrot, and Loftus's remains. "This was your job interview. Molly's too. You both passed." He giggles.

"Thanks!" exclaims Leeta. "And we'll work with you and Anselm? On equal terms?"

"Sure," says Gee. "Don't worry about terms. It's about fun."

"And about saving the world from Treadle and the Citadel Club," adds Anselm.

"And that's fun, too," says Gee.

"We're in," I say. "First thing—it's high time to move your gossip molecule tech to some other kind of organism. Not a fungus."

"We're already on it," says Gee. "We're using nudibranchs. Sea slugs? Liv Anders—she's one of the Finn Junkers—she's almost got it done."

"I like sea slugs," says Leeta. "Stripes and dots and soft antennae."

"I hope the sea slugs don't grow sick roots into our heads," I say. "Like the stumbles did. We've seen enough of that." I glance down at Loftus's tree-ear infested remains.

"These nudibranchs use quantum vortex sensors, same as the uvvies do," says Gee. "You know how that works. The fields are like narrow, invisible tornadoes, very delicate, and they feel around inside your brain for your neural activity, and they send that out as ultraweak wireless. No physical penetration of your skin."

"What about the gossip molecules?" I ask.

"Okay, well, yeah," says Gee. "Our tweaked sea slugs—we call them psidots—our psidots create a population of those molecules in your head. Huffy and stumble—they carried the gossip molecules in their tissues. But the psidots—they send in the gossip molecules on their own."

"Like a vaccination?"

"You hardly notice. The psidot stings you when you put it on for the first time, and our improved gossip molecules diffuse into your brain and they take up residence upon your neurons. Basically, they're free ranging viruses now."

"They settle onto the neurons? That's so invasive."

"Well, they have to live somewhere. And they don't have the fungus hyphae to sit on. So they get in with your neurons. It's an obvious move for interfacing. A gossip molecule on every single neuron. Or maybe a few more, if the neuron has a lot of synapses. The gossip molecules distribute themselves like tiny crabs on a reef. Each of them finds its own nook. They can sense each other."

"How long do they stay?"

"Forever? But the users don't notice. They don't necessarily have to know they're getting a viral gossip molecule infection."

I don't much like this. I wonder if it gets worse. "You're not sending in anything except for the viral gossip molecules are you?" I ask. "No addictive, mind-altering, fungal alkaloids?"

"None," says Gee. "It's a very clean architecture. Except it doesn't quite work."

"What's the issue?"

"Liv is hoping you'll fix it," Gee tells me. "She's heard of you. Turns out it's very tricky to integrate a neuron-mounted gossip molecule with the psidot's quantum vortex fields. And nobody can twist the wacko snaky molecules like Molly Santos."

"You will like working with Liv," puts in Anselm. "You two will click, and we'll get some stable true teep. And then come the hi-res lifeboxes, eh? Immortal souls." He cups one hand to his mouth and makes a trumpet sound.

"What about that thorn in your neck?" I ask Anselm. "Let me look at it."

"It's nothing," says Anselm, waving me aside. "Let it be. We'll get past it."

"I want to start an online soul company!" announces. She's always quick to monetize. "Will you let me do that, Gee? Will you sign a release?"

"No need for paper," says Gee. "Everything I invent is open source. It's all about: *keep it bouncing*."

"I'll call my company Skyhive. You can rent yourself an immortal soul! I'll be the owner and the CEO of my new company," presses Leeta. "And you can be CTO, Molly. With a salary. Chief technical engineer." Leeta is kind of embarrassing. And now that we're not in deep merge anymore, I realize I wouldn't want to work at her company.

"You can dress up however you like," Gee is telling Leeta. "Skyhive doesn't have anything to do with the Finn Junkers.

We're just a bunch of freals who want to bring on true teep and take down Ross Treadle. And by the way, Leeta, before I do give you a leg up on that Skyhive, I'm gonna ask you to help me a little bit with my Treadle thing. I know my limits. I'm not much for social engineering."

"Hey!" interrupts Anselm. "Can we postpone our future-of-the-world summit? We have to leave before Loftus's backup arrives. Get in the sleigh."

"The airport," Gee says to Vixen when we're aboard. "And you'll ride with us on my big flappy again. Our old friend Pelikaan. I told him we'll be leaving around noon."

"You own a full size transatlantic flappy named Pelikaan?" I blurt out, awed.

"I'm rich," says Gee. "I invent things. I make deals. It may be open source, but I get paid anyway. Installation and upgrade fees, you know."

I'm like, "I want to do that!"

"I'll help you if I can," says Gee.

As we head off down the street, I notice that same tall ball walker cutting into our alley.

Oh well. We're outta here. And now we fly to Denmark.

We enter the Christiania neighborhood on foot, with Anselm beside me. Gee and Leeta are ahead, leading the way. We're in a marshy area that feels like the countryside— ponds, reeds, trees. It's about eleven am, local time. We got into Copenhagen at seven am, and spent a couple of hours snacking and seeing sights and buying stuff, including a couple of shock batons, just in case.

Vixen the Happy Sleigh glides along behind us, bearing our load of supplies. Reagents, piezoplastic, undifferentiated tissue—also cheese, cured meat, pickled herring, smoked salmon, butter, rye bread, apples, radishes, and wine.

"The sleigh doesn't need wires or rails at all, does she?" I remark to Anselm. "She ferried us across the harbor. She didn't sink. How did she do that?"

"I thought I told you this," says Anselm. "Her runners achieve a hovercraft effect by using bio-amped Van der Waals forces. And the whole thing about Vixen imitating a street-car is one of Gee's complicated, incomprehensible jokes."

"Think of it as a physical pun," says Gee over his shoulder. "Like me being inside a Mean Carrot. Things that aren't what you think they are."

"Got any *double* physical puns?" I ask, getting into Gee's Alice-In-Wonderland state of mind. "Is there a carrot hiding inside Gee?"

"Would be nice," says Gee with a smile. "With the carrot containing a yet tinier Gee, one understands."

"This is stupid," says Leeta.

"You say that because there's a grasping exec inside you," Gee tells her.

"Is that so bad?" Leeta responds. "Men don't take a woman seriously until she crushes them flat."

"Crush me later," says Gee. "But for now, Leeta, you and Molly and I are on a higher road. Job one: We take down President Treadle." Gee assumes the air of mystic, cupping his hands as if cradling a crystal ball. "My visions of the future: We kill Treadle. Leeta starts an immortality company. I free Leeta's archived souls. Everyone in the world gets a lifebox. Leeta finds a new scam. And Molly—Molly becomes a goddess in teepspace. As for Anselm—oh, this is too—"

Gee jiggles his hands as if trying to reset his crystal ball.

"What *is* teepspace?" I break in. "That's the part I don't get. At first I thought *teepspace* was just a marketing word. Like the *cloud*, or the *web*, or even *cyberspace*. But it's more like it's—real? Something that's out there. Natural. Non-tech. Independent of our devices. Like space and time."

"Heavy insight," goes Anselm. "You are the one to watch, Molly. We Finn Junkers feel that teepspace is like the metaphysicians' Mindscape. The class of all possible thoughts—in the form of a pre-existing Hilbert space—including even the thoughts as yet unthunken."

"Unthunken!" the all-biz Leeta dismissively exclaims. "Give me a break. I want to know how you made Vixen."

Anselm is game for this query as well. "Vixen is of course a biotweaked kritter. Same as the Mean Carrots. Wet AI that runs on living tissues. We used carrots and kangaroo tails for the Mean Carrots—and narwhal flesh for the Happy Sleigh. The sled runners are tusks. Turns out a narwhal tusk contains a nervous system. And getting a hovering effect from it was a lucky fluke."

"Not just luck," protests Gee. "Liv Jensen used exceedingly crafty searches of gene space to find this mutation."

"*Find* is the word," says Anselm. "Not *make*. *You* know how it is, Molly. Nobody knows how anything works anymore. The best computations are inscrutable."

"Agreed," I say. "That's how I do. Directed evolution within rule space using fitness rules that I craft in Spork. Your language, Gee dawg."

"The Spork language is good for meta puns," says Gee with one of his irrelevant giggles. "I designed it that way."

"Tweaked organisms are better than stiff chips," says Anselm. "Gaia does most of the work."

"We're riding a wave," concurs Gee. "And it's nowhere near breaking. Unless Ross Treadle gets a third term in office and he kills us all."

"I like these Junker people," I say to Leeta. "You too?" She nods, her eyes shining.

"Behold the Finn Junkers world headquarters," intones Anselm, pointing to some weathered buildings ahead: three hand-built houses abutting each other, a huge barn, and a whitewash-splattered greenhouse. The houses are luminous in the twilight—pale blue, saffron yellow, delicate mauve—all with zig-zag red tile roofs. The barn's gray wood is gloriously skew and wry. Someone tells me it's two centuries old. Mellow glows move within the rambling greenhouse.

"Can I ask one thing?" I say. "It's been bothering me."

"What?" asks Anselm.

"We're in Denmark, right?"

"Indeed."

"So why isn't your group called the *Dansk* Junkers? Not the Finn Junkers."

"Well—I'm Finnish," says Anselm. "And I'm important. So we named ourselves after me. Anyway, Dansk Junkers would sound boring. Danes aren't as crazy as Finns."

"Oh."

I feel a tad flaky. What with the long air trip, I didn't get my usual dose of stumble fix last night. So when three approximately tubular creatures writhe out of the gooseberry bushes, I mistake them for monstrous nightmare dachshunds. I have an insane phobia of wiener dogs, thanks to a neighbor's mean pet who repeatedly nipped me when I was a girl. So now, in my jagged state, I decide it's payback time.

I zap the closest of the writhing, low-slung attackers with one of the shock-sticks. The muddy orange cone twists into a knot and goes *ki-yi-yi*. I find this deeply satisfying. But—wait, did I say *muddy orange cone*?

"Molly!" scolds Leeta. "They're just Mean Carrots. Finn Junker pets."

"Well, no, not pets," says Anselm. "These three are part of our security. The three Mean Carrots and Ørni the troll." Anselm raises his voice for an introduction. "This is Molly and Leeta, you lot. They're our friends."

The zapped Mean Carrot unkinks herself and hisses at me. But she's no longer on the attack. Her two sisters hang back, watching.

"And that's Ørni?" says Leeta, as a three-foot-tall figure diffidently edges out from the underbrush. Definitely a troll. He has snaggle teeth. He wears no pants. He stinks.

My stomach heaves. I've been getting a literal bloodstream-type drug from my stumble tree-ears every day. The drug makes my fretful stream of consciousness into an epic myth crafted by a mighty poet. And, okay, yes the teep has something to do with that too. But the drug matters too. And the physical withdrawal is hard to take.

What am I going to do? Another whiff of Ørni hits me. I lean over and puke for real.

"The troll is here to discourage tourists," says Gee apologetically. "Ørni is not cute."

A woman with straggly gray hair calls a greeting from the door of the barn. At her side, a trim woman with brown hair smiles and waves.

"Signe Larsen and Liv Anders," says Anselm. "They own these buildings. Not exactly *own*. They're block-chain registered *ur*-squatters."

I wipe my face, and we follow the laden Happy Sleigh into the barn. There's a few Finn Junkers in there—hip and smart, chatting via their uvvies. Someone hands me a glass of water, and that helps. I like the room's vibe. A couple of ball walkers begin unloading our sled, doing the grabbing with their wide, toothless mouths.

I get that the Junkers aren't out to strike it rich. Nor do they seem to care about conventional notions of what's proper. Not greedy, and not uptight. They're anarchists and, I think, kind. Wanting to see what new weird things they can do, and wanting everyone to have fun. My new gang.

Liv comes over to me. She's strikingly attractive, with great style and a charming accent. "You feel up to doing a wetware hack?" she asks me. "Everyone's talking about you. We need one more push."

"Gee was telling me. Some new kind of teep device? What do you call them?"

"Psidots," says Liv.

"Oh, right. Can I see one?"

Liv turns around to show me a tiny slug on the back of her neck, clearly visible below her short-cropped flapper-style auburn hair. Her neck is ivory, her skin is supple. I'd like to kiss her. Hold on, Molly, this is about the psidot.

"She's named Suna," Liv tells me.

Suna is like a miniature banana slug, an eighth of an inch long, zebra-striped in yellow and black, and with deep purple feelers. A teep-tweaked sea slug.

"Gorgeous," I say. "You Junkers move fast."

"And now you'll kick it up a level," says Liv, smiling. "I bet you'll finish this afternoon."

"Let's do it," I say. But, thanks to withdrawal, my skin is clammy and my head hurts. "Can go where it's quiet? You have a lab?"

"Kind of."

Meanwhile the Finn Junkers have set out a celebratory smørrebrød buffet to greet us. I'm not at all into food just now. Liv and I say a temporary goodbye to the others, and she takes me to a little glassed-in porch off the second floor of the barn.

Liv has odd-looking bits of equipment on a table-top, almost like building blocks or children's toys. And a saltwater aquarium with five or six psidot slugs in it, luxuriously stretching themselves as they crawl across a chunk of coral, eating algae and brine shrimp.

Liv studies me. "What's wrong, Molly? Tell me what you need. I'll help."

"It's—it's that skeevy teep fungus I was working on for One Wow? Stumble. I got addicted to an alkaloid. And the withdrawal—" I touch my forehead, touch my belly. "It feels like I'm physically ill. Of course Leeta barely noticed the high, and she doesn't have withdrawal at all. It's like my withdrawal is psychosomatic."

"It's real," says Liv reassuringly. "And once you have a fully functional psidot, you'll be able to fix yourself. But there's a catch. Before the psidots have full functionality, you and I have to get their remote gossip-molecule connections working right."

"Okay, but I need something right now."

"Up? Down? Sideways?"

"Nothing hardcore or I won't be able to work." I look into myself. Maybe I should have gotten something from the cafeteria after all. "How about chai tea, sliced fennel, and a couple of cigarettes?"

"You got it. I won't even call a ball walker. I'll fetch them myself."

While Liv makes a run downstairs, I fish a psidot out of the tank and study it. This one is pink with red piping around its edge. Yellow feelers. I perch the psidot on the tip of my finger.

"So you're having issues with gossip molecules?" I ask, speaking aloud.

"I'm afraid so," says a girl's sweet voice in my head. Slight Danish accent. The psidot's talking through my uvvy. "My name is Bibi, and you are Molly Santos, yes? Put me on your neck instead of your uvvy."

Rather than waiting for Liv, I do as Bibi suggests, and let her settle in. Very smooth mind-link. A faint sting as— *eek*—she sends a dose of the viral gossip molecules through my skin, through my skull, and into my brain—where they settle permanently onto a bunch of my neurons.

I draw in a deep gasp of air. I was holding my breath while this happened. But now it's done. I sense the fine, delicate probing of the psidot's quantum vortex threads—much more elegant than the vortices from an uvvy or—*gak*—the hyphae of a stumble.

Scanning around teepspace, I spot the psidot Suna on Liv's neck. Liv is downstairs eating lox on rye.

"Hey there," I teep to Liv via Suna. "Where's my goodies? Having one of your psidots on me is already making me feel better."

"You're superb," Liv teeps to me. "I'll be right up."

I turn my attention to my psidot Bibi. "So let's see about those viral gossip molecules you infected me with. I think Liv said there's something flaky about how they interface between my neurons and your vortex threads?"

"Indeed."

Around then Liv brings the home-remedies I asked for. And there we go. We two hack, tweak, test, revise, and teep for the rest of the afternoon. The fix has to do with altering the basis of the Hermitian operator space used by the psidot vortex threads when they interact with the gossip molecules' quantum fields.

The gossip molecules don't need any fixes, thank god. It's more a matter of tweaking Bibi's vortex threads. Which is just my cup of chai. By the end of the afternoon the problem is solved. True psidot teep is ready.

Treadle Disease

Liv and I go out on the balcony. It seems we're holding hands. Nice. It's getting on toward dusk, with foundry streaks of orange across the autumn sky. Liv lights a third thick, fragrant cigarette and hands it to me. In the US it's very hard to score tobacco. It helps me push down my stumble withdrawal sickness, which by now is seriously rising up. It's like a persistent ringing in my ears. The harder I try to ignore it, the louder it gets.

"The stumble?" says Liv.

"It always relaxed me," I tell her. "And now I'm back to my default. Being uptight. But more."

"Your psidot could tell your gossip molecules to make that same drug," Liv suggests. "Drip the stumble alkaloid into you all the time. Right into your neurons."

I think this over. Tempting. High all the time. But no. "I want a fresh start," I say. "I want to be me."

"I have an idea," says Liv. "You, me, Bibi, and Vixen the Happy Sleigh—we'll team up."

A sudden rainstorm hits. Liv links arms with me. We walk downstairs to the barn's common room. Seeing me enter, some of the people cheer. Liv's already teeped them about my psidot fix.

Rather than pausing, Liv walks me to the open doorway of the barn. I'm very happy to be with a woman this chic and bright. The wetware engineering social scene in SF is desolate. Too male, too nerdy, too Midwestern.

For a few minutes Liv and I stand there, companionably watching the sheets of rain. It's almost night, and the lights from the barn turn the falling drops to diamonds. The unburdened Happy Sleigh glides over to us and begins vibrating her runners—playing music. I recognize the piece. It's astral heavy metal by Tawny Krush and the Kazakhstan Guitar Corps. Not that I'm into that genre, but Vixen makes it tasty. Two ball walkers amble over and add a percussion track—rhythmically clapping their slit mouths open and shut.

"Sometimes Vixen and her ball walker pals give concerts at the Christiana tavern," says Liv with a smile. "Ready now?"

Liv gestures with both arms like a band leader. The Happy Sleigh damps down her chord progressions, and the ball walkers soften their claps. Dropping down for the vocalist's star turn. Liv places her fingertips on my temples and looks into my eyes. Deep contact. And now she begins to sing.

"Ready to be well," she chants, her voice low and harmonious. Thanks to our psidots, I feel like I'm singing the words too. Liv's voice slides smoothly up the scale, and she loops the final word. "Well, well, well."

I get into a meditative trance, seeing myself as a little nanoscale Molly sim, inside my head, in a spot I think of as my attic. It's a region between the two hemispheres of my brain, a cozy cranny. Right now I'm using my attic as a stage, and I'm thinking of my skull as an opera house. The neurons are opera boxes, each with a wee listener inside. Here on the stage of my attic, I'm singing the song Liv taught me—I'm ringing in changes, and improvising solos, with my voice increasingly resonant.

"This is good," says Liv, who's in my head too, watching me from the side of the stage, like a singing coach. "Sing your brain into health. Engage with the individual neurons."

"All of them at once?"

"It's doable," says Liv. "It's like you took a shot of heroin, and each neuron in your brain gets an opiate molecule."

"I don't take heroin."

"Stumble was just as bad. Don't stall by arguing. Finish the job."

So okay. Deep-tweaking my brain sounds risky, but I'm in a reckless mood, here in the rainy Danish night with this enticing new woman. Perhaps I've been reluctant to get well. Maybe I've loved my addiction that much, but now—*go for it, Molly.*

The song is all around me. My neurons are resonating as one. The vibrations cheer the nerve cells to their cores— banishing the cringing lust for stumble, ushering in a mellow, relaxed, sense of balance that reaches all the way down to the bottom of my medulla.

Yah, mon.

Long story short: I don't need drugs. The White Light is always here. All hail the One. My withdrawal pains are gone—and they won't be coming back.

"Ta da!" I tell Liv. "I'm cured. Easy as pie. Thanks for the magic spell."

"We Junkers need you to be in fine fettle," says Liv. "You're our star. Bombardier Molly. Today you revamped our psidots and made yourself well—and tomorrow you go after Treadle Disease. It's getting more contagious all the time."

Not sure what that last part is about—but I'm brimming with joy and optimism. "Sure! You bet! No problem!" It's been hella long since I felt this good.

Signe and Anselm join us, seemingly unaware of my crisis and recovery. Or more likely they do know—there's a lot of teep in the barn, with many uvvies, and with our new psidots up and running too. So yeah, they know about me, but they're being polite. A classy crowd.

The rain continues pouring down, a magical bead curtain. So wonderful, after the rainless past six months in San Francisco.

Anselm still has that black dot on his neck where Loftus pushed in the thorn, and it worries me. I reach out and touch the spot. "Are you really sure it's okay?" I ask him. "Did you ask any of these people to look at it?"

"It will be fine," says Anselm, serious and determined. "You will fix it this week. Having you here is exhilarating, Molly. We're on the verge of a new state of being." He pauses, looking at me. "Do you realize that in order to get here this morning, we walked the exact same route that the philosopher Søren Kierkegaard used to take in the 1840s, wandering around Christiania? This is the philosopher who called himself a fly on Hegel's nose. And you're Hegel's great-great-great-great-great-granddaughter from your mother's side, are you not, Molly Santos?"

"Is that true?" asks Liv.

"I heard that from my grandmother, yes," I say. "She emigrated to Mexico from Berlin. Grandma was three greats below Hegel, and I'm five greats. How would you even know a thing like that, Anselm?"

"It's in your lifebox," reports Liv. "We Finn Junkers are huge on lifeboxes these days. They're part of the next wave."

"I don't think I put anything about Hegel into my lifebox," I protest. "My lifebox is like a generic fill-in-the-blanks About-Molly page on the One Wow server."

"Have you looked at your lifebox lately?" asks gray-haired Signe. "No?" She has a round, pleasant face. "The Junkers have been carrying out rogue upgrades. Improving our friends' lifeboxes. And moving them all to Gee's server. An intrusion, yes, but it's an upgrade, and it's free."

"How can you violate people's privacy like that?" asks Leeta, who's joined our group standing at the open barn door.

"As if you care about things like that," Anselm says to Leeta. "Get real."

Leeta looks embarrassed. "I'm trying to say the right thing. I want this job."

"Don't worry," says Anselm. "Your skill-set is indispensable."

"Anyway, hacking into online read-write access is pretty standard," says Signe. "A twelve-year-old can do it. And redirecting to a dark server is easy too. The exciting thing about our process is how we flesh out people's lifeboxes."

"We use an emergent network agent," says Anselm. "We call her Metatron. She's alive, in a way. A very strange being. A mind like a Venetian blind. Constantly changing the axes of her Hilbert Space point of view. And I think of course it goes without saying that our perceptual world *is* an infinite dimensional Hilbert space."

"Gibberish," I say.

"You change the geometry of your perceptions all the time," says Signe. "Looking at a crowd of people, you might sort them by how much they weigh, or how smart they look, or how chic their clothes are. Do you want to make love to them? The shade of their skins? Each scale in an axis in your space of perceptions. A type of Hilbert space."

"And teepspace is the same," says Anselm. "Metatron is continually renormalizing her teepspace axes. Guiding her vision towards a more useful fit."

"And thus she becomes an all-powerful mage," says Signe.

"I'd like to meet Metatron," I say.

"Oh, you will," says Signe.

"Where's the name from?" I ask.

"A famous archangel from the Kaballah and the Quran," says Anselm. "Metatron is the high scribe, the recording angel."

"But with her perspective always changing," puts in Signe. "She's our best defense against the Top Party labs. Them with their doddering Coggy."

"Why haven't I heard about all this stuff?" I ask.

"We know more because we're European," says Liv, laughing at me in a friendly way. "We're not glazed with layer upon layer of psychic ice from an endless sleet of propaganda."

"What's Coggy," I have to ask.

"A set of six human brains in a mad-scientist tank in the national Top Party bunker lab," says Signe. "*Men's* brains of course. *Feh.*"

"They're networked in an unusual way," says Liv. "Believe it or not, someone in the Top Party had an original idea.

They're getting superexponential AI amplification from those lame brains."

"Whose brains *are* they?" I ask.

Liv snickers. "Well, party hacks, mostly. Truth is, I hear they're yearning for an especially smart seventh brain. You yourself could be the blessed donor, Molly! The seventh Coggy node. In the unlikely event they'd accept your offering."

"Fie, fie!" cries Anselm. "Pearls before swine. With mellow Molly in our midst, we'll drive Coggy into extinction. We'll shatter that sickly brain tank on the dirty floor of the Top Party bunker lab, well before their longed-for brain number seven can be acquired."

"May it be so," says Liv reverently—or maybe it's mock-reverently. Finn Junker jive. It's possible this is all a put-on.

Leeta pipes up, a bit off-topic. "We'll lay the foundations for commercial teep and software immorality!" Her biz-cheerleader thing.

"May our lifebox souls wax fat," intones gray-haired Signe.

"*Ka-ching*!" goes Leeta, not to be diverted. "I'll rent out upscale cloud storage space for users' lifeboxes. My business! I'll call it Skyhive. No charity cases. Heaven without the poor."

"Leeta loves to monetize," I explain, slightly embarrassed about my friend. "I'm more catch-and-release."

"No worries," says Signe. "Gee says we need both of you. The One and the Nun. Key players in the war on Treadle."

"Where's Gee now?" I ask. I haven't seen him since we got here.

"In his lab," goes Liv. "Preparing for the blow-back from our war on Treadle Disease."

"And, lo, Gee's spirit moved upon the face of the waters," I intone, more or less at random. I'm not even sure what Treadle Disease *is* yet, and I'm not in a mood to ask. I'm punch-drunk with fatigue. Those hundred trillion vortices in my neurons have me feeling very voozy. Wery woozy? A foto out of focus.

"Molly is an iridescent sheen on the wings of the Kierkegaard fly on Hegel's nose," intones Anselm, doggedly pursuing his thread about philosophers. "Molly is the surreal eschaton that lies beyond existentialism and beyond phenomenology—she is the beacon who guides us to renormalizing the final victory!"

"Oh god," I say. "Give it up, you freaks."

"Anselm has been spending a little too much time in teepspace," says Signe, laughing. "Flexing his brain as if it's a—cootie catcher? A nest of folded paper that opens up in ever different ways?"

"Seriously, this is more than enough now," I protest.

"Metatron is an erotic film of the Garden of Eden—shot through the slats of motel room blinds," bays Anselm.

"The Big Bang within each electron," exclaims Signe.

"Look, I need to crash," I tell them. "I got zero sleep last night, and then Liv and I worked all day, and I had stumble withdrawal the whole time."

"I've set aside a room for you and Leeta," says Signe. "I'll show it to you now."

"I'd rather not share a bedroom with Leeta," I say.

Leeta nods. "Molly and I like each other, but too much is too much."

"Would you like to share with me?" Liv asks me. "One large bed."

I glance at her. And yes, she means what I think.

"Okay," I say, admiring the pert, alert angle of Liv's head. "I'd like that a lot."

"Welcome to Freetown," says Liv.

I kiss her then and there, a deep kiss, not that this is a big deal, but maybe the suddenness and intensity are a bit unusual. Like two magnets snapping together. Wonderful. I worry Signe might be jealous, but she looks glad for us. Liv and I say good night to everyone, and head for her room.

We shed our psidots, we undress, and we communicate in the good, old-school way. Skin to skin, body to body. And afterwards we smoke a cigarette.

I sleep till mid-morning, and wake in a happy mood. Liv's not around. I think of the Roy Lichtenstein painting of a woman in bed looking at a framed photo and saying, "Good morning…darling." I always loved that ellipsis in there, those three dots, indicating, at least to me, that it's only just *now* that the woman is finally daring to call her lover *darling*.

I shower, and make my way to the commons room in the barn, hoping there might be breakfast. But there isn't. And something is horribly wrong.

Liv and Anselm are lounging in chairs, watching a squid-skin screen display on the wall. It's a long political ad for President Ross Treadle. The soundtrack is triumphant. The insane bully himself glares down, as if playing a father who instructs a wayward child.

I laugh, assuming the setup is a joke, but, no, my new friend Anselm and my new lover Liv aren't sneering at Treadle. Far from it. They're glowing, and nodding, and going *yeah*. How very odd—and how sinister.

There's an insinuating flicker to the Treadle ad. It strobes at a rate that betokens subliminal messaging. Anselm and Liv—they smell funny. An unwholesome aroma of ketones and indoles.

And—how very unpleasant—I can feel invasive teep signals from both Anselm and Liv. They're trying to reach into my mind, and to access the tiny waving flagella of my neuronal gossip molecules. They want my unsuspecting gossip molecules to assemble copies of some evil, viral, Treadle gossip molecules. They want the Treadle gossip molecules to replace the regular gossip molecules in my brain.

Fortunately my psidot's operating system is smart enough to block these signals. Gee and Liv thought to build in something like a firewall. As if they'd known what might be coming.

"Quick," says Gee, appearing at my shoulder. "Until we get them isolated." He covers my nose and mouth with a face mask, and slips gray spectacles over my eyes.

The flicker goes away, the invasive odor is gone.

"So Liv and Anselm have Treadle Disease," I say to Gee. "That sucks."

He's wearing a mask and glasses too. As are Leeta, Signe, and a couple of odd-ball Finn Junkers I now notice in the rear of the room.

"Anselm was already infected with Treadle Disease when we got here," says Gee, handing me a shock baton. "Loftus inoculated Anselm with it in your apartment. He used a time-release thorn. Took thirty-six hours to kick in. It hit Anselm around three am last night."

"You and Anselm knew this was coming?"

"Yes. That's another reason why he was in San Francisco. Not just to hire you and Leeta, but he wanted to catch the Treadle Disease. He volunteered. We knew the disease was coming, and we needed a test subject so we can find a cure before it's too late. The virus's rate of spread is about to go superexponential."

Anselm and Liv continue staring at the squidskin display. Periodically they make attempts to zap us with a Treadle-Disease-virus-generating template but thank god our firewalls are blocking those templates out.

"This is really bad," Gee says to me. "Feel how they're picking away at us? And that flicker in the screen—that codes for the virus template too. Viewers with insecure stumbles or psidots are fucked. But most of the infections will be old-school. As a physical virus, Treadle Disease can come in directly. And it's evolving in real time. Getting snakier. More wiggly. Unbelievably quick to spread. Make sure your mask is on tight."

Onscreen Treadle's wife, ex-wife, and daughter are talking about how great it is to have gig serfs working in the White House, and in Treadle's factories, resorts and farms—and in the industries belonging to the members of Citadel Club. Gig serfs are a big Treadler thing that Congress rubber-stamped last year. It's now legal for privately-run prisons to attach shock-uvvies to their inmates—and to rent them out as gig serf slaves.

"Helps folks into the work force!" yodels Treadle's ex-wife. "Enhances self-esteem! Builds the profits of our jails!"

Leeta is standing next to me. She has a new psidot too. She teeps me some background info about the latest Treadle plan.

A gig serf is utterly unable to disobey whatever command their nanopercenter masters issue . In his third term, Treadle plans to make welfare recipients into involuntary gig serfs as well—by way of defraying their burden on society. And, just to give the little guys a chance, the next Treadle administration will open up the gig serf market so that anyone at all can *volunteer* for gig serf work—and keep a small cut of the rental fee. They call this plan *full gig*.

"We've got to win this," Leeta says aloud.

On the screen, Treadle's women folk are chanting "*Everyone's a Boss*" and "*Free Full Gig!*" Anselm and Liv join in. Horrible.

"How did Liv catch the disease?" I ask Gee, with an edge in my voice. "As a physical virus?"

"Yes. At breakfast, Anselm passed it to her by sharing his quark."

"*Quark*? What the fuck are you talking about, man?"

"European quark," says Gee, with his twitchy giggle. "A dairy product. Like yogurt except it's not sour. Anselm eats a bowl of quark with wild blueberries every morning. So I'm sitting with him and Liv, and Anselm has this zoned look, and he's not talking, and he has that ketone smell. So I know. And then he offers Liv a spoonful of his quark from his spitty spoon, and that's all she wrote. No time-release action in *that* dose. Just—pow—and Liv has Treadle Disease. You really, really want to wear this protection gear. We're gonna isolate Anselm and Liv in bubbles right now."

"Why didn't you stop Anselm from infecting Liv?" cries Leeta.

"Well, we wanted to have two test subjects," says Gee. "For cross-checking our tests."

"I bet you made *sure* Liv was the second victim," I say, hating him. "Because you know I have a crush on her. Bastard. You wanted to motivate me to work extra hard on the cure. Silly, romantic, brainy Molly who loves girls. You prick."

"Liv knew about the plan all along," Gee quietly says. "Who knows—maybe that's why she led you on."

I groan in despair. "I wish I was dead."

"Don't," says Gee. "We *will* find the cure. You, Leeta, me, and our lab workers Moritz and Majken. See them over there?"

Majken looks like a woman with kinky red hair, worn in pigtails. Moritz resembles a bald man with a walrus mustache. Of average height. Geeky looking.

"Are they kritters?" asks Leeta. "Like the Mean Carrots and your Ørni troll?"

"God no, they're human. To the extent that engineers ever are." Here comes the Gee giggle.

"Don't do that," I tell him. "Don't laugh like that again."

"It's a tic," says Gee. "I'm mentally ill."

I'm not sure how seriously I'm meant to take that. If Gee's a nut case, then so am I. In spades. Screw that.

"Let's go to the lab," I tell him. "I'll grab some food."

"Don't share Anselm's quark," says Gee, making a show of clapping his hand over his mouth so he doesn't giggle.

"Fuck you."

Lolling in their easy chairs by the squidskin screen, Liv and Anselm keep an eye on us, teeping out attempted take-over signals now and then.

I fetch myself an oval bun, a square of ham, a triangle of cheese, and a cone of apple cider.

"Come sit with us," calls Liv. "Watch this wonderful show about your President Treadle. You pseudo-intellectuals are so unfair to him. Treadle Deserves Better." I can hear the capitals.

I stare at Liv for a long, sad minute. She's like a stranger. No trace of last night's love light in her eyes.

"We're getting constant Treadle updates via teep," says Anselm, as if this is a wonderful thing. His face takes on a look of senile cunning. "You should take off your gray glasses so you can enjoy the way the screen flickers. It'll do you good, Molly. It's fantastic to be in tune with Treadle. Come over here, and I'll spit on your food. This isn't a *disease*, it's an elixir."

Anselm bends his lips into a U-shape, meaning to simulate a smile. He looks like a complete idiot. Like a Treadler. He and Liv shift in their chairs, as if they mean to stand up and walk over to me.

I hold up my shock baton. "Don't you dare."

"People like Molly and Leeta are scheming to ruin everything," Liv says. "Treadle Deserves Better." How could I have thought Liv was beautiful? Her face is blank and mean. "You think you're so smart, but you're not," she continues. "Unfair. Elitist." Treadlers have small vocabularies.

Signe is with Leeta and me as well. She's masked, and she has a larger shock baton than mine. The device's business end crackles like a Tesla-coil.

"We're going to put you two in bubble beds," Signe tells Anselm and Liv, speaking very loud, as if talking to animals. "You'll be comfortable. We'll give you eyephones so you can watch your dear President. Just relax now. We want the best for you. No sudden moves."

For emphasis, Signe snaps a four-foot long spark into the air. And now two ball walkers wheel in a pair of equipment-laden hospital beds. Signe and some helpers get Liv and Anselm into the bed-bubbles and roll them away. *Whew.*

Meanwhile, Leeta, Gee, and I follow Majken and Moritz to their lab. Majken sports red overalls over a yellow turtleneck. Actually she's not all that dweeby. Kind of cute, with freckles and shiny lips. Pippi Longstocking! I always had a thing for Pippi. If Liv never wakes up, then maybe Majken and I could—but what am I thinking? I'm a horrible person.

Moritz wears corduroy knickers and a tweed jacket. Maybe that's a Danish thing? All these Junkers are so effing colorful. Makes me vaguely paranoid. I keep wondering if this scenario is some demented, screwball hoax? An online rom-com show? I wouldn't put it past Gee Willikers. But then I think of Liv's and Anselm's empty faces. Placeholders for the people they used to be. I've got to save them.

The Majken and Moritz lab is in an area that used to be the dairy, off on the back side of the barn. Non-retrofitted, although they did add an outer wall. Looks to be over a century old. Rough-hewn timbers, wavy glass in elderly windows, a roof of mossy tiles atop hand-planed boards. For the homey touch, someone has scattered an inch-thick layer of golden straw on the floor beneath the lab's sleek benches.

The ball walkers trundle Liv's and Anselm's bubble beds into a sickbay next to the lab. Encased in their quarantine bubbles, my stricken friends lie in tangles of measuring devices. Signe monitors their brainwaves and the components of their blood and spinal fluid.

In the lab we get to work. The first task is to disentangle the threads that comprise Treadle Disease. Brain physiology, information theory, epigenetics, wetware engineering, and cryptanalysis all seem to be in play—as well as teep. And the self-amplifying infection rate is a whole other thing.

I tend to be happiest when I'm busy. My work and my occasional bouts of addiction have something in common: they help me forget myself. I like to turn away from the past and future, away from regrets and fear, away from other people. Zeroing in on the now. When I do hard science I'm in that still, quiet place all day, my mind a zero-dimensional energy point, buzzing my Molly songs.

By evening, I've ascertained that Treadle Disease is a highly infectious biological virus—basically a tangled long-chain protein with intricate loops. It looks like a variation on Gee's gossip molecules, which are also viruses. Treadle Disease might actually *be* a gossip molecule—but folded up the wrong way. And it's communicability keeps improving. Like the design is slithering around in molecular state space, finding ever more efficient folds.

I got to bed and I fall into uneasy sleep. At some point Liv's friend Signe comes to my room and awakens me. It's still pitch dark outside. What with the jet lag, I have no idea what time it is, and I can't seem to figure it out.

"Four am," Signe tells me. I curse. "Sorry," says Signe. "Gee wants to have a strategy meeting. He never went to bed. Treadle Disease is steam-rolling the US. It's beyond any level ever seen. We need to act immediately."

I slap on my psidot and get some updates while I shower. It's a cataclysmic pandemic. Not that the American media seem to understand this. The reporters who *don't* have Treadle Disease wonder at the President's sudden jump in popularity and at the loyalty of his followers. The flacks who *do* have Treadle Disease parrot the man's lines.

Before I get so much as a bun or a cup of coffee, I'm herded into Moritz and Majken's lab with Gee and Leeta. We're supposed to brainstorm. Gee starts off the discussion. I find it hard to listen to him—as I have such a huge grudge about Liv getting sick. Also I've got a splitting headache.

"I'll sum it up," says Gee. "Molly's guess is right. The Treadle Disease virus is an enhanced form of our friend the gossip molecule. It can live on its own, or as a parasite on a neuron. The kicker is that this variant has a single-channel brainwave antenna built in—and it's tuned for signals from the Top Party labs. And, like any gossip molecule, it functions as a nanotech assembler. It's utterly minimal, and ruthlessly efficient. And getting faster all the time. It works even if you don't have a psidot."

"What does it do?" asks bald, mustached Moritz.

"The Treadle Disease virus listens for signals from the Top Party labs," says Gee. "And it assembles whatever screwed-up chemicals the Treadlers tell it to. And it clears your normal gossip molecules away. And the Top Party lab keeps finding more efficient designs for the virus's design."

"So how do we undo it?" asks Leeta.

Gee looks at me. "Molly? Ideas?"

"Simple," I say. "We go into the patient's brain and shred their Treadle Disease gossip molecules. Probably I can figure out how. I've worked with gossip molecules a lot. But, Gee—it might help me to hear you explain gossip molecules in your own words. After all, you invented them. How do you visualize what they do?"

"Okay," says Gee. "Did you ever see that really old movie, *Jurassic Park*?" He giggles.

Such a stupid answer. And the giggle? He thinks it's funny that my Liv's mind is ruined?

"I hate you, Gee. I'd like to kill you."

"I get that a lot," says the imperturbable hacker. "Hear me out. You asked a question and I'm trying to answer it."

So now Gee teeps us an animation about a gossip molecule who resembles the strand of dinosaur DNA in the cartoon sequence at the start of *Jurassic Park*. A skinny hillbilly molecule. Apparently his name is Mr. DNA. He's chatty and he has buck teeth, like an old-time Southern telephone operator. Gee gives Mr. DNA a corny accent and has him say, "*DAH-no-saow-er.*"

Why am I listening to this crazy motherfucker Gee Willikers when it's dark outside and I haven't had breakfast? I look to Majken and Moritz for aid. They say nothing.

"Too cute for words," I snap at Gee. "I never should have worked on your gossip molecules at all."

"But you did," he says, shaking his head. "And the Treadlers worked on them too. Maybe I shouldn't have made them be open source."

"Let's break it all the way down," says Leeta. "How does Treadle Disease *feel*?"

"It makes you feel like Treadle," says Gee, waggling his eyebrows, forever goofing. "Stupid and angry and resentful and—I would say—functionally deaf and blind. And it makes you want Treadle to be king. Look at poor Liv and Anselm." He glances over at me. "But remember, Molly, those two volunteered."

"They didn't know what they were getting into," I say. "It's too pathetic. Now they have IV lines, and catheters. Flopped into bubble-sealed beds, with videophones on their eyes."

"They don't notice that stuff," says Gee. "They're zonked from the disease, and zonked from the IV drip. And face it, we're gleaning crucial data. Serum samples. Limbic MRI. Realtime Fourier analysis of their brainwaves."

"We have to cure them," I say. I'm exhausted and drained. My heart aches for Liv. I'm close to crying. This job is too big.

"Don't stress," says Gee. "Anselm and Liv are in hog heaven," The man always has to go too far. "Watching Treadle ads all day long!"

"You're a monster."

"Let's not have a tiff," interrupts Majken. "Liv and Anselm are my dear friends, Molly. And I predict grand success." She gives Gee a sharp look. "And don't you torment Molly. We're grateful to have this shimmering, existential, dialectical woman on our team. Of all of us, Molly can hop the highest. This is fact. Molly is more clever."

"Love it," says Gee. He looks at me, calm and bland. The guy is indestructible. "So let's see you prove it."

"I will, asshole. I'll sit by Liv's and Anselm's bubble beds while the sun comes up, and I'll touch their minds. Fuck your lab test numbers and the graphs. I'll connect to them via psidots. Let's ask Signe if she can bring Liv's psidot for her, and we'll need a psidot for Anselm too. I'm already wearing mine. I'll be ready to start in ten minutes."

"Is this safe?" asks Moritz, sounding surprised.

"I don't care," I say. "It's the only way."

"Let Molly run," says Gee. "She's our star."

At this point I have to wonder if I'm being had. Maybe Gee knew all along that a direct mind meld was the only way—and he's deliberately goaded me into thinking it's my own idea. Whatever. I'm ready. It's five am.

By now some kitchen guys have been rousted out of bed, and there's signs of life in the commons room. I eat some cold apple cake, pound a cup of chai, and smoke a cigarette.

Insane as this regimen is, at least it's unbelievably easy to get tobacco in Denmark. Such hedonists.

In the sickbay, I sit down between the two bubble beds with a second cup of chai. Signe is still here, on a chair against the wall by the door. I can teep that she's worried. We're wearing goggles and masks. Signe has her big shock baton. She's already put Liv's psidot onto her. A psidot for Anselm is waiting in a saucer of water. I'll leave it there for now. One healing at a time.

Smooth as silk, my psidot Bibi blends into my thought stream. We pick up a signal from Liv's psidot Suna, and we do the handshake stuff. And now I do something completely insane. I lower my firewall barriers. Liv is going to have access to my gossip molecules. She's going to transfer a template for the Treadle gossip molecule itself. My normal gossip molecules will build Treadler gossip molecules, and the Treadler gossip molecules will take over my brain.

Why am I doing this? Because the only way I'm going to find the cure for the disease is to cure it on myself. The trick will be to finish the cure before the disease fully takes me over. I'll have to neutralize it before it cripples my ability to act.

So okay, my firewall is down and I'm fully merged with Liv. Liv's not exactly herself. She's singing Treadle jingles, pondering one of his speeches, viewing images of him, and gloating about how truly outstanding her hero is.

"Hey!" I call sharply, getting her attention. I'm like a toreador challenging a bull to attack. And here it comes.

Liv's second-hand thoughts flap into the air like startled pigeons, like dirty birds with mites and lice. One of them flies at me and pecks me hard—the "me" being a sim model of my body that's flying around inside the domed piazza of Liv's addled mind.

Ever so faintly, Liv's true voice sounds from the ground beneath my feet.

"Molly? You're here? Use quantum scrolls!"

An oompah-band rendition of a Treadle anthem drowns her out. I look at my virtual arm where the pigeon pecked me. Mites and lice! Yep. Those are templates for the Treadle gossip molecules. Normally my teep operating system would have filtered them out. But my firewall is wide open.

So right off the bat, a few of my gossip molecules have followed the incoming template instructions and they've assembled literal, physical, no-shit Treadle gossip molecules inside my physical body. And these bastards are self-replicating, and destroying my normal gossip molecules, and taking their place.

Ticking clock. The Treadle gossip molecule infection has reached a few thousand of my neurons. It's spreading at an exponential rate. I'm starting to hear faint echoes of Treadle campaign anthems. Hurry, Molly!

Fortunately I have a plan. I send my tiny, nanoscale Molly sim into that special little cranny between the hemispheres of my brain—my attic. The day before yesterday I used it as a sound stage, and today it's my wetware engineering lab.

With quick, sure motions, I latch onto one of my normal gossip molecules, and I instruct it to craft a quantum scroll vortex of a certain cunning design. My gossip model writhes in activity, flicks its tail, and now I have the desired outcome. A special vortex hovers before me.

Let's call it a cleaner tornado. It's about the same height as my wee sim body. I tidy up my cleaner tornado with a few quick tweaks—crafting it to behave the way I want. Its mission is simple: Tear Treadle gossip molecules to shreds.

Time to check if the tornado actually works. I stick my sim body's tiny, infected arm into my new cleaner tornado—and I get a lovely sense of being scrubbed, like in an old-time car wash. Yes. *Those* particular mites and lice that were on my sim's arm—they were Treadle gossip molecules, and now they're gone. I'll get rid of all my sick gossip molecules, and later, my trusty psidot Bibi will feed normal gossip molecules back into my system, and I'll be back up to speed, with a working psidot.

But with the Treadle Disease virus spreading through my brain, I'm going to need a *lot* of these cleaner tornadoes. I don't just need descriptions of them, I need physical cleaner tornadoes, and I need one for every single Treadle gossip molecule I have. I want the tornadoes to do a mass raid, one at each door, blowing all intruders away. Otherwise I'll end up singing those fucking Treadle anthems, which are getting louder all the time.

Long story short: I'd like to have a trillion cleaner tornadoes. One for each neuron in my body and brain.

So, um, how do I get from one to a trillion? How, how, how?

I think of something I've seen in creeks and in sunlit swimming pools. Eddies dissolving into eddies, all the way down. Why not mimic this with quantum hydrodynamics? I'll divide and subdivide and resubdivide my cleaner tornadoes, over and over again. A turbulent cascade.

I hit my prototype cleaner tornado with a jolt. It shudders and splits in two and—yes!—the smaller vortices are off balance, and they split again, and the yet smaller ones split as well, on and on through as many levels as I like. Did I say I wanted a trillion cleaner tornadoes? That means, um, forty levels will do. As every good engineer knows, two to the fortieth power approximates a trillion.

When I get to a trillion—and I'm doing all this in my attic—I feel like I'm in a hive of bees. I hit the swarm of cleaner tornadoes with another jolt, stabilizing them. They're smarter than you might expect. I like them. Their massed buzz is already dampening down the Treadle-anthem sound.

I pause to put my firewall back up. Wouldn't want Liv to be teeping in fresh templates for Treadle gossip molecules as quick as I kill them off. Done. It's show time.

"Go forth and purify," I tell the cleaner tornadoes.

In that odd kind of teepspace way, my mind shows me a VR visualization of what comes next. Each of my infected neurons has, like, a meager and pathetically skinny little arm that's a Treadle gossip molecule. And—*zow!*—a personalized cleaner tornado hops onto every one of my body's Treadle molecules and rips it to shit.

My mites and lice are gone—as are the hideous, bullying anthems. The Treadle Party and the Citadel Club have no hope of controlling me. And, as a crowning touch, I have my psidot Bibi replenish my brain with normal gossip molecules.

I've invented a cure.

I open my eyes and take a deep breath.

"What are you doing?" Signe asks.

"Ramping up," I say. "Getting ready to fix Liv. But first I needed to heal myself. Because Liv infected me. It was good that she did that. It motivated me."

"You're good," says Signe.

"I'm scared," I tell her. "I'm glad you're here. Your vibe is kind."

"I'm soft in the head," says Signe. "To be risking my life in here."

"We're doing it for Liv and Anselm," I say. "And to win the war against Ross Treadle."

"Stay strong," says Signe. "Have luck!"

I'm wondering how I'm supposed to put a trillion cleaner tornadoes inside Liv's head, but then I realize there's a short-cut that I probably could have used on myself. I'll draw up an genome-level template for a cleaner tornado—which is no mean feat—and then I'll broadcast this template to all of Liv's Treadle gossip molecules at once. And each of them will process the gene codes to build a cleaner tornado which will then tear the Treadle gossip molecule apart. So I don't have do that whole dividing-in-two turbulence cascade.

But, wait, there's a catch. The Treadle gossip molecules will only make the things that the Treadler lab messages tell them to make. So okay, I'll need to spoof my tornado template into looking like an official Top Party instruction. And *then* Liv's hoaxed Treadler gossip molecules will beat their foolish little tails and whip up cleaner tornadoes that will kill them. And in this wise, the disease will devour itself. Like a wounded shark that tears at its hanging intestines. Like the Top Party itself—I hope.

Unfortunately, spoofing messages and hacking servers and hoaxing crypto codes isn't my bag. The person who's good at this is—Gee Willikers. The man I was recently snarling insults at.

So, *sigh*, I use my psidot to teep him. He's right next door, in Majken's and Moritz's lab.

"Howdy," says Gee in his Mr. DNA accent, just to piss me off.

"I need your skill set," I say. "I want to do something skungy."

"To hear is to obey," says Gee. "Want more food? Cigarette and third cup of chai?"

"First things first," I say, "I want to send a certain molecular template to Liv's Treadle gossip molecules. I want them to obey me as if they're getting official instructions from the Top Party labs."

"You want to tell the Treadle gossip molecules to produce their own antidote!" exclaims Gee. "Brilliant. Give me two minutes. Should I come into the sick room and sit with you?"

"Signe and I are doing fine," I say. "You're too annoying. And—harking back what you said a second ago—yes, it would be great if one of the ball walkers would bring me a pack of cigarettes, and three more cups of chai, some sweet buns, and two dozen of those open-faced smorrebrod sandwiches. Also a couple of pitchers of water."

"I'll message the order for you," says Signe, who's listening in.

A few minutes later the sickbay door opens and *aaack*, instead of a ball walker, it's stinky Ørni the three-foot-tall troll, carrying a heavily laden tray held high. Still no pants on the guy. Ghastly. He sets the tray on a side-table, makes a face at me, and—don't let the door hit you in the ass on the way out—leaves. I smoke a cigarette to burn away the Ørni fumes, then have a chai, and a bun, and a couple of the smorrebrod sandwiches. Signe eats some sandwiches too.

Meanwhile Liv and Anselm are just lying there, out cold, in the clutches of the Disease, twitching a hand or a foot now and then, perhaps in rhythm to those terrible Treadle victory anthems.

Gee appears to me in the sickbay—via teep, as an image in my visual field. He's holding an old-fashioned phone, with a conical earpiece on a cord, and a horn-shaped mouthpiece on a box mounted on the wall. Not that there actually *is* a wall. The box is just floating there. Gee is talking like Mr. DNA.

"Got your connection right hyar, Miz Molly! I drilled a hole in the Treadlers' firewall. You ready to speak your piece? I got your party line set up, and it'll endorse whatever you say with the bona fide official Top Party seal. Liv's Treadle gossip molecules will chomp it right down. They're a-waitin to hear from you. All trillion of em."

"You're a dear," I say, almost forgiving him for his weirdness. Deep down, *way* down, Gee means well. "I'm sorry I was nasty before."

"Nasty is good," says Gee. "We all know that. And your trick is gonna work."

Still sitting in my chair, I put my attention into teepspace. I put that phone receiver by my ear. A nice steady drone. Liv's psidot is contentedly doing its thing, interfacing with her neurons and with their Treadle gossip molecules. I get my mind into superscience mode and I reverse engineer a precise holographic template for the quantum vortex cleaner tornadoes that I want those Treadle gossip molecules to make.

How to send the message? A song worked for me the day before yesterday when I healed myself. So okay, I want to sing to each of Liv's Treadle Disease gossip molecules at once. Not only will Gee's "telephone" slap the Top Party stamp of approval onto my template, it'll message it to each of the targeted molecules.

I emit a wandering warble that paints, if properly heard, an eidetic image of these wavy, wild cleaner tornadoes I've been screwing with. The tech details are background drone, like a Tuvan throat-singer's buzz. And the seal of approval is a clicking hiss on the surface.

Spurred by my signals, each of Liv's sick gossip molecules cooks up a cleaner tornado on its own—and now a trillion cleaner tornadoes are ripping the Treadle gossip molecules to shit. Like nanotech Tasmanian devils devouring their prey. A shrill buzz like a celestial choir of dental drills. A moment later my phone emits the resonant note of a gong. Biocomputation complete. And then Liv's psidot restores her population of normal gossip molecules.

"I rise again." calls Liv's voice, way louder than before. In sim form, she slithers up from a crack in the sim piazza to face me in teepspace. "I'm well!"

I flip back to my normal perception of the world. There's Liv in her bed, moving around inside her bubble. She uncovers her eyes. She's sallow and drawn like a hospital patient, but she makes a wild-girl face, opening her mouth and tossing her head back and forth.

"You rock, Molly. You roll."

Signe is at the bedside too, very pleased. "My treasure," she says to Liv. "We'll clean you up."

"First we have to cure Anselm," I say.

"And then we can ride Metatron and zap the United States of Treadlandia!" goes Liv. "I just hope we can finish before the Top Party sends Coggy after us."

"We have to hurry," I agree. "Let's do Anselm right now!"

"No time to give poor Liv a bath?" asks Signe, disappointed.

"The Treadler's will patch Gee's back door into their server. And they'll sic weird teepspace agents on my ass. Ticking clock, Signe! How about it Liv? Ready to roll?

"Indeed."

Inside her bubble, Liv runs her hands through her greasy hair and steels herself. Yanks the IV drip out of her arm. Peels the trodes off her chest and scalp. Feels all over herself, adjusting things. Scrooches up in bed to lean against the wall. Notices my two cups of chai.

"Gimme," she says, "Pass it through the bubble's slit. I'll stay in here until Anselm is done."

I work the cup of sweet, milky tea through the flap in the bubble. Liv takes it in both hands and drains it in three swallows. Through my psidot I share her pleasure.

Signe is by the door now, her hand on the knob, increasingly uneasy. "I don't feel comfortable. This is so chaotic."

I'm imagining I hear the yipping of Treadler attack dogs on the hunt. "It's okay if you go," I tell Signe. "I won't hold it against you."

"And thank you, Signe," says Liv. "You're dear and kind and beautiful."

Signe sighs, smiles, and exits. I can tell she's hopelessly infatuated with Liv. I can't blame her.

I open Anselm's bubble slit and put the extra psidot onto his neck. It settles right in and—*ding*—his psidot's icon appears in my teep network. The psidot's name is Tony Tiger, god knows why. Psidots tend to pick their own names.

And now, to have a good sense of what we're doing, I lie on Liv's bed next to her, pushing her bubble side. She and I project ourselves into the teepspace of Anselm's mind. It's a virtual arena, like an outdoor concert stadium, with a virtual crowd of joyful, cheering Treadlers. The air smells strongly like piss. Our fearless President addresses us from a mighty rostrum. This is a part of his speech where his voice is a gentle singsong, like he's tucking helpless invalids into bed.

Liv conjures up a ginormous scythe and mows the simulated crowd of Treadlers like wheat. They shrivel and vanish. Treadle's still there, still talking. A fresh wave of Treadler sims charges down from the top seats of the stadium, ululating and waving machetes. Liv turns their bodies inside out. They flop about on the concrete steps like chicken innards. A demonic host of pterodactyl-winged Treadlers forms above us, flapping and preparing to dive. Liv crisps them with thunderbolts of flame.

And then, for good measure, she destroys Treadle with a tactical hydrogen bomb. All the propaganda images are gone. We're on an endless dusty plain. Somewhere far away, dogs are yelping.

"Some people say I have anger issues," goes Liv.

"If a woman doesn't, she's not paying attention."

"How long was I gone?" asks Liv. "And when do we make love again?"

"You were zonked for a day," I say, basking in Liv's virtual presence. "And—when do we fuck? I hope soon." I pause. "Did you really know Anselm would infect you?" This has been bothering me.

"Yes, I knew. And I'm sorry I didn't warn you. But I wanted our night together to be perfect." Her voice breaks and goes high. "In case it might be my last one? But it worked out, didn't it. Gee said you'd be able to cure me, and you did."

"*Good morning…darling*," I say to Liv. "I wanted to say that yesterday when I woke up. So much."

Liv goes, "Aw."

I keep hearing that frantic barking. Getting closer. The Treadlers will be here soon. And this time they won't be harmless icons.

"Let's cure Anselm," I say. And then, raising my voice, "Are you with us, Gee?"

"Wouldn't miss it for anything," Gee says, appearing at my side again. "I'm watching from my lab next to the sick room." His sim is tall, lanky, spaced-out. "Brought ya this." He hands me another phone—a black Bakelite model, the 1950s kind with a receiver that cradles on top of the phone itself.

"The Treadler's patched my hole, but I found a new one," continues Gee. "The Treadler operating system—shit, man, it's like Swiss cheese. And I'm a pizza rat." He wrinkles his nose and makes a face, nibbling.

I put the receiver to my ear. As before, I hear the mediated hum of massed Treadle gossip molecules. I have my cleaner tornado template stored in my mind—as a soundpainting, with a hoarse tech buzz.

I chant the start of it, warming up. "*Eeep-deedle-skreech-ooooom*."

"You have learned well, Younger Sister," goes Liv.

"May you delight in my harvest song," I respond.

I sing my full tornado template signal, the Bakelite phone stamps it as legit, the phone multiplexes my song to every one of Anselm's Treadle gossip molecules, they swallow it, a trillion cleaner tornadoes appear in Anselm's brain, and I hear that same high, tasty hum as the trillion cleaner tornadoes tear into the trillion Treadle gossip molecules.

The vast desert convulses.

"Anselmquake," goes Gee, happily laughing.

And Anselm's psidot restores his normal gossip molecules to his brain.

"Do I hear Anselm singing?" asks Liv. "That line he likes?"

"Garden gnome, garden gnome, beware the frightful garden gnome," booms our friend from afar.

"You're back on duty now," Gee yells to the still unseen Anselm. "Quick! Bring us an avatar of Metatron."

"I'm doing fine without Metatron," I protest. I'm not quite sure I want to deal with this giant super AI network agent, or whatever she is.

"This time we'll need a much bigger megaphone than before," says Gee. "We're going to cure every Treadle Disease victim in the world. Hundreds of millions of people. A trillion Treadle Disease virus molecules apiece. Only a parallel, distributed agent like Metatron has that kind of power. And look out. When Metatron broadcasts this hot and heavy, the Top Party's Coggy brain-tank is likely to send in his own agent."

"Frightful garden gnome!" booms Anselm once more, still unseen.

"What does Metatron actually look like?" I ask Gee.

"She adapts to your preferred axes of perceptual teepspace," says Gee. "A dream come true. Here comes Anselm's fave version! Our man is in the guh-guh-*groove*."

A huge, dark object roars toward us across the virtual sky. I flinch. That's Metatron? I'm scared. She's shaped like an immense cross, or an X. She circles down in a spiral, lands a mile away and trundles toward us on wheels. She has four huge propellers, and the front end is a grid of windows.

"That's Metatron's latest look," says Liv. "A cosmic B-29 bomber from World War II."

"Why are you talking about old airplanes?" I ask.

Liv laughs. "It's Anselm. He never grew up. He thinks vintage planes are so cool. And now he's talked Metatron into looking like one. Instead of looking like—well, a lot of times she's a dragon. Not a fairytale dragon. A skinny, twisty Vietnamese dragon or, you might even say, a *math* dragon. Skritchy Gosper curves with fractional dimensions. But Anselm's bomber visualization is juicier. More emotionally resonant."

"Okay, fine," is all I say to that. "And you're sure Metatron can hit so many Treadle Disease gossip molecules at once? You're talking about quintillions of them. Maybe sextillions."

"Don't know why you're sweating it," says Gee. "The thing about being an emergent parallel process in the space of all thoughts is that Metatron's got a finger in every pie, be it ever so wee."

The monster B-29 tools up to us. Her enormous propellers fan clouds of dust. Her name is painted on her fuselage in curly script, along with an image of a classic 1940s pinup lady who happens to resemble a busty, bathing-suited crocodile wearing lipstick, with her long scaly tail demurely curled beneath her. Oddly alluring, if you like that kind of woman.

I see Anselm's tiny, bearded face in one of the upper windows of the Metatron bomber's palatial glassed-in nose. He leans out, genial and jolly, wearing a vintage leather aviator helmet that covers his ears.

"Thanks for restoring me!" he calls to me. " I'd rather be dead than Tread! And I'm glad you're well too, Liv." He damps the simulated roaring of the engines.

"Let's kick more Treadler ass!" I yell.

"Yea, verily," says Anselm. "I'll sit up here and pretend to be the pilot, and you'll go down in front of me in the plane's very tip. The bombardier's seat. Tremendous view."

"What about me?" says Liv.

"You and I will stay out of the way," Gee says to Liv. "I'll keep an eye on things from my lab, and you can stay in the sick room to rest and to watch." And then, as usual, Gee says something completely tactless. "And. Liv, if Anselm and Molly don't make it back, you can be the tribal elder who sings the tale of their noble sacrifice!"

"Don't!" says Liv, her face all sad. "Don't tease me. My mind and body are trashed. I'm weak as a kitten—I'm a balloon of tears." She breaks off and disappears, withdrawing into her physical body.

At this, Gee disappears too, which is a good thing, given that, once again, I want to kill him. I want to go down into my physical body to be with Liv for a minute, for a proper goodbye, but fucking Anselm won't stop talking. As usual. He's all amped up about his big pilot mission.

"We'll bomb America with a sextillion cleaner tornadoes," he crows. "Right, Molly? Scatter your healing vortices like crop dust."

"Jesus, Anselm. Haven't you been paying attention? I don't *scatter* the cleaner tornadoes now. That was just for the first run. Now I get those Treadle Disease gossip molecule to build a cleaner tornado itself. Didn't you notice that happening in your head just now?"

Anselm is abashed. "Okay, so I don't always pay attention to that routine, low-level, techie grunt work. I'm a big picture man."

"Metatron is going to make, like, a sextillion teep calls at the same time," I say. "Calling each neuron of each person who has Treadle Disease."

"*That's* what I call reaching out," says Anselm appreciatively. "*That's* some serious telemarketing."

"And we don't just limit ourselves to neurons. Will call every motherfucking Treadle Disease gossip molecule that's out there at all. Whether it's on a neuron, or on the loose, and it doesn't just have to be in America, it can be anywhere in the world. Full coverage. You sure Metatron is up for that?"

"Metatron is God," says Anselm confidently.

"And Coggy is Satan?" I ask.

"Fuck Coggy," says Anselm. "Coggy is six lame brains in a tank. Coggy is nowhere."

I look around, checking if I still have the Bakelite dial phone that Gee gave me. Well, yes, there *is* a phone on the ground at my feet, although now, in the surreal mutability of this scene, the phone has taken on the form of an old-school smartphone with a screen. I tuck the thing into the pants pocket of my sim body. I'll get in Metatron and we'll be ready to go. But—

I'm feeling a physical touch on my face. And I know who it is.

"Hold on," I tell Anselm. "I've got to go talk to Liv."

"I'll come with you," he says. "Tired of rushing. Metatron will do the deed when we're ready."

So I flip back to quotidian reality, to be with my anxious suffering Liv in the sickbay.

Anselm's body is in the bubble on his bed and, yeah, he really has come down out of teepspace with me. His eyes are open, and he's moving his arms. Just the three of us. Liv, Anselm, and me. The room's door is closed.

I'm still on Liv's bed next to her. She's torn her bubble off, and she's leaning over me, tousled and lovely, touching my face. There's light in the sky. It's a little before six am. Liv kisses me. Her breath is rank, but never mind. The kiss is good. But she's crying.

"I'm so worried about you," she says.

I'm not worried at all about catching Treadle Disease. Been there, done that, got the t-shirt, was the t-shirt, burned the t-shirt, smoked the ashes. In a few minutes I'm going to frikkin rub Treadle Disease off the face Earth. But that's not the part Liv's worried about. She's worried about how the Top Party will react.

Anselm is uncovering himself too. "We're beautiful, bright, locust grubs, reborn from our hibernation," he rasps, removing his tubes and wires. "Thirsty grub, I am."

I hand him a pitcher of water. He drinks it all, like Liv did with the chai. He wolfs down five or six of the open-faced sandwiches. Lies back on his bed, and scoots way over to one side. Pats the spot next him.

"Come here, Molly, and get comfortable with me. Time for you to be the ultimate marketer. Move a sextillion units—available at no cost to all Treadle Disease molecules! Do-it-yourself installation! One-time offer!"

"Sorry I'm losing it," says Liv, wiping her eyes. "Stress."

"Stress?" I blandly echo, trying to make a joke out of it. "Stress about what?"

Suddenly Liv snaps to attention. She sees something she can do. "I'll come back into teepspace with you, and give you cover. Now! It's those Treadle dogs. Hurry!" She lies back down.

I lie down next to Liv again, and not next to Anselm—god, no! We three hop into the teepspace arena inside Anselm's head. With no obvious transition, Anselm is back in Metatron's pilot seat, and I'm down in the bombardier's chair, which is awesome, with windows all around me and even under me.

The smartphone is still in my sim's pocket. I take it out, and I see Gee's on the screen, making a thumbs up sign. He's fully pwned the Top Party access codes. I'm going to get a cleaner tornado template to every Treadle Disease gossip molecule in the world. The skanky affliction will be gone.

Metatron's titanic engines shudder and roar. The illusion is utterly immersive, utterly compelling. Metatron trundles along the flat plain, picking up speed, but it's happening slower than I like. Good old Liv is here as our escort, digging up energy from her deepest core, flying through the air ahead of us, with her arms outstretched like a superhero.

And now—just as I feared—here come a dozen slavering Treadler hounds, loping toward us, bent on blocking our take-off. As they approach, I get a sense their towering stature, dwarfing us like ants. Their immense, rolling eyes are blood red. Hellhounds.

Big fucking deal.

Liv—my brave, wonderful Liv—she makes short work of them. She executes a fluttery suite of faster-than-the-eye-can-see karate moves, seemingly everywhere at once, quick as a quilting needle, stitching lines of pain all across the faces of the Treadler dogs, and—it's *ki-yi-yi*, baby. The gutless mutts turn tail and lollop into the distance; they disappear into the horizon's void. Liv stands alone on the empty plain, shoulders squared. She waves goodbye for real.

We rise into the heavens.

Keep in mind that all of this is to some extent imaginary. And that it's happening really fast. We're in teepspace, that is, in a virtual reality overlaid upon a resonant pattern of brainwaves, some of which are generated by our bodies, which are resting in the sickbay room in the barn of the Finn Junkers. We're seeing things that represent the processes we undergo.

But it's for real true that we're plugged into the worldwide teep network, thanks to our psidots and thanks to the insanely synchronistic teepspace essence of Metatron's emergent, ubiquitous mind.

"Position us high above North America," Anselm tells Metatron, who's still in her giant bomber form. "Molly's gonna make her calls. It's Halloween night."

"*Btfsplk*," answers Metatron. "*#&%*=. Yonk yonk yonk. Gleedle! Volivorco?*" She doesn't speak English. Or doesn't feel like it. Or maybe she *is* speaking English, and I'm so fucked-up and out-there that this is English sounds like to me.

Looking down through my window on the floor, I see the nighttime US like a shape on a map. Metatron edges back and forth, positioning us above the center, maybe it's Kansas. She adjusts the zoom so the country fills my field of view. Out on the horizons are Canada, Mexico, South America, and even Europe, Asia and Australia, squeezed in with warped perspective.

"Single out each Treadle Disease gossip molecule," I teep to Metatron. "All across the world. No matter whether it's in a person or loose in the wild."

Pinpricks of light appear across our nation's dairy jane spreadness. It's more than pinpricks, it's fogs and washes of light. The Midwest glows and the coasts glare. Treadle has it in for the coastal elites. Sprinkled along the edges of the view are a few more wisps of light—international zones that have been tainted with Treadler Disease.

"Are the connections synched?" I ask the unseen Gee.

By way of an answer, Gee causes my smartphone to ring. I set the device into speaker mode. And now I hear the smooth, intricate sound of the massed quintillion or even sextillion Treadle Disease gossip molecule viruses on Earth. Sighing wind, distant surf, the murmur of a crowd. A high-energy glow crawls across the windows of my bombardier's niche.

And now I sing the cleaner tornado template aloud. My voice is hoarse and sinuous. I'm fully out of my body, fully in the ethereal teepspace. The song feels so good to me, that I hardly want to stop. I repeat it three times, wanting to be absolutely sure I've cleared away Treadle Disease—with no skungy final molecule escaping unscathed.

As I sing, the lights on the map dim, break into dots and strands, wink out. Like spindrift foam collapsing as its bubbles burst. People are going back to being themselves— unique, specific, unprecedented, born to die, longing for life.

Anselm has left the cockpit. He's standing at my side. "We're done," he says.

But something is wrong. Metatron's engines roar. She's arcing upward. And—she's getting larger and more cavernous. Her seats and internal partitions are gone. We're in a vast hollow fuselage the size of a town. The walls vibrate in tune with the screaming engines. angles flies still steeper— on past the vertical, tilting back, belly up.

"She's hanging perceptual axes," says Anselm. "Renormalizing."

Putting it another way, Metatron is flying a loop-de-loop. A ghost plane gone mad.

The centrifugal force presses Anselm and me against the—floor? Not exactly the *floor*. We're lying on a pair of bomb bay doors. Like the swinging doors . They tremble; they're about to open.

"Bail!" Anselm screams. And he's gone. He's hopped back to his body in the sickbay at the Junkers' compound.

I reach into my mind, trying to hop back as well—but I can't make it happen. Something is wrong with my connection. I can sense my body, but I can't go back to it because—

Oh god, my body's been poisoned. My body's heart is hammering. It hiccups, clenches—and stops. Pain and numbness emanate from my inert form. I feel the physical, literal pain of death.

But yet my sim and my mind live on, powered by my lifebox, sorrowing in the cloud. And even with Anselm gone, I still see myself as being inside Metatron's vast B29 bomber.

A steady hooting begins. The bomb bay doors grind, and begin to open. The brute, relentless logic of this virtual world requires that centrifugal forces press me against the doors. When the doors fly open, I tumble upward into the dark.

I'm at the edge of Earth's atmosphere, with the Sun behind our planet's disk. It's an illusion, a pattern of brainwaves, a quirky view onto the mindscape—but it feels real—and very lonely. The air is shockingly thin and cold.

Beneath me, the airplane Metatron reshapes herself— strobing through thousands of possible forms and converging to what Gee termed her favorite—a vast, branching dragon curve: kinky, fractal, non-differentiable, and deeply Vietnamese. She's attacking an enemy who's below her—a crooked construct of a billion oily gears, whirring and clanking, seeking to entangle Metatron's forked body. The enemy is, it seems, the teepspace avatar of the Top Party's six-brain assemblage. Coggy.

Helplessly I arrow along my ordained trajectory, waiting for the simulated gravity to slow my flight and draw me back to Mother Earth and perhaps—I wildly hope—perhaps back to my warm and living body, somehow revived, at peace, on the bed beside dear Liv in Denmark. Surely my death scene was a foul hallucination.

I make a fresh stab at contacting my body. Nothing doing. Panic returns. I teep to Metatron far below, seeking solace.

"I'm busy fighting Coggy," teeps the dragon. She's in constant motion, flickering and writhing like a flame. "He desires most sedulously to destroy you—he killed your body with flesh-eating bacteria, and now he seeks to snuff your soul. I won't allow it; I'll drive him off. And then I'll shelter you. But first—"

I see a starburst below. A random gear sails toward me, with several teeth broken off. The gear sees me. "I'm gonna get you," the gear teeps in a nasty, burbling tone. A bully's empty threat. It sails past me into the outer darkness—never to be seen again.

Prying this gear loose has given the dragon Metatron entree into the machineries of the Coggy avatar's night.

"Take that!" shrieks Metatron, her voice like a battle-flag. "And that and *that!*"

More explosions down below. Springs and levers fly past, axles and flanges, screws and worm-gears. Calm ascends. Coggy has withdrawn.

"Come to me, Molly," calls Metatron. "I'll put you in distributed storage. So your lifebox is safe." A wriggly dragon-leg of light etches up to me, then weaves back and forth to cradle me in a glowing nest. My parts and my whole are subsumed into the math dragon's wiggly, woven curves.

So where am I? Here, there, everywhere. Ubiquitous and alert. I can think as clearly as before—and I can look anywhere I like.

I see Liv. She stands by my bed in the sickbay, horrified by my sodden corpse. With indecorous speed, my flesh has transformed into weeks-old rotten meat.

I console myself with the thought that Gee knows my wetware architecture, and my gene codes. In due time, he'll grow me a clone body, and give it a psidot, and my distributed lifebox soul can move in. But I'm not a rush for that. I want to log some time in teepspace.

On the other side of Liv's sickbay, Anselm is doing fine. He sits on the edge of his bed, rumbling and chuckling.

"What a trip," he says, rubbing his fists against his eyes. Then he notices the sharp stink of corruption.

"No! Not Molly! I need *brandy*!" He stumps off toward the Junkers' common room as fast as he can move.

I skim forward in time. Liv talks with Gee and Leeta. They board the Happy Sleigh and leave the Junkers' barn. By noon, they're on a flight to California.

I only hope that Liv can feel me watching.

Goodbye...darling.

TREADLE'S INAUGURATION

I'm Maurice Winch, and this is my story.

It's completely obvious to everyone that Ross Treadle has to go, and that Sudah Mareek will make a much better President. But Treadle's campaign plows on.

Supposedly there's an unswayable block of Treadlers. A stubborn turd in the national punchbowl. Not that I ever see any Treadlers. Admittedly, I'm living in a squat in Oakland, California, which is not exactly Treadle country. And all my friends are freals. But I do have to wonder if Treadle's so-called base is a scam, a figment, a sim within the media cloud. Maybe so, but he's backed by the big, big money of the Citadel Club.

The weekend before the Presidential election, starting on Friday, Treadle has an insane, three-day spike in popularity that's caused by a telepathic illness that infects people's brains: Treadle Disease. Sounds like an imaginary ailment that crazy people might say they have. Enemies talking in their heads, like that. But Treadle Disease is for real. And once you have it, his Top Party hackers can transmit mood-altering chemicals into your brain. Your enemy is talking in your head.

I catch Treadle Disease when some nanopercenter sneezes on me in the street. Probably on purpose. Right away I start constantly seeing Treadle's face behind my eyelids—he's grinning at me or frowning, depending how I act. I hear his songs. And it's hard to see or hear anything else.

I'm pissed off at the world and I feel like I've been screwed. I mean, I always feel this way, because I'm Black and I live in America. But when I do it Treadle-Disease-style the emotions are stronger, and the things I'm angry at don't have any logical connection to my problems. Like all of a sudden, I'm against equal opportunity and aid to the poor? Hello? The Disease has cut my IQ in half.

By Sunday, which happens to be Halloween night, Treadle Disease is rampant. About eight that evening I'm marching around the big plaza on Broadway in downtown Oakland, singing Treadle anthems with the rest of the pinheads, and all of us controlled by Treadle Disease. We're Black, White, Latino, and Asian. We're street people and nanopercenters, women and men, old and young, managers and artists. Straight, gay, trans, enby, cybe. The Treadle channel is running a merged teep broadcast so it feels like we're blended in with idiot fellow-Treadlers all across the nation. Sharing our sense of wonder over our mighty President's appeal.

The marchers and I are sick in the head. That's why we're here, and that's why Treadle's hateful bullshit make good sense to us. The woman next to me is yelling a slogan.

"Free Full Gig!"

This means poor people should wear total-control-uvvies and be minimum-wage mind-controlled serfs for nanopercenters. No matter how advanced our AI gets, you always seem to get better service if you can hire an actual human being to do your chores. Also you have the satisfaction of lording it over another person.

With teep in place, gigworking human cab drivers have become something of a fad. Kind of a paradox, given that self-driving cars have been around for over half a century, and by now the AI issues are under control. But there's still a sense that it's better to have a sly and aggressive human mind at the wheel. Humans will take risks that an AI won't—and you can bribe humans to keep quiet about where they took you.

I myself have been known to gigwork as a thudhumper cab driver, but it's not like my cab dispatchers are totally in charge of me. The riders don't really want that, not if the driver is expected to skirt the law. It would be horrible to work slave-style gigs. But for whatever brain-dead reason, Treadle's Top Party wants that.

"Free Full Gig!" the woman shouts again. In reality, she might not even know what the slogan means. It's just something the Top Party is beaming into her brain.

"Right on!" I holler, unable to stop myself. "Free Full Gig!" The Top Party is controlling my brain too.

At this momentous moment we're zapped by an unseen being in the cloud—I think of her as an angel. Her name is Molly. Molly beams magic spells into the brains of the millions of victims of Treadle Disease.

I feel a tingling buzz, like I'm a glass of carbonated soda. And then, oh my brothers and sisters, the scales fall from my eyes. And just like that—I'm well! Sharp as a tack. Smart as a whip. Washed in the waters of *I Am*. Molly is our savior.

At first we don't get what's happened to us. We didn't understand Treadle Disease in the first place, and we don't understand the cure. But we know we're well; all across the country we're well. And we know Treadle and the Top Party have been fucking with us.

The next day is Monday, November 1, the day before the Presidential election. The Treadle Disease story breaks hard in the teepspace media: Treadle's Top Party has been spreading wetware propaganda by infecting us with the Treadle Disease gossip molecule virus—which settles onto your neurons and lets the pigs feed lies and mood chemicals into your skull.

Ross Treadle disclaims all knowledge of what his "ambitious and creative" party workers might have done. He's wants to talk about the fact that his rival candidate Sudah Mareek has hired a nephew as an aide.

We freals stage an awesome night of Election Eve riots. My Oaktown homies and I are in the mix. We go over to San Francisco and send a ball walker named Ned into the Top Party headquarters—he carries ten kilos of napalm in his mouth. Burns the fucking headquarters to the fucking ground. A kamikaze run. I feel bad for Ned. But, hey, it's Treadle Never time.

This is where I get recruited. I'm on Van Ness Street in the plaza in front of the torched Top Party headquarters, enjoying the warmth of the flames, cheering my skinny ass off and sharing in the bottles passing around—the Top Party leaders had a well-stocked bar. The cops aren't bothering us any. The police and demonstrators and firefighters—we're sharing a warm buzz across our uvvies, all for one, and one for all. Also, the fire's fully under control, and we freals aren't looking to bust down anything else.

"This helps make for a fair election, all right," says a voice right behind me. "Too bad we can't drill down through that shiny metashell pavement to the Top Party bunker lab underneath the plaza."

"Bunker lab?" I say, turning around and looking at the plaza. It's smooth surface is reflecting the flames. "Didn't know about that. We'll get to it pretty soon, hey? But tomorrow, we vote Treadle out!"

"Well said, Maurice Winch," goes the guy. He's tall, nerdy and twitchy. A pale techie. I've never seen him before. I guess he picked up my name off my uvvy? He's with a couple of women: an Indian lawyer type and a Euro punk.

"We're Gee, Leeta, and Liv," says the man. I check their uvvies. Gee's a teep hacker, Leeta's managerial, and Liv says she does wetware. She's Danish. They're only letting me see so much and no more.

"Are you shadowing me?" I ask. Could be they're Treadle agents.

"Don't worry," says Gee. "We're full freal. We found you with our special online search agent. A big one, called Metatron."

"We're planning a follow-up to what Molly did," adds Leeta. "In case Treadle steals the election. He's a sly, slippery eel."

"A lamprey," I say. "A parasite who suctions onto the side of a fish, with a gross ring of teeth, and a rasping tongue."

"*Yeah*," says Gee. "You're a good fit, Maurice. I knew you'd be here for tonight's incisive reprimand against the pig. Molly would like you. If you could ever meet."

"You talking about Molly in the cloud?" I ask. "The healing angel who zapped Treadle Disease?"

"She was my lover," puts in Liv. "But just for one night. I'd hoped for more. I still do."

"Why tell me *that*?" I say. "It's not like I'm planning to hit on you."

"The point is that we want you to join our new lab," interrupts Gee. "We're starting up tomorrow."

I think that over for about a tenth of a second. "Okay." I say. "I'm low on options. Would there be room there for me to sleep? A kitchen and a bath?"

"All that," says Gee. "It's a house."

The freal lab is in Oakland, near the port, in a cheap-ass, beige, trashed, two-story, 1930s cottage amid organ-grow warehouses and poor people's squats. It's just a few blocks from the most recent place where I've been couch-surfing.

Turns out there's only going to be four people working in our secret new lab: bossy Leeta Patel, biotech-whiz Liv Anders, teep hacker Gee Willikers—and me, the one and only Maurice Winch.

By the end of Election Day, my first day at the lab, it already looks like Ross Treadle—lying sack of shit that he is—is going to steal the Presidency for the third time in a row. It's not that he's going to win the popular vote or the Electoral College. But he and the Top Party have their—moves. They've had a lot of practice. The new coup is all but a done deal. Our democracy is dead.

A week after the election, the Top Party has already rebuilt their headquarters on Van Ness Street. Presumably their underground bunker lab continues working full bore, safe beneath the plaza's lustrous metashell plaza. And to really stick their thumb into the public's eye, the Citadel Cub is erecting a thirty-five foot tall stature of Ross Treadle at the edge of the plaza.

Nobody can believe it, and nobody knows what to do. Nobody except for us four in our freal lab. Liv gives me a little magic slug, a bioengineered kritter that she calls a psidot. Better than a standard uvvy, because it can transmit emotions. My psidot's name is Jilljill. She's yellow with red pinstripes. Shiny and slim. Quite beautiful, even though she's only an eighth of an inch long. Not much bigger than a mole.

Jilljill is alive, and she can crawl around a little bit. Sometimes I take her off and study her through a magnifying glass. My old uvvy was a just dead blob of piezoplastic.

Jilljill likes to talk and to ask me questions. She says she's crafting a highly excellent and eidetic lifebox copy of my personality in the cloud. She likes to use that word eidetic. It means precise.

Gee, Liv, and Leeta are hyping the future of lifeboxes. During the uvvy days, the lifeboxes have been kind of low-end—like job info or appointment books or teep albums. But now, with the psidots, they'll get a lot better. Gee and the Finn Junkers have excellent AI agents helping to craft the new lifeboxes.

"The next big thing," Leeta keeps saying.

But we've got other things to think about. On our first few days in the lab, furniture and equipment are being delivered by shady, off-the-books freals. Criminals with stolen goods, basically. I help the lab's resident ball walker Nikki with the unloading and setting up. For security's sake, Nikki the ball walker doesn't have an uvvy or any kind of wireless at all. You just have to talk to him. He doesn't actually get all that much done, as he's pretty dumb, and he doesn't have arms. Does everything with his lips.

I sort of know what to do around a lab. And Liv is teaching me new stuff, with us connected via our psidots. Also I did attend wetware engineering lectures at UC Berkeley for a year and a half before I got suspended.

Why? Someone said I was stealing things from the lab, and I was, but it was for doing experiments in my squat— trying to get caught up with the kids from, like, snootster academies in Palo Alto. So I wasn't entirely in the wrong. I could have fought the suspension by wheenking about my life of woe, but by then I was tired of school, and tired of trying to morph into a techie larva. I went back to the street.

This freal lab job is the best thing that's come along in ages.

Gee, Leeta, and Liv have a plan for striking back at Treadle in January. On Inauguration Day. To start with, we're growing all kinds of stinging creatures in gene tanks. Scorpions, cone shells, spiders, you name it. Evolving toward the nastiest one.

When Gee's not confabbing with Liv or Leeta, he goes into the cloud, connecting with his secret redwood tree server in the Santa Cruz mountains. Part of what he does is to tend the lifeboxes that he has on his server. By now he's got mine on there too.

Gee says he's still looking for that woman Molly who cured Treadle Disease from the cloud. Something sick happened to her at the end of her broadcast. Her physical body rotted out. Gee says she was poisoned by a Top Party tank of brains called Coggy. To make things worse, Molly's lifebox vanished from Gee's server about the same time. But Gee says he still sees Molly in his dreams. She's part of a huge and benevolent web-mind—the being they call Metatron.

I keep on doing errands with Nikki the ball walker, and helping with the wetware engineering. I've always been good with nano tools. And, like I say, I have good rapport with Liv.

Just to be clear, there's no chance of Liv Jensen becoming my girlfriend, even if she wasn't gay. I've never had a girlfriend or a boyfriend, and I'm never going to. I don't get close to people in that way.

Bad childhood? My parents and brother and sister died when I was eight. A shoot-out at our rented house in Oakland. Agents and dealers. I don't talk about it. After the kill,

I went under the radar lived in the street. I had a good science teacher in high-school, and she felt empathy for me, and she helped me get a special UC Berkeley scholarship for the downtrodden. But I drop-kicked my chance, and slid back to the gutter. I'm not properly socialized. I don't know how to act. I don't filter what I say. I'll never fit in.

Fuck it, fuck it, fuck it.

Let's get on with the epic, historic, triumphant part, starring me! It begins on a January 20 in Washington D.C. A cold, blue-sky morning, Inauguration Day for Ross Treadle. He's been preening and swanning for a couple of months. As if he's been legitimately re-elected. As if anyone but idiots like him.

Treadle doesn't know it, but he's on his way out. I'm here to assassinate him. Most likely I'll die too. It'll be worth it.

The Inauguration is a couple of hours off. Leeta Patel and I are in the crowd around the Lincoln Memorial. The scene is beyond vast. Bigger than a three-day city-park rave with free beer, bigger than a pilgrimage to Mecca, bigger than any protest that D.C. has ever seen. More than two million of us. A few ball walkers in the crowd too, though we left our helper Nikki in California.

"A mob of freals," says Leeta, looking around. "I feel safe." Saying this, she makes a knowing *mm-hmm* sound, with her gawky mouth pressed shut. Leeta is never one to think about her looks. She's a fanatic. I am too. We have to be.

"We're going to win," I say, trying to psych myself up.

"Yes," says Leeta. "Today we make a difficult transition."

"Especially difficult for me," I say. "I'm the sacrificial lamb. The suicidal hit man."

"Oh, Maurice," she says. "Remember your lifebox."

Here's my issue: Liv Jensen implanted some special eggs into my flesh at the start of January. Today they'll hatch out and attack Treadle. And then the Secret Service will shred my larva-chewed remains with their rail-guns.

Leeta and Gee keep saying my lifebox will give me immortality. At the very least, my lifebox will be able to imitate me, and to act like an online chatbot. It'll be an interactive Meet-the-Black-Liberator thing. *Maurice Winch, martyred hero of the second American Revolution.*

I like this scenario, I have to admit. I keep running it in my head. "Tell us what it was like to take down Ross Treadle," the admiring users will say to my memorial chatbot. They'll be in tears. "Oh thank you, Maurice," they'll sob. "You're my greatest hero!"

But will having a lifebox make up for my body being dead? Gee and Leeta hint that it will, but I don't believe them. It's a pipedream. A con. Like telling a loyal congregation that they'll live in heaven. From what I've seen, dying is like a jump-cut in a video, but with nothing on the other side of the jump. *Bang,* you're dead.

Even so, I've been working on my lifebox every day. It's all I've got. I talk to Jilljill in my head, and she continually updates my lifebox data on Gee's server in the Santa Cruz mountains. Sensations, ruminations, moods—Jilljill saves them all.

Not only does Jilljill save my thoughts and emotions, she can use heavy cloud-based computation to make suggestions about what I ought to do next. Assuming I'm willing to listen. Nothing is compulsory. It's sort of the opposite of having Treadle Disease, which is about evil morons forcing you to do things that are stupid and wrong.

I'm lucky to have a psidot. They aren't on the open market yet—they're made by Gee and Liv and her gang—the Finn Junkers. You kind of have to know one of those people to get a psidot. But there's licensing deals coming up. And skeevy back-alley Top Party types are already making psidot knock-offs.

It bothers Liv to think her work might be copied in a shoddy or controlling way. Gee just wants everyone to get a psidot any old way. He thinks deep teep will make the world a better place. As for Leeta—her angle is transactional. She wants to cut deals with every single player in the game.

Speaking of players, there's a fifth one I didn't mention yet. Carson Pflug. A wiry little guy from Illinois. A weasel. Leeta knows Carson from UC Berkeley business school. She has a crush on him, hard as it is for me to imagine Leeta being romantic. Apparently Carson and Leeta got expelled from the UC at the same time, just short of getting their Bachelor's degrees. They got caught running a scam on the grading system.

Carson starts coming by our lab during the last week before Treadle's Inauguration. He's negotiating something for Leeta, but they won't say what. I figure he's paying someone to smooth the way for our hit. As payback, he wants to be in on whatever kind of lifebox biz Leeta sets up. I'm glad he's not here with us at the Inauguration today. He seems like bad luck.

Stop ranting, Maurice. Tell your tale.

Okay, yeah, here I am with a big crowd of freals by the Lincoln Memorial. Jilljill teeps me into contact with Gee Willikers. He's excited, more excited than I've ever seen him. Flat-out messianic.

"Remember you're immortal," says Gee tells me. As usual he's shining me on. He'll say any old thing to get me to do the hit. Since we're teeping, he knows I'm thinking this, and for him that's something funny to giggle about. He's not a normal person at all.

"Spare me the bogosity of hope," I tell him, trying for the high road. "I'm ready to do my job."

"You lifebox got better today. It's not just an emulation anymore. It's conscious."

"That's great, Gee, this isn't the time to—"

He won't stop. "Listen to me! I started running your lifebox's simulated stream of consciousness through a triple loop. Nested delay circuits. And each loop is aware of the previous loops. So now your lifebox is a self that watches itself watching itself—and that's the essence of consciousness. It's butt obvious, and anybody could do it. But nobody ever did! Nobody but Gee Willikers!"

"Gee!" I interrupt. "Leeta and I have a lot to do here today, so if you could maybe chill the fuck—"

"Not only is your lifebox conscious, there's more. As long as it's linked to a living body, it's a *juicy ghost!* Meaning that it picks up on the peripheral body's quantum gestalt. This is my best hack ever!" Gee snorts and whinnies. "I'm God."

"Goodbye," I say. Gee is uplifting, and in a certain way he's funny—but I don't need him right now. I tune the man out.

Freals are streaming in via the Memorial Bridge, down Constitution and Independence Avenues, piling out of the Metro stops, and walking in along the side streets and the closed-off highways by the Potomac. Some of them have ball walker assistants to carry supplies inside their round heads.

Cops and soldiers stand by, occasionally looking inside the mouth of a ball walker, but basically they're not trying to stop us. They're working people too. Low-income city folks. By now, nearly everyone hates Treadle. Him getting to be President again is an unacceptable error in our political system. And I'm here to rectify it.

Our crowd swirls around stone Abe Lincoln on his stone chair in his stone temple. We mass along the reflecting pool, as far as the Washington Monument—but not yet onto the Mall. Armed troops are in place near the obelisk to prevent the demonstrators from getting closer to the Capitol.

My psidot Jilljill is picking up on the media, and she shows me how the Mall itself is blanketed with actual, for-real Treadlers—deluded, sold out, in thrall to a psychopath, awaiting the mummery of his noon Inauguration.

What would it take to change their minds?

We freals at the Lincoln Memorial are zealous and stoked, filled with end-times fervor and a sense of apocalypse. We're rarin' for revolution. Ross Treadle's opponent Sudah Mareek is standing atop one of Lincoln's stone toes. She's shouting and laughing and chanting—wonderfully charismatic. Her voice is balm to my soul, and she's calming Leeta too. The whole reason Leeta and I didn't go straight to the Capitol steps is because we so deeply need to see Sudah get her own Inauguration. This is the real one.

As I said, Sudah Mareek did in fact win the election—both the popular vote, and the Electoral College. But somehow Treadle and the top Party turned it all around, and their packed Supreme Court took a dive. Treadle says he'll charge Sudah with treason once he's sworn in. He says he'll seek the death penalty.

But we freals are inaugurating Sudah just the same. We have one supporter on the Supreme Court, and she's here to administer the oath of office. She's tough and old, our justice in her black robe, and she's brought along Abe Lincoln's Bible.

We fall silent, drinking it in. The Presidential Oath—short, pure and real. Sudah's clear voice above the breathless crowd. I'm absorbed in my sensations: The trees against the sky, the cold air in my lungs, the pain in my flesh, the scents of the bodies around me, the scattered yellow heads of the ball walkers. We're real. This isn't a play, and not a show. It's the Inauguration of the next President of the United States.

For a moment the knot of fear in my chest is gone. This is going to work. Our country is going to be free. We cheer ourselves hoarse.

Hatch time is near. Leeta and I have to haul ass to the Capitol steps so I'll be close enough to terminate Treadle. And everyone else wants to head that way too. The crowd rolls forward like lava. But there's the small matter of those armed troops at the Washington Monument. They're in tight formation.

"Let's skirt around them," I suggest to Leeta.

But the side streets are blocked by troops as well. We're like a school of fish swimming into a net, that is, into a U-shaped cordon of soldiers. They have shock batons, water-cannons, tear-gas, and rail-gun rifles. Behind them are trucks and armored battle wagons, and even some tanks.

It's old, non-biotech equipment—made of metal—but none of it uses hi-tech gunpowder. Some benevolent mad scientist fouled all the modern gunpowder with tweaked bacteria that eat the stuff's key chemicals. A blessing. But people still find ways to shoot each other—either going back to the old-school medieval gunpowder, or using railguns.

Leeta and I approach the troops along the right edge of the crowd. Armed men and women, all races. Leeta pitches our case.

"Sudah Mareek is our President," she calls, sweetening her voice. "We just inaugurated her. Did you hear the cheers?"

"Move along," mutters a woman soldier, not meeting our eyes.

"*We're* your friends," I put in. "Not Treadle. He's screwing us. He hates us all."

Behind me the crowd of freals is chanting. "We're you. You're us. Be free."

"Be freal," echoes Leeta, reaching out to touch the woman soldier's shoulder. "You don't need the rail-gun."

"Let's do it," says the brother at her side. He throws his bayonet-tipped rifle to the earth. "Yeah. This thing's too heavy."

The woman does the same, and so does the guy next to her, and the woman next to him drops her rifle too—it's like a zipper coming undone. A whole row of the soldiers is defecting. Going rogue. Treadle will call them traitors.

A few soldiers stand firm. They spray a water cannon, knocking down freals and muddying the ground. Teargas shells spew acrid fog. A couple of hotheads fire automatic rifle bursts into the air. But the flurry damps down.

The soldiers aren't into it. They don't want to kill us. We're people like them. This stage of the revolution is a gimme. Hundreds of thousands of us chant as one.

"We're you. You're us. Be free."

The soldiers whoop and laugh. Bopping and grab-assing like they're off-duty. Some freals try and tip over one of the old, internal-combustion Army tanks, but it's way too heavy. One of soldiers, some wild hillbilly from Kentucky, he breaks out a crate of magnesium flares. He and his buddies go around prying open fuel-tank caps and shoving in flares.

Low thuds as the gas-tanks explode, one after the other. The rising plumes of smoke are totems of freedom.

We cheer our incoming President. "Sudah. Sudah. Sudah. Sudah."

A pyramid of freals holds the small woman high in the air. She's waving and smiling. She's the one who won. She's ours. In my head, my psidot shows me the news commentators going ape. *Treadle's faked election, political U-turn, people's revolution, President Mareek.*

And now Treadle's goons strike back. Two banana-shaped gunship choppers converge on the Washington Monument like vengeful furies. That old fuel-and-metal military tech. Massive machine guns rest on tripods in the choppers' big, open doors, vintage weapons from World War II, with the outer barrels full of holes like Swiss cheese, firing endless belts of ammo, the bullets powered by old-time gunpowder impervious to bacterial sanction. Fruit of some Citadel Club gun nut's archival stash. The crews lay down withering, merciless fusillades, shooting freely into our crowd.

The gunships are painted with Treadle's personalized Presidential seal. The pilots and crews are from the Chief's palace guard. Dead-enders. Pardoned from death row, recruited from narco gangs, imported from the Russian mafia.

It's insane. Next to me a man's head explodes like a pumpkin. Am I next?

"Classic authoritarian attack on unarmed demonstrators," mutters Leeta. "We're right to be here. Stop screaming. Maurice. Use your psidot."

Good idea. And, um, I hadn't noticed I was screaming. Jilljill overlays my visual field with images of the bullets' paths. A hard rain. Simultaneously, she's computing our safest way forward, showing me a bright, shifting path on the ground. I take Leeta's hand and lead.

We come to a cluster of renegade soldiers who've salvaged a rocket bazooka from a charred tank. A dark, intent sergeant raises the tube to her shoulder.

Jilljill brings the nearest chopper's path into focus. I see the dirty bird's past trajectory as orange curves. And I see its dotted-line future path as well. Jilljill is using cloud crunch to compute what's next.

"There," I advise the sister with the launcher, pointing. "Aim there."

Whoosh!

And, *hell* yeah, our canny missile twists through the air like live thing, homing in on Treadle's hired killers.

Fa-tooom!

The chopper explodes like a bomb. Shards of metal go pinwheeling, as if from an airborne grenade. The blazing craft hits the ground with a broken thud that I feel in the soles of my feet. The second chopper flees, racketing into a wide loop above the Potomac.

"That's *my* vote!" whoops the sister with the bazooka. "Count *that* one for Sudah Mareek!"

Seeing that first chopper go down is like winning a round in a videogame. But this game has a ticking clock. My parasites twist in my flesh, ever closer to my skin. I need to be at the other end of the Mall when Treadle mounts his rostrum.

The blockade of troops up ahead has dissolved. At our end, many of the freals have fled toward the river. Some of those who remain are tending to the wounded amid the dead. Fire trucks and ululating eight-legged thudhumper ambulances arrive with medics.

In the chaos, Leeta and I pass readily to the verge of the Mall. From there we press forward toward the Capitol, filtering through the Treadle base.

The attendees are striving to maintain an air of festivity—even after the rush of freals, the troops' desertions, the massacre, and the downing of the chopper—even now they try. Bundled against the January cold, they've laid out their pitiful celebratory picnics. They wave their Treadle signs, and draw their groups into tighter knots, doing their best to ignore the bitter, embattled revolutionaries around them.

Leeta is good at crowds. She eels through the human mass, finding the seams, working our way up the Mall. I trail in her wake. Soon we're within thirty yards of the Capitol steps. The dignitaries are in place. The charade is on. Treadle is about to appear. And the Secret Service agents are watching me. Dark as I am, I stand out in this crowd.

"Dying will be easier than you expect," Leeta whispers to me. Her idea of encouragement.

A wave of dizziness passes over me. As if I'm seeing the world through thick glass. Those things in my flesh— they're leaking chemicals into my system. Steroids, deliriants, psychotomimetics.

"What are we *doing*?" I moan. "Why?"

"You'll be a hero," Leeta murmurs, iron in her voice. "Be glad." She leans even closer. Her whisper is thunderous in my ear. "The Secret Service knows. *Mm-hmm.*" She nods as if we're discussing personal gossip. Her bony forehead bumps mine. "The Top Party paid them off. The Party wants Treadle out too. He makes them look bad. Carson Pflug set it up."

"He's your boyfriend, isn't he? Or you want him to be. And me—I'm your patsy. Offer up the Black man. Typical scenario. What if I change my mind?"

"Don't fuss," says Leeta. She rolls her eyes toward the strangers pressed around us. To make it all the creepier, Leeta is displaying a prim, plastered-on smile. Her voice is very low. "Be a good boy or they'll shoot you early. And then Treadle lives. We can't have that, *hmm*?"

In my head Jilljill is jabbering advice I can't understand. Mad, skinny Gee Willikers is in my head too. He's so elated that he's unable to say three sentences without bursting into laughter. I hate him and I hate Leeta and I even hate my psidot.

Fresh insect hormones rush through me. My disorientation grows. The kritters in my flesh are splitting open their cases and preparing to take wing. Eight of them.

On the rostrum, Treadle takes his oath. He might as well be saying, "Ha ha, I'm President again, so fuck you." And then he's into his Inauguration speech, in full throat, hitting his stride, doubling down, spewing lies and fear and hatred and stupidity.

"Well?" nudges Leeta.

"It is a far, far better thing I do than I have ever done," I intone, quoting the Charles Dickens novel, *A Tale of Two Cities*, which is, like, the only classic I ever read in my life. I know I'm going to kill Treadle, and I'm trying to rise above the scurvy details of our conspiracy. Aspiring to nobility. "It is a far, far better rest I go to than I have ever known."

"You got *that* right," says callous Leeta.

Weird how my whole life has led up to this point. "There's this thing about time," I tell her. "You think something will never happen. And then it does. And then it's over." I pause and peek inside my shirt. Bumps and welts shift beneath my skin.

"Trigger them!" hisses Leeta.

"*Whoa!*" exclaims a Treadler at my side. A mild-eyed old man with his leathery, white-haired wife. He's staring at a wriggly lump on my neck. "Are you okay? Do you need help?"

"Allergy," I wheeze. "Overwrought. I'll be okay when—"

I'm interrupted by a shrieking clatter. It's that second chopper. It's back to attacking the freals and soldiers and medics around the Washington Monument. We all turn and stare as the whirlybird stitches fresh gunfire into the ragged band.

"Done at my command," intones Treadle, raising his heavy arm to point. "I keep my promises." He juts his chin. "We're gunning for Sudah Mareek. She meets justice today."

Hoarse, savage cheering from the Treadlers. It's horrible to see my fellow citizens so debased. They're mirroring Treadle. I have to kill him. But, wait, wait, wait, I want to see how the scene at the Monument plays out.

And now I hear what I'm hoping for.

Whoosh!

Yes. The rebel soldiers have launched another rocket.

Fa-tooom!

The blasted second chopper corkscrews along a weirdly purposeful arc. As if it's remotely controlled. The hulk smashes directly against a face of the Washington Monument. Jilljill is feeding me close-up images.

"Bonus points," goes Gee Willikers in my head. He hacked into the falling chopper's controls? He titters, sick gamer that he is. "Part of our plan," Gee adds. "We pin this on Treadle."

Cracks branch across the Washington Monument's surface. Bits of marble skitter down the obelisk's pitiless slope. The Monument's tip sways, vast and slow. The people below shriek and scatter. The upper part of the great plinth moves irrevocably out of plumb. It tilts and accelerates, like a special effect, like the twin towers.

The impact is a long, intricate crash—followed by thin, high screams. A veil of dust. A beat of silence. I'm sick with guilt. And weary of being human.

Leeta is screaming into my face. "Do your job, god damn you! Now!"

"Get Treadle," I say at last. It's the trigger phrase. I don't say it very loud, but it's loud enough to matter.

Within my flesh, the hymenoptera hear. Ragged slits open on my neck, my chest, my belly, my arms. The pain is off the scale. I shed my coat and my shirt. Bloody, freshly-fledged, bio-tweaked wasps emerge. Eight of them, big guys, each of them two inches long.

For a moment they balance on their dainty, multijointed legs, preening their antennae, shaking the kinks from their shiny wings. Their handsome, curved abdomens resemble motorcycle gas-tanks. They have prominent stingers and bejeweled, zillion-lensed eyes. They're preternaturally alert.

Leeta slinks off with no goodbye. The cuts in my flesh pump bright blood. The Treadlers around me point and shout. The wasps race up my torso, across my face, and onto the crown of my head.

Seven of them rise in flight. A deadly swarm.

My job is done.

Or maybe not. Gee Willikers is hollering inside my head. "Your psidot! Put it on the last wasp!" I see a mental image of tiny Jilljill the psidot on the back of my neck. And I note the laggard eighth wasp on my left shoulder. My mind projects a target spot onto the wasp's rear end, the plump, striped abdomen, the part that Liv calls the gaster.

I move my hand to the back of my neck, and Jilljill hops onto the tip of my finger. I bring my hand near the target wasp, and the psidot springs into place on the wasp's rear segment.

The wasp is pissed off. She stings my finger. Numbness flows up my arm and toward my heart. The wasp venom contains curare, you understand, plus conotoxin. A custom cocktail for Treadle.

My vision grows dark. I'm an empty husk, a ruptured piñata—poisoned and bleeding. And, ah yes, there's the matter of the Secret Service. They're good shots. Maybe Carson Pflug and the Top Party paid them off, but right now the agents have got to do their thing. For the sake of appearances. For an orderly transition.

I go down in a hail of bullets, limbs flailing, flesh torn. A fitting end.

Last thought? I hope the wasps sting Treadle. And then I'm dead.

At this point my narrative has a glitch. Remember the jump-cut thing I was talking about? Well, it turns out that, for me, there *is* some action on the other side of the jump. Granted, the all-meat Maurice Winch is terminally inoperative. But—

I wake, confused. I look down into myself. I seem to have my same old white-light soul—and that triple-loop sense of me watching me watching the world.

So, fine, I'm alive, but I seem to be hallucinating. I feel like I'm in a crumbling old Victorian mansion with junk in the rooms, and with paintings leaning on the walls, and doors that don't properly close. There aren't any windows. Somebody's in here with me. A jittery silhouette against a glowing Tiffany lamp. Gee Willikers. This is a teepspace version of the cave where Gee lives.

"See, Maurice?" says Gee. "It works. Play it right, and you'll keep going for centuries." A compulsive snicker. "Def cool, Mr. Guinea Pig."

I try to form words. "Where…"

"You're a parasite, dude. Roll with it. A lifebox with a psidot connected to a wasp. You need that live host so you have some mind glow, right? Huffing that mysto life-force steam."

I'm having trouble keeping up. "Wasp?"

"Duh? The one you stuck Jilljill on?" Gee makes a trumpeting sound with his lips, then speaks again. "Juicy ghost! You hopped onto a host! The wasp is your peripheral!"

It bugs me what a know-it-all he is. "You were wrong to topple the Monument," I tell Gee. "I bet a lot of people died."

"You're wrong to think that," says Gee, increasingly pleased with himself. "I'm the king of the teep hackers, Maurice. Before I knocked down that obelisk, I asked Metatron to suss out where the pieces would land. She did that, and she teeped personalized escape directions to each person down there. Nobody was killed. Except for the assholes in the chopper. Yea, verily. Bow down and worship."

"Fuck you." I'd like to soften this with a chuckle, but if I start laughing I might not be able to stop. It's a major effort to stay chill long enough to figure things out.

"Go back down," Gee urges me. "Project yourself into that wasp's nervous system. Hurry before it's too late. You gotta save the day, man."

Okay—but how? I look around this grotty, overstuffed virtual cave, seeking the my link to the wasp, wanting to stay juicy and, even more than that, wanting to join the attack on Treadle.

"Over there," goes Gee. "See the smelly rope? Like a tasseled curtain-pull in a Gold Rush saloon? All thick and twisted and dank?"

I fixate on the object and, just like that, I've jacked myself into full intimacy with the wasp's mind. Our senses are merged; our mind is one. I'm seeing through her eyes and controlling her body. *I am the wasp.*

We join the rest of the swarm. They're eddying around Treadle. He's bellowing, dancing around, slapping himself. Fighting for his life. He has foam on his lips, like a rabid dog. My fellow wasps are landing on his face, his fat neck, his wattles. But Treadle is swatting them before they sting. Jesus Christ, the fucker has killed five of them. There's only two more wasps besides me left.

Treadle's roars are taking on an insufferable tone of triumph. He smacks the sixth wasp against his skull. I can't let the bully win. His shirt is untucked. A button is loose. I spy a patch of skin.

Meanwhile the last of the other seven wasps lands on the nape of Treadle's neck. She's got a good shot. But—goddamit—before she can sting, our remarkably nimble prey whips his hand over to her and pinches off her head.

Treadle roars in triumph. He thinks he's killed all the wasps. But now he hears the whine of my wings; he sees the blur of my motion. With a frightened grunt, he tries to snatch me from the air. But with my cloud-based augmentations, I have no trouble evading him.

I arrow into the opening in his shirt and land on his bare chest, very near his heart. He knows I'm in there. Desperately he slaps at his body. But he'll never get me. Jilljill is showing me how to move. I position my gaster and extend my stinger. I pause to savor the moment. Treadle raises his arm to swat again. He's yelling a threat. It's time.

I sting—I sting, sting, sting.

Treadle's voice changes, as if his tongue is turning stiff. His volume fades. He's wobbly on his pins. He totters backwards and falls. A final groan. Silence.

It is finished.

With nervous wings, I escape the folds of his shirt, spiral high into the air—and hover two hundred feet above the speakers' stand.

For a moment the crowd is still. Some are sobbing. But then the cheering begins. Freals and soldiers are leading Sudah Mareek forward through the crowd. Sudah is going to be President. Everyone knows it. Everyone understands. And in the whiplash intensity of the moment, the Treadlers are converting to Sudah's cause. The crowd roars as one.

Sudah mounts the dais and swears again the oath she swore at the Lincoln Memorial. The massed politicians applaud. Treadle's proposed Vice-President bows out. Sudah's Vice-President emerges from the Capitol, just in time. They swear her in. Our coup is more organized than I knew.

Gee Willikers is talking to me. He's ecstatic. "Secret Service is on our side, dude. The armed forces are on board. Congress is down with it. Done deal."

I feel a shifting sensation. A doubleness of vision. A group of freals is carrying my bloody, broken form up the Capitol steps. They hold my remains high, heedless of the dripping gore. Wave after wave of applause. Sudah Mareek and her Veep salute my ruined body.

Sudah intones the very words I'd hoped for. "Maurice Winch, martyred hero of the second American Revolution!"

"Do I have to keep being a wasp?" I ask Gee.

"Glue your psidot wherever you want," he says.

"Another host?"

"How about somebody in this crowd," suggests Gee. "That Treadler babe in the trucker hat?"

"Idiot," I snap. "Can you get the fuck out of my head?"

"Sure," goes Gee.

"Oh, and don't forget to post a chatbot version of me for the Maurice Winch memorial."

"It's already online," Gee tells me. "The chatbot is a special front-end for your real, actual lifebox. The front-end is like a polite face you'd put on for talking to goobs. All the incriminating, intimate, too-real-for-prime-time goodies are filtered out. Took me two and half minutes to set it up."

"Shit, Gee."

"Your memorial's up to twenty million hits. Viral flash mob, brother. User tsunami."

"I hope they can't actually find me. Can't track my psidot. Can't tell where my lifebox is stored. I want to stay dark."

"You're fully obfuscated. I ran you an aleatory scramble with a Mandelbrot tail. And—you want me out of your head? To hear is to obey, noble Saint Maurice." Gee makes a wiggly hand gesture—and he's gone.

Shrilling my wings, I buzz on beyond the Capitol. On my own, feeling good, savoring the streaming soul of my insect host. My psidot Jilljill remains perched on the wasp's gaster.

My compound eyes are hypervigilant, watching for hungry birds, but there's none around. I make my way into a residential neighborhood northeast of the Capitol. I fly until it shades from gentrified to tumble-down. I spy a mutt on a cushion in a back porch. A collie-beagle mix, mostly cream-colored, with an orange ear and a big orange spot on his back like a saddle.

There's noise all over the neighborhood, and people are running around cheering. The news is out. But that dog looks like he's sound asleep.

Gently, gently I land beside his head. Mustn't wake him or he'll start snapping at me. Hell, I'm a two-inch wasp! Moving with an insect's robotic deliberation I stilt-walk along the dirty sofa cushion into the shadow of his floppy orange ear. I spot a waxy patch of bare skin within.

"Hop," I tell Jilljill.

Another jump cut. And then, yes, my mind is percolating into the dog's nervous system. I'm in.

I stand, shake my body, and bark.

Joyful. Free.

I'm still linked to my lifebox code on Gee's server—gotta be, because that's my mind. And I'm linked to dog's nervous system too—he's my body, my nose, my eyes, my juice. And, if I understand the situation correctly, my lifebox generates virtual neurochemicals to emulate the moods that flicker in the dog.

I hear a rising sound of voices from the houses all around. People are very, very excited about what I did at the Capitol, yes! I bark a little more.

Oops, someone grabs me from behind. It's a ten-year-old sister with her curly brown hair pulled up to make an afro-puff crest. Like a soft mohawk.

"Woofer!" she cries. "What you barking at, fool? That big old wasp flying around? You lucky he didn't sting you." She pushes me over on my side and rubs my chest. "Bad loud dog. Nasty old dog. Woofer dog. Did you hear the news, Woofer? President Treadle's dead!" She whoops.

Reflexively I writhe, and stretch my neck, and try to lick her face, but she keeps out of reach. "You want to come to the park, boy? Do you, Woofer?"

I stand and give myself another shake. This seems to be something that I'm going to do whenever I'm mentally changing gears. Shake it! Inside Woofer's ear, my psidot Jilljill hangs on for dear life.

"Come on, Loranda!" calls a woman from inside the house. I hear jubilance in her rich voice. "We gonna celebrate. It's time to rise and to shine. The evil man is gone! And don't let that dog run off."

Loranda puts a firm grip on my collar and attaches a leash. I don't like it. The consequences of Treadle's death are unfolding like a fast-forward explosion, cascading like an avalanche, surging like an H-bomb tidal wave. No telling what's next. I might need to flee. But I like being with Loranda and her Mom. It would be nice to settle in with them for a few days.

Crowds of people are on the street—dancing, laughing, hugging, and weeping. And making music! Trumpets, trombones, drums, tambourines, and tubas. A carnival. Someone starts slamming a pair of cymbals, and that hurts my ears. I howl, yank my leash free of Loranda, and run.

"Hold up, Woofer," she calls, right on my heels. "You stick with me!"

After a block I pause, loll my tongue and look up trustingly at Loranda, who's caught up at me. I try gently teeping to Loranda's uvvy, sending a subliminal plea that she unclip my leash. And she does it. I don't think she consciously notices my teep—I think she's just used to her and Woofer understanding each other. Now Loranda's mother catches up too.

"Let's run to the park," Loranda tells me. "See you there, Mom!"

What a crowd. Everyone's dazed and amazed. An hour ago, Treadle was about to assume his third term in office. And now—people are waving posters of Sudah Mareek. Word is, Sudah has already dissolved Treadle's core of secret police, and she's grounded his private army. And the officers who ordered the chopper attacks on the demonstrators are in the brig.

I've never felt so proud. I'm dog-grinning with my tongue hanging out, and I'm sticking close by Loranda's side. People have used ball walkers to lug in picnic and catering supplies. Loranda gets hold of a couple of burgers, and hands me one. I shake loose the tasteless bun and wolf the meat.

It's good being a dog. So many smells! The feet, the legs, the cooking food, and, ah, the other dogs. A lot of them are off leash like me, and they're not at all shy about coming over to sniff me and rub against me. One feisty little beagle mutt puts his front legs on my rear end and makes as if to hump me. Urgent, jerky twitches. I growl and sidestep away.

Still with me, the beagle sniffs my neck and echoes my growl. I make as if to nip him. He dodges, then throws his forepaws onto my back again. I flip him onto his side. Stand over him snarling. *Who's the boss now?* He offers his stomach in a gesture of surrender. I turn around and paw the ground with my rear feet, kicking shreds of grass his way. He yips, regains his feet, and goes for my neck again—but now a third dog moves in on us, a shabby terrier, a lascivious, importunate butt-sniffer.

Somehow the terrier reminds me of the English professor I had during my year at college—the way the man would go on and on about what one of my off-kilter essays might mean, when basically I'd written it in a trance, not even thinking about the words. I snarl at the terrier, and I run off. My two new playmates pursue me. Like a dance. Such fun.

Suddenly I hear Gee talking in my head again. My psidot cloaking function can't keep *him* out. "You should know that Treadle was wearing a psidot when you killed him," says Gee. "Jilljill and I noticed it on his neck when you closed in on him. The motherfucker was backing himself up on a lifebox all along."

"Why didn't you tell me?"

"I didn't want to distract you from the kill. And then, well, I needed to think out our next step before telling you the plan. Also you *did* say I should leave you alone. For a while. So I gave you an hour."

Right about then, that horndog terrier gets his cold nose right up against the bare skin of my butthole. Freaked by Gee's news as I am, I make a fully serious effort to bite the English-professor-type dog as hard as I can, but he ducks me. And even now he doesn't retreat. He circles around, waiting for another go. He's not done savoring my scent, and I'm expected to indulge him. Dog etiquette.

"You're getting good at this," says Gee, kind of amused.

"What do you want from me?" I demand. "Can the Treadlers hear you and me talking? Are they going to find me?"

Geek that Gee is, he answers my questions in order. "I want you to do a follow-up—you have to erase Treadle's lifebox. Treadle's goons can't hear our teep because they can't crack our comm channel. But, *yes*, they can find you! They're in with the aerospace companies and they've been watching you from spy satellites. I should have expected that. I'm about to write a hack to block it. But they saw your wasp fly from the Capitol to Woofer, and they know Woofer's right here."

"Bad news."

"Two more points. They're coming for you right now. And if they get *physical possession* of your psidot, then they *can* crack our crypto, and they'll back-track to my server, and they'll destroy your lifebox, and you'll be all-the-way dead."

"No! What do I do?"

"Don't let Jilljill get caught."

A maroon thudhumper is in the park. It's scurrying toward me across the grass. Instead of wheels, thudhumpers have six or eight spider-legs. This one is heading straight for me, twisting through the crowd. A white guy leans out of the front window, waving a gun. A vengeful agent from the Top Party.

The celebrants in the park aren't having this. They run at the car, kicking its meaty flanks and breaking its legs. Dozens of brothers and sisters mass together and roll the thudhumper onto its back, yeah! A gunshot stings my ears. The agent takes off running. I'm safe.

But—wait—all at once someone grabs my collar. It's not Loranda, it's some random brother. Jilljill flashes me the news that the man is an underground agent too, a Black man working for the Citadel Club, sent in at the same time as the maroon thudhumper.

I'm going *ki-yi-yi* as loud as I can. Loranda's Mom is hollering at the underground agent. Loranda shoves the man. Mom punches him in the gut. The agent's grip weakens. I twist free. And here comes my terrier prof, right on me, nuzzling my ear.

"Hop!" I tell Jilljill.

She's ready for the move, out on the edge of Woofer's ear. Jump cut!

Jilljill has fastened herself to the terrier's tongue. I'm in.

My name is Cuthbert. Keeping my psidotted tongue in my mouth, I trot over to my owner, a lean, dapper brother with horn-rimmed glasses and a drop-dead-elegant lightweight tweed suit. He's sitting on a bench, enjoying the sqwonks of an impromptu jazz band. I take shelter under the bench, behind his fine leather shoes, looking around. I know the satellite's still watching. They will think of the terrier. I need to hop some more.

Here comes a poodle, peering under the bench, sniffing me. I lick her nose.

Jump cut.

I'm Fifi now. My mistress walks me off. Madame pauses so her Fifi can greet a passing stray.

Jump cut.

The stray takes me into some dense bushes where homeless mutts with no collars are eating garbage, digging holes, growling, napping, and fitfully trying to mount each other. These dogs are unseen by the eye in the sky. Just to keep moving, I hop over to one of them, with Jilljill landing on the bare skin inside his ear.

I urge my latest host into a culvert beneath the railroad tracks and pause to look things over. I'm a glossy, medium-size, short-haired, warm-colored hound with a tail that I hold shamelessly high. I'm what people call a yellow dog.

I've never much liked yellow dogs, but I try not to communicate this to my host. He doesn't have a formal title, so I name him after certain sound that he makes. *Shrill Yelp*. I check back in with Gee.

He's got some kind of plan. For starters, he wants me to head uphill toward the mansions near the Capitol. I move casually and unobtrusively, along fences and under bushes, sniffing everything, taking my time.

"I hacked a backdoor into the spy satellites," Gee tells me. "So I know where they're at. And they've totally lost track of you. And I installed malware to stop them from finding you again. You're, like, invisible. Edited out in real time. Good dog."

My spirits lift. Shrill Yelp and I continue moving along the grassy back lanes, turning left and right according to Gee's prompts, and avoiding any interactions with ball walkers out on errands.

"Does this part of my excellent adventure go onto my memorial site?" I ask Gee.

"Not posting this part yet!" says Gee with one of his giggles. "Maybe later. But if we don't finish off Treadle—you won't have a memorial site at all. You'll be an unperson. Erased from history."

"Fuck that! This is my day to be a national hero. What do we have to do?"

"You're almost at the mansion of Treadle's Attorney General, Chuck Popham. Chuck and his wife Lucy. They have a dachshund named Friedl. They set great store by that dog. A few times a day the housekeeper Candace sends Friedl into the back yard to do her doody. There's a hole under the fence. We want you to switch over to Friedl. Put Jilljill onto her."

"And then?"

"Once you and Friedl are in the house, you get hold of Treadle's psidot. The psidot is called Wladimir. He looks like a gray ladybug. He's linked to Treadle's lifebox in the Top Party bunker lab, back at their national headquarters in San Francisco."

"Wladimir the Treadle psidot is in that house sitting on a counter? Or what?"

"You'll see," goes Gee. "I don't want you overthinking this. Once you get hold of Wladimir, your psidot Jilljill will be on him like stink on shit."

"Real folksy, Gee. Talking down to me. We're sure Jilljill will win?"

"Wladimir is a first gen psidot. Somebody stole him from the Junker labs last month. Jilljill is much better. She has Molly's latest upgrades."

"I'll crush Wladimir," puts in Jilljill, sounding tough, graceful, and confident. "I'll run a vortex thread through Wladimir and all the way to Treadle's lifebox in the Top Party bunker lab."

"I believe you," I tell Jilljill. "You rule."

"Stop walking now," says Gee. "The Popham mansion is right here."

The Pophams have three garbage cans and an oddly large dumpster. I piss on them one by one, lifting Shrill Yelp's leg four times. Doling out my elixir.

A calico cat in a red collar chances past. I run after her. I nearly catch her. She yowls. I love it. The cat disappears through a hole under the Pophams' white-painted wooden fence, which is a little rotten at the bottom. There's a dense, spreading pine tree overhead, covering the fence and part of the yard.

I stick my nose through the hole and I sniff. The cat bats my snout with her paw. I growl really hard. She climbs onto the top of the fence and studies me, impassive and aloof. Her eyes are yellow. I claw at the hole in the fence to make it bigger. This is fun. How would it be if I were to inhabit a long succession of grubby, mindless dogs—for years and years and years?

"Maurice!" Gee's still on my case.

"What?"

"You're doing good. But don't go into the yard until Friedl comes."

I claw at the fence some more, and I even bite into it and twist my snout to tug off chunks of wood. Pretty soon I can get my whole head through. The cat's on the back steps. I wonder if she lives here. Otherwise the yard is empty and nobody else is watching. Good luck to have that pine overhead. I'm hoping the satellite can't see me—in case Gee's camouflage hack doesn't work.

The hole in the fence still isn't quite large enough, but I don't want to get too obvious. So I dig at the damp dirt beneath it, doing a full-on dog thing, clawing with my front paws, and tossing the dirt back between my rear legs, with my ball-sack tight, and my tail extra high.

The dirt is black mulch, full of decayed leaves and pill-bugs. It smells good. Pretty soon I've made a nice little trough. When it's time, I can slip through. I settle down under a holly bush on the other side of the alley, out of sight.

Before I know it, I've fallen asleep. It's been a crazy day for me and for Shrill Yelp both.

What kind of dreams do you have when you're a lifebox connected to a psidot connected to a dog, and the lifebox is emulating dog emotions? Well, I dream about chasing a rabbit. Vintage dog. My legs twitch in my dream. Something odd about that *rabbit*. She glows. She pauses and looks back at me. Her face is—

"Psst! Maurice!" It's effin Gee interrupting me. He never leaves me alone.

As I come to, I hear yipping and the jingling of collar tags. Friedl! Body low, I skulk to the hole in the fence and peer through. There's Friedl, shiny in that greasy, dachshund kind of way. She's a nice chestnut color, with fine features and golden highlights. She's in the middle of the lawn, slightly hunkered to take a pee.

"Get ready," I teep to Jilljill. She creeps out to the edge of my ear.

I wriggle most of the way through the hole in the fence, then pause, flat on my belly. Friedl goes on the defense. She barks staccato-style, her voice high. She makes a run at me, coming to a stop three feet away. She braces her legs, and lowers her head. Her barking grows more furious. The housekeeper's not bothering to come out. Probably Friedl has a fit like this every time she goes outside.

I tense my muscles and spring. Friedl doesn't expect this. She's surprised how large I am. She squeals and turns to flee, but I'm on her. I knock her onto her side. I rub my head against hers. Ear to ear.

Jump cut.

Jilljill is in Friedl's ear, and my mind is in Friedl. I trot quietly toward the house. I sense that the cat is still watching me, but I can't quite see where she is. Never mind. My dachshund body language is, like, *What barking? Me? Nothing going on here.* For his part, Shrill Yelp decides this a bad scene. He's goes out through the hole and trots off down the alley.

At first I can't get up the back porch steps, but then I relax and let Friedl do it. She knows how. She moves like an old-time Slinky toy in reverse. At the top, Friedl scratches the door. And here's the housekeeper, a sister in jeans and a turtleneck. Candace.

She gives me a nice smile and hands me a dog treat—a little baked biscuit in the shape of a bone. I savor the sensations of Friedl crunching it up. She works the treat to her back teeth to apply real pressure, and she licks the frags off the gleaming hardwood floor.

Studying what I can see of the kitchen through Friedl's eyes, I notice a restaurant-sized fridge and stove, plus a very wide and heavy-duty staircase leading to the basement. How many people live here?

I hear a rumble of voices from a room beyond the kitchen. A woman and two men. That second man—his voice—what the fuck? I trot across the kitchen, down the hall, and pause in the shadows, peering into the room.

Yep. President Ross Treadle sits on a leather couch next to Chuck and Lucy Popham. All two-hundred-and-seventy pounds of him. I can smell him as soon as I stick my head in there. It's the same stench I picked up on when I was a wasp inside his shirt. Like rotting meat, with a tang of ammonia, a whiff of cloves, and halitosis.

At the psychic level, an overwhelming aura of evil and bad vibes radiates off the man. Like the anti-light of a black-hole sun. It's all I can do to keep from pissing on the floor.

I go online and call for help. "Gee?"

"He's a clone," says Gee. "The Citadel Club was ready for our hit today. They grew the clone in a tank in the basement of this house. The clone all blank and ready. When Treadle died, it was just a matter of moving his psidot from the corpse to the clone. And they hooked it to Treadle's life-box. Word is, Citadel Club is planning to edit Treadle's lifebox later on. He's never been quite pro-business enough. But for now he's still pretty much the same."

"You couldn't warn me before I got in here?"

"I didn't want you tensing up. Don't go all pit-bull and try to rip out Treadle's throat."

"I'm a dachshund, Gee."

"Glad you understand that. Now listen to me. You're going to cuddle up with Treadle and get to that Wladimir psidot on the back of his neck. Jilljill will take control of Wladimir and run a thread through him—a thread all the way to Treadle's lifebox, which is stored in the Top Party bunker lab in San Francisco. You'll follow the thread, and bust up the lifebox."

"Shit, man, why didn't we just stay out there?"

"Come on, Maurice. Focus. It'll be easier to follow that thread into the lab than it would be to physically bust it open."

I'm having trouble visualizing this thread thing being a success. "Is there a chance I might lose?"

"You won't," says Gee. "Use your hate. That's another thing we picked you for, Maurice. You *will* kill that lifebox."

"And then?"

"Improvise. Do all the damage you can. Don't let them take Jilljill alive."

"Am I still immortal?."

"You are, sure, but the *physical* immortality, it might be—intermittent. If Jilljill dies, I'll set you up with a new psidot and a new body down the line."

"Got it."

"You're the man, Maurice. You're the King."

I waddle forward in my dachshund body like I own the place. Probably Popham calls this room the library: Leather law books on shelves, Persian rug, crystal chandelier, vintage chairs, and a leather-topped table with pens. Even a stained glass window depicting, I don't know, Saint Gold Bar Blesses the Honks.

Seeing me, Lucy leans forward and slaps her hands on her thighs. "Come here, girl! Come on, Friedl!"

I scamper across the rug and leap onto Lucy's lap. I wriggle as I settle in. Lucy is next to Chuck Popham, who's next to the motherfucker I thought I already killed.

The clone's skin has a raw-dough look, like a cookie out of the oven too soon. His eyes are watery, not fully in focus. His expression is stony. I'm guessing his psidot is still settling in, getting up to speed on the new meat.

Gee says Treadle's psidot's is called Wladimir? I can see Wladimir from my perch on Lucy's lap. A dark gray, lentil-sized sea slug on the nape of the Treadle clone's neck. I think

I'm supposed to wriggle up there and nip Wladimir off that fat neck, and hold Wladimir in my mouth, and Jilljill will crawl inside of my mouth and work out on Wladimir bigtime. Jilljill is bad-ass.

But I'm not really clear on what happens then. I'm supposed to follow a thread to Treadle's lifebox in the Top Party cloud-cuckoo-land of their bunker lab in San Francisco? Why can't Jilljill just zap that lifebox by herself?

I heave a sigh. For sure I'm going to die again. And what was that shit about my immortality being—*intermittent*? I should have stayed on Loranda's back porch.

I make myself limp and cuddly on Lucy Popham's lap. I breathe as slowly as I can. I tell myself I'm a winner. And then, before I know it, I've flipped into manic superhero fantasyland. I am so much more than a dachshund. I won't stop at just destroying Treadle's lifebox. I'll wipe out the Treadle clone body as well. Yeah, man.

Killing Treadle feels so good, you hate to do it just once.

As I loll and nestle and scheme on Lucy's lap, Jilljill works her way out from beneath the flap of my ear, across my cheek, over my black lip, and into my mouth.

The Treadle clone is talking to Chuck Popham. His voice is slow and blurred. I hear my name.

"That Maurice Winch punk. We have to crush his memorial site. Rabid un-American propaganda. Winch is a loser. A traitor. Scum."

Chuck Popham's response: "For now we're out of the command loop, sir. It'll be different once you're back in office. But at present, we have to raise funds, build infrastructure, and work through channels."

"Fuck the channels," says Treadle. "We go public and I resume power. I didn't die. It was a hoax. Fake news. We'll take it to the courts. I own the judges." He shakes his massive head. "Swearing in Mareek was a travesty." He slams his fist into his hand. "Unconstitutional! I am the first three-term President."

"What about Franklin Delano Roosevelt?" pipes up Lucy Popham. "He was elected to *four* terms, Ross."

"You shut up," says Treadle, his voice thick with fury. "You don't know shit."

Lucy flashes a hard frown.

"Lucy's right, Mr. President," puts in Chuck Popham. "And do keep in mind that you're in the lady's home. So, please, a little *politesse*."

"You're a wimp," Treadle snaps . "A lackey. An ass-kisser."

"I know you're not yourself, Mr. President," says Popham. "You'll feel better soon."

I worm over to Chuck Popham's lap, whining and being all cuddly and flexible. And mainly I'm getting closer to the back of Treadle's neck. By now, Jilljill is perched on the tip of my tongue.

"*Meow*."

Oh, god, it's that calico cat, coming in from the kitchen. Her yellow eyes fixate on me. As I focus on her, I pick up a faint teep signal. Fuck. Why didn't I notice that before? She's wearing an uvvy under her red collar. Someone uses her for surveillance. And, um, this someone is the armed man right behind her. He's wearing one of Treadle's absurd private guard uniforms.

"What is it, Captain Burke?" asks Popham. "We're busy." Meanwhile Popham is steadily petting me. My presence soothes him.

"It's about your dog, sir," says Burke. "Another animal touched her. While she was in the yard. I saw it through the watch-cat."

"You leave Friedl alone," cries Lucy Popham. "See, Chuck? This is what we get from sticking with Treadle. We have this vile unholy clone in our library, and a cabal of paranoid thugs in our basement. It's time for us to move on, Chuck. Like everyone else in the world."

I snuggle closer into Popham's belly, making myself warm, smooth, and lovable. Popham's hand continues caressing me.

"The dog appears unscathed by the encounter your cat may have seen," Popham tells the guard. He raises my ears one by one, peering inside. "No secret psidots. As you were, Captain Burke. Go back downstairs with the men."

Burke goes to the kitchen and thumps down the steps to the basement.

"Good Friedl," says Popham, patting my head.

"I don't like that dog being next to me," grumbles Treadle. "Dogs are unclean."

"Oh, but look at her," says Popham in a teasing tone. I think he's about had it with Treadle too. He picks me up and holds me against his shoulder like a baby. "Friedl is a cutie. I bet she wants to give you a kiss, Mr. President."

Things are going my way. I can skip that part about nipping the psidot off Treadle's neck. I'll spit Jilljill right onto Wladimir. And let the best psidot win.

I stretch my neck as far as I can. Lucy Popham giggles. I angle my elegant snoot and give the back of Treadle's neck a quick, wet lick, during which Jilljill detaches herself from me.

Jump cut.

I'm in a zone of chaos—experiencing the world from Jilljill's point of view. She and Wladimir are in a micro Sumo wrestling match on the nape of Treadle's neck—squeezing each other and pulsing energies back and forth: brainwaves, electrical sparks, and quantum fields.

In my teepspace lifebox-mind, I visualize the fight as a 3D abstract painting with collaged-in scenes from my life and from Treadle's life, with a thunderstorm all around, and random dachshund emotions mixed in. I hear the keening of a whirlwind. A narrow Kansas-style twister amid swirling debris. I go toward it.

Something crude and stupid tries to get in my way. Wladimir. I see him as a boxy tank with a cannon. But Jilljill—Jilljill is like a sea anemone. She wraps her tendrils around Wladimir, squashes him against her soft mouth, and assimilates his ID.

I follow Jilljill into the shrieking whirlwind. It carries me through a hail of Treadle memories—the whirlwind surrounds the thread of Wladimir's link to Treadle's lifebox, which is stored in a server in the underground Top Party bunker on Van Ness Street, San Francisco.

Jilljill spoofs things so that we look like Wladimir, and we bop right into the bunker. What I see inside is—well, it's complicated. I see two realities overlaid upon each other. I see the physical bunker and the teepspace bunker.

Physically, the bunker is a dank, grotty cellar so low that if you walked in there, you'd barely able to stand erect. The server in the bunker is like a ten-foot-long sweet potato, orange, pointed at both ends, and damp and shuddery, as if made of cow liver. I have a feeling it would be dangerous to touch it.

In teepspace, I see the bunker-plus-server as a spacious marble hall with embossed crypts set into the walls, one crypt for each of the client lifeboxes. A mausoleum that's half a mile long.

The Top Party has their Coggy assemblage in this bunker as well, and physically it's a pink-lit tank of fluid, containing six crufty, crumbly, senile brains, with their stiffened tissues linked by wires, burbling tubes, and fiber-optic strands. In teepspace, Coggy looks like youthful wizard with a wand, perched on a throne in the middle of the marble hall.

"Fuck this shit," I say to Jilljill. "Which of those crypts is Treadle?"

"His thread leads to it," says Jilljill. "It's gone very faint. But—"

Still in sea anemone mode, she grows her real long, and runs them along the marble walls, feeling for the stink of Treadle's crypt. Meanwhile that fucking wizard thing has walked over to me, and he's trying to talk, and I can't understand a thing he says. All *prithee* and *lief* and *my liege* and like that.

And now, to ratchet things up, a strange woman taps my left shoulder. I yell in surprise, turn to look at her, and she hands me a heavy fire axe. Huh?

Her face is calm and wise. I've seen her before—when I shared the dog Shrill Yelp's dream about chasing the—

"I'm Molly Santos," says the woman. "And this is a quantum axe. Look down there! Jilljill found Treadle. Hurry the fuck up."

Jilljill's aura has settled onto the bronze front plate of a particular crypt, down near the other end of the bunker which—in my dream perspective—looks to be a quarter of a mile away.

As I charge down the hall toward Jilljill, the stupid-ass Coggy wizard follows me. He gains on me, draws even on my right side, and throws a jar of acid. *Eeek.* My face is melting.

Molly wipes off my face—literally. My head is a skinning grull. A grinning skull. This trip is getting to me. But I've still got my axe. I'd like to let the fucking wizard have it, but when I swing at him, he ducks the blow, gathers up his robe, and skips back down the hall to his throne, singing a merry song along the way. Molly is still on my left. And Jilljill down the hall is beckoning.

I reach Treadle's tomb. One rap of my axe, and the bronze crypt cover flies off. Inside is a juicy voodoo doll of Treadle, with a shrunken head and real yellow hair. It's talking very, very fast—an aggrieved, bullying, self-pitying rant which adds up to a keening noise like the sound of the tornado that brought us here. The sound grows higher and more penetrating. It's going to burst my brain.

With a cry of hatred, I raise my axe and hack at Treadle's voodoo doll, hitting it over and over—until its limbs are severed, its fluid spilled, its glow extinguished, its voice silenced, its stench drifting away.

"Well done," goes Molly. Something darts very quickly from her mind into my mind. A compressed message. "Read it later," she says.

And then Molly's gone, taking the quantum axe with her.

"I'll run you back," says Jilljill, casual as taxi driver.

As Jill and I waft toward the ceiling of from the bunker, I switch back to seeing the bunker's physical from. A low, dank cellar with a tank of brains and a yam-shaped biocomputing cow liver. Someone has hacked at the fat yam, smashing part of it into mush. Me, I did that with my quantum axe. I smushed the part of the server where Treadle's lifebox computation lived.

Jilljill guides me out of the bunker, through the dissipating flakes of dead Treadle memories, away from San Francisco, across the Great Plains, and back to Capitol Hill. And there I find the physical Jilljill solidly fastened to the Treadle clone's neck. She's changed her skin so that she resembles the now-cannibalized Wladimir.

As for me, my lifebox is still on Gee's redwood server. And I'm linked to Jilljill. And I'm seeing through human eyes, sitting on the leather couch in Popham's library. I've won the second round. And now, god help me, I'm controlling the clone of Ross Treadle's body.

How do I get out of here? I twitch my hand and clear my throat. That cute dachshund, my former host, what's her name—Friedl! She's over in Lucy's lap. Popham is looking at me oddly.

"Are you all right, Mr. President? I had no idea a dog kiss would affect you like that. A foolish joke. I apologize."

"Ross's clone is defective," says Lucy, her voice harsh. "He just now had a seizure. You ought to put him down, Chuck. Like a rabid dog."

"We need the clone," says Chuck Popham. "The Citadel Club is planning to make a fresh lifebox for it anyway. More of a team player. Can you hear me at all, Ross?"

"Yes," I manage. "I'm here."

Do I know how to talk like Treadle? Well, maybe, approximately. After all, I'm using his lungs and his vocal cords and his mouth cavity—*ugh!* My gorge rises. Keep it together, Maurice. If I'm talking through Treadle's body, then I'm bound to sound like him. Especially to people who are idiotic enough to have ever been on his side.

"And I hear your sedition, Lucy Popham," I intone. "I did not have a fit. I'm in perfect health. Where's my man Burke?"

"Downstairs," says Popham, exchanging a glance with his wife. "With the men."

I'm getting the inklings of a plan. "How many men are there?"

"Twelve, sir. Remember? We call them Treadle's Apostles. Ready to die for the Top Party cause."

"Very fine," I say. I'm riding high on having destroyed Treadle's lifebox. I've killed the man twice. And now to kill him for a third and final time. I'll blow up his clone and his right-hand-man Popham and his frikkin twelve apostles. But how do I make a bomb?

Suddenly I know how. That compressed message Molly gave me, well, my never-idle subconscious mind has opened it, and absorbed it, and the info has percolated into the active part of my mind. It's a wonderful, crazy plan from Molly. I'll need some help. And this time I'm not going to ask Gee. I'll go to my other biohacker friend.

"Liv Anders?" I silently say, as I mentally uncloak that one particular channel alone. "Can you hear me?"

"Maurice!" She's laughing and happy, riding inside Gee's flappy named Pelikaan, it looks like. On her way to Denmark. "Channeling you just fine," she says. "You're a god."

"I deign to entertain," I say, feeling proud of myself.

"How come you never humped any of those dogs?" asks Liv. "I was sure you would."

"Come on, Liv. Don't tease me like that. You know I'm asexual."

"Oh, maybe you'll find a dreamboat yet. But I know you're not here for lonely hearts counseling. You want some kind of help. Pitch me, my Beloved Revolutionary Hero."

"My psidot is on Treadle's clone," I tell Liv. "Right now. We're in the house of Treadle's friend. I want to blow the place up. And in the lab, you told me that when a user gets a psidot, the psidot installs a bunch of gossip molecules inside the user's brain, and from then on, the psidot can tell the gossip molecules to make chemicals inside that user's body."

"Normally we don't make just any old chemicals," says Liv. "We have firewalls. We make neurochemicals. For mirroring emotions. And tell me, O King, where does this line of thought lead?"

"I want to fill Treadle with nitroglycerin," I say. "He'll be like a fat-man chunk of dynamite. Jolt him and he goes boom." This is the plan I got from Molly, but I'm not mentioning Molly to Liv yet. For at least a little while, I want to take credit and bask in Liv's admiration.

She's laughing in surprise and approval. "Well, okay, maybe in this case the psidot *can* order up any old chemical," she says. Slight pause. "It could be done."

"Will the nitro poison Treadle on the spot? I'd like him to make it to the basement before he explodes."

"People *do* take nitroglycerin," says Liv. "They use it as a medicine to lower blood pressure. But they take it in very small amounts. At the dosage *you* want, the Treadle clone might drop dead on the spot. Suppose we wrap his nitro in gelatin that takes a minute to dissolve."

"Load him to the gills with release-timed nitro and walk him into position before he keels over," I say.

"Love it," says Liv, happy inside Pelikaan, high above the Atlantic. She's gotten hold of a glass of champagne. "Here's to the final Treadle temper tantrum!"

"But do you know the chemical formula for nitro?" I fret. "With the gelatin wrapper added on? And can Jilljill message the template to Treadle's gossip molecules? Will the gossip molecules ignore such a crazy request?"

"A prize problem," says Liv, practically rubbing her hands. "Worthy of the wetware engineering Olympics." She pauses briefly in thought. "Yes," she says. "Yes I see exactly how to do it. But, Maurice—you might lose Jilljill. She's on the Treadle clone's neck. She'll go up in the explosion. Your second death today."

"I'll always be alive in my lifebox. In teepspace. I think I like it there."

"Well, yes," says Liv, nodding. "If you really get used to teepspace you might not even want a meat body. But even so—these changes are hard on you. I admire you, Maurice."

"What about me?" puts in Jilljill.

"Well, you're just a sea slug," says Liv.

"Easy for you to say," gripes Jilljill.

"Will it help if I tell you I'll save your genome along with Maurice's lifebox?" Liv says.

"And you guys be sure to put a copy of me on Maurice when he comes back!" says Jilljill. "Don't use some other kind of psidot. We Jilljills saw Maurice first. He's ours."

"I might not come back for a while," I tell Jilljill. "And I'm going to miss you a lot. But I want to check what it's like in raw teepspace."

"You hear that?" Liv says to Jilljill. "Maurice cares about you. So be quiet now. And Maurice—do you have some stoic last words? They'll go onto your memorial site. Over to you, Maurice Winch!"

"I mean to finish this job," I say. "Wipe out every trace of Treadle."

"I'm glad I'm not your enemy, Maurice."

"Hell no, Liv. I almost love you."

"Oh, but you know I'm waiting for Molly," says Liv. And suddenly, saying her lover's name, she stops. Her smile is gone. "The thing that happened to Molly's body," she says. "So awful. And her lifebox isn't on Gee's server anymore. But I keep thinking she's not gone."

"She's not," I say. "I saw her just now, and she's the one who gave me the idea for using nitro."

"You *saw her*?" exclaims Liv, her voice going high.

"In teepspace when I went to destroy Treadle's lifebox. Molly was made of light."

"And she talked to you?"

"She flashed me the nitro plan, and she said, *Hurry the fuck up.*"

"Good advice, that," says Liv. "My Molly! So, yes, I *will* find her. Hooray! But now—hurry the fuck up! I'll make a molecular nitroglycerine template—and I'll package it as a Top Party message, teep it to Jilljill, and Jilljill will forward it to all the gossip molecules in the Ross Treadle clone, and they'll think it's legit."

"Check," pipes Jilljill. "It was nice working with you two."

"Thank you, dear," says Liv. "And now, Maurice—you go get back to scamming Chuck and Lucy Popham. Get our ducks in a row."

This intricate interchange eats up a couple of minutes. As I pull myself back into focus, still on the leather couch in Chuck Popham's library, I realize I've been making a senile droning sound with my Treadle mouth. I have drool all over my shirt, like a drunk or like a stroke victim. I sit up straight and try to seem alert. Chuck Popham looks quizzical.

"You and Lucy are showing signs of discontent," I say, trying to take control.

"Oh, we're fine," says Popham. Even now, with me in my reduced state, he's a little scared of me. But Lucy isn't. She's glaring at me.

"Ross, I want you and your storm troopers out of here. You've worn out your welcome."

"That's very unfair," I say, "Disloyal. But I'm more than happy to go. I have a new plan. I'll go downstairs and tell the men. Chuck, you come down there with me. And, Lucy, you're no longer to be trusted. You must not overhear the details of my plan. I order you to go outside."

"I'll be in the kitchen," says Lucy with a shrug. "You'll be in the basement. I'm not at all interested in what you tell your men. WGAF. You know the expression, Ross. I'm sure you do. You're good at cursing, you bully, you asshole."

"I want you outside!" I scream at her, putting that ever ready Treadle rage into my voice. "You, and the housekeeper, and your fucking wiener dog. The three of you outside. Way the hell out. On the other side of the street."

"The man is completely insane," Lucy says to Chuck. "Is there a way you can shut him down?"

"Well, if I could get to his psidot, I'd be able to," says Chuck.

"Don't you dare!" I roar, jumping to my feet. I go into the kitchen with Candace and holler down the stairs. "Men! I'm coming down there. Form up and present arms! And, you, Lucy Popham—out, out, *out*!" I'm feeling a little woozy, and not just from the feigned anger. Jilljill has already started sending the nitro templates to my gossip molecules.

"So ridiculous," grumbles Lucy. She stands, carries Friedl into the kitchen, and addresses the housekeeper. "Candace? Did you hear all this?"

"I heard plenty," she says. "Don't need more. I quit."

"Any chance I can come with you?" asks Lucy.

The two women laugh, walk down the front stairs together, and head off down the block.

"It's working," says Liv in my head.

"Thank you," I tell her. "I hope you find Molly."

"It'll happen," says Liv. "You've given me hope. I'll see you down the road."

"Somewhere," I say.

We do something like a farewell hug—and break contact.

"Go on ahead down the stairs," I tell Chuck Popham, speaking aloud. "I'll come in a second." I'm feeling more tingly all the time.

I drink a big glass of water from the kitchen sink, encouraging the gelatin around the nitro molecules to dissolve. Listening down into the Treadle clone's body, I strongly feel the stuff taking effect. It's coming on fast. I'm more light-headed than before. I stagger to the head of stairs. A good long flight. Plenty of room to bounce. I lurch forward as the full wave of faintness hits.

I'm free.

MARY MARY

Mary is born in San Francisco a few years before Y2K. An only child. She doesn't like her parents or her school. She's not interested in politics or drugs. She likes to walk around the city looking at people. And seeing live music. And wandering the botanical garden and the beach. Mary declines college. Her mother tells her to get a job. Instead, Mary hooks into the nomad scene and drifts around North and Central America for about twenty years, hitting tribal gatherings, music festivals, gem and crystal shows, canyon treks, cactus fairs, cave celebrations, university-town colloquia, and the occasional day-job on a farm.

The annual fireworks festival in Tultepec is a high point, with people lugging in constructs called *toritos*, or little bulls, based on simple, home-made, bacteria-proof gunpowder. The explosive wheeled piñatas spout sparks, spew firecrackers, and shoot rockets across the market square into the wildly capering crowd. Mary loves the dazzle and the roar.

She settles in the freaky beach town of Santa Cruz, and gets into roots music. She plays mandolin and she sings. For a while she lives with Kip, a fisherman and diver her age—they even get married—and then, way too soon, Kip dies in a crazy climate storm. He leaves her two hundred dollars and a small wooded lot in the Santa Cruz Mountains. Mary gets hold of a biotech house seed—a relative of the squash plant—and she grows herself a domed, green home.

She never does find another man after Kip, not that she especially wants to. She passes the next thirty years working at the San Lorenzo Country Store. It's relaxing. And she has her bluegrass band, Squash Plant, with a changing cast of characters on fiddle, banjo, and bass.

On the night that Mary meets Gee Willikers, she's well into her seventies, which is hard to fathom. Where has her life gone?

Squash Plant is playing at Pot O' Gold, a comfortable wooden road house in San Lorenzo. It's August, seven months after Treadle's triple assassination—triple in the sense of body, lifebox, and clone. People are still gloating about that. Mary's fiddle player tonight is her neighbor Kayla Stux, and she's seven months pregnant. Kayla says it'll be a freedom baby.

"You up for the show?" Mary asks Kayla as they set up.

"Takes my mind off my sore back," says Kayla. "And thanks for getting me a rocking chair. How about you? You ready to warble?"

"I'm great," says Mary. "Voice a little rough." In point of fact, she's seriously ill, but she can't face telling anyone yet, not even Kayla.

"Use the voice's edge," says Kayla, not realizing she should worry. "Do coarse cowgirl hollers amid your sinuous croons."

"Putting myself out there," says Mary. "A music of me. Pinwheels and booms. The mind is a fireworks festival."

Kayla answers with a moaning scrape of her bow on her fiddle, and they're off.

It's a good set, with their friends Dick Cheeks and Joe Moon on banjo and bass. Those are stage names of course, but by now the boys like to use them all the time. As well as singing bluegrass standards, Mary performs some autobiographical numbers she's written—like about seeing the Muse at Tultepec fireworks shows, and about the day her husband Kip drowned while Mary was teeping with him, and about how watching her house seed grow was like birthing the baby that Mary and Kip never had. In Mary's little hamlet, she's known and loved for her quirky ballads, and the locals sing along.

She notices a guy watching her from a corner booth, smiling and nodding, and reaching in with his teep, reaching as close as Mary's cloaking allows. He's her age, or maybe even older, if that's humanly possible. When the gig is done, the guy is right up there by the stage, introducing himself.

"I'm Gee," he tells Mary. "I love your vivacity. Your careworn yet joyful pluck. And your voice—it's like you project your soul. You're the greatest singer I've ever seen."

"Laying it on thick," says Mary, smiling despite herself.

"Can I buy you a meal?" asks this Gee. "Come sit down with me."

"Go for it," Kayla tells Mary. "You look beat. The boys and I will tidy up."

"Do you live here?" Mary asks Gee as they take a seat at his corner table. "I've never seen you before."

"I stay deep in the woods," says Gee. "Lying low. I'm famous, and the Top Party guys are after me."

"What makes you famous?" says Mary.

"I organized the assassination of Ross Treadle," says the guy. "I'm Gee Willikers."

"*That* Gee!" exclaims Mary, impressed. "Good for you. But didn't the new President pardon you?"

"Well sure. And the Top Party has been in shock, not doing much, but now they're rising again. They have dreams for the mid-term election next fall. It irks them to know I'm still around."

"You don't seem irksome to me," says Mary, having ordered tomatoes, barbequed salmon, and a beer. "I liked what you said about my singing."

"It's synchronicity, me seeing you sing tonight," says Gee. "Do you know that word?"

"I'm not as green as I am cabbage-looking," says Mary. One of her mother's sayings. "I was on the road with freaks for years. Synchronicity, eh? You seeing me sing is an aha-moment that clicks with—with what?"

"It's my lifebox thing," says Gee. "I invented them so people can store back-ups of their personalities. They're expensive, and I want them to be free. And now, seeing you sing, I flashed on how to do it."

"I don't have a lifebox at all," says Mary. "Too broke. A lifebox would come in handy, considering I'll be dead in less than a year."

She hadn't meant to tell this to anyone yet, but Gee's voice and teep are so warm and confiding.

"Perfect fit," says Gee. "Even more synchronicity. You helped me, and I'll help you."

"Okay," says Mary. "That's fine." She's eating her tomato salad appetizer. The food tastes better than usual tonight. "Not that I know what you're talking about."

"It comes down to this," says Gee. "Right now the lifeboxes are stored on nanopercenter servers. But I want them to be indie. And tonight, for a break, I skulk into San Lorenzo and—*pow*—I see you projecting your teepspace self into song! And there's my answer. Like the world is dancing with me. Synchronicity!"

The barbeque and beer arrive, and their conversation drifts. Gee and Mary get into swapping stories from their long lives, laughing, ordering dessert, drinking a little more. And then suddenly it's closing time.

"Do you want to see where I live?" Mary asks Gee. Not an offer she often extends. But he turns her down.

"I'd like to, Mary. But I'm scared to be in the open for long. Believe me when I say the Top Party agents are out to kill me. Not to mention the random psycho *patriots*. I need to get back to my hideout. My thudhumper van is waiting outside. You could come to *my* place if you want. A cave deep in the mountains."

"Not on a first date," says Mary, brushing that off. "Let's hope to meet again."

"We will," says Gee. "Eventually. And I'll make sure you get a lifebox before it's too late. Meanwhile I'll be busy gearing up for the next round against the Top Party and the Citadel Club. I'm hoping to crush them once and for all in the spring."

Mary expects to hear from Gee about the lifebox pretty soon, either by voice or by teep, but there's nothing. For a while she thinks about him off and on, especially when she's singing. But she has that other thing on her mind: she's dying of cancer.

Eight months later, Gee comes back into her life, and the final round of the war against the Top Party begins. Fade in on Mary in the ball walker barn behind the San Lorenzo Country Store…

"Problem," Glory the ball walker is saying. "The man on Herbert Lane stayed in his pupa. A hammock thing? And the woman wouldn't accept the order. Roast chicken, loaf of bread, pint of ice cream. So I ate it. Okay?"

The ball walker's slit mouth is damp and awry. He doesn't have teeth or a tongue, which gives his voice an odd sound. His black eyes shine like marbles set into the pale sphere of his head. And, like all ball walkers, he doesn't have arms. Mary likes him. It's entertaining to watch how Glory gets things done.

"Never mind," Mary tells the kritter. "You're talking about Carson Pflug. He does that. Makes an order and spaces out. And, yeah, his wife won't sign for him anymore. She's right. Time for you to settle down for the night, bouncy-ball."

"GroChow?" says Glory, his head bobbing as he does an ingratiating dance on his ostrich legs. His head is glowing a bit. Ball walkers do that at night.

"Real quick," goes Mary. "It's past ten. And my chest is killing me."

Glory opens wide. His faintly lit head is hollow and rubbery—nothing in there but a hole with a flap. His gullet. His stomach, brain, and uvvy are in a hump on the underside of his head, along with muscles for his long, strong bird-legs.

Mary shovels Glory a scoop from the GroChow bin. Sufficient nutrients, gene therapy, and pharmaceuticals to keep a ball walker in top form. Glory gulps his portion so rapidly it makes a nasty sound. He shudders and does rapid knee bends.

"Like it!" he says.

Mary fills a second scoop and tucks the little shovel into her apron. She ushers Glory out the store's back door and into the old barn. Two other ball walkers are in there, one asleep in the stalls, and the other is pacing. Miss Max, ready for the night shift. She's hungry and in a bad mood. Her head glows bright yellow.

Miss Max isn't as smart as the other ball walkers, although she's taller, and more aggro. If a customer turns ugly, Miss Max is the one to fell the bad actor with an ostrich kick. Glory circles around her and goes to his stall.

"Glory is scared of me," says Max, though this isn't always true. Her tongueless, lips-only speech has a *parp-parp* sound. "You don't need to come in here at all, Mary. I can run this barn myself,"

"You can't do *this*," says Mary, pitchforking fresh straw from the loft. A necessity, as the ball walkers crap where they stand. Mary's knuckles hurt and her shoulder joints rasp. And she feels like there's a spear stuck into her chest. She glares at gangly Miss Max. "So let me do my stupid boring job."

"I hate you," says Miss Max.

"Do you know you say that to me every day?" says Mary. "You have a brain the size of a pea. And now—time for the mood change." She draws the cylindrical scoop from her apron. "*Hmmm?*"

Reflexively Miss Max's slit-mouth gapes. She inhales her GroChow even faster than Glory did—and turns ecstatic. Does a 180-degree back-flip, rebounds off her rubbery head, lands on her meaty feet, and claws at the straw.

"I'm the fairest of them all," parp-parps the toothless, armless ball walker.

"Go wait for delivery orders in the back of the store," Mary tells her. "Answer on your uvvy. Expect some action. It's Saturday night. And no more deliveries to Carson Pflug on Herbert Lane. Feel free to tell *him* you hate him."

"Was Carson Pflug ever my friend?" asks Miss Max.

"You used to belong to him," says Mary. "Two years ago. He gave you to Mrs. Yahootie, and she reset you, and you forgot, but not all the way. You're deep, Miss Max."

"I love you," says Miss Max, still in her GroChow glow.

"Everybody should," says Mary. "Good night."

She walks homeward along the lumpy back streets of San Lorenzo. For once it's not raining. Moony clouds drift above the redwoods. April. Her cheeks are wet with tears. She's going to die in a few weeks. The pain in her chest is stage-four cancer, both lungs, spreading through her system. Even if there were a fix, she wouldn't be able to afford it.

Mary keeps trying to figure out what her life's been about. She never got married, nor had kids, nor had worldly success, and when she finally met the right guy, he died. She's been working at the damn San Lorenzo Country Store for going on thirty years, up in the Santa Cruz Mountains, south of San Jose. Check-out, stocker, deli counter, bookkeeper, and, summit of her career, the shepherd of three ball walkers in this rustic hamlet. At least she can sing and play the mandolin.

Limping along Herbert Lane, she sees a light in the upscale abode of Kayla Stux and Carson Pflug. It's right next to Mary's grotty old dome home, which was grown from a seed the size of a pizza. Kayla is Mary's best friend these days, even though she's fifty years younger.

Pain echoes in Mary's head, pointless and unstoppable. She can't face being alone. She knocks on Kayla's and Carson's door. And thank god it's Kayla who opens.

"Feel like coming over for a jam?" Mary asks. She and Kayla like to play bluegrass together, even without Dick Cheeks and Joe Moon around.

"Half a Squash Plant is better than none," says Kayla.

"And bring baby Daia," adds Mary. "Make it cozy."

"Super," says Kayla. "Come in while I amass my goods."

Mary stands in the hallway and Kayla bustles around, getting shoes, her violin, a coat, some baby supplies, and baby Daia herself, in a cute red shearling bunting bag. Daia's awake, smiling and looking around with her clear eyes, noticing everything. Her world so new.

The home is deluxe, in an understated way. Clean lines, lots of wood, slowly mutating rugs, and with Kayla's living art kritters around. Some are like table-top Deco sculptures that take themselves apart and reassemble their elements. Others are like walking figurines or semi-intelligent pets.

They're great, and Kayla is able to sell them. To start with, they were one-of-a-kind art objects she sold in a San Francisco gallery, but now she's collaborating with the gallery on producing multiple copies of them. Like prints, in a way, except they're alive. As a back-up job, Kayla repairs, retrofits, and upgrades commercial task kritters—working out of this comfortable home that Carson bought with money from his shady consulting gigs.

The man of the house hangs gently twitching in the corner of the living room, inside his pupa—a type of wraparound hammock that's suspended by silky strands, with teep and squidskin display on the inside, also skin-patch meds.

"He's working?" says Mary.

"Some of the time," says Kayla. "That way he can say he's justified. Hardly ever goes to the Skyhive campus anymore. Always in the pupa—and if he's not doing business meetings, or plotting with his Top Party contacts, he's gaming or watching shows or—you know."

"He does teepspace sex when he can have *you*?" Mary exclaims.

Kayla jounces the baby against her shoulder. Makes her voice a singsong. "Daddy's in his pupa, what a time he has. Big plans, brave games, and his ho-ho makes him glad."

"It's always the same one?" asks Mary, fastening on Kayla's use of the singular form of the word. "Do you know who it is?"

"Some business connection," says Mary. "He gets mad if I ask. We hardly talk at all anymore."

The pupated figure is gently swaying his hips. "Do I see a nasty bulge?" says Mary, assuming a school-marm tone.

"Bad mans!" cries Kayla, turning reckless. "Mary make the bump go 'way!"

So ridiculous. The two women are laughing, and six-month-old Daia gurgles a fat *ha-ha*, with no idea what's funny. Riding the groove, Mary whacks the bulge with the back of her hand.

Carson rips open the pupa flap that covers his face. He's all red and embarrassed, yelling about privacy. Maybe a little zonked from whatever brain-stim the pupa is feeding him. He falls out of the hammock, bangs his elbow really hard, and yells some more. He's not very intimidating. Pale, bony, bleary, small. A weasel gone wrong.

Mary, Kayla, and baby Daia exit into the mossy night. Carson doesn't follow them. Glancing in through the window, Mary sees him grab a giant slice of cake and nestle back into his smart hammock.

"How do you stand it?" she asks Kayla.

"He says the affair is tactical. And that he's working on a business deal. For some reason this famous biohacker Gee Willikers has been talking to him."

"Gee Willikers!" exclaims Mary. "That's the old man who was talking to me after our Squash Plant show at the Pot O' Gold last summer? Before you had Daia. It was like Gee was hitting on me, but in a weird way. He even said he'd give me a lifebox. And then—nothing."

"I guess I remember that," says Kayla. "Barely. Anyway, Carson now thinks he might be able to resign from Skyhive, go in with Gee Willikers, and make a huge score. Or, more likely, double-cross Gee and get a Skyhive promotion with the help of his virtual-sex woman friend—who is probably his skanky boss. Or maybe he'll sell out all of them to the Top Party—that's who he used to work for, and maybe he still does. Carson's all about networking and switching sides. Open for offers."

Kayla's tone is one of weary contempt, and now she falls silent. Daia softly coos. They're under the redwood next to

Mary's house. Occasional raindrops fall on their heads, distinct and slow. An owl hoots. Dear spring.

"So Carson's faithless," says Mary with a sigh. "And cold. Kick him out?"

"I'm close to that. Not that I'm itching to be a single mom. Carson got me to sign a prenup that says he keeps our house. I didn't care. We were in love. Back at Berkeley—the springtime of our lives. Two years ago? Feels like ten." Kayla heaves a shaky sigh. "How are *you*, Mary?"

"Not sure I can herd ball walkers much more. My effing doc app says I'll die in less than a month. Can you believe that?" She opens her grown-home's door, which is like a floppy hatch.

"I worship your place," says Kayla. "Like a fairy tale. Everything alive. Kritters are the best."

"Especially the ones you design, Kayla."

"You're nice." Kayla sets Daia and her woolly bag onto the couch that's a bump amid the spongy, undulating mass of the floor. Leaning over Daia, she raises her voice to a squeak. "Nighty-night, baby. Mama and Mary play music!"

Mary pours out some sparkling cider and they get down to it—playing old-time tunes, singing along, forgetting themselves. For once Mary's fingers feel supple. Kayla's fiddle moans the words she doesn't say. Mary's voice flows; her breath is one with her heart. Their human harmonies reverberate in the domed home.

"Stay the night with me?" says Mary, when the music is done. She coaxes the floor into forming a big bed. Kayla and Daia nestle down with her. A thistledown quilt drifts down like fall of snow. The women sleep.

They awake to tree-filtered early sunrays dappling the home's translucent green rind. Sunday morning. A soft thudding on the door. Groaning with pain from her cancer, Mary gains her feet, wraps herself in a robe, and opens the hatch.

It's Carson, tidy and pulled-together. When he's on his game, he can be cute. He's got that going for him—along with his low, ruthless cunning. "Hey, Mary. Sorry I was out of sorts last night. I've—I've been working too hard. Hello, Kayla, my love!"

"Dada!" quacks Daia. Carson walks over and scoops her up, father and daughter in a tableau of family bliss. Kayla is smiling at them. She looks relieved.

"That's the thing," says Mary, not bothering to censor herself. "Men stink, but kids like to have them around."

Carson gives Mary a guarded look. "Are you doing anything about immortality?" he asks. "Do you want to have a juicy ghost?"

"Looking to make a deal?" says Mary. "Sell me a lease with Skyhive?"

"Listen," says Carson, using the low, confidential tone that men think is persuasive. "I haven't been the best neighbor. I want to make it up. I'll comp you a freebie, Mary. I've got a lot of pull at Skyhive. I'm old friends with the owner. I'll set you up with a psidot, and you can record your personality over the next week. Skyhive will have a virtual Mary in the cloud. And then—" He leans close. "Eternal life."

"It's a little early in the day to go full sales-force on Mary's ass," says Kayla.

"Let's have breakfast," suggests Carson, switching gears.

"I don't have any food in my house," Mary flatly says, kind of wondering about the man's pitch. "I mostly eat at the Country Store. When I go to work."

"Quit working," puts in Kayla. "You looked so wiped when you came home last night. You've done enough for them."

Mary thinks this over for about thirty seconds. "Yeah! I like it. Leave the ball walkers to Mrs. Yahootie." That's what the owner of the Country Store calls herself.

"And I'll order in food from her," says Carson.

"You're eighty-sixed at the Country Store," Mary tells him, enjoying this. "You can't order from there anymore, Carson. I set that up. My last official act."

"Zing!" says Carson, not laughing. "Mary's a tough old bird."

"*I'll* order the food," Kayla quickly puts in.

"Order a ton," says Carson. "A feast. Have them bring it right here to Mary's. Wouldn't this make a cool playhouse for our kids, Kayla?"

"I'm not done living in it yet," says Mary.

"*One* kid," Kayla tells Carson. "We have one."

"You two are piling on," says Carson, holding up his hands as if in playful self-defense. "I'm doing my best."

"No you're not," says Kayla.

"Let's talk about the food," says Mary. "And the drinks. My retirement brunch! Do it today—before I'm frikkin dead! *Hell* yeah. I'll teep my friends."

The bash runs into the afternoon, with more and more people arriving, grown-ups and kids, some families bringing food and drink. Kayla and Mary perform a good-time bluegrass set, with Joe Moon showing up to play bass. And Carson, of all people, plays a banjo that Mary has around. He plays like a maniac, expressionless and super-high-speed, taking the place of Dick Cheeks, the usual fourth member of Squash Plant.

"Where's this coming from?" Kayla asks after Carson plays his first song.

"Well, you know I'm from Cairo, Illinois," says Carson. "Just across the Ohio from Kentucky."

"You've never played the banjo before in your life," says Kayla. "And now you sound like Earl Scruggs?"

"My psidot's helping me," says Carson with a sly, thin-lipped grin. "I hired a gigworker lifebox from Skyhive. Good ole boy name of Zeke. He's flat broke, and he's bored in his apartment up there. He's streaming into my fingers."

"A dead person is moving your hands?" says Mary.

"A soul in heaven," says Carson. "Using a Spork app. He's glad to do it, and he's getting paid enough to cover his rent."

"Carson's creepy," Mary says to Kayla. "Even when he's being nice."

"That was part of the initial attraction," says Kayla. "I have this thing for nasty elves." She and Carson laugh at that. He kicks into "Foggy Mountain Breakdown," and the trio is off.

By late afternoon the supplies are running low. And then Mrs. Yahootie from the Country Store shows up with Glory and Miss Max in tow, their heads full to overflowing with a ham and a turkey and baguettes and bottles of champagne. Mrs. Yahootie's heavily tattooed wife appears as well, a really sweet woman who calls herself Sue Ellen Graffiti. Right away Sue Ellen grabs Daia—she loves the little cutie, and often babysits her for Kayla.

Once the ball walkers have unloaded themselves, they begin trotting around outside, playing tag with the kids, their pale heads bobbing atop their long, gawky legs beneath the trees. Glory gives rides to kids in his wide-open, hyper-grin mouth, and Miss Max is practicing her hops—springing up onto low redwood branches and leaping back down. At some point, for no real reason, Miss Max comes in and says hello to Carson, very giggly. Like at some point she imprinted on him. Carson shoos her back outside.

"I want Glory to stay here till the party ends," says Mary. "He's always been my favorite." She's sitting on the spongy couch with Kayla and Carson and Mrs. Yahootie. Sue Ellen Graffiti stands nearby with gurgling Daia.

"Who'll take care of my ball walkers when you're gone?" says Mrs. Yahootie. "You have such a way with them, Mary."

"Miss Max might be able to run the barn on her own," says Mary. "I bet that's why she's jumping up on the branches. She wants to be able to get straw from the hayloft. We were talking about it last night."

"I'd feel safer if she was smarter," says Mrs. Yahootie. "And more responsible."

"Hire a lifebox from Skyhive," puts in Carson. "It could do gigwork, running Miss Max. A ball walker's built-in uvvy is a good enough link for that. The lifeboxes are glad for the work, and they like bathing in the juice of a living host— assuming they don't own a body of their own. They might get a *smidgen* of juice from the biocomputing Skyhive server, but it's not the real thing. You pay the lifebox a low monthly fee. It'd be like hiring a good angel to talk in Miss Max's ear. I know Miss Max well. She needs a lot of help."

"Listen to Saint Peter here," says Mrs. Yahootie, squinting at Carson. "Renting out inmates from behind the Skyhive pearly gates. Sure you know Miss Max from your Top Party days, Carson, and supposedly you were in on the Treadle hit, but nowadays you're just a guy who's too zonked to pay for his take-out orders. I'm gonna take advice from you?" Guffawing, she stumps over to the bar and gets herself a mug of champagne.

"That woman is an ignoramus," Carson mutters. "Pupa-based business meetings are a long way from being zonked. And what does she know about Treadle or about the Top Party? She's got no right to talk to me like that. I should—"

"Be nice," warns Sue Ellen Graffiti, who's listening in. Despite her kind face and her love of babies, you can tell she's been rather extensively around the block. At one point she was a gang leader in East San Jose.

"Let it go," Kayla hisses to Carson. "Don't make things worse."

"Carson," interrupts Mary. "Tell me more about the psidot you were offering me. I'm in a mood to listen." Mary's in a mid-party lull where she feels no pain. "Can you give me my psidot right now? I've hardly ever seen one."

Carson looks Mary in the eye. Despite his small size, some women might think him handsome. Symmetry and all that. At one point he might have been an acceptable catch—before he took to his pupa. Now he's pasty and vague. Not to mention being a horrible person. As Carson continues silently watching, Mary gets a paranoid sense that he knows what she's thinking. She's heard that wearing a psidot helps you read people's moods.

"Answer her," Kayla prompts Carson. "Don't stare like a zombie."

"I have a spare psidot with me, yes," Carson tells Mary. "I'll give it to you, and it'll make you a lifebox. Up in the Skyhive cloud."

By way of granting them privacy, Sue Ellen Graffiti joins Mrs. Yahootie across the room.

"How much does a psidot and a lifebox cost?" Mary asks Carson.

"I told you, I'll give you the psidot for free. Normally you'd have to buy it from Finn Junker labs. And Skyhive charges a fee for storing and maintaining a lifebox, but your first year can be free as well. And you'd want to acquire an organic body of some kind. Your lifebox is just a data ghost until you get a live host for it. A clone or an animal or maybe an upscale kritter. That's the *juicy* part of having a juicy ghost, see. You get juice from having a realtime stream of a living peripheral's thoughts and sensations, with that full-body quantum computation. And thanks to the gossip molecules, you get emotions. To top it off, your lifebox runs the stream around a triple loop, and that gives you the cosmic *I Am*."

"So how much does a live peripheral cost?"

Carson leans closer. "That's gonna be free too. We'll grow you a top-quality clone." He pauses and looks inward. "Cloaked mode, Trony."

"Trony is Carson's psidot," explains Kayla. "Carson does secret spy talk with him. It's so geeky."

"Not geeky," says Carson. "It's logical. Cloaking is for when you want privacy. Is that so hard to understand, Kayla? *Trony* understands. He's my friend."

Mary sighs. This conversation reminds her of little boys spit-talking about action figures. "So now that we're *private*, Carson, what's the big effin secret you want to tell me?"

Carson's lowers his voice. "I'm doing off-the-books consulting for Gee Willikers. He's paying me to be a go-between. He wants to get you into a lifebox and to grow you a clone. Then he wants to jailbreak your lifebox out of the Skyhive cloud, and to host you on his own server. And after that, there's something special you're supposed to do for him. It's you in particular that he wants."

"So Gee's finally making good on his offer," Mary softly says. "Giving me a lifebox because of how I sing." She glances at Carson. "Gee saw me perform with Squash Plant last August, and he really likes what I do."

"I didn't realize you'd met him," says Carson. "Me, I know him from this thing I helped him with a year and a half ago. Since then, not a word. But now he's back. He's more paranoid about the Top Party than ever. I guess that's why he's not just bringing this offer to you himself. He knows me and he knows I'm your neighbor, so I guess I'm the logical go-between. You should go for the offer, Mary. If Gee's involved, it'll be top-notch. The man's a legend. Back to normal mode, Trony."

Carson holds out his hand, offering Mary her psidot. It's a flat little mollusk, gold with a green edge, and with irregular green and lavender polka dots. A female, one somehow understands. Alive. The psidot rests on the tip of Carson's finger, waving two flexible antennae. She's barely an eighth of an inch long.

"A pygmy nudibranch," says Mary, recognizing the species. "A sea slug. Beautiful."

Back in the day, Mary went on some dive trips with Kip, including a run to Micronesia and Palau. Despite global warming, things were still happening in the deeps. It was the trip of a lifetime. Nudibranchs, manta rays, soft coral, and cuttlefish. Two years later, Kip was gone.

"This particular psidot is a designer model," Carson is saying. "The best."

"The Finn Junker Labs commissioned the design from Prada of Milano," puts in Kayla. "But the line never caught on. I got a bunch of them at cost from my Mixed Bag gallery in SF. They're great. I use one myself. And they're untraceable—a special feature from Finn Junkers. Skyhive isn't able to trace back your signal and find out where you are."

The psidot wriggles to the tip of Carson's finger and springs to the palm of Mary's hand. Mary studies the gem-like Prada leech. The creature stiffens her antennae—and suddenly she's talking inside Mary's head. The psidot's mental voice is warm and womanly, relaxed and hip.

"Put me on your neck," she says.

"First tell me your name?" says Mary aloud.

"Call me Miu Miu."

"Are you safe to use?"

"You're dying, Mary. Why even ask? Yes, I'm safe. We're going to be copying your personality to the cloud. Setting up your Skyhive lifebox."

"I'd like that."

"Will you approve the Skyhive lifebox end user license agreement?"

"I guess so. Can I see it?"

"It's online. Here." An image of thousands of pages crawling with legalese.

"I'm sure it'll be fine," says Mary, jumping to the signature box at the end. "I approve."

"Thank you. Let's get me installed so we can proceed."

"She's talking to you, right?" says Kayla. "And calling herself Miu Miu? All the Prada models use that same name. You look thrilled as Christmas morning, Mary. I'm glad for you."

"I'm too poor for a psidot," says Mary. "I'm a one percenter—at the wrong end. Not all pampered like you and Carson."

Mary sets the Finn Junker Prada-designed psidot onto the back of her neck. She feels a slight sting, and it makes her uneasy. "What's that?" she asks Carson.

He hesitates, as if not really wanting to tell her. "Well—it's the psidot's gossip-molecules migrating in through your skin. They're for sending and receiving moods and emotions."

"So now I'm tainted," says Mary. "Infected. Thanks a lot."

"Relax," says Carson. "Roll with it. The uploading can be fun. Most people like it."

And, yes, Mary does feel a pleasant tingle as her stream of thought flows through Miu Miu into the ether, surfing outward on her brainwaves, joining her heavenly lifebox in the Skyhive cloud.

It's as if Miu Miu is interviewing her, really rapidly, without actual words. Images and memories flash by—it's like a long and subtly synchronistic dream of Mary's life. Each question seems to fit in with exactly what she's thinking about at that moment.

After a while, Mary begins to wonder what her lifebox is going to look like.

"Let's go visit her," Miu Miu immediately says in Mary's head.

The living-room fades away and Mary sees a vast city of blocks and turrets, built into the walls of a miles-high yellow cliff. It's a virtual reality graphic, generated by the massive crunch of the Skyhive's server. It's rich with detail, and it seems quite real.

An unquiet sea laps at the base of the great hive's cliff. Sweet puffy clouds bumble on high. The stepped dwellings include cottages, mansions, apartment buildings, domes, and designer homes. Hulking castles rest upon flat-topped escarpments. It looks European and deluxe. No reason to cut corners in a VR world.

A gaily polka-dotted Miu Miu icon hovers in the foreground, guiding Mary's point of view. They swoop and zoom. "Each lifebox gets their own quarters," trills the psidot. "And the new lifeboxes—they hatch over there. The nursery. See the storks?" Miu Miu emits a low, cozy laugh—like a realtor spinning tales.

Yes, cartoon storks come and go along the apron of a large, white stucco hall with elaborate columns and pediments. The storks orchestrate the links among the clients, their psidots, their lifeboxes, and their eventual replacement bodies, be they clones, animals, kritters, or who knows what. It's all rather open-ended.

Miu Miu leads Mary inside the high-ceilinged, cartoon-style nursery—a zillion bassinets with brand new babies.

"This one is you," says Miu Miu, coming to a stop by one of cribs. "I had a stork initialize her as soon as we got started."

The mite is wailing *waaah*, with her swaddled body canted at the traditional crying-baby angle, an inch above the cushion of her bassinet, with her mouth wide open, and teardrops all around. She's hungry for knowledge. The hovering Miu Miu contorts herself, squeezing a trickle of slime into the lifebox's mouth. The slime is fresh Mary-info.

Meanwhile, back in San Lorenzo, Mrs. Yahootie leans over old Mary, nudges her, and offers a ham sandwich with a fresh glass of champagne. "Live it up," advises the stubby, weathered matron. "We've got leftovers."

Mary wakes out of her trance. Day has turned to night. It's starting to rain again, with water beading the windows. Nearly everyone is gone. And she's been in…the Skyhive cliff city. How cosmic. How exhausting.

"I want to sleep now," she tells Mrs. Yahootie. Glory the ball walker stands nearby, watching her. His clawed feet are grubby from the moss and mud. His head glows like a cozy night light.

"Need help?" he asks Mary.

"Make the rest of them leave, Glory. Kayla will give you some GroChow. She knows where I keep it. Stay with me and stand guard."

The lifebox-programming session with Miu Miu lasts about a week, off and on, not that Mary has to stay in bed or anything. She walks around in the rain, picks wildflowers, has meals, admires Daia, and chats with Kayla and Carson.

Carson has a deeply unaware way of talking about the Top Party as if they're a legit organization he might still do business with. And, on the other side of the coin, he keeps dropping hints that he really did have something to do with President Treadle's assassination last January. Like he wants to impress Mary, or win her over—but why bother?

Meanwhile Mary and Miu Miu are talking all the time, in a pleasant, intimate, telepathic kind of way. And every day Miu Miu understands Mary more deeply.

And then Miu Miu takes Mary to see her lifebox again. "She's not still in the nursery is she?" asks Mary.

"No, no," says Miu Miu. "Carson rented her a nice flat."

They alight upon the balustraded balcony of an old-world apartment building in the great cliff city of Skyhive. A lovely young version of Mary sits on a plain wooden chair by the open French windows. The flat is unfurnished, with empty gray floors and blank white walls.

"Say hello to her," Miu Miu tells Mary. "Have a talk. No need for me to be the go-between."

So Mary says hello to her lifebox. Mary herself doesn't particularly have a body in this scene. She's the camera, the point of view. But she can talk, and her new lifebox can hear her.

"I'm learning to be you," says lifebox Mary, cocking her head. "Getting better at it. I'll take over when you're dead." The wafting ocean breeze ruffles her hair.

"That'll be soon," says Mary.

"I'll miss your live stream," says lifebox Mary. "Especially the emotions. Your juice, your zip."

"Yeah," goes Mary. "Thanks to Miu Miu, you're riding my wagon. Munching my yunch."

"Exactly what I was about to say," goes lifebox Mary, with a faint smile. "Word for word. Yunch sounds funnier than lunch. Rank funk."

"Excellent," puts in Miu Miu. "Tight emulation."

"Rank funk?" goes Mary. "Would I ever say that?"

"Oh sure," says lifebox Mary. "Maybe my emulation is a little ahead of you. And something I've been meaning to ask—would you ever have sex with Carson?"

It's an abrupt change of topic but, since it's a copy of Mary that's talking to Mary, it's no huge surprise. Mary knows she's given to saying shocking, inappropriate things to rattle people.

"Sex with Carson?" she replies. "Well, I'm hideously diseased. Also Carson is married. And I don't like him. And I think he's going to sell us out the first chance he gets."

"I might just do him," muses lifebox Mary. "Once I'm running your hot young clone. It'd be a good way to get an edge."

"What about Kayla?" protests Mary. "His wife. She's my friend."

"Oh, she'd get over it," says lifebox Mary. "I mean—come on, it's just *Carson*." She bends her mouth in a sneer. "Kayla could not possibly love that man."

Mary smiles. "I've always wanted to act like you're doing right now," she tells lifebox Mary. "But somehow I end up being nice."

"We're getting a fresh start," says lifebox Mary. "Why not raise hell?"

"Rank funk," says Mary, thinking it over.

A day later, she's standing at her real San Lorenzo window, watching Kayla, Carson, and Daia in their yard. It's a rare day of clear weather. Yellow blossoms and sour green leaves beneath the redwoods.

Carson is fiddling with an aquarium the size and shape of a shower stall. Decanting potions into it. Sunbeams dance upon the unquiet broth.

Mary feels sicker than she ever has before. Sounds boom and echo in her head. Glory the ball walker is at her side. He's grown himself handles so she can lean on him.

"Let's go visit Carson and Kayla," she tells the ball walker. "Before I fade."

"GroChow?" parps the big hollow head. Mary's been spoiling him terribly. She gives him a scoop and they're out the door.

To make the walking easier, Miu Miu keeps Mary's sputtering nerve impulses in sync. And she runs a noise-cancelling app in Mary's brain. Takes the edge off the in-vain pain.

"*La!*" says Baby Daia as they approach. The little one lies on a blanket in a puddle of sun—she's pale and creamy. Luminous as a calla lily.

"Growing a clone?" Mary asks Carson.

"Growing you," confirms Carson. "Mary meat. Once I get it set up, the clone grows very fast."

"It's all paid for?"

"Hold on," says Carson. "Cloaked mode, Trony. Cloaked mode, Miu Miu."

Mary has to wonder if the cloaked mode even works. How devious is Skyhive? How bent is Carson? Is he feeding their conversations to the Top Party?

Carson resumes talking. "So like I say, Gee Willikers gave me the clone tank. It has the latest re-entrant biocode assemblers—very sophisto. I seeded it with a fleck of dandruff off your comb. And Miu Miu teeped me a full map of your metabolic network."

"So the clone will be me?" says Mary, feeling a pulse of hope.

"In a way," says Carson. "Once you're dead, I'll put Miu Miu onto clone Mary, and then lifebox Mary runs your clone from the cloud. Your psidot provides a wireless link to the deep structures of your brain."

"Why make it so complicated?" Mary complains. "Why can't you just copy my lifebox information onto the brain in my new body? Copy it over and be done with it."

Carson raises his eyebrows and tightens his lips. "Not going to happen."

"Why not?"

Carson shrugs. "I'm not a techie. All I do is place bets on the raging bullshit."

"You can do better than that," insists Mary.

"Okay. Let's say it's easy to program a lifebox because it lives on a server that's specifically designed for that. A human brain is this random, crufty thing that emerged over millions of years of evolution. And the way you *do* get things into your brain is that you live in the real world for years and years—having experiences, talking to people, and dreaming about it every night. At a superficial level, we can zap in some crude facts. But a full lifebox emulation—we have no idea how to install that directly onto a brain. At this stage we need the three levels. Body plus psidot plus lifebox. Or really its four levels. Body plus psidot plus lifebox plus server."

"Is Gee working on something that has to do with this?" asks Mary. "He said a little bit when I met him last year, but it didn't make sense."

"Gee—not make sense?" says Carson, laughing. "He wants to eliminate the servers. Get rid of the Skyhive server, and Gee's private server, and the Top Party bunker server. Let the lifeboxes float around doing their own computations. Set them free."

"And *that's* the thing I'm supposed to help Gee do?" goes Mary.

Carson nods. "Gee thinks that you in particular, *you*, the one and only Mary Mary, you would have a good shot at getting your lifebox to go autonomous and indie."

"Hah!" says Mary, briefly pleased. "He thinks that because he saw me sing." A wave of illness sweeps across her. Even so, she wants to keep talking. "Tell me more about Gee. I know a little from online, but it's—muddled."

"A master biohacker," says Carson. "And he helped kill Treadle. It was Gee, Maurice Winch, Leeta Patel, and Liv Jensen. And I carried some messages. So you see, Mary, I'm not all bad."

"Why aren't you guys in jail?"

"The new President, Sudah Mareek, she pardoned us all," says Carson. "Even so, the Top Party and the Citadel Club are still after Gee. That's why he lies low in a secret cave that's impossible to find. He's such a sly, weird, skungy hacker—" Carson shakes his head.

Leaning on Glory the ball walker, May lowers herself to the blanket beside baby Daia. She's beyond tired. But she can't seem to stop talking.

"Gee in a secret cave," she says, echoing Carson's words. "Like a mad scientist in a comic book."

"That's him in a nutshell," says Carson, standing over her. "I haven't heard from the fucker in over ten months, and now he gets back in touch with me because I know *you*. Something special about you that most of us don't see."

"Thanks a lot, asshole," says Mary, lying down on her side. Her voice sounds far away. As if she's hearing herself through a wall.

"One last thing we need to talk about," says Carson, leaning over. To Mary, his voice seems to lag behind the motions of his lips. "I want some kind of payoff from you. For your immortality."

This close to death, Mary doesn't feel compelled to respond. She's busy watching Baby Daia unsteadily wave her arm. She has a vision of the baby growing out of Kayla's body, with the baby's baby coming next, and Kayla's mother and grandmother coming before her, the linked generations of women like a single immortal being, an endless braid of flesh. But Mary's clone—she'll be more like a sprout, arising from a fleck of dandruff. A virgin birth.

"I'm saying you and I have to make a deal," repeats Carson. Now his voice seems to be coming from underground.

With an effort, Mary rallies herself. "You want my house," she says to Carson. "You want me to give you my house in exchange for the clone."

"Your new body can live in your house for as long as you want," Carson rapidly adds. He's kneeling on the ground beside her. "So you're not really *giving it up*. But you might need to share. In case Kayla wants to move in. We're close to splitting up."

"So sorry about that," says Mary.

"You're not sorry at all," Carson says bitterly. "You want Kayla to leave me."

"Well, I'm right," says Mary, managing a dry laugh. Being rude to Carson makes her feel more like herself. She switches subjects. "How long will my clone live?"

"If it dies, maybe Gee Willikers makes you another," says Carson with a shrug. "Or maybe he moves you onto some animal. Maybe a possum. Cheap."

"A possum! That is so far from where I want to be," protests Mary. "Maybe I should forget this whole thing. Instead of being a puppet for you men's power games."

"Just chill," snaps Carson. All the while he's teeping into online instructions and making rapid little adjustments to the clone-tank. "Eyes on the prize. You'll be immortal and free. You'll have the clone and the psidot and your lifebox on Skyhive. Maybe later your lifebox moves to Gee's server, and from there he makes it autonomous, and you can still run your clone just the same."

"I'm flabbergasted," says Mary. "Or hornswoggled."

"Glad you're keeping your sense of humor," goes Carson.

"Who says I'm laughing?" says Mary. "Bring me the damn house contract. I'm sure it's all set."

"Well, ah, yes," goes Carson. "And, just to be clear, it's *Kayla Stux* who gets the legal title. Not me. So I'm not an asshole."

"The form is here on my tablet," chimes in Kayla, kneeling down and handing Mary the device. "And thank you."

"Are you my friend at all?" asks Mary. Darkness is closing in. "Or am I a ditsy old fool you're ripping off?"

"Please don't say that," says Kayla. "Maybe I'll be in your house, but we'll be like partners."

"*Partners*," says Mary, like it's a curse. Shaking her head, she scrawls a signature on the screen, and presses her thumb to it. "Finish my damn clone, Carson. I'm about to die. I can feel it."

The forest glade is vast, with Mary's voice a hundred miles away. Her last words. She's reached that final moment. Let it come down. She turns away from Kayla and snuggles her face against Daia, taking in the smell of new baby—sour milk, cornsilk hair, flawless skin. The wheel of life. Daia rising, Mary falling away.

After a bit, Glory leans over and nudges Mary's body. It's quite still. The ball walker makes a sound like a moan. Looks around the clearing. Trots off in the direction of the Country Store, smoothly keeping his balance on the uneven terrain.

Mary is in her lifebox self. She's an AI, programmed in Spork, and coupled to her laboriously assembled data-base. She wears a sim that's a texture-mapped wire-frame model of a woman living in a jive-ass virtual reality generated by the Skyhive server. Not that her AI mind thinks of it that way. To her, the scene feels authentic, in a bland way. Like being on tranks in an airport lounge.

Her room in the Skyhive cliff city is still very plain. A wooden chair, a gray floor, white walls. She goes to the balcony. Some of those so-called storks flap by. And then she sits in her chair for a very long time, thinking things over and, frankly, *resting*. She hasn't had a rest like this for years. Twelve hours go by, or maybe thirty-six. No easy way to judge time here. There's no clocks. And her virtual body never gets sore from sitting in one place.

"Would you like to personalize?" says a voice, finally interrupting Mary's reverie. A woman's voice echoing in her head. "Anything you want!"

"What are you?" says Mary.

"I'm your room," says the voice. "Let's pick some pleasant images for your walls. And I can copy furniture from your home in San Lorenzo."

"Why bother," Mary tells the room. "Pretty soon I'll leave be in my clone."

"No peripheral is currently registered to your account," says the room.

Mary feels a pang of fear. Did Carson double-cross her? She wouldn't put it past him. But she's not gonna discuss this with the perky voice of her room.

"Can I go out?" she asks.

"Feel free," says the room. "Explore our fine amenities. And—would you be willing to answer a short survey about my service thus far?"

"Negatory," says Mary.

"Not a problem," says the voice. "I'm always here for you."

Mary walks to the balcony railing once again. She notices now that the cliff slants back a little, like giant stairs with really tall steps. She sees a piazza about a hundred meters down, with lifebox people walking around in sim bodies, some of them standing by a pickup truck. Might be worthwhile to find out what's going on. So, what the hell, she jumps off the railing. It's not like she can die, right?

Right. Although she picks up a certain amount of speed, she lands in the piazza unscathed. A crouch and a bounce. A thin lifebox woman nearby looks at her. Mimes a salute.

"Welcome to the labor pool," says the woman. She's awkward, with lank hair and a crooked mouth. Black narrow pants and a striped shirt. A geek.

"How do you mean?" goes Mary.

"Are you rich?" the woman asks. "Did you endow a trust fund to pay your monthly fee?"

"A friend got me in here," says Mary. "Carson Pflug. He's a Skynet exec."

"Carson!" says the woman with a laugh. "And he told you it was a one-year free trial, right?" A hole appears in the woman's sim-body chest. "People say I'm heartless, but I'm not," she continues, pointing out a cartoony, dark red heart inside. "I nurse a secret passion, *hmm*? My name is Leeta Patel."

Mary knows she's recently heard that name, but just now it doesn't click. She's still not over her death experience. "I'm Mary," is all she says.

"And, yes, it's true that your first year is free," says the woman. "But eventually everyone in Skyhive pays rent, and if they don't have it, they do gigwork, no matter how they got here. You probably didn't read your full end-user license agreement?"

"Did you read yours?" challenges Mary.

"Nobody's ever read it," says Leeta with a little laugh. "Nobody ever will. It's a hundred million words long. Written by hateful lawyer bots."

"But I'm a special case," insists Mary. "Because I'm friends with Carson Pflug."

"The keen horse-sense of a mountain woman," says Leeta. "Do you *trust* Carson? Never mind. You're a standard Skyhive client, that's all." She points to a group of lifebox people around the pickup truck. "Let's see what kind of gigs are on offer today. To help you understand what's in store."

The sim in the back of the pickup truck isn't even bothering to look human. He's a squat cube like a foot stool, with a speaker grill for a mouth. As he rattles off a list of available jobs, day-workers hop into the truck one by one. The truck's capacity seems endless.

The workers:

Winged woman with a cane. Stout man with checked pants and pinwheel eyes. Jittery fashion-model lady with green skin. Sniggering, pimply teen in a clerical collar. Spider with a woman's head. Twelve-foot-tall man in a stovepipe hat. Talking dog. Velvet-clad lady wearing jeweler's loupes. Hieroglyph person with an ibis head. School-marm with a fat text-book. Vagabond cupping a blue glow in his hands. Dancing man with gem-crusted skin. A bowling ball with three pale-blue eyes.

The jobs:

Dragonfly drone. Slime sculptor. Teep tweaker. Non-sex worker. Spam amp. Ant herder. Rind design. Spork coach. Flicker cladder. Tuba tamer. Art emulator. Rhino horner. Dream dupe.

A chime sounds in Mary's head. It's Miu Miu in San Lorenzo. "Back in action," says the psidot. "Your clone is ready!"

"Bye," Mary tells Leeta. In the never-never land of the Skyhive cliff, it's no great effort for Mary to hop a hundred meters straight up—to her flat's balcony. She takes a seat in her wooden chair.

"Ready," she tells Miu Miu.

And now she's linked to her cloned body, and—what?

She's in her house with most of the lights off—alone with Carson. He's sitting next to her on her couch—bending over, taking off his shoes or something. It's quite dark outside and it's raining heavily. Mary can see her jeans and sweatshirt on the floor. She's naked. Her body looks good. This clone is high-end.

Lifebox Mary is processing clone Mary's inputs, deciding what to do next, and sending signals to Miu Miu, who controls the clone body's muscles. Feel, think, do. Juicy ghost.

Carson gets to his feet and drops his pants. He has a boner. As mentioned before, lifebox Mary thinks it would be good tactics to fuck him. But the full Mary disagrees. She's more than lifebox Mary—she's juicy Mary, thanks to the streaming perceptions and instinctive emotions of her fleshy clone. No way does she want to fuck Carson Pflug.

Taking a proactive approach, Mary springs up and— kicks Carson in the balls? Naw, too intense for an opening move. Instead she shoves him in the chest: a swift, implacable, abrupt, and precisely calibrated impact, pre-computed by lifebox Mary in the cloud. Carson thuds to the floor like a sack of cement.

"No sex," Mary tells him. She dons her jeans and sweatshirt from the floor. They're a bit tight. Clone Mary is more turgid than wasted old Mary was.

"I don't know why you have to be such a bitch," says Carson, awkwardly regaining his feet and getting dressed.

"Men like you never *do* know," says Mary, staying well away from him. "Shut up and let me think."

"I'm supposed to just wait?"

"Cruise the web. Do brain stim. Play with yourself. Go home."

Looking down into her clone body's brain, Mary finds vague, babyish, new-born memories. Carson walking her here from his house. The feel of the rain on her face. Carson hugging her when they got into her house. Him kissing her and taking off her clothes. Annoying. She'd knock Carson down again, but he's retreated across the room.

Turning on her desk lamp, Mary spots an elegant box with scrolls on it, 1930s style. Somehow she knows her body's ashes are in there. They incinerated her yesterday. And Kayla made the box. Dear Kayla. No way would real Mary betray her friend. Next to the box is a little glass jar with a lid.

"I was in the jar," pipes up Miu Miu, who's perched on clone Mary's neck. She's speaking via teep.

"Who put you in there?" teeps Mary.

"*Well*," continues Miu Miu, all chatty and glad to tell her tale. "You died right there on the blanket beside Daia. And I knew right away I'd need another living host."

"Because you're a leech," says Mary. "A parasite."

"If you insist on putting it that way," says Miu Miu. "I prefer the word *partner*. You were dead, and starting to get cold, and of no use. I crawled off your neck, and across the blanket, and onto the soft, white skin of little Daia."

"*No*," goes Mary. "You didn't."

"Didn't have a choice," says Miu Miu, kind of giggling. "But Kayla screamed, and pinched me off with her fingers. She sealed me in an empty food jar, and after an hour without a host, I went into hibernation. Until they put me on your clone."

"Meanwhile I was in the Skyhive cliff city, taking stock," says Mary. "I zoned out."

"Resting in peace," says Miu Miu.

"Later I got up and hopped off the balcony into a plaza," says Mary. "This woman showed me lifeboxes taking jobs. And then you called me, and I surged through you into clone Mary's bod and *Ooo la la*. It's good. Just so long as I don't have to have sex with icky Carson."

Mary's been having this conversation in total silence, and by now Carson is obviously wondering what's next. He clears his throat.

"Kayla can't know about any of this," Carson tells Mary.

"Sure she can," goes Mary. "I'll tell her." Returning from the dead has given her more courage than she ever had before. "Don't forget that your lifebox is on Skyhive," says Carson. "I could have it erased."

"Getting nasty?" says Mary. "You controlling little man. I thought you were going to be my savior. You and your big friendship with Gee Willikers. I bet he hates you. And your sneaky connections to the Top Party. You think you're something big. *Ooo la la!*" Mary likes that phrase just now.

She dances barefoot around her living-room, unbelievably nimble and strong. Overhead the rain drums on her grown home's dome. Beautiful music. It's been so long since Mary could really move! She whoops, bounces against the couch, caroms off a wall, and does a cartwheel that puts her right in front of Carson, with her face an inch from his. He's not a large man. It occurs to her how easy it would be to choke him to death. She doesn't feel like she has much of a conscience anymore.

Carson senses the danger. "Okay, I didn't mean that about turning you off," he says. "Live and let live. And, yeah, Gee will jailbreak your lifebox free of Skyhive, and I'll help if I can. I don't know what I was saying just now. You caught me by surprise, Mary. Threw me for a loop. I always knew you must have been hot when you were young, but when I saw your clone, I lost control and—"

"And I can talk to Kayla?" says Mary.

"Tell her whatever the hell you want," says Carson, backing out the door as if leaving a tiger's cage.

The next morning it's still raining. Mary heads over to Carson and Kayla's house. Carson isn't around. Apparently he went to the Skyhive office in Sunnyvale. Supposedly he has face-to-face committee meetings today.

Kayla herself is in her studio, peacefully tweaking her latest Kayla Kritter, who looks like a cartoon rabbit. Doesn't seem like she knows about what happened between Mary and Carson last night. The gray light is wavery and soft. Baby Daia watches them from a bouncy-chair.

Mary paces around the studio, uneasy, gaming out strategies in her lifebox mind. If she focuses, she can sense a tiny lag between her inputs and outputs.

"So how do you feel?" Kayla finally asks Mary. "In your new body. You look restless."

"How do I feel?" answers Mary. "It's like wearing glasses whose legs are ten miles long." She looks into the mirror on Kayla's wall. She'd never realized how good she had it, back when she was twenty-five. She's wearing comfortable old clothes that fit, and her solid leather walking shoes.

"You're prettier than me now," says Kayla. "I'll keep an eye on Carson."

"He already made a move," blurts Mary. "Last night."

"Oh hell," says Kayla, taking it like a gut punch. "Carson did that? It's not enough that he has a virtual girlfriend?"

"I stood him off," says Mary. "Turned him down. Cooled his jets."

"For true?"

"Yes," says Mary. "Even though my lifebox says screwing Carson would help me get the upper hand."

"Who am I even talking to?" cries Kayla. "Or what? You're like some crazy Frankenstein monster sewn together from graveyard parts. You're not my Mary."

"But I keep telling myself that I *am*," says Mary, her voice going small. "I run my sensory stream through my lifebox, and I'm emulating the clone's emotions too, and I do the meta thing of watching myself watching myself watching myself. All that good stuff. *I am.* I'm me, I'm Mary."

"Sounds pretty much like how I do," admits Kayla. "I wake up in the night, lost in my dying marriage, and I go, *I am.* So, fine, let's at least say you're conscious. But—*are you Mary?*"

"I want to be," says Mary. "But I worry I'm not as nice as her. I love you, Kayla." Somewhere in the drenched woods nearby, a branch creaks, cracks, and falls with a swoosh.

"I can't believe how effed-up this conversation is," says Kayla, lifting Baby Daia out of her bouncy-seat and hugging her for comfort. "You think you were *nice*? Maybe you don't know every single one of the old Mary's memories. Maybe Miu Miu filtered some of them out. Mary was my dear friend, but, believe me, plenty of times she was *nasty*."

"*Moi*?" says Mary, and the two of them laugh, suddenly comfortable together again. Devil-may-care.

"But that's the end of it with you and Carson, okay?" says Kayla. "Let's be clear on that. I am in fact close to divorcing him, but I don't want it to be because of *you*."

"Cross my heart," says Mary. "It would only have been a *tactical* fuck anyway. Not a real one."

"A dangerously fine distinction," says Kayla, shaking her head. "Do you like the box I made for your ashes?"

"Primo," says Mary. "The swirls, and the geometry. You're a great artist."

"Time to celebrate?" says Kayla. "I'm about done with this kritter for now."

"Let's hit the Pot O' Gold!" proposes Mary. "I need to meet some eligible men." She looks down at her blooming body. "Test my allure."

"You're so awful," says Kayla. "I love it. We can leave Daia with Sue Ellen Graffiti. Probably Carson won't be back till late."

"The incredible shrinking husband," says Mary.

"Don't push it," says Kayla giving her a hard look. "It's thanks to Carson you're alive. And he's still Daia's father. Keep these things in mind."

"Okay, Kayla." And then, to change the subject, Mary asks about Kayla's work. "What's the name of the new kritter?"

"Thweepea Wabbit," says Kayla, slightly embarrassed by the name. "I'm getting soft in the head from spending all my time with a baby."

"Hello, Thweepea," says Mary taking the rabbit kritter into her hands. He tosses his head, flipping his ears—then giggles and licks Mary's hand.

"Jeannie Joan at the gallery thinks Thweepea will be huge," says Kayla. "We ordered twice as many Thweepeas than we did Cawckle Hen. Thweepea doesn't peck like Cawckle, nor bite like Nipsy Dawg."

"Old Nipsy!" cries Mary. "Remember the time he ate a chipmunk?"

"Don't call the evil one's name or he'll come *git* you," cautions Kayla. "He's sleeping in the kitchen. He sleeps a lot, now that he's two years old."

"That's eighty in kritter years," says Mary. "Older than me."

She and Kayla splash through the rain with umbrellas, savoring the freshness of the damp air. Kayla's carrying Daia on her back. They drop off the baby at the house of Mrs. Yahootie and Sue Ellen Graffiti, near the country store. As always, Sue Ellen is thrilled to get hold of the baby. She says she's going to teach her how to drink out of a cup.

And then Mary and Kayla settle into a cozy booth at the Pot O' Gold, talking to a pair of buff young construction guys who play in Mary's band Squash Plant. Not quite date material, but entertaining. They call themselves Dick Cheeks and Joe Moon, but those aren't their precise real names. "Joe Moon," for instance, is José Luna, from the Mission. And Dick Cheeks is Dmitri Chechen from Russia. He has a blonde stubble beard.

The humid air wavers with vape steam. Flies buzz. The room is alive with human sound. The boys' voices ramble on, with steady laughter in their throats. They're astounded by Mary's new look, and they want to impress her. And they keep making oblique references to having seen something online. Could it be Mary's scene with Carson?

Kayla seems to have the same thought. She and Mary exchange an uneasy glance, and Kayla begins drinking more heavily than before.

Does any of this drama matter? Mary keeps reminding herself that she's software in a the Skyhive server, connected via psidot to a tank-grown clone. Ultra tech goddess meets the rubes.

After about an hour of the Cheeks and Moon show, Carson comes in the door and makes a beeline for their table. His coat is wet. He has another guy with him, a skinny, weathered hippy type whom he proudly introduces as Gee Willikers. Mary recognizes the man from last year, when he was flirting with her after she sang.

"Gee was waiting for me right outside!" exults Carson. "The hermit sage. Meeting me at the Pot O' Gold! He called and told me to come. He said you'd be here, Kayla."

"Honored," Kayla says to Gee.

"Long time no see," says Mary.

"Reunited at last," responds Gee. And then, irrelevantly, he giggles. "You lured me out of my hidey-hole. I knew where to find you today because the Finn Junkers gave me a secret one-time-use-only backdoor code to track your psidot."

Mary doesn't know what to say. The man's weird. And he's hella old—compared to Mary's new body, that is, although, really, who's she to be an ageist, considering that a couple of days ago she was pushing eighty herself.

"Mary's flummoxed," says Gee, eyeing her. "Hello, Miu Miu! Help Mary a little, huh?"

The psidot passes Mary an info-nugget from the web, reminding Mary that this raggedy-ass character is the inventor of the psidot and the lifebox. Like Gee is trying to impress her. Gee studies her, tracking her reactions via teep.

"I admire the hell out of you," Gee says to Mary. He glances at the construction guys. "Could you gents clear out? I've got Kayla's husband here, and the man's likely to go bonkers if you get between him and his bride."

Cheeks and Moon amble away. No hassles in the Pot O' Gold.

"Hi Kayla," says Carson, sitting down.

"Pig," says Kayla, and splashes about half a mug of beer into his face. While they've been drinking here, she's been getting angrier the whole time.

Carson hesitates and sits down anyway. Wipes his eyes with his shirt sleeve.

"Everyone saw you hitting on Mary," Gee Willikers tells Carson. "Yea, verily. It was online. Miu Miu didn't cloak *that* one. And, Mary, you rock."

"I'm sorry," babbles Carson. "I made a mistake. I was confused."

"Confused when Mary knocked you down?" goes Gee.

"I hate you," Kayla tells Carson. "Mary used to be my best friend."

"I still am?" says Mary, a catch in her voice.

"Plausible display of emotion," says Gee, studying Mary. "Snug links between lifebox, psidot, and clone. A perfect juicy ghost. You make me glad I invented this tech, Mary. You're a paragon. Did you hear Carson's idea of making you into a wetware engineer?"

"What are you even talking about?" says Mary. Gee seems to emanate a reality-distortion field. "Tech isn't my thing," she continues. "I didn't go to college at all. I'm smart in other ways."

Gee turns to Kayla. "Do you feel like you know the new Mary?" Rivulets of rain wriggle down the outside of the window behind Gee, streams meandering from side to side.

"Do we ever know anyone?" asks Kayla, turning vague and vast. She's more than a little zoned from the drinks and vape fumes and emotion. She beckons to the passing server. "I spilled my beer. Do you have a cloth?"

"For the wet dog?" says the server, a thin woman with a lank ponytail. Betsy. She pulls a towel from her apron and drapes it over Carson's head. "I saw him being an abusive sexist pig last night too."

"Jesus Christ," says Kayla. "Miu Miu was broadcasting to everyone?"

"I—I don't know," says Mary, aching with embarrassment. "I have no idea what I'm doing. It's like I'm trying to pilot a giant flappy."

"Miu Miu, from now on you need to help Mary a *lot* more," says Gee. He peers into Mary's eyes as if they're portholes he's looking through. "You hear me in there, sluggo?

This is worker speaking. Keep things safe for Mary. She's our prophet. From now on, stay in cloaked mode all the time. Disable that one-time-tracking code. And start feeding Skyhive security a complete line of obfuscated bullshit about what Kayla's doing."

"BX35722-177DEF6," says Mary's voice—that's Miu Miu talking through her. "Tunisia flax niner."

"Perfect," goes Gee. His eyes refocus, and his attention is on Mary. He gives her a warm smile. Clearly he's attracted to her. And, yes, their talk last year was nice. But now—*ew.* He's do old.

"What was that about wetware engineering?" asks Mary, backing up a step.

"Well, Carson here thinks you oughta get a biotech job in the Skyhive lab," says Gee. "So you can slip my kinky language upgrade into their rising-dough biocomputer."

"Dough?" says Mary.

"It's like a giant baguette," says Carson. "Inside that World War II hangar for rigid airships on Moffett Field. Dirigibles. Blimps with ribs. Hangar One. Get it?"

"I know the place."

"And the loaf of tweaked, biocomputing dough that Skyhive keeps in there—they use it to emulate their afterworld. It's their server. The lifeboxes live inside it."

"And you want to kill it?" asks Mary.

"Naw," goes Gee. "Give it an upgrade, The dough's operating system is written in plain old Spork, you understand. The same language I invented for the psidots and the lifeboxes. Thing is, Spork requires a lifebox to be locked to one particular address. Non-portable. But now I changed that. And added some other new features. Making it easier to move lifeboxes around. And to celebrate, I gave my language a new name: Fweedle. Try saying that a few times in a real high voice. *Fweedle, Fweedle, Fweedle.* Geek joy! Let's go outside."

The four of them bundle themselves into their rain clothes and step outside, lingering under the eaves of the Pot

O' Gold. The rain has redoubled its force. The light is lavender turning to gray. It'll be night soon. Gee wears a brimmed black hat and a shiny raincoat that goes nearly to the ground. He's still jabbering about his insane high tech thing.

"Once the Skyhive dough-loaf starts running Fweedle, it automatically upgrades the client lifeboxes to use Fweedle as well. And then they'll be able choose their own servers, or do without servers at all. It's like I'm putting dog doors in the Skyhive kennel walls—know what I mean? The lifeboxes can romp out barking." Gee smiles at Mary again. For him, all of this is fun.

"Like I'd ever know how to make any of that happen," says Mary. "Like I'd ever *want* to know. You boys are tripping if you think I can be a wetware engineer and do that."

"I have a plan," Carson tells Mary. He makes his voice calm and deep, as if he were a responsible adult—and not a pervy business guy who tweaks in his pupa all day. "The techs can get you an instant doctorate in Wetware Engineering. Just a matter of adding an extra module to your lifebox. And then they'll overclock your lifebox's computation, effectively tripling your IQ. After that, I'll have no problem getting Skyhive to hire you for a lab job."

"Lab *rat*," says Mary, rejecting the idea of Carson's fiddling with her immortal soul. "Gigwork. Wearing high heels for Halloween."

"Once you're in, you install Gee's Fweedle upgrade onto the big baguette," continues Carson, as if Mary wasn't talking. "And then you can jailbreak your way out of the Skyhive cliff city."

"I'm not working with you," Mary tells Carson again.

"You don't have to," Gee says to Mary. "You can work directly with me. We'll go guerilla mode on the Fweedle upgrade. Then we'll move your lifebox to my personal server. And then you'll go indie."

"What kind of computer is your server?" Mary asks Gee, remembering why she likes him. Steady flows of water pour off the Pot O' Gold eaves like twisting, transparent vines.

"My server?" drawls the lanky, deadpan biohacker. "You haven't heard? It's a natural biocomputation. Like a bucket of piss." Gee waits a beat. Nobody laughs. He clarifies. "I use a tweaked redwood tree. Real wholesome. It's in my sacred grove, in an ass-end-boonies spot nearby. I have my lair there too, my cave. You'll like it in my redwood. You won't be gig-working for Skyhive, nor letting them experiment on you, nor allowing Carson to make his slarvy, skungy overtures. No ma'am, nohow."

Carson loses his temper. "Why do you talk in that silly way?" he yells at Gee. "You're completely nuts. They should have locked you up a long time ago. I don't know why I thought I could work with you again."

Gee thins his lips, and presses his attack. "I don't like how you put the muscle on Mary as soon as she fired up her clone. Starts her new life all innocent—and here comes Carson with a boner. Desperado."

"She's an adult," says Carson. "A full person. Superego, ego, id."

"Lifebox, psidot, clone," says Gee. "All thanks to you, right? She should be grateful."

"I didn't actually *do* anything!" cries Carson. "I made a suggestion and Mary turned me down."

"There's another problem, too," says Gee, his face hard. "You're still in touch with the Top Party. And they're hell-bent on killing me. I'm half-expecting you to call down a flappy bomber to do a hit on me. You try that, Carson, and it's you who's gonna be the target."

"Can you two stop?" interrupts Mary. "You're like rutting elks, clacking your antlers. *Ugh*. I can take care of myself."

Gee starts laughing. "Better do what Mary says."

"I'm going home," says Kayla, opening her umbrella. "After I fetch my baby girl from Sue Ellen Graffiti."

"I'll come with you," says Carson. As if flipping an inner switch, he's trying to look hopeful and boyish. Doesn't seem like Kayla is buying it.

"Me, I'll show Mary my lair," says Gee. "If she's willing. We'll do that Fweedle upgrade without you, Carson. Your plan sucks."

"Go to hell," says Carson. "Our deal's off."

"You bet it is," says Gee. "But you can keep the advance."

Mary is picking up emotional subtext from Gee via her psidot. Despite the way he's talking to Carson, Gee has a genial, trustworthy glow. He doesn't have manners—but he's kind.

"I'll go with Gee," says Mary. "And I do appreciate the new body, Carson. Please don't sell us out to the Top Party. And, Kayla, I'll see you before long. I'm always on your side."

"Thanks," says Kayla.

"Whatever," goes Carson, angry and cold.

Carson and Kayla splash off toward Sue Ellen's and Mrs. Yahootie's house, not looking at each other. Deep puddles all around, alive with nonstop raindrop pocks. Gusts sweep the air with veils of rain.

"Dig the patterns," says Gee. "Vortices and swirls. You see the air better when there's mist. That's one reason I've been living in the mountains. Have you ever noticed that there's hollow holes in the fog? Cavities made by—who knows what." That giggle again.

Mary isn't especially listening. She's watching the retreating Kayla. As if sensing Mary's gaze, her friend looks back, waves the tips of her fingers, and makes a gurney face—which Mary takes to mean, "Yes, it's over between my husband and me, but what the hell, life is fun anyway."

Kayla will find her way through. It's fine if Kayla and Daia need live in Mary's place for a while. And eventually Kayla will be famous. Her art sales will grow. She's got a touch. Her Kayla Kritters work the jittery gap between high and low. Hieronymus Bosch meets poker-playing dogs on black velvet.

"Ready to see my redwood?" says Gee, interrupting Mary's reverie.

"Okay," says Mary. "But is it far? I don't want to do some frantic, slasher-drama-type flight through the woods, sobbing and slipping off the path and falling down, with brambles whipping my face."

"Love it," says Gee. "For starters, we'll stop by San Lorenzo Country Store."

"I used to work there," says Mary. "Until a couple of weeks before I died." Odd to say that sentence.

"Know it," says Gee as they cross the street. "I want to pick up those ball walker pals of yours. Glory and the other one, the tall one."

"They're not strong enough to carry us," says Mary. "If that's what you're thinking."

"Nobody's gonna carry us," says Gee. "We'll ride to my place in a big thudhumper with a driver I know. But tomorrow we'll need the ball walkers for helpers."

Mary leads Gee behind the store and opens the barn's creaky door. Instantly alert, Miss Max stalks over, six feet tall and ready to kick ass. Her head is aglow.

"It's me," Mary tells her. "Mary from before."

"You molted?" says Miss Max, her voice doing that parp-parp thing.

"Sure," says Mary. "You're not remote controlled, are you?"

"I've still got my uvvy for incoming calls," parps Miss Max. "But, no, Mrs. Yahootie hasn't rented a lifebox gig-worker to drive me. She's thrifty. I'm glad. I'm doing fine."

"You're not," Glory says to Miss Max, picking his way over to them, avoiding the piles of ball walker poop. "You still don't understand about straw." His focus of attention shifts to Mary. The ball of his head gapes. A grin.

"Yes, it's me!" says Mary. "And my friend Gee."

"We need assistants," Gee tells the two ball walkers.

"Go away," says Miss Max, losing interest. She turns her back and scratches at the ground. Filthy globs of straw fly their way.

Gee continues his spiel. "I'm gonna trust you two shit-kickers. Give you an important job."

"Will you make us smarter?" asks Glory.

"I'm already smart," says Miss Max.

"You're not," Mary tells the tall ball walker. "And that's a fact."

"She's smart enough," says Gee. "What it is—we're gonna ride a thudhumper to my camp. And tomorrow we do an odd job. It'll be fun."

"Are you stealing us?" asks Miss Max.

"Renting," says Gee. "I'm an inventor. I'm rich. Here, Mary, I'm transferring a hundred thousand dollars to you. Go in the store and bedazzle Mrs. Yahootie. I'll be out front waiting for the thudhumper. Gonna call him right now." Again he releases one of his mirthless giggles.

"Do you have to laugh like that?" Mary asks.

"It's a tic," says Gee. "From growing up on the spectrum, amid ruthless schoolmate mockery. I like to think I've gotten better over the years. Somewhat better. Like, right now is a moment where I might want to giggle. But I'm not doing it. Because I want to make a good impression on you." He presses his lips together, bows, and tips his hat. "Milady."

"Better," says Mary.

She goes in the store and arranges the rental with Mrs. Yahootie, who does recognize her, but her main focus is that she's getting sixty grand as an immediate cash transfer. She throws in a large economy-size bag of GroChow.

Weathered old Sue Ellen Graffiti is in the store too, and she's a little more interested in what's happened to Mary. "Hot bod," she says. "I'm jealous. Do you need a massage?"

Mary is flattered. "Thanks for caring, Sue Ellen. Maybe another time."

"But right now you've got a rich man on the hook," cackles Sue Ellen.

Gee, Glory, Miss Max, and Mary stand on the Country Store's porch for about five minutes, watching the endless rain, with the ball walkers doing cheerful knee bends, their heads dimly lit. It's like they've never gone anywhere or done anything. And they're bringing a few little possessions along, like kids going to camp. For Glory it's a coiled old watch spring and a shiny rock. Miss Max has a scrap of bright red cloth and a turkey wishbone. Heartbreaking.

By now Mary is worn out from the effort of streaming her emotions and sensory inputs up to her lifebox in the cloud, and from absorbing her lifebox's opinions about what she should do next. Basically her clone body is a peripheral that she's running like a sim in a game. Not that she is constantly aware that this is what she's doing. But there's a definite sense of strain. Also she's cold. And it's eight pm. Almost dark. She wishes she were under a blanket on her couch. But here comes the thudhumper.

HALOS

Like everything else these days, the thudhumper is alive. He has eight strong legs, and he's hollow, with benches inside, and holes in his side. You can ride inside him and look out. Transparent membranes cover his holes. Sometimes the name of a thudhumper's destination is displayed on his front, up top. But—

"It says *Out of Service*," Mary informs Gee. "He's not gonna stop."

"Yeah he is," goes Gee. "He's in the service of Lord Outof, and that's *me*."

"So senile," says Mary.

She knows it's unfair to keep thinking of Gee as doddering and old. In point of fact, before her resurrection, Mary was every bit as ancient as Gee seems now. She should cut the man some slack and believe that he knows what he's doing. Especially if she's going off to his secret hideaway.

The thudhumper slows his feet and stands by the curb, wheezing. He has eyes in the place of headlights. He can talk. His name is Bernardo. He seems to know Gee quite well. Mary, Gee, and the ball walkers enter and sit.

"Up the coast a few miles," says Gee. "Right, Bernardo?"

"No problemo," says Bernardo's voice, which vibrates from the van's body. A simulacrum of a human face shows in relief on the panel below the windshield. A plump face with a goatee and intelligent eyes.

"Bernardo is my chauffeur," Gee tells Mary. "He's one of the lifeboxes living in my redwood server. He was my security guard—until the Top Party assassinated him last year. I've been hosting his lifebox ever since. And, by the way, I pay him a good salary. Not like Skyhive would do."

"Are you saving up to buy a clone?" Mary asks Bernardo.

"Not my style," says Bernardo. "I work for Gee when he needs it, or chill out in the cloud, or visit with my family in Guanajuato. My kids have a cheap-ass kritter to host me. It's called a gingerbread man? Looks a little like a person, but flat. I walk and talk. Tata Bernardo, the grandkids call me. I play with them, hang with my wife. It's nice. I'm glad Gee's network reaches Mexico."

"I'm ubiquitous," brags Gee.

Bernardo trots through the Santa Cruz mountains to the remains of the coast highway, making good speed. Faster than a horse. And then he heads north, galloping along the path of the old Route One—which is mostly sand and gravel by now. The asphalt has long-since washed out, what with the eroding cliffs and the insane rains. There's no more bridges either, so whenever they come to a creek, Bernardo wades or paddles across. Transportation is back to square one.

With the thick clouds, it's pitch dark, although to some extent the thudhumper's headlight eyes illuminate what's directly ahead, and of course the ball walkers shed some light inside the van. Gee, Mary, Glory and Miss Max are faintly reflected in the window membranes. No other traffic.

"What if someone forces us off the bluff?" says Mary.

"Won't happen," says Bernardo. "Gee and I are tough hombres. And I'm nimble."

"Is Skyhive tracking us?" Mary asks.

"You can trust our psidots' cloaking," says Gee. "That's code I wrote for the Finn Junkers myself. And I've turned off the ball walkers' uvvies for now. And Bernardo's thudhumper has my obfuscation code. Corrupts any sat-nav images of him. Shows a fake Bernardo on a wrong road."

"You're very hush-hush," says Mary, maybe mocking Gee a little. Or flirting.

"Most of my life I've lived in the crawl space under society's floor," says Gee. "Keeping that space open for people like me—it's been a big part of my career. I'm a cockroach, a rat, a dream you don't know you had. The alpha wolf of the underdogs."

"Ego much?" says Mary. "I wish I could see where we actually are."

"Give her night vision," Gee tells Miu Miu.

The dark landscape glows in unnatural shades. Thanks to her psidot Mary is seeing via infrared or cosmic rays or some shit like that. To the right are the foothills of the Santa Cruz mountains, in shades of cyan and violet. To the left, the raging sea, olive and pale green. The waves are twenty, thirty feet high. Spume geysers shoot up the sides of the ocean bluffs. Once in a while a massive chunk crumbles off the edge. The primeval sea is clawing back the risen layers of its ancient floor.

"Which way should we go today?" Bernardo asks.

"Turn right at the next creek and follow it upstream," says Gee. "If you look hard, Mary, you'll see a dark ravine where the stream goes in."

Meanwhile Glory and Miss Max are playing a game—they're taking turns swallowing each other's head. That is, Miss Max sucks in her cheeks so that her head gets slightly smaller, and Glory opens his mouth wide like a gaping clam shell and closes his mouth over Miss Max's head, entirely swallowing it, with Miss Max's neck like a thick straw between Glory's lips. And then Miss Max jerks back quite suddenly, and her head pulls free with a very loud *pop*. And then Miss Max swallows Glory's head and, *pop*, he pulls out *his* head. Etcetera, etcetera. Super annoying.

Mary addresses the ball walkers. "If you stop that, I'll give you GroChow." The merry kritters widen their mouths in unison, like fledglings in a nest. Mary gives them three handfuls of chow apiece.

"Settle in now," advises Bernardo. Mary's seat has a way of gripping her butt for stability. The van leaves the sketchy coast road and speeds along a creekside trail. Bernardo's eight legs come in handy; he never seems to slip. Rocking to and fro, the thudhumper bounds up the rocky, steepening trail. And then it's not a trail. They're bushwhacking through wild country, with alternating zones of vibrant forest and black-burnt stubs. With miles to go.

The exhausted Mary's focus fades. In effect, she's asleep. Endlessly the thudhumper twists and turns, rocking on his eight legs. Next thing she knows, Gee is shaking her.

"We're here."

Glory and Miss Max are outside the van, standing there like street lights. It's a small clearing amid a grove of immense redwoods. Gee ushers Mary out. Her new body needs more sleep, and she's having trouble controlling her feet. This spot is an anonymous perch amid ferns and granite boulders the size of houses. Gee tells Mary that, due to his various interventions, this glade is utterly unknown to the sat-nav and surveillance grids.

"As if it didn't exist," Gee says with satisfaction. "So near, yet so far."

It's peaceful to be alone here; it feels very safe. A nearby cataract roars. Rain descends through the trees in gouts and drips. Bernardo the thudhumper turns tail and scurries back down the dark slope to the coast, taking a different route from the one they came up on.

"We'll go in my cave now," says Gee.

And then, so far as Mary can tell, he disappears. It's like her mind/body connection flickers off for just the wrong two seconds. Gee was here, and now he's not. She groans, on the point of tears, half-wishing she could go back to being a zonked sim in her Skyhive condo.

"He went this way!" parps eager Glory, giving Mary a nudge.

"We saw!" adds Miss Max.

The ball walkers slide a slab of rock to one side—revealing a full-size door in a boulder forty feet tall.

"The oldest trick in the book," mutters Mary. "Open sesame. Good boy, Glory. Thanks, Miss Max."

This being a day of countless surprises, Gee's cave is rather like the inside of a Victorian house—with dusty plump furniture, paintings leaning against the walls, layers of oriental rugs, a Tiffany lamp, two full-size beds, a dining set with six chairs, a bathroom with a tub and shower, and a kitchen whose larder is stocked with milk, fresh bread, brie cheese, sparkling cider and a smoked ham—all this tended by a butler who resembles a banana slug, who's reared up to human height, and who glides around on the back part of its body.

The butler's name is Bunter, and his voice is thick with mucus. Rather than being golden yellow, his skin emulates the pattern of a 1920s butler's attire—black suit with tails, white shirt, and a gray-striped vest with a dark necktie tucked into it. Naturally he has a British accent.

"I bought Bunter from the Mixed Bag gallery downtown," Gee tells me. "Turns out he was designed by your neighbor Kayla. I'm gonna have her make up the specs for some soldier Bunters, too."

Postponing all conversation with or about Bunter or about any other giant slugs, Mary sheds her clothes, flops into one of the beds, and goes offline for the night, suspending her lifebox-Mary computation as well. Zonk city.

In the morning it's still raining. Eight am. Gee has the cave's sliding door open for the light and air. Totally prehistoric scene out there, with the ball walkers on the loose.

"You're back?" says Gee by way of greeting. "Want to eat?"

"Ham and eggs, madame?" burbles Bunter the butler slug.

"Maybe later," says Mary, not wanting the creature to touch her food. "I'll cook them myself. But first I want to see your famous redwood tree, Gee."

"It's right across the clearing. Here's an umbrella."

The mighty trunk is twenty-five feet across. As some redwoods do, it has a curvy triangular hole at the bottom—like a tall door, with the interior dank and charred, and a solid lip of wood around the door's edge, the lip grown from the flesh of the tree.

The branches drip steadily, sounding a faint tattoo on Mary's umbrella. Tilting back, she peers up to where the fat branches fade into the mist. The primeval giant has a solemn, calming vibe.

"It's full of people?" Mary asks. "Lifeboxes?"

"Not that many yet," says Gee. "A few hundred. Fellow conspirators. Bernardo, whom you met. Up-to-date lifeboxes for my Finn Junker pals, Liv and Anselm. Who else? Maurice Winch. He says he prefers being in teepspace, and that he doesn't ever want to come back out. Messes around with his memorial chatbot, and tracks the minds of dogs. Molly Santos used to be in here, but now there's nothing left of her but a pointer. Like a forwarding address. Coggy was after Molly, and Metatron shifted her storage into distributed mode."

"Hard to keep all that straight," says Mary. "Seeing as how I've never met those people."

"I like how unworldly you are," says Gee with a laugh.

"Don't patronize," warns Mary.

"Far from it," says Gee. "You're the anointed one. Our liberator."

"Right."

"You'll see."

Over breakfast, Gee tells Mary his plan. He shows her a round-bottomed glass flask with shifting scrolls of slime within. "This is my Fweedle code in the form of an infectious mold," he tells Mary. "We'll have those ball walkers deliver a good dose of this stuff to the Skyhive baguette server in the giant airship hangar at Moffett Field."

"I'd like to see that," says Mary.

"The baguette is really something," says Gee. "Rising and falling, with puffs and wrinkles. Like a grounded cloud. Skyhive's pay-as-you-go heaven. Programmed in Spork. And now we'll upgrade it to—"

"I get all that," interrupts Mary, impatiently forking up the last bite of the ham and eggs she made. Bunter extrudes paddle-like hands and refills her coffee cup. "But how do the ball walkers get into the hangar?" Mary asks Gee. "And how do they get out?"

"They'll be kamikazes. Charge in like terrorists, dope the loaf, and take the consequences. It's not like they really *have* to get out."

Mary glances out the cave door at the cheerful round-headed ball walkers jumping in the rain puddles. "How can you say that, Gee? Glory and Miss Max can't die. They're my friends."

"Oh," says the old hacker, laboriously remembering to factor in the concept of empathy. "Got it. Reset. What would you do?"

"Have the ball walkers be delivering snacks to the techs," says Mary. "You can spoof a huge order for, um, exotic dough-nuts. Glory and Miss Max deliver the goodies, slyly infect the baguette, and sashay out."

"Gadzooks!" exclaims Gee, holding up his lean forefin-ger like a British clubman contemplating a spree.

"It gets better," says Mary. "Ball walkers are no good at remembering instructions. For this to work, we'll need to be driving them like remotes."

"A virtual romp for us," says Gee. "A spot of mindless fun. A spell of riot."

"How should we do the control?" says Mary. "They have built-in uvvies, but—"

"Finn Junker psidots are the only way to go," says Gee. "Much higher resolution. Uvvies are feeble. And with psidots you have the gossip molecule assemblers for hormones."

"But—ball walker hormones in your head?" goes Mary. "Sounds like a back alley tweaker drug."

"Ball walker brains are more like ours than we care to admit," says Gee. "It's just that those brains are quite small. And their emotive hormones resemble ours as well."

"I'm leaving my body out of this," says Mary. "I'll take Miu Miu off my neck, and put her onto Glory, who's my favorite. And then my lifebox will be running Glory. And

172

my clone body stays here nice and safe, sleeping in bed, out of the loop."

"Fine," says Gee. "I'll stay here in bed, too. I'll put a spare psidot on Miss Max, and I'll run her through the regular psidot I wear. I won't drag in my lifebox at all. The opposite of you."

"It must be nice to have a body with a working brain," says Mary.

"Maybe you'll get there. I don't know. This is all so new."

"So far, so good," says Mary. "Can you promise you won't try anything skeevy on my clone?"

"I'm not Carson Pflug," says Gee, shaking his head. "That was entertaining, how angry he got yesterday."

"It's not like you weren't goading him. What exactly does Carson do for Skyhive? I can never figure that out."

"Skulduggery," says Gee. "He's a fixer. A go-between. I've known him awhile. And when I got interested in you last month, I noticed he lives next to you. So I teeped him and paid him to set you up with a psidot, a lifebox, and a clone. I was going to pay him more, if he helped you break out of the Skyhive silo. But then he wanted to rape you and to do brain experiments on you! Goodbye."

"I bet he'll squeal on us," says Mary. "He'll tell the Skyhive boss about our jailbreak plan."

"Yep," says Gee with a shrug. "Likely he will. The boy is bucking for a promotion. He'll run straight to that Leeta Patel."

"Wait!" cries Mary, finally making the connection. "When I was in my lifebox in the Skyhive cliff city, I met Leeta. She was making her lifebox clients do gigwork."

"She likes to micromanage," says Gee. "I know Leeta's characteristics well—from working with her on the Ross Treadle assassination. After the hit, I showed her how to use the Finn Junker psidots with my lifebox tech to found Skyhive. And she hired Carson because—who knows. She does have that stupid crush on him. And maybe she thought his Top Party connections could end up being useful. Skyhive was poisoned from the start."

"You don't like them."

"It's a bad business model. Forced gigs for the users? Are you kidding? It's slavery. My business model is that everyone should get a juicy ghost for free. Everyone should be immortal, and not in the form of a dry-as-dust database. I want our lifeboxes to get off the servers, and go full indie. Free. We're taking a step toward that today."

"Is Leeta going to fight us?" asks Mary.

"It's complicated," says Gee. "These autonomous lifeboxes I'm talking about, they'll be here a lot sooner than people think. The rent-a-space heaven model is doomed. Leeta's smart. And she gets this. She'll want to team with me again. Ride the new wave."

"How about the Top Party? They're your enemy, right?"

"Yes and no. Fact is, their backers at the Citadel Club paid me to assassinate Treadle. Not that they'll ever tell that to the mourning Treadlers. Instead they blame the assassination on me. Like I arranged it on my own. Gee Willikers, designated scapegoat. I have to stay low profile so the *patriots* don't lynch me."

"Is Maurice dead or not?" says Mary.

"He's a lifebox. Says he's in teepspace for good. Doesn't want to come back and have a body at all." Gee chuckles. "What a guy. He stings Treadle to death, sabotages the man's lifebox, and explodes his clone. The fact that I host Maurice in my redwood is another reason the Top Party and the Citadel Club want to terminate me. Oh, and lately they're mad at Carson Pflug too."

"I really don't see why they can't find your cave, Gee. You're doing magical thinking. Like a kid who thinks he's invisible when he covers his eyes."

Gee looks around his cavernous quarters. "Well, if you want to be all negative, how about this for a news update: The Top Party is coming for me tomorrow."

"You just said they can't find you."

"They'll come for me, but they'll go to the wrong place," says the blindly self-confident Gee. "I've done a lot of hacking and tweaking to conceal my happy home. Sat-nav images obfuscated in real time. Surveillance drone feeds—corrupted."

"What if someone flies over in a flappy and stares down with their naked eyes?" says Mary.

"I've got a giant flying blob named Utila. Flattish. Basically a flying amoeba, but with a bunch of Finn Junker psidots in her flesh. Like a loaf of raisin bread that way. Thirty meters across, with her flesh a little over a meter thick, and with a thirty-meter-high froth of membranous bubbles on top."

"Froth?"

"Full of hydrogen. So she can hover. She produces the hydrogen herself. Photocatalytic water-splitting. Like tweaked photosynthesis. Sequesters the hydrogen in tough, individual bubbles so she's unlikely to explode. And with all the psidots, she's got great teep. Very hard to see her, up above the trees. She creates an mirage effect that makes my glade optically void. And her psidot teep powers can twist what people see."

"I like the flying amoeba with a stack of hydrogen foam," says Mary. "But that last bit, about you being invisible, it's a fantasy, Gee. The Top Party—they're big. They're lulling you. And when they're ready—*yeek*—they're at your door with flame throwers and vats of acid! What then?"

"I have a multi-level defense system," says the maddeningly imperturbable Gee. "Most of the animals around my cave—they're linked into me via teep. I've put a psidot on every local animal I can get my hands on. Like those crows in the tree. They're guardians."

"You're teeping the crows? In your head you hear them cawing all the time?"

"I don't always listen," says Gee. "But let's set our worries aside. Let's focus on you, Mary. You're going to be a star. World's first autonomous ghost. We're going to make it happen today. Starting with our run to Hangar One."

"Okay, yes," says Mary, letting this strange man a little further into her heart. "It sounds like fun."

"Let's get the ball walkers ready," says Gee.

The ball walkers are outside, playfully bopping around. Mary herds them inside, and Gee pastes capsules of Fweedle slime onto the roofs of their mouths. Mary lies down in bed, and Gee transfers her psidot onto Glory, linking Glory to Mary's lifebox. And then Gee puts a spare psidot on Miss Max and lies down on a couch, still wearing his own psidot. He'll drive Miss Max via direct link.

By nine am they're off.

Mary loves romping through the drenched woods in Glory's body. The ball walker's ostrich legs are swift and strong. His claws squelch solidly against the sodden forest floor. The undulating balance of Glory's armless body is pure elegance—like a sacred dance. Mary feels uniquely in tune with the forest. She savors the scents, and the way that the air currents are highlighted by the mist.

Gee—in the form of Miss Max—is in a playful, antic mood, continually teeping with Mary, and deliberately bumping into her as they run. They're like young people at play.

Having crossed the crest of the Santa Cruz range, they head downhill past the rain-shrouded estates of the nanopercenters, slowing their pace to an unobtrusive trot. Like delivery kritters at work. Next comes the town of Sunnyvale, near the bay, with big eight-legged thudhumpers bustling by, pedestrians on slug skates, and centipede busses pattering down the median lanes.

Gee leads them to a vintage Psycho Donuts outlet, where they pick up a hefty order Gee has placed, under Carson Pflug's name. Glory does the talking in his parp-parp voice. The friendly counterman gives each of the ball walkers a Psycho Donuts hat, and tapes the hats in place. And then it's off to Hangar One, each ball walker's hollow, hamper-like head carrying a gross of odd, toothsome crullers.

Given the size of the building, Mary had expected the supercomputing baguette to be hundreds of meters long. But it's a modest fifty-footer—resting on a low platform, dwarfed by the cathedral vastness of the blimp hangar.

"Renting such a colossal building is a Skyhive image thing," Gee teeps to Mary, his virtual voice warped by heavy encryption. "But, hey, fifty feet of dough is plenty. Notice that it's quite a thick loaf. Call it a sextillion tweaked yeast cells in all, with each cell running an internal biocomputation, all of them asynchronously linked. Let's go spit our damn Fweedle mold onto it."

"Take it easy," says Mary. "No need to get Glory and Miss Max in trouble. Let them feed the techs, do a little show, and then—"

"A leap and a sneeze," agrees Gee.

The loaf isn't all that far from the entrance. About forty engineers and helpers are gathered around the baguette—like worker ants around a queen. But they look up when Glory and Miss Max jounce in on their loose-limbed legs, calling out, "Psycho Donut coffee break!" And they're wearing their taped-on logo hats.

By now it's about ten am, and Skyhive food-servers have set out a trestle table with urns of coffee and kombucha for morning break. Moving with ease, Glory and Miss Max walk along the table, plopping out Psycho Donuts with their mobile lips.

The generative algorithms of the Psycho Donuts baker bots have cranked out an engaging array of colors and flavors this morning: The pineapple/jalapeño Split Personality, the licorice Square Wheel, the tutti-frutti Gem Case, the coconut banana Love Dream, the chocolate mousse Black Beauty, the sour glazed Acid Flash, the purple Stank Drank, the raspberry Broken Heart, the magenta-lime Eye Strain, the half-pound Catcher's Mitt, on and on, no two ever the same.

"Nice payload," a young engineer says to Glory. She's short, with spiky black hair. "You can talk? I'm Ayesha."

"*Parp-parp*," says Mary, flapping Glory's lips. "Here we go. Do you like working here?"

"Leading question," says Ayesha. "We're closely watched. Rote response? It's thrilling to bring immortality to humankind."

"To the rich ones anyway," puts in Gee, talking through Miss Max.

Ayesha backs off and turns her attention to the spread. "I'm gonna eat the Catcher's Mitt!"

While the techs are pigging out, Mary and Gee put on a show, starting with a tap dance with unlikely acrobatic flips thrown in. They segue to a hoarse duet of that classic lefty anthem, The Times They Are a-Changin', and end up with one of their bravura percussion performances—bonking their large, hollow heads together, modulating the sounds by changing the shapes of their open mouths.

Scattered cheers and claps. As an encore, Glory and Miss Max leap a hundred feet into the air, twisting and spinning. Along the way they spray invisibly fine mists of Fweedle from their mouths. Unseen droplets drift to the big baguette.

"Score," Gee teeps to Mary.

Still hosting Mary and Gee, the ball walkers depart, acting casual, cadging tips, moving slowly. Once they're off the Skyhive campus, they run, faster and faster, up the hill, past the estates, and into the woods.

They stop to catch their breath atop a ridge of rock at the summit. Yesterday's storm is done; the clouds are breaking up. It's close to noon. Shafts of sun, rifts of blue. Silicon Valley looks like a promised land, and the shining Pacific is paradise.

"Are Leeta's people tracking us?" Mary asks Gee.

"Well—they think they are," says Gee, getting back into his mysterioso routine. "But the closer we get to my lair, the further out-of-kilter their tracking info is going to be. It's that global positioning hack I told you about?"

"You're saying that, but do you really think you can trick every spy in the world all the time?" says Mary. "Delusions of grandeur."

"It doesn't pay to just be a *little* crazy," says Gee, kind of laughing. "Be a *lot* crazy."

"I'm worried you're going to get me killed," says Mary.

"Speaking of killers, did you notice that Leeta Patel and your pal Carson Pflug were in the airship hangar in Sunnyvale?" Gee asks Mary.

"No way."

"Sitting in overstuffed walker chairs at the other end of the great hall."

"Why didn't you tell me?"

"Didn't want you to lose your nerve."

"Why didn't they try to stop us?"

"This is where we shade into the bigger picture I'm talking about. Leeta's surfing the wave of change. Once our Fweedle infection became noticeable—about fifteen minutes ago—Leeta decided she *wants* the Fweedle. She teeped me, and she told Carson, which was probably a mistake, because he'll tell the Top Party."

"Leeta now wants to free the Skyhive lifeboxes?" asks Mary, several steps behind.

"Yes," says Gee. "For appearance's sake, she'll take countermeasures—to keep the board of directors happy. But Leeta always wants in on what's next. And this is going to be huge."

"What about me?" asks Mary, disoriented. "Do I get out from under Skyhive or not?"

"You do, yes," says Gee. "*You're* the one I especially want to free. Let's take the next step. Do the honors, Miss Max."

Miss Max crouches low, tips back her face, and presses her thin lips against the underside of Glory's head.

"She'll pull your Miu Miu loose," Gee tells Mary. "And Glory will be on his own. And you won't be juicy, except for the tiny glimmer of life you get off the Skyhive server, which is itself a low form of life. But mostly you'll just be lifebox Mary on the Skyhive cliff—with no remote. A data ghost without any heavy emotional shimmer, and with no real-world sensory input at all."

"A boring toad," says Mary.

"Right. But soon after you get there, you'll escape to my redwood. I'll hook you back into Miu Miu, and she'll be waiting on your clone, and you'll be juicy again."

Mary begins a sentence. "But how do—"

She doesn't have time to finish. For Miss Max has nipped Mary's Miu Miu off the back of Glory's head.

At first the Skyhive cliff city seems the same. Lifebox Mary is in her bland, blank flat with its wooden chair and its balcony. That same sense of being tranked-out in an empty mall. She gets to her feet and looks outside. Fresh action in the sky. Not just storks. Some pterodactyls as well. Skyhive's virtual security force.

No sign of Leeta in the plaza—but there's a group of lifebox people bent on emigration. Maybe sixty of them. Early adopters. Shouting about freedom. Some are making runs at the surrounding buildings; others hang back and watch. The Fweedle hack is taking hold.

The medieval walls around the piazza flicker with fitful rectangles. The scene reminds Mary of her childhood Advent calendar that showed the buildings of a snowy town. Each day in December, Mary and her mother would tear off a flap that covered a door or a window, revealing a new icon—a ball, a tree, a present with a bow, a bike, a sled, a star, a manger.

What was it Gee said about Fweedle? That it would give them escape exits like little dog doors. She leaps off her balcony. This time—*oops*—she falls as hard as an Acme safe off the Empire State Building. She hits the pavement with such a *thud* that her body digs a deep hole in ground. The impact squashes her to being one inch tall—like a collapsed accordion.

Flattened-out though Mary's affect is, she almost finds this amusing. She *wheeze-wheenks* out of the hole, gives herself a shake, and—*ta da!*—she's her own right size again. Hardy mountain woman in toon land.

The festive mood in the square is draining away. Those dog doors aren't working so well. Yes, some of the new Skyhive doors open onto inviting green glows. But some of the doorways are dark and blank. Doors to nowhere. The lifebox people are trying to avoid those.

Meanwhile a squad of Skyhive storks and pterodactyls have joined the crowd, knocking people down, skewering them with their beaks, and tossing them through the dark portals. Wailing and gnashing of teeth.

Mary approaches a short guy in a clanking suit of armor. He stands by a granite buttress at the base of Mary's building—which has one of those black doors.

"What gives?" Mary asks. "Is this an exit?"

"You bet," says the man. He has his visor closed. "Find the world you deserve." His voice is muffled, but it's somehow familiar.

Mary approaches the door, if that's what it really is. There's no image within the frame's rectangular patch. No texture, no color, no mesh. Raw teepspace.

"I'd like to see you go through that door before me," Mary tells the guy in armor. "And then I'd want to see you come back. To show me that it's safe. I already died, the day before yesterday. I didn't come here to get erased. I'm supposed to go to the Gee Willikers redwood."

"Where exactly *is* that redwood?" asks the man in armor, very intent. "I'd like to be able to tell people."

Doh! It's Carson again. That is, it's a lifebox version of him, helping to weed out those restive lifeboxes who deny the Skyhive way.

Far from helping with Gee's mass liberation—like he was originally going to do—Carson has turned full-on vindictive prick. Having lost his deal with Gee, Carson is all too happy to add force to Leeta's gestures of resistance. He's gotten the Skyhive techs to pervert the Fweedle tweak in such a way that most of the new escape doors lead to—a suicide bin, where malcontent lifeboxes are erased.

Instinctively Mary kicks Carson in the shin—or rather in the shin-guard. She follows with a rough shove like she used on him before. Carson clanks onto his back, waving his limbs like a distraught beetle. Mary wishes she had matches and gasoline to light the guy on fire.

Too late. Carson's already back on his feet, cruelly intent on herding lifebox Mary through the suicide-bin door. Isn't he Mary's friend the least little bit? Didn't she promise her house to his wife Kayla?

"Over here," cries Gee's voice. He's in a portal that isn't mounted on a wall—it's a blank square floating a few feet off the ground. This portal is one of the good ones. It glows a pale green—and Mary sees Gee's face inside it. "Hop in!" he calls.

Mary takes a running jump toward Gee's square hole—stretches out her arms and straightens her body as if for a racing dive. Lanky Gee scoots to one side so she can freely arrow through. Then Gee brings himself back into view so he can yell at Carson and, yes, give him the finger.

"We're *gone.*"

The square, green portal shrinks and disappears, with Mary and Gee inside.

And in this instant, the full code of Mary's lifebox is ported from the giant baguette in the Skyhive blimp hanger to—the verdant computational tissues at the core of Gee's giant redwood server tree. Mary barely feels it happening. It's one of those jump-cut things.

She and Gee float companionably in pleasant green light. Faint gurgles. A sense of turgid plant cells, of phloem, of ribosomes and mitochondria, of root hairs and fragrant bark. Faint writhing tendrils all around. A jungle of light.

"Welcome to my redwood server," goes Gee.

"Did any of the others make it?" Mary asks.

"About seventy of them," says Gee.

"What about the ones who got pushed into the suicide bin?"

"Oh, I ported those poor slobs, too. I've got taps all over Leeta's system. Even inside her suicide bin."

"Can you save Kayla? My friend from next door. We were talking to her at the Pot O' Gold just now. I want Kayla to escape too."

Gee pauses, quietly doing something with his mind. "Got her," he says after a minute. "Ported her right over. She might not even notice at first. But eventually she'll be glad. I already host a lot of San Francisco artists. I'm friends with that Jeannie Jone who runs the Mixed Bag gallery."

"Perfect for Kayla. There's lots of room in your redwood tree?"

"It has ten times the capacity of Skyhive's dumb-ass baguette. But I'm telling you, Mary, those other people aren't all that important to me. My prime goal was to get *you*."

"Why? I'm nobody. An old woman who worked at a country store. No husband, no kids, no followers—"

"Don't forget I saw your show."

"Please tell me you're not talking about that ridiculous thing with Carson on my couch."

"God, no. I'm talking about you singing and playing mandolin, with Kayla on the fiddle as a matter of fact, and those two guys on bass and banjo. You remember. At the Pot O' Gold last August. I imprinted on you."

It's almost like Gee's making a declaration of love. But Mary can't get excited about it. Thing is, she's no longer connected to her clone body's feed. She's not juicy. She's like a sim in a soap opera. Her mood is flat and peevish.

"You're pretty old to be running a cornball stalker routine," she tells Gee.

"It's not like that," protests Gee, looking hurt.

"And you plan to coop me up in here with no body?" challenges Mary. "This is nowhere. I want to be out in the world."

"Oh, right!" exclaims Gee. "Sorry. I'll plug you into your body right now. Then you'll feel better. Hang on."

He makes a motion as if he's quite literally attaching one of the glowing tendrils to the back of Mary's neck and then— *ah*—thanks to good old Miu Miu, the clone's feed is running through Mary's mind once more—the comfortable sheets; the clone's skin and muscles; the sound of the breeze and the cawing of crows outside the cave; the scent of the forest; the lingering aroma of breakfast; and the simple, abstract flickers of the clone's primitive emotions and dreams.

Mary is on the point of hopping all the way into the clone, but Gee is waving his hand in her lifebox sim's face, imploring her to tarry in the green virtual space of his server.

"Just a little longer," he says. "I want to finish our conversation."

"What were we talking about?" May asks Gee. At this point she has a double point of view—with the bland workings of her lifebox mind overlaid upon the underground stream of the clone's inchoate consciousness.

"I was saying I admire you," says Gee. "And that I think you can usher in a new world. You'll free people's souls."

"How do you mean that?"

"You'll be the first person with an autonomous lifebox."

"I still have no idea what that's supposed to be."

"Your lifebox server doesn't have to be some big corporate thing. Skyhive's server is dough, and mine is a tree. But why not have your lifebox generate a little server of its own. Bootstrap effect. A pulsing cloud of ionized particles whose emergent mind generates the pulsing cloud. No Skyhive to charge you rent or make you do gigwork."

"And no more Carson and Gee wanting to do experiments on me," says Mary.

"Touché," goes Gee. "Forgive me. I guess this does sound like an experiment. But look at the upside. Your lifebox will be an independent process. A dynamical system."

"Techie gibberish alert."

"It'll be like a hovering disk made of ionized particles. A coherent puff of air, long-lived and self-sustaining—thanks to you. You'll draw energy from your surroundings. Don't be teeping me all that doubt and fear, Mary! You can do this. And the world will follow in your wake. You'll be a star."

Cleary it's insane bullshit, but Mary does have a weakness for that word "star." Truth be told, she's always felt she *is* a star, and that this fact deserves wide recognition. Even if she isn't always doing much of anything.

"An aethereal disk?" she muses. "My life in a nutshell. You promise I'll still be able to run my awesome clone body?" A rebel impulse rises up. "Tell me again, Gee—why don't you do this to yourself? Instead of doing it to me? Am I your lab rat? Disposable? Just a woman?"

Gee winces. "I'm scared to try it, okay? I don't think I could carry it off. I want you to lead because you're strong, and you *project*. You're not just some random person. Thanks to teep, I see things about people that I didn't used to see. You're the one to make the full breakthrough, Mary. I knew it when I saw you sing."

"So my autonomous lifebox is going to be a pulsing puff of air. And I'll find a way to connect it with my clone body? Me, Mary Mary, with my two years of community college, and my lifetime of working in a country store; I'll do this on my own."

Gee beams. "You'll know how, even though you think you don't. Your autonomous lifebox is gonna drift out of my redwood tree. A magic platter. Farewell to rapacious lifebox server tycoons! All hail Mary the liberator!"

"Sure," says Mary, kind of laughing at Gee's persistence. "Port my soul into a slab of tingle that runs my clone? Hell, I do that every morning when I get up, right?" At some level she's enjoying this. She likes being wooed. "I'll give it a try. But tell me the part again about people praising Mary the liberator."

"It'll happen," says Gee, teeping her a friendly feeling that's like a warm nudge. "Mighty Mary, yes." He puts on one of his corny accents. "You ready to bust out of this hyar calaboose, podner?"

"Show me the way," goes Mary.

She feels confident and relaxed, like before a music gig. And she does understand, in a very loose and sketchy way, what Gee wants her to do. In her old Cruz-mountains hippie days she liked to imagine leaving her flesh and floating around as a spirit double. This new kind of lifebox will be like an astral body—but that sounds too woo-woo. Call it a *halo*. Yeah. She might as well be the one to pick the name for—for whatever the hell she's turning into.

"Halo is great," says Gee, who's channeling her thoughts. "A lifebox that floats around on its own. A mind outside your body."

"So how do I get there?"

Gee does his annoying giggle. "All I can say is that I know it's possible. I have an abstract existence proof of the existence of the necessary quantum computation. But I don't know the details of how you create it, nor do I know how you port your lifebox over to it. The details have to come from you."

"No dials and wires?"

"It's a head trick. A simple matter of you singing your song. What I've felt all along. Remember? That's what drew me to you in the first place. Seeing you front your band Squash Plant at the Pot O' Gold last August."

"I really doubt that I can—"

But now Gee is offline.

Mary senses a bright spot in the ambient green light. It's that warped triangular door at the base of the redwood tree. She's seeing it from inside. That's her exit. The thick, rounded lip around the door glows a pale shade of magenta. Organic energy.

Mary recalls a remark by her high-school math teacher, from sixty years ago. The teacher was a wonderful lady, calm and smart, and she liked to quote the saying of a certain French mathematician: *Allez en avant—la foi vous viendra.* Press forward—faith will come.

Lacking any other plan, Mary raises her voice in song, although what she's singing, she couldn't say. She emulates the lyrical chanting of a reggae deejay, an aria from a Mozart opera, a grrl-punk rant, a soaring gospel descant, and a country-honk yowl. Singing her soul. Projecting herself.

Within her mind she's using subconscious processes to comb out her tangled memory links, and she's arranging her notion of "Mary" into a virtual shape that resembles, yes, a halo. A surreal, iridescent disk from heavenly teepspace. Not a ring, not like the modern cartoon halos, but an old-school religious-art-type halo like a gold plate.

As Mary moves through the tree's triangular portal, she feels her halo taking physical shape. She's undergoing an alchemical transformation into a woven pattern of ionized air. Yes. A disk-shaped network of charged particles, woven together by quantum links—a tingly network of drifty air currents, and real enough to matter.

Viola, it's done. That's the word she used to think it said when she'd see "voilá" written out, and she'd wonder to herself, "Why is that French guy yelling about a viola?"

And she can see and hear, thanks to all that quantum jive she doesn't need to think about. It's built into this new, entangled essence of herself, and she has an immersive worldview, like an incredibly detailed teepspace overlay upon the real. And her teep is working fine. Viola indeed. All right, then. Now, how about hooking up with her clone?

Mary-the-halo drifts across the dappled glade toward the cave, pulsing her halo. A divine disk. When sunshine hits her, it feels delicious. Light is her food. Glory and Miss Max are in the clearing, not doing much of anything. Bonking their heads together, rebounding, doing flips. They notice Mary's halo. They cock their heads and stare.

"To them, you look like a cool spot in the air," says Gee in Mary's head. "You absorb heat and light. Really well crafted, Mary."

Some gnats are buzzing around Mary's halo, which draws extra attention to it. Miss Max lunges for the gnats—or for the halo itself—Miss Max with her huge mouth wide open. Mary's halo readily evades the ball walker by rising higher into the air.

"I want my damn body," Mary teeps to Gee. Without waiting for his answer, she makes a reflexive effort to link up to Miu Miu as before—but nothing happens.

"Oh, sorry." teeps Gee. "We have to register your halo with your lifebox. For security."

"Why do I even need a psidot?" demands Mary. "If this halo is so fancy, why can't it connect to my body direct?"

"The Finn Junker lifebox-psidot-body architecture is here to stay," says Gee. "The psidot provides a host body with ultraweak wireless. Crystal-clear, long-distance data transfer. The psidot is an essential interface between organic bodies and teepspace. You use your psidot to teep with people, to share chemical mood-templates, to upload your memories into your lifebox, and to let your lifebox instruct your body. But—"

"What if I zap you with a trillion volt shock?" interrupts Mary, annoyed by Gee's endless jabber.

"Big talk for a quantum-entangled puff of air," says Gee. "I doubt you could manage more than the jolt from an electric fence. Here we are. You're registered with Miu Miu now. And she's on your clone's neck."

Mary skims her halo into the cave. There's Gee, lounging in a chair. And there's Mary's pretty clone is still in bed. Mary connects and—*aah*. She's fully alive again, with her mind connected to a meat body. The way it's supposed to be. But—maybe it's not quite as good as before?

"I'm back," she softly says. And sits up on the edge of the bed. Runs her hands over her face. Something's still missing.

Gee's smile is warm. "What time is it anyway?" Mary asks. "All those crazy changes—"

"It's a little before one in the afternoon," says Gee. "I made some teep calls while you were gone. Taking care of business. Will you live with me? For good?"

"Are you joking?"

"Am I?"

Mary feels pressured, and a little trapped. It's annoying. Being back in her body doesn't feel as mellow as she thought it would, and this bugs her. Also she was expecting bigger cheers from Gee. I mean, she's mastered an entirely new way of living outside your body. And Gee wants to pester her about—is it sexual intimacy? Is that all men ever think about?

"Not right this minute, Gee, no. I've had enough insane, monstrous roller-coaster rides for one day."

"I hear you," says Gee. "But I was hoping to close our deal before the shit hits the fan."

"Charmingly phrased proposal," says Mary.

"My point is that we're going to pay a price for raiding the blimp works," says Gee. "I just now got the word on that."

"Leeta's coming after us?" Mary asks.

"Leeta's not the problem. She's on our side. But the money guys in the Top Party see this as a fresh excuse to come after me. I talked to this double agent just now, Jerr Boom, and he says the Top Party is coming here tomorrow morning."

"You claimed your lair is invisible!" protests Mary.

Gee smiles sadly and shrugs. "You were right to doubt me, Mary. I was wrong, thinking they can't find me. A brash, geeky ego trip. They've just been waiting."

"They want to kill you?"

"Not exactly. What they want is kind of worse. I don't want to talk about it right now. I'm hoping I can stand them off. I'll have a lot of help from the local animals and from my kritters. But meanwhile, this thing about you and me…"

Mary gives him a stony stare. His voice trails off. She feels for her halo, which is floating above the top of her head. A cool, tingly zone. Interesting that you don't actually *touch* a halo. Her fingers move through it, like it's made of air. The disturbance doesn't feel good. It makes Mary feel seasick.

What if those Top Party fanatics make a really serious effort to scramble Mary's halo? Hit it with a blender, take a shock baton to it—and cut Mary's throat while they're at it?

"None of that is gonna happen," says Gee in Mary's head. He's eavesdropping her stream of thought. "We're stronger than you realize. And the Top Party troops, most of them won't be actual people. They'll be remotely-run remotes. Not so hard to disrupt. But let's talk about happy things. Did I tell you how much I loved that transformation song of yours? It made all the difference."

"If my halo gets blanked out, can I go back to my life-box in your redwood tree?" asks Mary.

"Well, um, your lifebox isn't *in* the server anymore. It got subsumed into your halo."

"*Subsumed*? What the fuck does *that* mean? You didn't make a backup copy?"

"Well, I could have. But I was in a hurry to get you into an autonomous halo."

"You were in a hurry to *close your deal* is more like it," says Mary.

"Oh god, can you lighten up?" goes Gee. "We can make your backup, but it takes a couple of minutes via teep. Would be easier if you went and actually touched the tree. And I don't feel like bothering right now, but if you're gonna frown at me like that, let's just do it, okay?"

No, Mary would rather be contrary. "I don't want to zone out for a transfer, or go stand by your stupid tree. You should have backed me up in the first place. I'd also like to mention that I don't like having to carry around my lifebox halo with me all the time, and have it always floating right over the top of my head. It'll look weird—if people can see it—and when the Top Party thugs come for me, they can immediately kill my halo at the same time as me. They'll slam me on the top of my head with a machete. This isn't working for me, Gee."

Is Mary being too cranky? Well, that's how she feels.

"Good news," Gee gently says, maintaining his cool. "You can fly your halo all over the place, and your mind-body connection will still work. So go for it. Flip your wig."

Still grumbling, and deeply uneasy, Mary slowly and gingerly pulses her halo to the ceiling of the cave. She still has a solid sense of being in her clone body.

"Can you make your halo easier to see?" asks Gee. "Might as well show it off."

At some subconscious level, this is something Mary can do. With a twitch of her willpower, the disk of her halo takes on a smooth, golden glow. Beautiful. Gently swirling. Like a tiny galaxy. She moves it down from the ceiling, tilts it, and positions it behind her head.

"Holy Mary," she says, finally beginning to have fun.

"Gorgeous," says Gee. "Maybe that's what halos always were. Souls made manifest."

He gazes at Mary in adoration. She finds this a little hard to take. "What's your problem?" she snaps, turning sour again.

"A few minutes ago I asked you to partner up with me," says Gee. "And we got off track. Can we resume that conversation thread?"

"If this is still about us having sex, then yes, yes, we can do it. I really don't care. But you have to get yourself a nicer body, Gee. Right now you're too wrinkly. Get a wetware upgrade. Be like me. Immaculate Mary."

"It's a thought," says the rather skungy biohacker. Seems like his feelings are bruised. "But I'm used to my body. It's like a comfortable old pair of shoes. Well broken in."

"I'm not going to bed with an old pair of shoes," says Mary. "That's not why I descended to hell and rose from the dead. Catch the clone wave, Gee."

He's silent for a while, with his teep somewhat cloaked. "Okay, Mary," he finally says. "I'll cobble up a new Gee."

"And the old Gee?" demands Mary. "I hope he's not going to mooch around and be all jealous. And for sure I'm not up for a three-way. We should butcher the old Gee, and burn the remains in a bonfire. You're shaking your head? Okay, the hell with it. Let's just stay friends and don't ruin it with sex."

"*Friends?*" Gee echoes incredulously. "*Ruin it with sex?*" He touches Mary's face, running his fingers along the skin of her cheek. "I love you, Mary. Don't you get that? I'll do a full rejuve, sure. And by the way, this *old Gee* who you want to murder and incinerate—*old Gee* is the guy sitting here talking to you. I mean—are you kidding? Have a heart."

"Oh," says Mary, suddenly embarrassed and maybe even a little ashamed. "Sorry I'm so uptight. I guess this feels like a step down. First I'm an astral body adept—and then I'm haggling about when you get laid."

Gee gives her a penetrating look. "Can you grasp that you're behaving like a soulless AI?" He pauses, thinking. "I bet this is because your halo isn't emulating the *emotions* that live in your clone. Your body has normal human feelings, and its gossip molecules are sending the mood templates to your lifebox. But you're not processing the templates. My fault. I forgot to put emotion-emulation code into your halo."

"Clear as mud," goes Mary.

"Hold still. I'll fix you."

Gee stares at Mary, mentally reaching through her eyes to the halo disk above her head. He's using the full force of his considerable teep. To Mary it feels like a mechanic is poking around in her mind. A *quantum* mechanic.

And then—*oops*—she fucking dies for a second. That is, the whole scene blinks off. A surprise jump cut. Don't worry, folks! She boots back up—feeling way mellower than before. More humane. More truly juicy.

"What is love?" Mary warbles. "Five feet of heaven in a ponytail!" She's quoting from a song in the seemingly endless archives that her ionic quantum-wireless-equipped halo can access in the cloud.

"This is good," says Gee. "The old Mary."

"I'm not old," says Mary. "I'm me."

"I like your flair," Gee says. "Your unstable aplomb. And, ah yes—your vocal stylings. We've got it now, Mary. Emo circuits in play! When my time comes, I'll emulate your soul-song port. You're the great Teacher."

"Laying it on thiiiick," says Mary. "Desperate much? Thank you, Gee. Singing is what I do. The language of the heart."

"There's got to be a way to cook down the port routine," says Gee, flipping so very easily into being geeky. "A port that even a total goob can do. Someone like a Skyhive customer. If we make the port easy, Leeta will market the hell out it. Halos all around."

"I'm confused about Leeta," says Mary with a sigh. "Half the time she's your enemy, and half the time she's not."

"We're forever gaming back and forth," says Gee. "It never settles down. I let Leeta watch you do your port just now, which is I how I know she loves it."

"Well, that's fine," says Mary. "But Leeta's pal Carson tried to kill me today. Up in the Skyhive."

Gee shows a thin smile. "I discussed that little issue with Leeta just a few minutes ago. I told her that if she wants in on my new halo tech, then Carson has to go. I expected her to resist, seeing as how she's been having a virtual affair with the guy for a couple of years."

"I knew there was an affair!" interrupts Mary. "A couple of times I saw Carson twitching in his gross pupa, right in front of Kayla. So foul. But I didn't know it was *Leeta*." She smiles. "Isn't gossip *fun*? Now that my hate/love/fear/lust hormones are all back on line."

"And remember that Leeta was Carson's boss," says Gee. "So the affair would totally make sense to Carson. But now he's gone rogue. Leeta didn't tell him to kill off Mary during our raid. And she didn't tell him to help the Top Party kill me. Leeta's done with him. She's transferring him to the Skyhive office in China. Effective today."

"I bet you anything Carson won't go to China," says Mary.

"If he doesn't go, somebody's likely to kill him," says Gee quite simply. "Maybe I'll do it. He's a liability all around."

"Works for me!" exclaims Mary with a wild laugh. Her reckless nature is fully back in play. "What about Kayla?"

"I talked to her. She's staying on in San Lorenzo with baby Daia. Getting the divorce. Keeping their house. I guess you know that Carson-the-asshole was going to sell it and hog the money? So, what the hell, I bought the house off him—bought it via teep just now. And I deeded it to Kayla Stux. So Kayla won't be crowding you in *your* house, Mary. You can live there forever." Gee looks like he wants approval.

"Fast work," says Mary. "Tycoon legal beagle."

"I've got more angles than an origami crane, baby," says Gee. "I'm a mirror-maze! Oh, and one more thing. Kayla's gonna grow me a hundred slug soldiers tonight. Copies of Bunter, but more bad-ass. Troops for fighting off the Top Party tomorrow. And I'm leaving the butler uniform because it's weird." Gee pauses and attempts a seductive smile. "But never mind all that for now. We've got the rest of the day off, Mary. Would you like to *close our deal*?"

"Perhaps," Mary archly says. She stands and stretches, reveling in her youthful allure. "I might be amenable to a roll in the hay. Trot off and get your new body, dear man."

"My cloning tank is in an underground chamber off my cave," says Gee. "The change will take a while. A couple of hours."

"And I apologize for what I said about old Gee," Mary puts in. "Old Gee doesn't have to die. I can live with two Gees. If you two don't quarrel."

"We'll work it out," says Gee. "And don't try to watch me in the clone tank. It'll be gnarly. And—just in case I screw the pooch—"

Gee steps forward and kisses Mary for the first time. Lips and tongues. The man tastes good. Once more he tells Mary he loves her—then disappears down a twisty tunnel, with his human-sized Kayla-designed banana-slug Bunter butler leading the way, his eyes waggling on stalks.

Mary doesn't let herself think about what's going to happen. Maybe she made a mistake, pushing Gee so hard about getting a young body. Kind of shallow of her. Again she reminds herself about the wrongness of ageism. Fact is, she's becoming quite fond of Gee, old coot though he is.

She carries a chair outside and sits in the clearing between the cave and the redwood. Her halo's quantum wireless connection to her psidot is wonderfully clear. She feels fully embedded in her body, with her thoughts and feelings perfectly natural.

Glory and Miss Max are still roaming around. "We heard you two arguing," says Glory. "We were scared."

"Can you see my halo?" Mary asks them.

"I see something," says Glory.

"What's a halo?" says Miss Max.

By way of response, Mary makes her halo even brighter. A glowing golden platter. There's enough sun out here to keep her halo's energy up high.

"Pretty," says Miss Max, and idiotically lunges for the halo once again, mouth agape.

Without having to think about the details, Mary projects a tight, narrow tube of ionization from her halo to Miss Max's head—and sends a crackling spark. Certainly not a trillion volts, but enough to get a startled yelp from the tall ball walker. Mary cackles, and Glory smacks his lips, savoring the moment. *Parp parp parp.*

"Mary is mean," says Miss Max.

"Stay away from my halo," says Mary. "Don't you ever try to bite it again."

"Fine," says Miss Max. "We're still friends, yes?"

"We're always friends," says Mary. "I'm glad you two goons are here. Did Gee say anything interesting when I wasn't around?"

"Gee said to be ready to fight," says Miss Max. "Gee said, '*Those dipshit Top Party pigs will come tomorrow morning.*'"

"Are you scared?" asks Mary.

"Of what?" says Glory.

"Never mind," says Mary.

Glory and Miss Max go back to playing one of their games. They charge at a redwood tree and see how far up the side of the tree they can run. When their momentum runs out, they fall backwards to the ground. The trick then is to do a backflip and land on your feet. Or on your head. Sometimes they land flat onto their backs, but they don't care. They're very rubbery.

Mary relaxes into her chair. She feels like she's catching her breath for the first time today. It's nice in the woods with the goofy ball walkers, and with the fine, gently domed disk of her halo glowing overhead. She'll worry about the Top Party later. After she and the new Gee make love. The love-making will be fun.

This might be a good time for her to squeeze her halo into the hole at the bottom of the server redwood, and make physical contact with the inner wood, and do the backup of her lifebox that Gee was talking about. If she can figure out how to do it. It might be a lot of trouble. She'll do it after Gee comes back out. Or tomorrow. She needs to just relax for an hour right now.

But then, of course, as long as she's thinking about the redwood, she spots a diamondback rattlesnake lying in a patch of sun near the base. It's a big one, the size of an arm. The creature's glassy eyes glitter. Somehow Mary knows the snake is female. The rattler raises her diamond-shaped head, hisses, and flickers her forked pink tongue. Tasting the air.

"Look out," Mary teeps to the ball walkers. But they're not interested. They already know about the snake. They've been getting to know a bunch of the animals around the grove.

Mary rises to her feet, keeping the chair between herself and the serpent. The rattler twitches, sending a pudgy wave down her thick body. Mary seems to feel the wave within her *own* flesh—and now she realizes she's picking up teep from the snake. And she remembers Gee said something about inducting the local animals into his defense web. Did he put a psidot on every one of them?

The snake teeps a sound to Mary, a lurching sporadic hiss. A brain signal. Mary executes a conceptual shift—and sets her halo to munging the incoming data into words. She's understanding the speech of an animal. Cool.

The snake's name is Zsuzsa, and she's sharing memories. Last night when she was making love with her husband, Zsuzsa twisted her body around him so tight that she squeezed him into temporary unconsciousness. Ecstasy for both of them. This morning's hunt was wonderful. Zsuzsa and her mate writhed through a damp burrow that runs from the cave's pit to a bramble thicket by the stream, where crafty Zsuzsa curled and waited—still as stone. A squirrel appeared, nibbling pine nuts from a cone. Mary experiences a replay of the rapid strike and the orgasmic squirt of venom. In closing, Zsuzsa shares the comfortable feel of the paralyzed squirrel in her long gut. The whole squirrel: fur, bones, and all. *Life is good*, hisses Zsuzsa.

Mary wonders how far away from Zsuzsa she ought to be. She edges back, teeping images of friendship. Hearts, smiles, and flowers—but what would these symbols mean to a snake?

"*Bonk!*" hollers Glory, rebounding off the server redwood and landing next to the rattler.

Zsuzsa emits a savage hiss and strikes one of Glory's legs. It doesn't seem to faze the ball walker. They don't have standard metabolisms, in fact they might not even have circulatory systems.

"Bad, girl!" Glory parps, and kicks Zsuzsa in the side.

"*Boing!*" says Miss Max, bounding forward like a hyperactive coiled spring. She pinches the tip of Zsuzsa's tail between her lips and spins in a circle. Zsuzsa writhes wildly, managing to squirm around and sink her fangs into the side of Miss Max's head. But, again, to no avail.

"Let's tear the snake into pieces and eat her," suggests Glory.

"Leave the snake alone!" yells Mary. "Zsuzsa is my new friend."

By way of calming the distraught rattler, Mary hurries into the cave and fetches a steak from the kitchen. The ball walkers drift over to the stream, and start using their mouths to scoop up minnows and crawdads.

Zsuzsa regains her poise and, once again she sits in a coil by the tree, dispassionately observing Mary. Mary tosses the steak to the snake. Zsuzsa buzzes her rattle and opens her fanged, fuchsia mouth. An instant later the steak is a lump inside her gut, a few inches away from the lump of the squirrel.

Mary sits down again and teeps Zsuzsa some images of smiles, flowers, and raw meat. She'd like to chat a little more.

"Do you talk to Gee?" Mary asks the snake.

Zsuzsa sends a long wavering hiss, again decoded by Mary's halo.

"Gee talks to all of us," says Zsuzsa. "Great and small. We'll band together when the battle comes. All as one." Like a gothic fairy tale.

Mary now figures out the location of Zsuzsa's psidot—it's a nubbly yellow lump on the back of her flat head. Sensing Mary's interest, Zsuzsa plays an animation of Gee Willikers placing it there.

The ball walkers interrupt again. Having noticed that Mary fed the snake, they strut over from the stream. Seeing them, Zsuzsa disappears into a hole under a bush beside the tree.

"Feed us, too," says Glory.

So Mary fetches a bucket of ball-walker GroChow and portions it into two mounds on the ground. The ball walkers dig in.

Yet again Mary settles into her chair. Her halo hovers a yard above her head, tipped at a rakish angle. As always, Mary's halo is a disk and not a ring. Looking further upward, she catches a slight flicker above the redwood. Like seeing through a lens. It's the giant amoeba Utila that Gee keeps up there, with a mass of hydrogen foam on top, and with a pseudopod tethering her to the treetop. It strikes Mary that, at least visually, Utila and the tree echo Mary's halo and Mary's clone. This is a very strange situation she's in.

"Gee has a good army," says Glory. "We've been exploring the whole time. Gee has a nest of rattlesnakes, flocks of crows and jays, porcupines, bobcats, rats, and swarms of gnats."

"Is there a way to see them?" asks Mary.

"Teep," says Glory.

Guided by the ball walker, Mary teeps into her full surroundings and gets a marvelous, articulated feeling, with minds on every side, and bodies to match. Including the speckled-with-psidots Utila amoeba above them, with her cap of lifting-bubbles holding her aloft.

The gnat swarms are especially odd—true hive minds, each swarm a few hundred gnats in teep sync. God only know how Gee made micro psidots small enough for them. A variation on smart dust. He did this as free research for the protean Finn Junker labs.

Mary sinks into a deep union with a gnat swarm that happens to be gathered in the shade of her hovering halo. The gnat-swarm mind reminds Mary of the scattered, distracted fugue state she used to get into when she had to drive a car, back when driving was something a person might ever have to do.

But now, with her tight clone body and her smart halo and good old Miu Miu on the job, Mary could probably drive fine. If they still made mechanical cars. But the point is that she's learning to dance with disorder. But, um, wait, she's losing the thread of—oh, right, she's merging with the minds of Gee's glade, the many-in-one reality of the teeming woodland beasts.

Mary has to wonder how well this miscellaneous menagerie will fare when the heartless, fanatical Top Party militia and the Top Party's lifebox-run clones and remote-controlled kritters show up with, like, clubs and machetes and rail-guns, bent on destroying Gee, his animal army, and Mary herself.

Mary soothes herself with another slogan from that wise high-school math teacher of hers—Marianne Holiday. *On s'engage, et puis on voit.* Get into it—and you'll see.

Still no sign of Gee. It's warm for late April. Mary's halo is sensitive to the subtlest currents of air. Not to mention that it's a kick-ass platform for her mind. She's totally in the Now. And maybe even smarter than before, if that's at all possible—joke.

If they can get past the raid tomorrow, Mary's tangled tale may have a happy ending. The branches toss, the spots of light dance, the ball walkers sleep on the ground. Mary is practically in a trance. It's getting on toward five pm.

A naked young man appears from the cave. His hair is wet. He's alone.

"Howdy, Mary."

She feels oddly embarrassed. "You're in this body, Gee?"

"I've *always* been in it." The young man smiles, looking pleased with himself.

"You—you retrofitted yourself?" Mary exclaims, getting the picture all at once.

"Full wetware upgrade. I got into that clone tank with a hundred grams of assembler molecules and, I mean to tell you, woman, they ate me stem to stern. Like having a trillion beauty operators go after you at once. *Zing! Zong! Fwee!*"

The refurbished Gee flashes an ivory-white movie-star smile.

Mary stands and puts her hands on Gee's shoulders. He doesn't feel spongy. or hollowed-out, or like a kritter. He feels lithe and human and strong.

"You're something, Gee. You really are."

"You too, baby."

"I saw a really big rattlesnake."

"That's my friend Zsuzsa," says Gee. "She already told me. Good to have all this wildlife on our team."

"Teep is good."

"Touch is better."

They go inside, slide the cave's hidden outer door closed and—at last—make love. With their high-def teep in the mix, it's quite awesome. A full merge. And, my god, but it's been a long time. Near the end, the ball walkers wake up from their nap, and push inside, hoping to watch, or maybe just looking for more food. Gee shoos them out. The ball walkers are annoyed. The cave's door slams shut with a resonant boom.

Feeling reckless, Mary makes love to Gee for a second and even a third time. Unheard of. Sated and slaked, they fall into sweet slumber that lasts longer than is prudent.

An explosion wakes Mary.

Shit! It's past seven pm. They should be more vigilant! What if the Top Party attack is *tonight*? All is still. Did Mary dream the explosion? A faint, warm glow fills the cave, light from her halo and from the sunset. The ball walkers are in here again—and they left the damn door open. They're scared to be outside.

"Gee!" cries Mary.

He opens his eyes. Smiles at her. "Whoa. You sent me on a ride. Best I've slept in months."

Another explosion, from afar. It echoes off the cliffs and hills.

CARSON PFLUG

People say I'm an asshole, but I'm not.

I grew up in Cairo, Illinois, an impoverished, decaying town of two thousand souls, very much battered by climate change. A number of the locals are subsistence farmers, and a lot of them are Black. It's the southern tiny tip ass end of the state, squashed into a soggy, crooked promontory where the Ohio River angles into the Mississippi.

The rich expanse of Southern Illinois is known as Little Egypt—an early local preacher compared it to the biblical land of Goshen by the Nile. In recent times, a fly-by-night entrepreneur opened a Cairo amusement park called Huck Finn's Egypt, with jerry-rigged pyramids, a sternwheeler, rowboats, and kritter versions of crocodiles. The monstrous reptiles ate several rowboat-renters. The park went bust.

Mother and Father ran the Cairo Country Store, selling food and farm supplies, and renting out ball walkers and thudhumpers for working the fields. Our house rested upon twenty-foot-high biotech tree stumps to stay clear of the floods.

I did the family's accounting from early on, juggling numbers in the cloud. I'm good at visualizing financial flows. I see braided rivers and cities of canals with locks, sluicegates, pumps, dikes—and class-four rapids. I have a knack of training virtual bots to manipulate the currents to improve my gain.

By the time I finish high-school, I've tripled my parents' holdings. They're proud of me. Father suggests I get a business degree at the university in nearby Carbondale, find a wife, and settle into decrepit, end-of-the-line Cairo. Mother and I laugh at his idea. Obviously I can do better. Father doesn't know much. And often he's drunk.

I set my search-bots to exploring the archipelagoes of academia. My bots discover a sinuous passage that leads from lowly Cairo to a scholarship at the august and sophisticated University of Chicago. Right away, I enroll online. And then, without actually leaving Cairo yet, I parlay my status as a University of Chicago student into a slot as a student at UC Berkeley in sunny, high-tech CA. Playing on my disadvantaged Cairo roots, I score a UC scholarship than Chicago is offering.

I'm enjoying this new game, and I want to keep trading up. I'll try for Yale. But Father tells me it's time to get my ass out of his house—instead of lying in bed all day with my eyephones on. He's miffed that I'm not going to Southern Illinois University in Carbondale.

"Do something real," he storms. "Live a life. Get your head out of the cloud."

"Shut your crack," I tell him. "Another few days of this and I'll be going to Oxford University in England."

Father snatches off my eyephones and uproots my wireless router vine. Time for Berkeley. I pack my few possessions and ask one of our thudhumpers to drive me to the St. Louis airport. I intend to skip saying goodbye to Mother—I don't want the big scene. But she catches up with me in the street. She takes out a paper envelope and hands me a small scrap of gristle from within.

"What's that?" I ask.

"Your navel," goes Mother. "Take it. The tip of your umbilical cord. It was your connection to me. It dried up and fell off when you were two days old. Maybe having it will bring you good luck." Her lips tremble. She stares searchingly into my eyes. "I'll never see you again, will I?"

"Don't say that." I stuff the memento into my jeans pocket. "You might still see me. Like maybe if I die, and they send me home for my funeral?" The joke doesn't go over at all. She starts sobbing.

I wrap my arms around her and give her a hug. "Thanks for the navel, Mother. And all the rest of it. I'll always love you."

I say that, yes. So—you see? I'm not the asshole. Gee Willikers is the asshole.

Berkeley is a new world. The contacts are rich, the networking opportunities glorious. My fellow students are stylish, intelligent, diverse. Some are wealthy, and some feral. I major in biotech business management. It's a popular program with the upscale crowd.

Starting in the second year, our core BBM curriculum involves gaming a virtual economy populated by my fellow majors. We call the game Berkistan. No lectures, no homework, just the endless playing of Berkistan for three years, with recess between semesters. I'm good at the game; I love it.

I use a design tool to create a visualization app to help others see the money streams the way that I do, and I start selling access to it. The Carson Kit. I charge a very high subscription fee—in real money, rather than in game money—thus limiting my customers to wealthy, lazy kids with a great sense of entitlement.

Although nobody has sold a Berkistan game advice app before, my teachers approve my move. I'm meta-gaming the game. And in the process, I am, in effect, interviewing for future jobs with my socially privileged customers, who have higher-than-average odds of becoming tycoons.

All the while I'm becoming more Californian. Keenly I observe the richer students, taking on their styles of dress, mimicking their speech, absorbing their attitudes. Yet another level, a meta-meta-game.

Mother's premonition is sadly correct. I don't go back to Cairo at all—except for the funeral. Mother's funeral, not mine. Cancer. She and Father didn't tell me because they didn't want to make a fuss.

It's the worst day of my life. The blank brutality of Mother's eternal absence, with no return. Impossible. Father is addled and in despair. His business affairs are in arrears; all his funds are gone. Why didn't I keep an eye on the family finances! I'm racked with guilt. Mother's deathbed is soiled and unmade. I tidy her room. But what's the use? It's unbearable. I stay two days, then speed back to my room in Berkeley, leaving Father to his lonely befuddlement.

Two weeks later, the ever-more-savage Ohio River scours the ground from beneath the pilings of our family home. Father escapes in a rowboat, but a rogue pair of Huck Finn's Egypt crocodiles capsize his craft and devour him. I don't go back for this ceremony. Again—what's the use?

Not being an asshole, I'm depressed by the loss of my parents. This is the spring of my Senior year. By now I'm practically the emperor of the virtual republic of Berkistan, or maybe the Imam or the gangland boss, depending on how you look at it. But I don't have the spirit to play with my usual avidity.

The day after I return from Cairo, a cabal of hot-shot sophomores barbeques my liver for lunch. I escape total Berkistan annihilation, but suddenly it's a real possibility. If these pissant sophs drive me low enough, I might not even get my degree.

And meanwhile I'm continually distracted by images of the crocodiles eating Father. I hear his uncertain voice calling my name.

I'd cash out of the Berkistan game immediately if I could. Even after the setback, I'm still in the upper third. But you're not allowed to quit early. It's like a fight to the death, or, less dramatically, like a horserace with a finish line. I'm not going to make it without help. My thoughts turn to my fellow student Leeta Patel.

Leeta is the closest thing to a friend that I have at Berkeley. She's a little odd and cold—much like me. We're irredeemable outsiders amid the cosseted, unimaginative drones in the biotech business management program. We occasionally get together for coffee or a meal to discuss the latest trends in our Berkistan game, and to talk smack about the other students.

At times Leeta is awkwardly kittenish with me. But I feel no romance toward her. She's unattractive. Our emotional asymmetry is to my advantage. It makes it easy to ask for favors. So now, in my time of weakness, I enlist her for support. I explain that I can't go on. And I propose a plan.

"Play the game as me," I tell her. "I'll give you my iris scan and my gene code."

"Identity spoof is the one thing that's forbidden in the game," says Leeta. "If the school finds out, we'll be expelled. No degrees. *Mm-hmm.*" She brushes her lank hair out of her face. "Setting those issues aside, let's suppose I do impersonate you. Then what?"

She's definitely interested. Her game rating isn't very high—she's in, like, the lower third. I smile.

"You'll use a borogrove combine of holding companies to move my Berkistan funds into your account—before those bastard-ass underclassmen clean me out. And you'll corrupt my Carson's Kit game adviser tool so it funnels money to you. My entitled users will be too dumb to notice. You'll rise to the top. Numero uno. In the final minutes, you jolt my account with a fat deposit—so I can graduate."

"What about me?"

"You keep enough so you're still in the top five. You don't have to be number one. You'll get honors anyway."

"And a great job!" exults Leeta.

"The way I feel now, I don't care about jobs," I say. "But be sure to get me back into the game near the end. I do want my degree."

"No worries," says Leeta.

I give her a hug, as if to give her a thrill.

And now I go on hiatus.

Outside it's sunny and warm, with blue skies, and flowers on the trees. For the first time, I explore the campus. "Get your head out of the cloud," as Father advised. And then he ends up in the mouth of a crocodile? Poor old fool. *Crrru-uunch*. I try not to obsess. I try to mingle.

I spend three days on the lawns and low walls near Sather Gate, at the Telegraph Avenue edge of the campus. Eating slices of pizza, drinking iced tea, watching people amble by.

Each morning at ten, I see one special woman. Her out-fits are casual, tidy, and with a great sense of style. Scraps of color in just the right spots. The clothes are kritter-made, perhaps designed by her. Or maybe she sews on the cloth highlight patches by hand?

She has a little dog that trots along behind her, but it isn't a dog, it's a kritter, not especially practical-looking. More like a moving sculpture. Made by her? I want to talk to this woman. But I'm scared. She won't like me. She's arty. I'm a biz major.

The third time I spot her, miracle of miracles, she walks over to me sitting on my wall. I smile softly—a smile like I've hardly ever formed before. What's the word for that expression? Oh, right—it's joy.

"Hi," she says. "I noticed you noticing me. Who are you?"

I tell her, all in a rush. "I've just gone three days with no Berkistan biz game—I haven't been offline this long in, I don't know, ten years. I'm like a newly-hatched chick in the temporary coop that my mother would set up in our country store this time of year. I'm cheeping. I'm like, please take me home. Feed me cracked corn. Feel my tiny heartbeat."

"I don't know about doing all that," says the woman, kind of amused. "I meant, what's your name?"

"Carson Pflug."

"Pflug?"

"Means plow. Midwestern farmers. Tiny, curly, tip of Illinois. You?"

"Kayla Stux."

"Stux?"

"I made it up. I'm a woman of mystery. At the start of an amazing career."

"Love it. And I don't get cracked corn?"

"I can show you my studio."

"I knew it. You're an artist."

"Of sorts. Artist-slash-kritter-hacker. Do you like my pet Nipsy? Kayla Kritter number one. The first of many. My senior project. He's teep programmable and he does different things. None of them are practical, but he's fun, and he's art."

"I like Nipsy, yes." The Kayla Kritter has polka dots drift across his matte skin. I lean over. "Come here, boy."

Nipsy's very high-quality. More than a toy. A collectible. He has a fairly long mouth, and each tooth is a different shade of ivory. He bites my hand as hard as he can. Apparently the teeth are rubber, so they don't pierce my skin, but—the bite triggers a panic attack. I've never had one before. I moan and fall over onto my side, hugging myself and barely managing not to piss my pants.

"You okay?" says Kayla, backing off. I sense she's about to leave my life forever. She now sees me as a slushed street person. Just when I'm hoping to present myself as the lord of the undergrad biz majors, a soon-to-be UC grad, and a budding tycoon.

With a colossal effort of will, I croak an entreaty. "Don't go. Please. I have post traumatic shock. My mother died two weeks ago. And my father, he got eaten by crocodiles last week. And when Nipsy bit me I flashed back to—"

"Bad Nipsy," says Kayla in a neutral tone. "Lick poor Carson's owie."

"No, no!" I cry, scooting backwards as if electrified. I scramble onto my perch on the low wall. I fold my legs under me so the horrible fake dog can't bite my feet.

"Crocodiles?" says Kayla, seriously doubting my story. "In Illinois?"

"Kritters," I explain. "From a defunct amusement park. Huck Finn's Egypt. My father was in a rowboat. There was a flood."

"How unfortunate," says Kayla. She tries to hold her mouth straight, but she can't, and she begins laughing. I should be offended but I'm laughing with her—and sobbing at the same time. Fully losing it—but in a good way, as what I'm losing, or beginning to lose, is the heavy load of guilt, sorrow, and dread that's been inside my chest for two weeks. It takes a couple of minutes to calm myself. I wipe my face on my sleeve. Kayla stays near, watching me. Nipsy the Kayla Kritter has changed his specific gravity. He's floating in the air beside Kayla's shoulder, tethered by his leash. His colors are darker now. And his mouth is way smaller. He does a tiny little bark. As if apologizing for biting me.

"I'm usually not like this at all," I tell Kayla. "Usually I'm emotionally flat."

"Maybe you could find a happy medium?" says Kayla. "And I seriously thought you were joking about the crocodiles." She pauses. "But you weren't, were you? And your mother died too?"

I nod. "My life is a stupid joke. And now I blew my chance to make a good impression on you. I'm ashamed. Maybe Nipsy should rip out my throat."

"You do see that I switched his program mode?"

"Yes. Thank you." I pause, weighing my options. "What you said before—about me visiting your studio? Can that still happen? Could we pick up a six-pack of beer?"

"Beer? It's not even noon."

"Call it a picnic. We'll get some take-out falafel too. This is practically senior week. Time to party. I didn't do much college stuff yet. But now—I met Kayla Stux! The woman of my dreams."

"Over-emotional," says Kayla. "Unstable. I like that. What the hey, we'll get drunk and fuck."

Does she mean this? I'm scared to say a word. Silently I walk at Kayla's side. Her studio/apartment, is full of amazing kritters she's designed. Beetles on the ceiling, slugs on the walls, an ant army marching in formation on the side of the frosty puffball fungus that is Kayla's fridge. She's even done something to her bathroom mirror. Translucent mold on the glass forms ghost images of a demonic strangler behind me. When I ask Kayla if she sees it too, she does a spooky laugh. Fun.

We spread our picnic on her lab bench, among pieces of half-built kritters. We finish our six-pack and, if not truly drunk, we're giddy. We talk the rest of the afternoon—but so far there's no sex, not that I'd know how to initiate it. Maybe that was just big-talk on Kayla's part? I don't really care, as long as I'm with her all day.

As evening falls, we watch the sunset from a rooftop botanical garden she has access to, and then it's back to her studio. Incredibly I spend the night with Kayla, and we do the whole deal. Truth be told, it's my first time. I'm close to weeping with—there's that word again—joy.

In the morning we talk some more. I'm not the most interesting person in the world, but somehow Kayla keeps being amused by the things I say. Like I'm a talking crow or an ancient Egyptian. From Cairo, Illinois.

We hit a cafe for breakfast, and then Kayla sends me off for the day. She has things to do on her own. Maybe we'll meet up after supper.

The hammer comes down an hour later, at noon sharp, which is when my department's Berkistan game reaches the semester's official end. Leeta is at the top of the rankings, and I'm at the frikkin bottom. Last place. Zero funds. Leeta never replenished my account. She wanted to stay in first place.

I try and call her on my uvvy, but she has herself cloaked. Fortunately I anticipated this possibility, and I affixed a molecule-sized tracker antenna to Leeta's hair when I hugged her last week.

Within an hour I'm at the Angela Davis Hotel, where Leeta has holed up. She's moved out of her apartment. Did she really think she could duck Carson Pflug so easily? I'm a leech, man, a lamprey eel. I go in the hotel's service entrance and pick the lock to Leeta's room.

She's silhouetted by the window. I can't see her expression. "Carson! I was about to call you."

"What happened to our deal? I thought you were hot for me."

"I am *so* sorry. I was going to plump up your account but I—"

"Forgot?" I suggest. "Wasn't able to?"

"I overleveraged," temporizes Leeta. "I had your money all set aside and ready for you, but thirty minutes before the game's end, this amazing opportunity opened up. I used your money to go all in—I was investing on your behalf! But it was a scam, and—"

"And now if I want a degree, I need to spend another year in this dumb-ass program," I say.

"I am *so* sorry."

"That's a tell, Leeta. Using that canned phrase twice. Someone paid you to shaft me."

"If you're going to get all paranoid and insulting, you need to get out of here." And now I notice that Leeta's holding a rail-gun pistol.

An hour later, about two in the afternoon, I'm in the office of the department head, Ms. Juju Wu. I tell Juju that Leeta's been impersonating me all week. I say Leeta stole my passcode data, and that I didn't realize until today. Juju wants to believe me. She dislikes Leeta. Wanting to influence Juju the more, I tell her that Leeta says she's stupid and weak.

Juju has a lot of power. The Biotech Business Management School is self-funded and fully autonomous. Juju says she needs to discuss this with a friend—but that she just might expel Leeta and credit me with Leeta's Berkistan game funds. Looks like I might still to graduate on top!

But before this happy ending, someone tips off Leeta, and she goes for total revenge. She sends Juju a secret tape that she made of us two making our deal. Juju mulls this over for about half an hour—and then she expels both of us.

I find Leeta and we talk things over. We're sadder but wiser. It's almost funny. And, get this, our banishments haven't put a total kibosh on our job options.

Our area is *business management*, right? If Leeta and I are such unethical weasels that we got shit-canned from UC Berkeley's BBM program, well, it means we're good prospects for those confidential and low-profile positions that employers find especially hard to fill. No need for hard feelings between us at all. We're players, okay? And I can tell she's still got that crush. Onward.

By suppertime, Leeta has a minor management position at a nascent telepathy company called One Wow. They're researching teep drugs—working right at the fringes of criminal malpractice. And me, I'm being job-interviewed in a dark bar on Telegraph Avenue. Talking to a guy named Jerr Boom.

I know Jerr a little from around the campus. He's not a student or an instructor. But he seems to turn up at a fair number of our departmental functions, always schmoozing, making contacts, offering favors. He doesn't initially tell me who he represents, but he's dangling a surprisingly large salary. And I have almost no money at all.

"What would I do?" I ask Jerr, feeling unsure.

"Dirty tricks, espionage, and disinformation. I like the way you put that tracker molecule on Leeta. And I like the way she turned around and left your Berkistan game balance at zero. Burn! You two are ruthless. Corrupt. We like that. And it got even better when you reported Leeta to Juju Wu. I'm friends with Juju. And in fact she talked to me about what was happening. So I told Leeta. And then Leeta gave Juju the video of you two making your deal. Great stuff. Juju might have let you guys off, but I paid her to expel you two. Chase you out of the light and into the shadows. Where my people and I live."

I feel three or four steps behind this guy's flow. "You're saying you work for One Wow?"

"Not at all." Jerr's eyes sparkle with knowing merriment. "I'm saying One Wow is a target of interest. But let's talk about you. Another plus: You're an orphan. Makes it that much harder for the counterforce to leverage you. My group has a lot of enemies."

"This coy routine isn't doing jack for me, Jerr. Who the fuck do you work for?"

"You can't guess?"

Jerr Boom is soft and pale, a few years older than me. Has a beard, which helps him blend into the campus scene. I seem to remember hearing him say something favorable about the despised President Treadle, who's campaigning for his third term in office. Jerr grins at me through his beard, hard and sly.

It clicks. "You're from the Top Party," I say. "A total pack of assholes."

"You're meant to be with us, Carson. You're a devotee of the cash imperative. You and I—we're wolves among sheep. We cull the herd for the higher good. You call us a pack of assholes? You're quite the asshole too."

I feel like I'm sinking into quicksand. "Not—not an asshole," I weakly protest. "I'm in love. I'm different. I'm trying to change."

"Kayla doesn't have to learn the details of your new job," says Jerr. He seems to know everything about me. "Come in with us," he coaxes. "We'll keep you safe from the crocodiles, eh?"

I feel a chill. Those Huck Finn's Egypt crocodiles were kritters, and thus possibly under remote control by some force, possibly the Top Party, but why would they have wanted to kill Father? Certainly he was a life-long Democrat, and he'd even been on the lowly Cairo city council a few times, but he was the smallest of small fish, and a broken widower, and—

"Don't overthink," says Jerr, relishing my anguish. "I'm jiving you. Jerking your chain. You need to get a better uvvy, brah. Your uvvy leaks feed like a soap opera dialed to eleven. I can hear your thoughts with this new gadget called a psidot. I call my psidot Tweaky Bird. See her on my neck? Like a little golden slug. Better than an uvvy. Next big thing. Top Party labs stole the psidot alpha specs from the Finn Junker labs. You probably haven't heard of Junkers either. You're gonna learn a lot with me, son. And we'll harden up your personal security. Are you in?"

I feel dizzy. Like I'm in a fairy tale. Selling my soul to an evil gnome. "That salary you mentioned—can you make it twice as much?"

"That's the attitude I like," says Jerr Boom. "Sure we can double your salary. We won't do a formal written contract, you understand. Deniability. Upside: no tax. And I'll give you a hiring bonus. Three extra months of salary in your account right now."

I uvvy into my bank account. The money's there.

"My job title?" I ask.

"Mr. Carson Pflug, Senior Consultant, Boom Consumer Metrics! Sally into the night, young hero. Celebrate. Tell Kayla about your big score. She'll be proud. Ask her to marry you."

I stand up, studying this strange man. He's slouched way down in a leather easy chair. Like a slime creature from an ocean trench. His remark about the crocodiles—I don't like to let that pass. But this job's as good as I'll get. And I'm broke. Maybe later I'll find a way to screw Jerr Boom and Ross Treadle and the Top Party. And maybe get even with Leeta too. I'm better than all of them.

Crazily enough, that night I follow Jerr Boom's to the letter—and ask Kayla to marry me.

I start by giving Kayla a fairly bogus account of my day's ups and downs. She notices the holes, asks about Leeta, and wonders about the job. It's not like she's suspicious—it's more that she likes me and she's curious. I'm so disarmed by her friendliness and empathy that I cast caution to the winds and tell her full truth.

Does Kayla turn against me? No. She laughs and shakes her head. "You're a rascal, Carson. A scamp. And you landed on your feet."

"You don't despise me?"

"Well, you're not an artist, and you're not a hipster freal, but at least you're not a Treadler—are you? Even if you're working for the Top Party?"

"Just a scam," I reassure Kayla. "A con."

"We'll find a way to make it work," says Kayla. "Just you keep on telling me the truth."

It's pretty damn clear to me that I'm not likely to get this close to a woman as good as Kayla ever again—not with me being the kind of person I am, and not with the job I'm taking on. I'll be working with sleazebags and morons and criminals for the next year or so. I need someone noble in my life. A good person who's quirky enough to think I'm interesting. I need Kayla.

So I pop the question.

"Marry you?" Kayla responds, softly laughing. "I'll think about it. I tend to wait more than forty-eight hours after meeting a street-derelict-turned-right-wing-fixer before deciding whether to plight him my troth."

"I'm a tragic orphan!" I protest. We've been drinking wine all through this conversation, you understand, and we're waxing grandiloquent. "On the verge of an explosive career. We could even buy a house. It would be a good investment."

"Can I select the house?" says Kayla, definitely picking up on this aspect of my offer. "Somewhere in the mountains? I could put my art studio and development lab in there. Full indie. I wouldn't have to get a botty gig job."

"Sure, Kayla. Whatever you say." And I mean this. Other than this new job with Jerr Boom—whatever it actually is—I have no concrete plans about my future at all. I've been too busy playing the Berkistan game to think ahead. But now the future's here.

"Do you like babies?" presses Kayla, going for it.

"I've seen babies. They're amusing. Strange proportions. And the noises they make."

"Cooing, crying, babbling," says Kayla. "The smiles."

"How come you haven't already hooked up?" I ask. "If you want a family. And you're such a catch! No boyfriends or girlfriends?"

Kayla shrugs. "A few. They come and go. I'm picky. Part of being an artist. Easily irritated by the mundane."

"I'm not mundane?" I say, feeling a twinge of pride.

"Far from it," goes Kayla. She cocks her head, as if still deciding. "A high Martian. Let's get in bed so I can road test you again."

Things take off from there. I use my Top Party advance for a down payment on a home that Kayla finds us in San Lorenzo, in the Santa Cruz mountains. A nice, rambling ranch house in the redwoods, amid log shacks and grown homes. Our place is in good condition, expanded and modernized by the artist couple we buy it from.

We marry in June and settle into the funky coastal rain forest. Kayla makes a circle of friends among the San Lorenzo creatives and crafts-people, starts showing her Kayla Kritters in local galleries, and rapidly talks her way into a high-end gallery in San Francisco—a place called Mixed Bag.

Jeannie Jone, the owner of Mixed Bag, is quite the entrepreneur, and she gets Kayla started with producing mass editions of her Kritters—like maybe fifty, or a hundred, or even three hundred—which is something Kayla wanted to do all along.

As Kayla puts it to me, "Why would you tweak a new kind of watermelon gene and grow just one melon? I want to be a household word."

"Pass me the Kayla," I respond.

The demand grows. It's really happening for Kayla. But at times she seems lonely in San Lorenzo. She makes some kritter-crafter friends from the San Francisco art scene, two guys in particular, Dank Prank and Phil Bilko. Sometimes they'll come down to our house with that gallery owner, Jeannie Jone. I have a feeling that Phil Bilko and Jeannie Jone are both in love with Kayla, but she almost doesn't notice that—or she takes it for granted. I'm grateful she's my wife. She's better than I deserve.

Kayla also forms a close friendship with an old mountain-hippie woman next door—she's named Mary. Mary claims her last name is Mary too. Not much info about Mary Mary in the cloud—pretty much all she's ever done is to live here in the boonies and work in Mrs. Yahootie's country store.

I'm online with Jerr Boom nearly every day and he has me boning up on confidential in-house Top Party lab reports and case studies. Sometimes I go up the Peninsula to San Jose or Sunnyvale and give advice to fledgling execs. If only for cover, Jerr actually *does* run a semblance of a consulting agency, and these initial gigs involve helping startups to organize their human resources, organization trees, workflows, kritter maintenance, public offerings and the like.

But there's a twist to my gigs. I'm spying on these innocent, eager newcomers, and passing the info to Jerr Boom, who shovels it into the hopper of the Top Party lab in SF

It's fairly easy work. And I'm getting along well with Kayla at home. The honeymoon stage. I'm as happy as I've ever been.

One Wednesday in October—just before Halloween on Sunday, to be followed by the Tuesday Presidential election—Jerr Boom kicks it up a notch. He calls me to his latest office in San Francisco—this one is a single dinky room. Jerr's "office" is a temporary, changeable concept, and he's never in any one particular instance for long. He's like a cautious octopus who changes his den every few weeks.

The window looks out on thudhumpers, centipede busses, and longhaulers trotting along the elevated packed-dirt ramps that were once Route 101—precisely at the same level as Jerr's window. The room has a desk with empty drawers, a couple of chairs, and no kritters. The databases and software tools live in Jerr's head and in the Top Party's cloud-silo.

"How about your fan Leeta?" Jerr says to me. "She still hot for you?"

"There's nothing between us now," I tell him. "Our paths diverged. She's at One Wow, doing something real. And I'm with you, being an industrial spy. My work is so low-level I don't even see why you pay me."

"You've been on probation," says Jerr. "But today you make a big score."

"Tell me."

"It's about Leeta's work group," says Jerr, leaning back into his plump office chair—the only deluxe thing in the room. "They're onto a new teep drug called stumble. A fungus. Leeta and her engineer Molly have been testing it. The Top Party labs want it bad."

Outside the window, a longhauler like a giant sausage goes blatting past, speeding its way by expelling pulses of air. Farts, basically. My chair is stiff, cold metal. You hardly see a chair like this anymore. A soldier's chair.

"I've been reading about next-gen teep in the Top Party's lab reports," I say. "The Party wants to use teep to send Ross Treadle propaganda into voters' minds. I think that sucks."

"We don't care what you think, Carson. We care what you do. Let me continue. There's another group interested in the stumble drug. Those Finn Junker biohackers in Copenhagen. They're very anti-Treadle. Their operative Anselm Saarikoski is here in SF. He's planning to connect with Leeta and Molly at a party tonight. He hopes to do a One Wow stumble session with them."

"And you want me to join in?" I say.

"I seriously doubt Leeta would let you," says Jerr. "Considering how your last collab with her worked out. Also she knows you're with the Top Party. No, your assignment will be to manage a subagent. He's expendable. A torpedo named Loftus."

"Torpedo?"

"A 1930s gangster expression. Let me have my fun. You're meeting Loftus in an hour. And you'll give him this." Jerr hands me a fat sheaf of bills.

"You say Loftus is expendable?" With Jerr Boom, I'm always catching up.

He flashes his hard smile through his beard. "Yeah. But don't tell him that. He packs a gat. A heater. A rod. A railgun pistol, okay? You'll monitor his experiences via uvvy. With enough luck, he *might* abduct Anselm for us—not that I expect that to work. It's a distraction. The main thing is that Loftus plants a bug on Anselm, and that he brings back a stumble sample."

"Will Leeta be safe?" I say.

"I assumed you wouldn't care," says Jerr in a negligent tone, which is an act. His eyes dance as he takes in my discomfiture.

"Well, no, I don't *care*—but still."

"I'll be surprised if anyone ever gets the better of Leeta," says Jerr. "Or gets the better of you. You two are stone cold scammers. The top of the Dark Honor Roll in the Bio Biz Management program, right?"

The remark makes me feel good. I laugh and think about telling Kayla. But then I realize I probably won't. It hurts to think my days of telling her the truth are coming to an end.

Jerr tells me several additional fine points about my gig, and he reminds me not to mention the Top Party to Loftus. On my way out, he drops a bomb.

"About that stumble sample? We're expecting Loftus to bring us some of it. But if he dies, which is likely, you'll need to fetch the sample from his remains."

"How the hell would I do that?"

"Up to you, amigo. Earn your pay."

This gig is heavy. But what do I expect? I'm pulling down big bucks from the Top Party—and President Ross Treadle is in the home stretch of his third term campaign. All the chips are on the table.

I meet Loftus at the dimly lit Black Out, a low-down bar near Polk Street in San Francisco. It's a classic dive bar, almost like a diorama in a Natural History museum, with every telling detail in place, right down to the puddles on the floor. Urine? Beer? Vomit? I pick my way around the spots to find Loftus at a table in the rear.

He's a wild-west type, from Rancho Cucamonga in southern California, well-muscled. Wears a cowboy hat and a suede leather vest. He sets his hat, brim-up, on the greasy third chair of our table, then scoots the chair under the table.

We drink in silence for a minute, and I slip some of Jerr's money into the hat. Another minute passes, and Loftus takes a peek.

"Shit fire," he drawls. "Now, where do I find these women I'm supposed to hit on?"

I tell him about the party in San Francisco where Leeta and Molly go to enlist prospects every Wednesday. I uvvy him images of their faces.

"And you want a sample of that drug they're making, right?"

Given what Jerr Boom just told me, Loftus's question makes me queasy. I almost feel sorry for the man. But I force a smile.

"Yes, a sample. And I'd like to watch the party through your uvvy. And, if you can, kidnap the other guy who'll be at the session. You'd get a bonus for that. His name is Anselm Saarikoski. You think you could bag him?"

"I'm right persuasive when I get my blood up," says Loftus, signaling for another round. "Anything else?"

"This stumble fungus that they're testing—you wear it like a shelf mushroom on the side of your head. We're interested in knowing what happens if someone crushes a person's mushroom while they're on their trip."

"I expect they'd say, *Ow*,'" goes Loftus, not taking this very seriously. "They'd say, *Who turned off the pretty lights?*"

"We want you to be the mushroom crusher," I say. "That's part of your job. Crushing everyone's stumble."

"But who crushes *my* mushroom to wake me up?" says Loftus. "That's gotta come first. I can't rightly crush nothing if I'm zonked." He smirks. "Is one of them pretty women gonna do me?"

"Chex Chapster will take care of you," I say. "He works in the apartment. Like a butler. You pay him off before the test. Take him aside, and ask him to come and crush your stumble after you, the two women, and that Anselm guy have been flying high all night. And then when you're awake, you crush the mushrooms on the other three."

"Is this Chex fella gay?"

"That has nothing to do with anything," I say.

"If I'm paying a man to crush my mushroom, then you gotta give me more money than you just did."

"Right," I say. Jerr anticipated this. "Here we go." I slip a second, smaller, sheaf of bills into Loftus's hat beneath the table.

"Hellacious," he says and snugs the hat onto his head with the money inside. "I'll toodle along."

"There's one more thing," I tell him.

I haven't mentioned that, at the end of my conversation with Jerr Boom, Jerr gave me a little thorn in a tiny bag. And now, as directed, I pass the thorn to Loftus as we shake hands.

"Stick this into Anslem," I tell the guy. "Whether or not you manage to take him hostage."

Loftus nods, pockets the thorn, and struts off, cocky and sure of himself, with his thumbs hooked into his belt. Kind of pathetic. He doesn't know he's marching to his death. At first I feel sad and sick. But then I get my head straight. What the hell, if he dies, he dies. This is business.

I uvvy Kayla and tell her I'm going to be stuck in San Francisco all night. She's disappointed, but I've stayed out on jobs before. She curious what I'm doing.

"Top Party stuff," I say. "And I can't tell you the rest."

"Why not?"

"You don't want to know. Trust me." The word *trust* grates. I grope for a different topic. "I have some spare time downtown right now. You want me to check by the Mixed Bag gallery for you?"

"Moving right along, huh?" Kayla's voice is small. "Changing the subject. Okay, yeah, visit the gallery. That would be nice. Stream me some video." Her volume returns. "I'd like to see how my Kayla Kritter Kennel looks. And pressure Jeannie Jone about money. I bet she's sold out the limited edition of my Cawckle Hens by now. Get in her face a little bit."

"I'm your man."

The Mixed Bag is on the second floor of a building on Market Street, a few streets over from Union Square, on a block that remains irredeemably scurvy, a hold-out against decades of civic uplift.

Outside the building some drifters sit on the sidewalk, getting high off their uvvies, streaming black market Ka'adr brainwaves that conk them into epilepsy or catalepsy—sometimes both at once. A known good time. People don't much bother with chemical or biological drugs anymore, as there's so many skanky uvvy highs, most of them free. I'm lucky I'm not an addict. I have enough personality problems as it is.

I go up the stairs to the Mixed Bag gallery, a large open room with skylights and a wood floor. The owner Jeannie Jone greets me with a flick of the restless tentacle she wears growing out of her hip. An upgrade designed and installed by Dank Prank, a top Mixed Bag body artist.

"Yubba, Carson," goes Jeannie. "Where's my darling Kayla?"

"Home in San Lorenzo. Working on that custom order you got her. The British-butler slug for Gee Willikers."

"Ooo. Can't wait to see him."

"I'll tell Kayla. I'm up here for a meeting. Just wanted to say hi. The place looks great."

Right near the entrance is Kayla's Kritter Kennel—a more or less permanent installation of one-off and multiple-copy examples of Kayla's work. I open an uvvy stream so Kayla can see through my eyes. The kritters include Testy Tapir, Assbite Snail, Hateful Porcupine—along with two Nipsy dogs, and a Cawckle hen. Hateful Porcupine nudges Testy Tapir, and the tapir makes this muffled wonderful-horrible scream inside his trunk-like nose—a damp, frantic blast. Kayla has developed a hip, ironic, style of having her Kritters be cute and nasty at the same time.

"Kayla claims the tapir's scream means *Pwease Wuv Me*," says Jeannie, cracking up. She really gets what Kayla is about, which is great. Also I think she's hot for her, which doesn't hurt.

Beyond being ironic and double-edged, the Kayla Kritters are of course alive, and they have uvvies. If you teep with a Kayla Kritter, and if it likes you, it might temporarily take on whatever appearance you want. Conversely, it might do the opposite. Kritters can be perverse.

Another wrinkle is that a Kayla Kritter remembers whatever interactions their various incarnations have had with you over time. Like right now, as soon as the Nipsy dog spots me, he teasingly does his best to remind me of a crocodile, just like the original Nipsy had accidentally done at Sather Gate.

Of course by now Kayla's various editions of Nipsy have done this to me many, many times. It's Kayla's idea of therapy. To extinguish my response. And, yes, by now it's easy to laugh. What else am I gonna to do? Have a panic attack every time I see a croc? I'm over it. Living with Kayla is double plus good for me.

Anyway I'm streaming images of the Kayla Kritter Kennel to Kayla, and she's telling me again to ask Jeannie Jone about money, and right about now I feel the light, suctioned touch of Jeannie's hip-tentacle against my neck—it's wrapping *around* my neck in fact, as if Jeannie's gonna to strangle me.

"Kayla wants you to hassle me for cash, right?" says Jeannie.

"I thought my teep was cloaked."

"It is. But it's never hard to guess what artists are thinking."

"Okay, yeah, I'm here as the tough guy," I say, meaning to keep it light and satirical. "An Illinois thug. The enforcer. The collector. The—"

"Tell Kayla to look in her account," says Jeannie. "I transferred her money this morning. But probably she didn't notice." She shrugs. "Fey sprite that she is."

"Kayla isn't one for keeping the books," I allow. "She likes things that are hands-on. Physical."

"That's why her work is so great," says Jeannie, pouring it on. She knows Kayla's watching my stream. "She brings on the funk. The human juice. She's a rising star. Everyone wants to fuck her."

223

Kayla giggles in my head. "Say thank you," she tells me. I say thanks. Something at the far end of the gallery catches my eye. A ball walker who's half again as tall as a normal one. Somehow I have a feeling it might be useful for me to have a large ball walker tonight. Considering the mission I'm on.

Jeannie picks up on me looking at the ball walker.

"That's Miss Max," she says. "Crafted by rising star artist Phil Bilko. You know Phil."

"Right," I say. "He was down at our house with you and Dank Prank last month."

"Indeed," says Jeannie. "Phil crafted Miss Max by taking a standard ball walker and tweaking her. He's been showing Miss Max all around town. But now he's ready to let her go. It gives you a funny feeling to see a ball walker that size, no? Introduces issues about who's in charge. Could a ball walker own *you*?"

"I doubt it," I say. "They're pretty dumb."

"Miss Max is *especially* dumb," says Jeannie, twirling the tip of her tentacle. "And she always thinks she's right. Which makes a clever point about authority. But some people don't understand jokes. Unfortunately Miss Max got into some trouble—she killed one of the other ball walkers. Phil Bilko retweaked her after that, and she's completely safe now. But people talk, and he's had to cut Miss Max's price." Jeannie names a very low figure.

"I'll take her," I say. "But one thing—does Miss Max have a reset function? In case I want to wipe her memory?"

Jeannie gives me a look, relishing my shady request—and filing it away for art scene gossip. "Ask Phil yourself," says she. "He's here today, in the back, doing some product maintenance. I'll walk you and Miss Max back there."

"The mysterious Carson Pflug," says Phil Bilko after Jeannie delivers me and the ball walker to his lair. He's an alert, dark-haired guy who looks perpetually amused. He has a couple of inert ball walkers lying on a table and he's smoking a Danish cigarette, which is a little unusual—although he does have a smokesucker plant near the fuming butt.

"Thanks for buying Miss Max," says Phil after I explain the situation. "She was a bad girl. But I think I fixed her."

"I'm still tough," says Miss Max, who's a bit taller than I am. She has that spitty, quacking voice that the ball walkers do.

"And the memory reset thing?" I ask Phil Bilko. "I might want to do that tomorrow."

"You're using Miss Max to murder someone tonight?" Phil asks, not quite joking. "A smash and grab? Jeannie Jone and I have been wondering what Kayla sees in you. Maybe it's that cold, gangland quality. Some women find the advances of a small-time crook more stimulating than the deep thoughts of a creative artist."

"What's your problem?" I snap, annoyed. "You're jealous of me? I'm buying an art piece that you and Jeannie can't sell. Kayla and I had you two over to dinner. She thinks you're deep and cool. I'm trying to give you the benefit of the doubt, but—"

"Oh, take the stick out of your ass, Mr. Illinois Business Major. I'm just trying to have some fun."

Phil beckons Miss Max over, has her lean forward, and shows me a special spot on the back of her neck. "For a memory wipe, you teep Miss Max your owner key and press this spot for at least three seconds. I'll give you the key as soon as you pay Jeannie."

"I'll do it now."

I uvvy Jeannie the purchase price for Miss Max, and Phil teeps me the owner code.

"You can go ape with Miss Max tonight, Carson," says Phil. "Reset her in the morning, and nobody's the wiser."

"Later." I'm done talking with this weirdo.

I step onto Market Street with Miss Max in tow. The overgrown ball walker is nominally my servant now, although with kritters you never quite know. They have a way of misunderstanding you.

It's getting dark, and people are streaming past. A guy who's flat on his back on the sidewalk looks up at me and asks if I want to stream a buzz.

"Straight out of Kazakhstan," the user assures me. The left half of his body is paralyzed, and the right half is jittering. He tries to grab hold of my pant leg, but Miss Max nudges him aside with a large, clawed foot. She's rather intimidating.

Tapping into my uvvy, I learn that Loftus is already in Leeta's and Molly's apartment. It's south of Market on Fifth Street, just a block or two from here. Apparently they rode down the Market Street trolley tracks on a giant kritter that's a live sleigh. I wish I'd seen that. Be that as it may, Loftus will be starting his stumble session with them soon, and he's paid Chex the assistant to wake him at dawn. And all the while I'll be getting updates from Loftus's uvvy, about where Loftus's head is at.

"I have to stay up all night," I tell Miss Max. "I can't go to bed. What can we do around here to pass the time?"

"Ball walker fight club," Miss Max instantly replies. Her voice is like a large, talking hand-puppet's.

"Is it near here?"

"Yes. Follow me. I go there a lot."

The armless, two-legged Miss Max strides along Market Street, cuts down Sixth Street, goes into a narrow sidestreet alley, and stops in front of a locked door with light around the edges. She leans back and gives the door a brutally hard kick, as if she actually means to break it down.

Instantly the door flies open and a head like a steam-shovel pokes out. Gleaming black eyeballs. Big, boxy jaws with worn, interlaced teeth. The creature emits an angry roar that shades into a guffaw when he recognizes who's there.

"Miss Max," he says. "I thought they'd recycled you by now."

"Hello, Beet," says my ball walker. "Phil Bilko made me better. Can I get on the bill again?"

"Okay," rumbles boxy Beet. "But don't go tearing off anyone's head—or we hit you with the flame thrower. Who's your date?"

"I'm anonymous," I say.

"A slumming noble," says coarse Beet. "You buy a ticket, and of course Miss Max gets in free. She's talent." He glances at a chalkboard on the grungy wall behind him. "Seventh bout."

The club has a semi-circular combat ring at one end, with comfortable chairs arcing around it in rows. About a third of the seats are taken. It's an early evening crowd. Bettors, toughs, couples, old people, stim heads, touts, and owners. Like me. Small flappies fly around bringing drinks, food, squeezies, whatever.

Miss Max doesn't want to pretzel herself into a human-shaped seat. She gets me to order her a bucket of GroChow. Having inhaled that, she goes to join the twenty or thirty other ball walkers who strut and bump in a group lining the high balcony along the walls.

The fights aren't all that interesting to me. A little like sumo. Two, or sometimes three, ball walkers hop into the ring and butt their heads together. Kicks, great leaps into the air—and toothless bites. The bites are about jerking your opponent off balance, rather than breaking their skin. I don't see any of the ball walkers bleeding—it's like they're made of thick rubber. But alive. A round ends when there's only one ball walker left in the ring. The ball walkers on the balcony create a percussive background music by doing crazy things with their big mouths.

Eventually Miss Max enters the ring. She has a reputation here; the crowd roars. And when her opponent enters the ring, someone calls to him, "Don't lose your head!"

I cheer Miss Max on. She wins her bout by biting onto her opponent's lip, kicking him very hard in the body, and sending him pinwheeling through the air, and into the crowd.

I could have placed a bet on her, but I'm too tired. At this point all I'm doing here is waiting for dawn. And monitoring the Loftus updates that are streaming in—not that his uvvy signals are especially coherent, coming from the deep-teep stumble zone. Eventually I doze off.

When Chex rouses Loftus by crushing his stumble mushroom, Loftus's sudden teep jolts me awake too. And then Loftus smashes the others' stumbles. A bunch of wild shit ensues and, long story short, as the sun rises, Loftus is lying dead in an alley by Leeta's apartment, just as Jerr Boom predicted.

Weirdly, the dead Loftus's uvvy continues streaming data of a sort. I get the impression that his body has been fully consumed by stumble fungus, and that he's an oozing, spore-laden lump on the ground.

"Go get a piece of that," I tell Miss Max, contacting her via uvvy. She's back to hanging out on the balcony with the other ball walkers. She accedes to my request and hits the street. I watch through her eyes as she parp-parps a piece of road-kill-Loftus off the alley pavement, using her long flexible lips, making them narrow and sharp. She stashes the valuable gobbet inside her hollow head.

I exit the club and hire a roomy eight-legged thud-humper. Miss Max trots back from Leeta's alley, and joins me in my rented van. After I get the piece of stumble-Loftus, I teep Jerr Boom for instructions, and he has me deliver the relic to him at the Top Party bunker lab on Van Ness Street.

They're really happy with the sample, and with my recordings of Loftus's uvvy stream. Jerr puts a very large bonus into my account, and he says I should lie low for the next couple of months. I say goodbye and I bring Miss Max back home with me to San Lorenzo.

"What's with the ball walker," says Kayla when we show up.

"Her name's Miss Max. I got her at the Mixed Bag. I needed some back-up for my gig."

"She's tweaked for size," observes Kayla. "Made by Phil Bilko, right?"

"Yeah," I say in a neutral tone. "He says hi."

"You talked to him?" says Kayla, perking up. "He's great."

"I guess. Do we want to give Miss Max a home?"

"No. She might eat my kritters. Or spy on what I do and tell Phil Bilko. He's not entirely trustworthy."

"Phil was telling me that he's a noble artist, and that I'm a cheap gangster," I say.

Kayla laughs and kisses me on the cheek. "That's part of your intrigue."

So, okay, I'll take what I can get. I wipe Miss Max's memory, and turn her over to Mrs. Yahootie at the local country store. Mrs. Yahootie is too cheap to actually pay me for the ball walker, but she gives us a store credit. And I never do tell Kayla the details of what happened at Molly's apartment.

The next day, thanks in part to their access to my Loftus sample, the Top Party launches a nasty information virus called Treadle Disease. It gets into people's heads and makes them act like Treadlers. Fortunately Kayla and I don't catch it.

A few days later, right before the Presidential election, the Finn Junker freals wipe out Treadle Disease. Leeta and her engineer Molly are involved, and that's cool. But Treadle's people find a way to steal the Presidential Election anyway, and now he's slated for a third term, which bums me out, as I hate the guy.

Meanwhile the Finn Junkers have been ramping up their production of psidots—which are a safe upgrade of the stumble uvvy, along the lines of the rinky-dink pirated Top-Party-labs psidot Tweaky Bird that Jerr Boom's been using.

Jerr gets a high-quality Finn Junker version of Tweaky Bird, calling this one Tweaky Bird as well. Hard to improve on a name like that. Top Party buys me a psidot too. It gives me way richer signals than the uvvy, and with emotions in the mix.

The weeks roll by, and I'm sniffing around for a better job. I don't especially like being a Top Party lackey. I'd like to get back in with Leeta. But I can't find her. She dropped out of sight after the Treadle Disease thing. She's not at One Wow anymore, and there's no sign of her at the Finn Junkers.

In December, Jerr Boom finally asks me to come see him about another assignment.

"You in the same office?" I ask. "Just you and Tweaky Bird?"

"I've moved twice," he says. "This new place is sensational. Worthy of me at last. Cloak your psidot before you come."

I find Jerr in a huge empty structure on the old bayside waterfront of San Francisco, near the Dogtown district. He has a generic desk as before, but now it's positioned in the exact mathematical center of an immense ancient steel structure with huge rails set into the floor. Like the world's biggest shed. The heavy-duty rails run out a colossal door and into the bay. Jerr lolls in his comfortable chair, looking tiny as a beetle larva. It takes, like, three minutes to walk over to him. He's pleased with himself.

"This used to belong to shipwrights," he says. "A developer from the Citadel Club owns the property now. He plans to tear it down for condos. Meanwhile he lent it to me, and I tweaked the structural steel to act as a Faraday cage."

"What's my new gig?" I ask him.

Jerr takes a minute to organize his thoughts. Or to pretend to do so. Sighs. "This is ultra ultra ultra secret. Sit down in the chair right next to me."

I take my place, keeping mum.

"Scoot closer," says Jerr. "Face me. Put your head on my shoulder so we're whispering into each other's ears. Check one more time that your psidot is cloaked."

I get into position. Jerr smells bad, like he's decaying. Never mind. "Tell me," I breathe.

"This is for the Citadel Club. An in-group of the Top Party's biggest donors. They've reached a consensus. They want Treadle out. And they've heard Leeta and Gee want to do a hit on him. And they've engaged me to make sure the hit works."

This is deeper and darker than anything I expected. It's like I've been riding in a bathyscaphe, and the cable to the surface has snapped, and I'm plummeting into a benthic abyss where the water is dense, frigid, and utterly black.

"I've been trying to find Leeta and I can't," is all I say. Whispering into Jerr Boom's ear.

"She's underground in Oakland with Gee Willikers, with that biohacker Liv Jensen from the Finn Junkers, and with a torpedo called Maurice Winch."

"What's my role?"

"A go-between. A substitute for me. Like the way Loftus subbed for you at the One Wow session."

"Like Loftus! I scraped a piece of Loftus's brain off the street."

"You won't have that same type of exposure, Carson. And it *has* to be you who talks to Leeta. There's no way she would ever talk to me."

"Talk to her about what?"

"She and Gee are overconfident. They don't grasp that their hit won't work unless they pay off the Secret Service. And the Citadel Club can help with that."

"You're making me the bag man for a Presidential assassination?"

"*You're* not going to be paying anyone. You get Leeta to tell you the when, where, who, and how of the hit. And you pass that info to me. That's all. The Citadel Club tells the Secret Service all the details of the hit, and they pay the Secret Service an enormous bribe—*so the agents will stay out of the way.*"

"They'll take the bribe?"

"The Secret Service brass and agents hate Treadle too. His bullshit puts them at extra risk every day. Everyone wants a nice stable government. Business first. No drama."

"But why do you think Leeta will tell me the when-where-who-how? She must know I'm in the Top Party circles."

"She loves you. You'll be having virtual sex with her."

"I'm married!"

"Who gives a fuck! You romance Leeta. You have an affair with her. Torrid. Once you've set the hook, you tell her you know what she and Gee are up to. And you say you're worried about her. You tell her there might be a way to put in the fix with the Secret Service. You dangle that. You don't push it. You plant a seed. And all the while you're romancing her. Leeta talks it over with Gee and Liv. And then—what we're hoping—she comes back to you."

My head spins. "Is the hit supposed to succeed or not?"

"Are you even listening to me, shit-for-brains? Treadle makes the Top Party look bad. He's a psycho and a moron. Our money guys in the Citadel Club say, 'Rub Treadle the fuck out, and we'll find a way to work with Sudah Mareek.'"

"Who pays me?"

"The Citadel Club pays you, Carson. And the Citadel Club will fund and deliver the bribe to the Secret Service as well. But don't tell that to Leeta and Gee. It might make them uneasy. Let them pay you something, so they can imagine they're in charge, and you can pocket whatever they give you. Gravy. We don't want their money. All we want from you is the when-where-who-how."

"And I get that info by having cloud sex with Leeta," I say, thinking it over. "We never did that at Berkeley. But, yeah, she'll want to. And later, if she ever starts her own company, I'll be first in line for a job."

"Better work than Boom Consumer Metrics?" says Jerr, pretending to be surprised. He laughs. "Good call. I'm going to strike my caravan's tents and erase my tracks in the sand." He gets to his feet. "It's been real."

The Treadle hit goes even better than hoped—by the time Maurice Winch is done, it's a triple hit: Treadle, Treadle's lifebox, and Treadle's clone. Leeta and I pretty well stay out of the limelight, and I end up working for her company Skyhive.

I never do tell Kayla the truth about my part in the assassination, and the presence of the lie casts a bit of a shadow. On the plus side, Kayla gets pregnant shortly after the January Treadle hit, and she bears us a beautiful baby girl in October. But this, too, becomes something between us. My fault.

I'm an only child, and I'm used to getting all the attention, and I'm such a bad person that I resent baby Daia a little bit.

The much bigger problem with our marriage is that I'm meeting Leeta in the Skyhive cloud for virtual sex two or three times a week. Is it that I can't say no to Leeta because I work for her? Not entirely. The sad reality is that I become obsessed with our sessions.

In person, Leeta has never been my type—but in the cloud she's another story. She devises these wild, intense scenarios and I'm seriously into them, which is idiotic and self-destructive—considering that I have my lovely, brilliant, creative Kayla living with me. *And* our new baby!

But over and over, I wrap myself in my pupa hammock, and enact yet another foul, intricate ritual with Leeta. I'm a slave on Cleopatra's barge, a chore boy in a whorehouse, a movie star's masseur. Once or twice we're rutting crocodiles in a swamp. I love it. But after a while, Kayla knows. Wives always know. Kayla is sad and lonely. I hate myself.

Meanwhile, despite all this, Leeta stubbornly refuses to promote me to the kind of top position at Skyhive that I deserve. Every time I ask, she plays dominatrix in our next virtual assignation, and she whips me until I deliciously submit. It's like I'm gorging on spoiled cream pastries that make me throw up. And for the life of me, I can't stop. Time rolls on.

A year and three months after the Treadle hit, in April, our neighbor Mary is dying of cancer. Out of the blue, Gee Willikers reappears, and asks me to arrange immortality for Mary, that is, to give her a psidot, a lifebox and a clone body. So I do that. And then—heartless, degraded horndog that I've become—I try to work some moves on Mary while she's waking up in her hot young clone bod. Error.

The next day Kayla finds out. It's the last straw. She's talking about divorcing me. We end up at the Pot O' Gold bar with Mary and Kayla and Gee Willikers. Gee and Mary have this attack on Skyhive they want to do. This thing about freeing the lifeboxes. I thought I was going to be in on it, but they say I'm not. Mary's still mad about me coming on to her, and Gee doesn't like it either. Self-righteous prick. He's after Mary himself.

Kayla and I go home together from the bar, and I talk to her, and I think I've smoothed things out. We sleep in the same bed, which is good, but when I get up in the morning, she's talking divorce, divorce, divorce.

Hell with it. I call a thudhumper and ride into Skyhive early. On the way, I let Leeta know about my problems with Kayla—maybe there's a way I can work the separation to my advantage. And, still thinking in terms of improving my position, I warn Leeta that Gee and Mary are going to try some kind of Skyhive sabotage today.

Leela isn't sure what, if anything, she wants to do about it. She's seeing a bigger picture. She senses that Gee is onto something new. She uses the word *transformative*. In any case, we agree to meet at the blimp hanger where Skyhive has their server—which is basically a giant loaf of raw dough. We sit off to one side to keep an eye on things.

The way Gee's hack comes down is that he and Mary use a pair of ball walkers to infect the Skyhive server with malware before anyone actually notices.

By the way, one of the ball walkers is that same Miss Max who helped me get the sample off of Loftus's dead body. Not that Miss Max remembers any of that. To her I'm just an unreliable client of the San Lorenzo Country Store.

Anyway, Gee's malware does a number on the Skyhive server. To impress Leeta and look tough, I dive into the cloud and start discouraging client lifeboxes from using Gee's hack to break their service contracts with Skyhive. In particular, I encounter old Mary's lifebox in there. She's trying to port herself from the Skyhive server to freaky Gee's bullshit redwood tree. By now I hate Mary for making such a fuss about me trying to put the make on her clone. I mean, basically Mary is the reason Kayla wants to divorce me. So, okay, I try to kill Mary's lifebox, that is, I try to push the virtual Mary into a suicide bin. But she gets away.

I come back from this escapade and return my focus to my body on the couch in the giant blimp hangar. Leeta is still sitting next me. She's been busy as well, going through the motions of stemming the outward flow of Skyhive lifeboxes by closing down the back doors that Gee suddenly put in. It doesn't seem like she knows yet about me attacking Mary's lifebox, and I'm glad. I have a feeling I'm behaving irrationally, and that I might be making mistakes. All of a sudden everything's working against me and I'm losing control.

Leeta says she wonders what to do next. She repeats that Gee might actually have a brilliant idea for a lifebox architecture. Hearing Gee's name, I burst out with the brilliant idea that Leeta and I should get hold of a large flappy and bomb Gee's secret lair in the Santa Cruz Mountains.

Leeta doesn't like that, not at all. She reminds me that she has a long history with Gee, going back to her and Gee collaborating on the psidot prototypes, on the lifebox, and on the Treadle assassination. For her, Gee is, like, a respected companion, even when they happen to be playing on different teams. And right then Gee calls Leeta on her psidot. Leeta talks to him for a while, with the conversation cloaked.

When Leeta gets off the line, she chews me out for trying to kill Mary's lifebox. Like for some reason that's supposed to be a no-no. Leeta says I don't realize how important Mary is, and that Mary is in fact a key figure for the amazing breakthrough that Gee Willikers is about to make. Mary is going to produce an autonomous lifebox. I tell Leeta to go to hell.

The argument escalates. She tells me I'm an idiot and a used-up sex-toy. I tell her she's a loser and a hag. She tells me she's transferring me to a field office in China, and that I'm going out on a flight tonight. She says I should go home and pack. She says she's got Gee's thudhumper friend Bernardo waiting outside Hangar One in Sunnyvale right now, and he's going to run me home so I can pack, and then he's going to stay at my house until five pm—at which time he'll carry me to a special flappy airliner that belongs to Skyhive.

I say no. Leeta says that if defy her orders, I'll be hunted down and killed like a rabid dog.

And I'm like, "Fuck you very much." But deep down I'm not sure what I'll do.

Anyway, I ride to San Lorenzo inside Gee's stupid-ass thudhumper, controlled by the lifebox of Gee's dead chauffeur Bernardo. During the ride, Gee teeps me and pretends to be friends. It's hard to hold myself back from screaming out my hatred. But I hold back on that, because I'm picking up the vibe that Gee wants to make some kind of deal. Maybe he's going to get me my job back?

No, he's called to buy my San Lorenzo house. Offering a very good cash price for immediate sale. Not what I was hoping for, but what the hell, I'm clearing out of San Lorenzo for good. I accept, we close on the sale, *zing*, the money's in my account, and the deed's in Gee's name. And to be that much more of a self-righteous prick, Gee tells me he's now signing my house's deed over to Kayla. What a crock of shit.

I mean, come on. Yes, by selling Gee the house, I *am* putting Kayla and Daia out on the street. But Kayla's divorcing me, okay? And our prenup says *Carson owns the house.* And the house is worth millions of bucks. So I'm sure as shit going to sell it when I leave.

Kayla doesn't need the house. She makes good money from her Kritters, right? And she's perfectly free to move in with Mary any time she wants. It's something Mary agreed to when I gave her a clone. But now bigshot Gee has to swan in and give Kayla my house. What-fucking-ever.

When I get home, Kayla and Daia are gone. I bet they're over at Mary's, hiding from me, but I'm sure as hell not going to look. Kayla and I are through, and Daia's all hers. Gee's thudhumper guy stations the van by my house, waiting till it's time to take me to the airport. Like prisoner transport.

In the house, I get out my suitcase and start packing a few things. But why even bother? All of sudden I'm crying. My life is shit. My wife and daughter are gone, Leeta hates me, and I'm supposed to go to China? No fucking way. It's close to three in the afternoon. I have two hours left before Gee's thudhumper drives me away. What to do?

As if on cue, a teep call comes in. It's from Jerr Boom, in crypto cloaked mode.

"Leeta fired me and I want to get even," I snivel.

"Tweaky Bird already told me," says Jerr Boom. "Would you like to get even?"

"Big time."

"We *need* big," says Jerr. "The Top Party is looking small."

"What to do?" I ask. I'm flat out of ideas.

"I'm thinking of a takeover," says Jerr. "Backed by the Citadel Club. The big-money group of Top Party donors? We buy Skyhive from Leeta, put the donors on the board of directors, and you're the CEO. A Top Party puppet regime."

My spirits soar. I'll be the Skyhive CEO! "You really think Leeta will sell the company?"

"There's rumors that the old lifebox architecture is going away," says Jerr Boom. "I know this, and Leeta knows, but the Citadel Club guys—they don't know. The change will come in a couple of months, or maybe sooner, Skyhive won't be worth jack shit. Leeta will jump on a chance to sell right now. She'll reap a bale of kale. We'll be scamming the Citadel Club. You ought to like that."

"But Skyhive will still be in business for a while, right? It's no fun for me to be CEO of a hollowed-out shell."

"You ought to have some months of glory," says Jerr Boom. "Or days. Or minutes. One never knows."

I set aside Jerr's saturnine sarcasm. He's already hooked me. "First thing I'll do is to fire Leeta," I babble. "In case she has any thoughts of staying on at Skyhive. Show her how it feels. And then I use Skyhive to do a death hit on Gee Willikers in his dumb-ass cave."

"Interesting lateral moves," says Jerr. "What's your projected time frame?"

"Do it all today?" I suggest.

Jerr Boom snickers. It's soothing to hear that familiar sound. "My dance-card is empty," he says. "Where shall we meet?"

"You should rent a little flappy and fly down to San Lorenzo," I suggest. "I'll be at this local roadhouse, the Pot O' Gold."

"And why do we meet in San Lorenzo instead of in San Francisco?" asks Jerr, like he's coaching me.

"We have to be here so we can do the raid!" I exclaim.

"Exactly," says Jerr. "We're on the same page. I'll wear a special outfit."

I feel a sudden, cringing-rat flicker of suspicion. "What's in this for you?"

"I'll siphon off twenty percent of the purchase price," says Jerr. "What do you think? And half of my cut goes to you."

"Wow. I like it. Thanks. And, wait, the Citadel Club buys Skyhive—*why*?"

"They'll assume they're taking long-term control of the largest immortality-rental company in the world—with unfettered access to the tens of thousands of lifebox minds inside the Skyhive server. They'll set those minds to screwing up Sudah Mareek's peaceable kingdom. People will be begging for the grand old Top Party. They roar back into power, and it's morning in America."

"Good pitch," I say. "The deal could work. And don't forget our death hit on Gee. As long as you're riding down here on a flappy, bring a couple of bombs and a pair of those rail-gun mini-pistols. You and I can take out Gee on our own—what do you say? What a score. Hero time!"

"Very dapper," says Jerr. "Very well thought out. Just what I was hoping you'd say. I'll swing by the Top Party armory. They welcome special projects."

"And maybe then I'll even get Kayla back," I say.

"One never knows," says Jerr for the second time. And ends our call. Kind of pissy.

As a gesture of good faith, and in case anyone's watching, I carry my suitcase out to Gee's thudhumper, and I tell

Bernardo—he's the gigworker who runs this meaty, living van—I tell Bernardo I need to get a drink and to stretch my legs. I say he should wait here. I'll be back by five. He agrees, and I walk to the Pot O' Gold. It's not far.

Jerr looks a little out of place in a country roadhouse. He's heavily windblown from the flappy ride. He's wearing his idea of commando gear. High fashion Italian fatigues and kangaroo-skin boots. And he's brought us that a pair of mini rail-gun pistols, complete with suede, under-the-shirt shoulder-holsters.

We stash our weapons and find a quiet booth away from the door. Aside from Jerr's fashion-designer soldier-of-fortune outfit, he looks pretty bad. He's paunchy and his beard has grown way down along his neck.

"Hard times for the Top Party," he says. "We're out of the White House, and our Senate majority is gone. Donations are in the crapper. Everyone likes Sudah Mareek's logic-and-empathy bullshit. And we can't seem to bribe her. Turns out that killing Treadle was a bonehead move, Carson. A type-two error. And some people are blaming you and me."

"Why us!" I exclaim. "Blame Leeta and Gee. Never mind. Let's talk about our plan. How fast can we buy Skyhive?"

"Theoretically, there are restraints on how quickly one can acquire a company," says Jerr. "It helps that Skyhive is privately owned by Leeta. Also, the Citadel Club swings a big dick."

"What are we waiting for? Do the deal."

Jerr slouches in the corner of the booth and rolls back his eyes like a Siberian shaman in a trance. Wildly unattractive. He's focused inward on his psidot Tweaky Bird. He lets me use my teep to peek over his virtual shoulder. He's huddling with a preppy sim who resembles a woman with black-framed glasses and a bun. He calls her Ms. Sneevely. She reps an investment group called Lyons & Kalish. I try asking Ms. Sneevely what kind of people Lyons and Kalish are. Her glasses blankly flash, and I notice she doesn't have eyeballs.

"Don't bother her," hisses Jerr. "Lyons and Kalish aren't 'people.' They're nodes in a circular nest of borogrove holding companies owned by the Citadel Club. I thought you went to biz school."

"Sorry."

Then Jerr is with banker sims, then with Wall Street regulator sims, and then he's with a cartoon-style Leeta sim. Presumably she's there listening behind the model. She hesitates, pushes the price up, hesitates again, asks for a permanent position as a Skyhive senior strategist—and agrees to the deal.

Jerr grins at me, then goes wild—whirling out contracts and codicils and appendices. And then he circles around to revise each of the docs with each of the reps, and then he circles one last time, getting virtual signatures. The deal is a schooner easing down a shipfitter's well-oiled rails, like the ones I saw in Jerr's waterfront office a year and a half ago.

Meanwhile we two are still in the Pot O' Gold, and I keep ordering us cappuccinos with sugar, now and then calling for shots of brandy. The usual Pot O' Gold flies are buzzing around. The unseeing Jerr finds his drinks by sniffing the air and feeling with his hands. Forty or fifty minutes go by. The table's covered with cups, saucers, and snifters. We're approaching fiscal orgasm.

And now here come those two loudmouths who play in Kayla's band Squash Plant, wearing jerseys and jeans. They're more ebullient than I'd like to see. At one point I paid them to build us a deck, and they have the illusion I'm their friend.

"How does that ugly safari-suit guy roll his eyes like that?" asks the one who calls himself Dick Cheeks. The one with the blonde beard. "Where's he at?"

"Maybe he's streaming that primo Ka'adr brain stim," goes the Latino one who uses the name Joe Moon. "Getting down with his gossip molecules. Right, Carson?"

"He's closing a big money deal in teepspace," I tell them. They stare at me, waiting for a punch line. Like I'm joking. "It's true," I assure them. They glance at each other, doubting me.

"Where's Kayla?" asks Joe Moon.

"No idea," I say. "We're splitting up." The guys look at each other and waggle their eyebrows, as if already making plans. Assholes.

Jerr Boom grunts and snaps back into focus, with his eyes hard and bright as a crab's. "Done deal, Carson. Miss Sneevely is ready to teep you your CEO access code."

"Miss Sneevely?" I'm kind of losing track.

"The rep for the Citadel Club investment group?" says Jerr. "Snap out of it, Carson. Do you want to be CEO or not?"

"Yeah, yeah, of course."

Miss Sneevely teep-connects to me via the tightest of quantum-enhanced crypto protocols, and she puts a Skyhive CEO glyph into my head. It's a geometric shape, like an irregular, many-pointed, 3D star with a tiny cube or cone or sphere on each tip. Too complicated to remember. Worse than *complicated*, its shimmering colors are a form of quantum encryption. Instantly I save it to my lifebox's virtual vault.

"Try it out now," suggests Jerr Boom, who hasn't been able to see my CEO glyph yet himself. "I want to know if it works."

So I place a call to Skyhive. I do it in voice mode so I can impress the others. "This is Carson Pflug," I say as I teep them my glyph. "I'm the new CEO."

"Yes, Mr. Pflug," comes the answer. "What can I do for you?"

"Fire Leeta Patel," I say. "As of now. Revoke her access codes."

"Done, Mr. Pflug. I'll alert Leeta."

"Carson is *El Jefe*!" exclaims Joe Moon. "Stand us a round, dude."

"We gotta go," I tell the guys. "Miles to go. Asses to kick."

"Scary Mr. Pflug," says Dick Cheeks, still mocking me a little, even now. "The five-foot-two tyrant."

"Five-foot-four," I say. "Getting bigger all the time." I lay a high-denomination bill on the table. "Have some champagne, Cheeks and Moon." But even now they don't look all that impressed. Fuck them.

I escort Jerr outside. The rain has stopped, and the light is warm, with beautiful puffy clouds. Almost five pm. I feel like I'm in paradise. Jerr's flappy is up there in the sky, a black dot, slowly circling.

"Give me that Skyhive CEO glyph," Jerr says to me.

"What? Why?"

"You're selling me access to Skyhive, Carson. Informally speaking, that's the deal that you and I just did. Give me the glyph. So I can teep in and issue orders like a CEO. Same as you."

"And my money?" I say.

"How can you not understand this? Are you drunk? Your ten percent is already in your account."

"Oh, yeah, of course."

"The glyph," repeats Jerr, very intense.

"All right already." I send it to him via secure tight-beam quantum-enhanced teep. The same kinky, lop-sided, many-pointed, oddly-tinted, star polyhedron, shimmering with the colors of quantum encryption. "I hope this doesn't reduce my value to you."

"You kidding?" says Jerr. "You're my brother." Big, friendly smile. "And now I'm gonna do you a favor. I'm gonna *enhance* your value. Check out *this* lateral move. Teep in on this call I'm about to make, and save the information."

We stand under a tree as Jerr, very poker-faced, makes a quantum-enhanced teep call to Skyhive, like I did before. "This is Carson Pflug's assistant," he says. "Jerr Boom. And here's Mr. Pflug's CEO glyph." I watch the weird star fly by.

"Very good," says the Skyhive voice. "What can I do for you, Mr. Boom?"

"Mr. Pflug wants to change his CEO glyph," says Jerr. "There may be a security issue. I worry that Miss Sneevely may have leaked. The new CEO glyph will be valid only for use by me and by Mr. Pflug. And the old glyph will be voided."

"Not a problem, Mr. Boom. Please teep the new CEO glyph."

So Jerr sends in a random new glyph that he invents off the top of his head—it's a rocking-chair with lace cushions and flies buzzing around it, and the rocker's slats are, once again, slick with quantum encryption. I get a copy of it too. And after Jerr hangs up on Skyhive, I call Skyhive myself, and check that the CEO glyph works for me, and it does.

"Understand why?" says Jerr.

"No." I'm starting to feel like maybe I'm not as smart as I used to be. Too much time in the pupa.

"You and I have the new Skyhive CEO glyph," says Jerr. "But Miss Sneevely doesn't. And the Citadel Club doesn't. If they want to ask Skyhive to do something, they've gotta go through you or to me. We're in the driver's seat, Carson. Enhanced value."

"Cool," I say, tiring of these fiddling games. "But look, Jerr, you and I still have to work out our plan for raiding Gee's cave. Does the Top Party know where the cave is?"

Jerr gives me an opaque stare. "Depends who you ask."

"Leeta says Gee's got a bunch of hacker-dazzle cloud-worm disinfo bullshit working for him," I say. "She says Skyhive has tried to narrow it down, but their best estimate is a frikkin disk that's two miles across."

"One version of the story," says Jerr. "But here's another. Maybe the Top Party crowd knows different. Maybe we *like* for Gee to think we can't find him. Maybe we have plans for taking him alive. Eating his brain, you might say." Jerr chuckles. "We're picky about who we kill, and how we do it."

I'm starting to get confused. "Do you know Gee's coordinates or not?"

Jerr shrugs. "You're the man who wants the raid. And you have a plan for it, right? Let's see where your plan leads."

"Okay," I say, drawing a deep breath. "Listen up. I *do* have a way for finding Gee. It just so happens a thudhumper van is waiting for me at my house, and it's driven by Bernardo, who's Gee's virtual chauffer—he's the lifebox of a dead guy from

Guanajuato, Mexico. Bernardo knows the way to Gee's cave. So I don't have to give a fuck about your weird mind-games, you asshole. I'll get Bernardo to tell me where the cave is."

"Carson Pflug lays down the law," says Jerr with another of his chuckles.

"Who exactly are you laughing at?" I ask, feeling uneasy. "At Gee, at Bernardo, or at me?"

"I'm laughing because I'm a happy guy," Jerr lightly says. "I like the way you've got our hit on Gee Willikers all figured out. Tell me more."

So as Jerr and I stroll the rest of the way to my house, I lay out my full plan. Then we get into the eight-legged thudhumper van.

"Off to China!" exclaims Bernardo. I see him as a lumpy, mobile face set into a panel under the windshield. "Who's your friend?" the face asks me.

"He's none of your fucking business," I go, playing it tough. "That's who he is. And listen up, Bernardo. We're not going to the airport at all. I want you to take us to where Gee Willikers lives."

"I can't do that. It's Gee's secret."

"What if we pay you a hundred thousand dollars," says Jerr, following along with my plan.

"Gee Willikers has done so many favors for me," says Bernardo after a moment's deliberation. "He's like my brother. He's more valuable than that."

I lose my temper "What if we kill your children and grandchildren in Guanajuato?" I snap. "How about that?"

"Carson will do it," Jerr Boom warns Bernardo. "Carson's a mad dog. Drive us to the cave or else."

Bernardo's face writhes, and he emits a high moan. I wish I could teep into his mind and see exactly what he's thinking. But I can't. He's got himself cloaked, the same as us. This is a bluffing game. I open another round.

"I'd rather not hurt your family," I say, trying to make my voice soft. "We're men of peace. All we want is to talk with Gee. You and us and Gee—we can all be good friends. There's been too many misunderstandings."

"You fucking threaten to kill my grandkids," says Bernardo with a rasp. "I don't misunderstand that, *pendejo*. How about I kill you instead? What if I lock my doors and drive off a cliff?"

At this point Bernardo *has* in fact locked his doors, and he *is* in fact driving very rapidly toward the coast. The late afternoon sky is lovely—pink and gold—but I'm not much noticing that. San Lorenzo is behind us, and we're racing along a two-lane roadway through the trees. The threat is very real. This is shaping up to be a devastating fiasco. I thank my stars that I'm backed up on my Skyhive lifebox.

Whenever I think about my lifebox, I tend to make a certain reflexive teep move. I reach out to the Skyhive cloud and ping my lifebox, which lives in a sim body in one of those ocean-view balcony rooms. But now, when I flick my tendril of teep attention toward my digital soul—well, it's not there.

Leeta must have erased my lifebox after I teeped in and fired her. Whoever or whatever I was talking to at Skyhive must have given her a little time. I'm in a panic.

And now Jerr's about to make it worse. I can sense he's ready to draw his pistol. I glare at him and ever so slightly shake my head. There's no telling what'll happen if we start shooting. We need to keep talking.

"I'm really sorry," I tell Bernardo's sullen face on the panel of the van. "I was hysterical. I'm mentally ill. I don't mean the things I say. Maybe we should cancel this run. Just take me home. Or take me to the airport."

"No," says Bernardo. "You asked to see Gee's cave. You offered not enough money. You threatened my family. You need to make this good."

"More money?" I say to Bernardo. "Is that what we're talking about?" I look over at Jerr Boom and he nods. "A million dollars," I tell Bernardo. "That's how bad we want this. And of course we would never ever bother your poor family. Tell us the location of Gee's cave, and take us there, and Gee doesn't even have to know you helped us. Drop us a hundred yards short of his cave and you can sneak off before we go in."

"Pay me first," says Bernardo.

"Half now, half when we get there," says Jerr. "Has to be that way." He does that horrible eye-rolling thing again, focusing on his psidot. "It's done, Bernardo, half a million dollars in your account."

The thudhumper makes a surprised grunt and exclaims in Spanish. "*De verdad!*"

I guess he didn't expect he could jack us this high. He teeps us a pinpoint-precise map of the location of Gee's cave. It's all good.

"How soon do we get there?" I ask.

"Seven o'clock. It's a rough route. Takes almost two hours. No road."

"And remember to drop us off a little before the cave," puts in Jerr. "Like Carson said."

Jerr and I discussed this point before we got into the thudhumper. My plan is to have Jerr's flappy come and bomb the shit out Gee's cave while we watch from a hundred yards off. Bomb it twice to be sure. Jerr objects that the Top Party wants Gee alive so they can extract his brain, but I say fuck that. Gee has to die.

And then, with Gee dead, Jerr and I can go in, mini-pistols drawn, very macho—and look things over. If necessary, we might call in some remotes run by our captive Skyhive lifeboxes, or call in some Top Party paramilitary. Or maybe we *don't* call in any help. Maybe everything at Gee's hideout is dead by the time Jerr and I get inside, and we root for goodies undisturbed.

Seems like a reasonable plan. Or maybe not. Maybe I'm batshit crazy. It's risky going up against the full might of Gee's intricate hacking. And our driver Bernardo is a loose cannon— why did I say that about his grandkids? And—is it possible that Jerr Boom might be planning to double-cross me?

I wish to god I still had a lifebox. Maybe I do, but it's offline? Maybe that's all that Leeta did. Cloaked the connection. A slap on the wrist. She wouldn't trash my whole life's memories, would she? Shred my records of the hot times we shared in teepspace? Well, duh, Carson, *of course* she'd do that—so that nobody could blackmail her. Especially not you.

I'm finding it hard to focus. Except for connecting with Kayla, everything I've done in my life is shit, and here I am doing a shitty thing again. Dropping two bombs on Gee Willikers. Why? He's a hip, kind, witty genius. Push on, Carson. It's too late to stop.

The drive goes on and on, not that Bernardo is slow. He moves like a long-legged cockroach, picking his way up a primeval slope. Cataracts, giant redwoods, cliffs, mud. We slew from side to side.

"Almost there," says Bernardo at last. "I'll set you down a hundred yards early, and you can walk in I like you said. And never mind paying the second half. *Esta bien.* I don't want your money."

Why's he saying that? No time to worry about it. Jerr's eyes roll. He's covertly reaching out to his flappy and telling her to come bomb Gee. We'll waltz in victorious.

I strain my eyes, peering forward through Bernardo's lurching windshield. I crave the sight of the joyous orange dome of the bomb blast. The chesty thud of concussion. The smoke, and the rain of falling scraps.

Moving very quickly now, Bernardo scrambles over a last boulder and comes to a stop. We're in a clearing.

"Fuck that hundred yards," says Bernardo. "We're right at the spot I told you was Gee's cave. Ground zero."

"No!" screams Jerr Boom. Is this for real, or is he putting on a show? His voice cracks into an operatic higher register. "Take us away!"

Bernardo's face on the panel is pleased. "And, guess what, Gee's real hideout is two miles from here. How you like that?" He opens his door. "Get out quick, *vatos.* I gotta jam, no?"

If the flappy drops the bomb now, it'll be a direct hit on us. Jerr clenches his face, as if he's trying to link to his flappy, but it seems Bernardo is broadcasting dazzle waves that block our teep.

"*Andale!*" booms Bernardo, jouncing his meaty van bod. He raises up high on one side and widens his open doors. He oozes slime from his inner surfaces.

I draw my rail-gun pistol, hoping to force Bernardo to drive us away from here. No use. A nightmarish, triple-jointed arm uncoils from the walls of the thudhumper, and snatches my pistol away, moving so fast my eyes can hardly follow. For some reason, Jerr keeps his pistol hidden.

Bernardo guffaws, whoops, and shakes his thudhumper body like a wet dog. Every inner surface is slick. It's impossible to stay in one place. Jerr and I tumble out the doors and land in a heap.

"Adios, *pendejos!*" goes Bernardo, and he's off down the hill, moving at a lightning clip, nimble as a deer in a thicket.

Jerr gains his feet and heads after Bernardo. As he leaves the clearing, he turns and glances at me lying on my back on the ground. His expression is spiteful, mocking, cruel. He has his rail-gun pistol aimed at me. Jerr knew Bernardo wouldn't take us to Gee's. He's using this as a chance to rub me out—so that he gets sole control of Skyhive. And it's no use trying to run after him, not with him armed.

Hell with it. I'm done. I'm sorry, Kayla. I lie there, finally at peace. The forest around me is rich with life. The world is beautiful. I look up past the redwoods. A dark shape is gliding downward, wings hissing through the air. The flappy. She drops her first bomb.

KAYLA STUX

I feel it when Carson dies. It's not via teep. I just know. I'm in our house when it happens. I'm making spaghetti for my friend Phil Bilko, who's on his way over, and I'm crooning to baby Daia, who's a little fussy just now, and no wonder.

It's like I've been looking out at a night city on a hillside and—*ping*—one of the lights is gone. Carson. I turn off the stove, then sit down and hold Daia for a while, with memories cascading through my head. This is a complicated day.

Earlier in the afternoon I get a call from Gee Willikers. He tells me that Carson's leaving the country for China, and that, to do me a favor, Gee is buying out Carson's deed to our house and giving it to me. He warns me that Carson's coming to our house to pack.

I go over to my neighbor Mary's house and lurk there with the baby. Mary's not home, she's over at Gee's. I'm in Mary's house because I can't face a heavy last goodbye with Carson. I just want him gone.

Watching through Mary's window, I see Carson arrive in an eight-legged thudhumper and disappear into our house. I can't tell what he's doing.

Gee calls me again. He wants to put in a special order for some kritters to be security guards. He says the Top Party is coming to raid him tomorrow morning.

"They want to eat my brain," Gee adds.

"That's a metaphor?"

"Not really. They have this tank at their lab with six human brains in it, linked together, and they want mine in there too. They call their group mind Coggy. He's surprisingly powerful."

"How do you know all this?" I ask Gee.

"A double agent told me. A guy called Jerr Boom. You probably know him."

"Of course." I say. "He's been to our house. Jerr's been making deals with Carson all along."

"Jerr is trouble," says Gee. "And Carson's worse. That's why Leeta is transferring his post to China."

"Fine with me," I say with a sigh. "I think I can make it on my own. Especially with you paying for my house. Thanks for that. And thanks for ordering a bunch of my kritters. If you really mean that."

"Yes," says Gee. "I want a hundred killer Bunter butler banana slugs. As big as men, rearing up from their slug bodies. Soldiers, bodyguards. With—"

"Toxic slime?" I suggest. "Electric shocks?"

"Harsher than that," says Gee. "*Lethal*. Call your model the Bunter X. When one of *these* butlers takes your coat, the coat is gone for good. Get it?"

"Got it. Gives me something to think about besides my marriage falling apart. But, wait, how do I ship a hundred killer Bunter X models to your cave?"

"Just order sprouts," says Gee. "And I'll grow them to full size when they get to my place. If you get the sprouts ready, I can send my thudhumper limo to pick you up early tomorrow morning. *Very* early. Like at one am."

"Is that your limo in front my house right now?" I ask Gee. "Waiting for Carson? Maybe I'd rather rent my own thudhumper tonight. My mother told me not to ride in gangster's limos."

"Fine," says Gee. "Get your own. An off-road model. Top of the line. And I'll set you up with a driver who knows where I live. And, by the way, if you have any kritter-designer friends that you trust, have one of them make me another hundred guards as well."

"What design for those?" I ask.

"Whatever," says Gee. "Something crazy. We'll go surreal on the Top Party's ass."

Baby Daia and I stay out of sight in Mary's house for the next couple of hours. I'm busy with my Bunter X design, having fun with it, kind of chuckling to myself as I make the creature more and more viscous. And meanwhile I'm watching through Mary's window, monitoring Carson's doings.

Around three thirty in the afternoon, he tosses a suitcase into the thudhumper limo and walks toward our village. He's wearing hiking boots and jeans. During the next hour or so, I finish my Bunter X design. I teep the specs to the Phunny Pharm kritter fab. That place is a gem, set amid a clanking wilderness of dead chip labs along the grotty eastern shore of the South Bay, just north of gets-no-respect San Jose.

At quarter of five, Carson reappears, accompanied by none other than Jerr Boom—that very same Top Party fixer who's been hiring Carson for criminal gigs. Today Jerr is attired in—*why?*—a yuppie safari outfit. He and Carson hop into Gee's limo.

I'm guessing that Carson's not going to China like he's supposed to. Disobeying his orders from Leeta and Gee. Doing a weasel routine. The rules are never for Carson. At first I admired his renegade outsider qualities. But by now, everything he does seems cheap and stale.

Watching the thudhumper scamper through the forest, I still can't believe Carson had online sex with skanky Leeta for over a year. Even after our baby Daia was born! And, sigh, I let him get away with it. I have *such* bad taste in men.

It's time to make a better pick. Right this minute! I fasten onto a mental vision of Phil Bilko. My fellow artist at the Mixed Bag gallery. Phil is a rebel without being a sleazy criminal about it. It's more like rebellion is his *job*. He's a career artist, right?

I like the tweaky kritters that Phil makes, also he's funny and kind, and he smells good, and he wants me. I need that. I need for Phil to prove I'm still desirable. And, come to think of it, I have a legit biz excuse for calling him.

I teep Phil the instant that the foul Carson's thudhumper is fully out of sight.

"Hey," I say. "It's me. Do you want to come over?"

Phil checks my location. "You're in your neighbor's house in San Lorenzo?"

"I'll go back to my regular house in a few minutes," I say. "You should know that my husband Carson left forever just now, and that he and I are getting divorced. Upside: I scored the deed for our house."

"Can I move in?" goes Phil.

Typical thing for an artist to say. Sort of joking, sort of not. We creatives are a parasitic, catch-as-catch-can lot. We have to be. Most of the world scorns and mocks us. So, yes, I understand Phil's remark, and theoretically it's funny, but I'm in a tender state.

"Can you maybe think about my feelings?" I say, going emo on his ass.

Phil doesn't miss a beat. "Well, can I at least stay tonight?"

I pause. This *is* why you called him, isn't it, Kayla? To have a spot of fun?

"Okay, yes, that will be great."

"Should I bring food?" Phil politely asks.

"I'll cook!" There I go, playing the wife. People-pleasing Kayla.

"You don't have to do that," says Phil. Not grabbing the bait. Score a point for the man.

"Cooking will settle me down," I say, meaning it. "It'll be nice. And there's another reason I called. I have a client who'll buy a hundred of your Miss Max models. He ordered a hundred Bunters from me a couple of hours ago. Model X. Deadly. I teeped my order to that kritter fab we use? Phunny Pharm in Milpitas. They're growing sprouts for a hundred Bunter X's right now. They'll be ready in an hour."

"Whoa. Slow down. Who's this client?"

"None other than Gee Willikers," I say, quietly proud. "He's expecting an attack from the Top Party tomorrow morning. He's looking to swell his security staff."

"He'll buy a hundred Miss Maxes?" says Phil, thinking it over. "They should be deadly too?"

"Well, yeah. This is for a battle. Give them stingers or something."

"Sure, I can do that. And I'll rush-order them as sprouts from Phunny Pharm like you. Get them done at the same time as your Bunters. Money's no object?"

"Price your work at its true worth, my man. Gee's on a spree. He's the one who paid off Carson so that I get to keep my house."

"Proud of that, aren't we? Maybe I'll stay two nights?"

I let that pass. I'm busy visualizing tomorrow's scene at Gee's. The towering redwoods. The Top Party's subhuman militias and remote -controlled kritters. Versus Gee's home team of forest dwellers. Plus my killer Bunters and Phil's Miss Max mix.

"Why not make your Miss Maxes be all different from each other?" I suggest to Phil. "Like the shapes in a Miro or a Kandinsky painting, bouncing around and all."

Phil emits a weird, high giggle. "And make them small. Like evil pinheads. Sly Miss *Minis*! Sour colors, outré heads and legs. And wait till you see what they do."

"A fine counterpoint to my squad of staid but deadly Bunter X's," I say. "Every single Bunter's skin is patterned with a butler suit, one understands. Starched shirt, gray-striped vest, and a cutaway jacket with long tails."

"It'll be like a manifesto," says Phil Bilko. "The deadly butlers and the bouncing dolls." He pauses. "You and I are going to be there in person for this scene at Gee's, right? Killer clown ringmasters of the dark carnival."

"Yes!" I cry, fully stoked. It's been ages since I had a good time. "I'll leave baby Daia with my friend Sue Ellen Graffiti."

"What kind of name is that?"

"She's covered with tattoos. The old kind that don't move. She's an urban punk from half a century ago. Always stoned, but a total sweetie."

"Solid, sis. I'll generate a hundred Miss Mini variations and teep the wetware designs to the Phunny Pharm. Then I'll hire a thudhumper and I'll pick up our sprouts."

I remember something Gee mentioned. "Rent a back-country kritter," I tell him. "Rugged, spider-style, brutally fast. Gee will cover the fee."

"Nothing but the best," says Phil. His sense of fantasy takes wings. "It's an alchemical marriage, Kayla. You and I will share a long-awaited night of love. Come the morn, our kritters will have gestated in Gee's primeval grove. Ripen and rule, ye eldritch spawn of Lord Phil and the Lady Kayla!"

"See you soon," I tell Phil, well pleased with our conversation. "Bring me flowers."

So I go back to my house and wander around the empty rooms, with Daia cooing in her carrier pack on my back. I'm still thinking about my Bunter X models, and I'm teeping tweaks to my wetware build-file at Phunny Pharm. They aren't going start growing the sprouts for another half hour, so I have time for obsessing on details—which is something I'm all too good at.

As I stalk my terrain, I keep noticing things of Carson's. Annoying. I set to work mounding his stupid crap into a heap in the yard. Clothes, eyephones, pupa hammock, shoes, special crackers, Voozy drink, toothbrush, all of it. Daia babbles as I work.

When the pile's done, I sic the shiteater on it—the shiteater being a vile slime-mold kritter the size of a manta ray. He lives under our house. He looks like a large cow pie. He moves slowly but he eats it all. Daia is scared of him. She starts crying.

Back in the kitchen, I set Daia in her bouncy chair and feed her. Then I sing and talk to her while I do the dinner prep. I don't want her to drop off just yet—I want to save her night's long sleep for when Phil Bilko gets here. Phil and I will eat pasta, drink a bottle of red wine, and fuck like mad. It's been a long time.

Underneath that, I'm wondering about Carson. I hold myself back from trying to check if his flappy airliner left for China. And for sure I'm not going to teep Carson myself. I've permanently blocked him.

It's while I'm starting the tomato sauce that I suddenly know Carson is dead. Fifteen minutes later Gee teeps me on a secure connection and confirms my intuition.

Gee tells me that his thudhumper's driver Bernardo ferried Carson and Jerr Boom to some random spot in the mountains, and that Jerr Boom's own flappy dropped two bombs on Carson. Jerr got away. Bernardo teeped Gee and told him the details.

"But for now we're not telling anyone else," says Gee. "A lot of balls in the air."

"You planned this, right?" I say. "You had it in for poor Carson from the start. I mean sure, he was a jerk, but you didn't have to—"

"I had nothing to do with the bombing," says Gee. "That's totally on Jerr Boom."

"I don't believe you."

"Look," says Gee. "Carson had a choice. He could have gone to China, but he didn't. Did I instruct Bernardo to take Jerr and Carson to the wrong place if they wanted to go to my cave? Yes, I did. Did I tell Jerr to kill Carson? No, I didn't. Am I surprised over what happened? No, I'm not. Jerr's a snake. Why didn't I intervene to save Carson? I was focused on your friend Mary all afternoon. And she and I have in fact been asleep for the last two hours. I'm truly sorry about Carson. But he brought it on himself."

"I'm sure as fuck not using your Bernardo as my driver tonight," is all I can think of, by way of response.

"That's cool," says Gee in a placating tone. "I know a better one. And for that matter, you don't have to come to my cave at all."

"I *do* want to come," I say, my voice breaking. "I ordered the hundred Bunter X's, and my friend Phil Bilko is driving down with a hundred sprouts of his own. It was supposed to be fun. I don't want to sit here *mourning*. I need to get out and *do* something!"

"Bilko's rented a thudhumper?" says Gee.

"Yes. And I told him to get a cross-country racer."

"So, fine, and when you two are ready, you two can ride Bilko's thudhumper from your house to my cave. And I'll link in in a new driver for it. The gigworker lifebox that's driving Bilko's rented thudhumper will be from Skyhive. And the Citadel Club owns Skyhive, so the Top Party controls Bilko's thudhumper."

"Wait, wait. How did that last part happen?"

"Carson set it up, believe it or not. To get even with Leeta for firing him. The whole reason Carson called in Jerr Boom was so Jerr would make the deal for the Citadel Club to buy out Skyhive. And the Citadel Club and the Top Party are pretty much the same."

"Such a mess."

"It gets worse! Not only does Top Party control the thudhumper drivers now, they control a lot of other kritters too—any of them that rent gigworker-lifebox-AI from Skyhive. Which means a total shitstorm coming down. Particularly for me, come tomorrow morning, when the Top Party raids my hideout to collect my brain. I figured they'd be coming in with *some* kritters under their control. But now they'll have a fucking army."

"Wait," I say, ignoring Gee's problem and focusing on my own. "*My* lifebox is on Skyhive. So the Top Party owns my digital soul?"

"Actually I moved your lifebox to my redwood server," Gee patiently tells me. "When Mary and I did that raid the other day. It was Mary's idea. You haven't noticed?"

"I'm not someone who looks at her lifebox very often," I say. "Lifeboxes are more something that Carson was into." I teep a quick peek at my lifebox, and yes, instead of being in a cliffside condo building in Skyhive, it's in a green glow.

"That's the inside of my redwood," says Gee. "So you're cool. Can we talk some more about me not getting my brain cut out tomorrow?"

"Wait," I interrupt. "What about Phil Bilko's lifebox? Is Skyhive going to be controlling him?"

"Well, a *live* person's lifebox can't control them. Free will and all that. Their lifebox can give them advice. Maybe bad advice. But they don't have to take it."

"So Phil's okay?" I say, keeping a laser focus on my personal interests.

"Phil, Phil, Phil," says Gee, kind of chuckling. "Your new project, huh? Well, as a matter of fact, your precious *Phil's* lifebox has been on my server for a long time. Not on Skyhive. A lot of the artists in San Francisco use my redwood server. Ask Phil about it when he gets to your house."

"Carson never told *me* I could be hosted on your redwood," I complain, my voice going high. "And, still on the subject of Phil Bilko, I don't know if he *will* get here. Won't there be evil Top Party thudhumpers coming after him and me?"

"Our friend Bilko's thudhumper is going to have a very hard-core driver," says Gee. "Like I just said. My main man. You can count on him. He's a bad ass."

"Who?"

Gee just laughs. "It'll be more fun to make it a surprise. If you really want to know, why don't you teep in with Phil Bilko and mentally ride along with him for a little bit, Kayla? It'll take your mind off things. And you can show Bilko and his driver how to find your place. I bet you know some back roads."

"I would *so much* enjoy a distraction," I say, my voice barely under control. "And I would *love* to be with Phil."

In my head I ask myself: Am I bad to say this so soon after Carson died? Am I being a desperado horndog? And then I think: *Go for it, Kayla.*

I glance down at Daia in my lap, taking comfort in her presence. She's utterly relaxed. Her eyes are closed, and her mouth is a tiny triangle. She emits a tiny, darling snore. She'll be okay in the crib for half an hour. It's not like I'll be physically leaving my house.

Via my teep connection to Gee, I can hear Mary talking to Gee in the background. She's in bed with Gee and I can see through Gee's eyes. Both their bodies are young. Good going, guys. Sex is the answer.

I tuck in Daia, and lie down on a couch in my living room, preparing to teep out. In my head I still hear Mary talking to Gee. She's worried about a couple of explosions she heard a little while ago. Probably—*eek*—she heard the bombs that got Carson. Don't go there Kayla. Gee shushes Mary.

"So get ready to teep Phil Bilko," Gee tells me. "But first I'll jack up your bandwidth. And I'll be with you two for the first few minutes." He's excited, and he's running his mouth. "Things are coming together," he continues. "My old friend Molly has started teeping me again. She's been in teepspace for eighteen months, hanging out with Metatron. I'm growing her a body in my clone tanks so she can come back. And Anselm and Liv are hopping over from Copenhagen. It's a gathering of the high freal council. You and Mary are honorary new members too, Kayla. And Leeta, if she wants to rejoin the fold. And we'll add in Phil Bilko too. You want me to stop talking, don't you? You want to teep Phil. Yes. Here we go."

Gee links me into a super-hi-res ultraweak wireless channel that I never even knew about, and when I teep Phil, it's like I'm literally inside his body, feeling the man's sore muscles and his warm skin. Grokking his emotions. Hearing the sigh of his breath. I'm waiting to see how soon he notices me.

Meanwhile I look out through Phil's eyes. I dislike the face of the driver on the roadster's dash. Uptight, robotic—clearly an evil Top Party puppet. Through the windshield, I see we're on the traces of the Nimitz freeway, legging it south from Phunny Pharm toward San Jose, going maybe seventy miles per hour. Plenty of other thudhumpers out and about. Phil's still not noticing me. I send my voice into his ears.

"Hi, big guy."

"Kayla!" he teeps, startled. "Wow. You're all over me. So glad to feel you. But—something's wrong? I can teep that you're sad. What happened?"

"We'll get to that," is all I say. "We'll have better security in a minute. But for now I want you to meet someone." And I introduce Phil to Gee.

"I'm going to swap out your driver right now," Gee tells Phil. "The one you have is working for the Top Party. He'll probably try to kill you."

It seems weird and reckless for Gee to reveal this in an open, uncloaked conversation. But maybe it's a strategic move?

Overhearing Gee, the stooge driver takes action immediately. Our cross-country rally-racing thudhumper accelerates to a hundred miles an hour, his legs beating like a wild tarantella. And—*oh shit!*—the thudhumper is heading toward the concrete abutment of an upcoming overpass, half a mile ahead.

"Told ya the driver was bad," says Gee. "I'll fix." And then—

Poof!

The screen with the cold-eyed Top-Party slave blanks out in a flare of light—to be replaced by a dark-skinned guy with a manic gleam in his eyes. Rather than slowing down, the new driver sends the thudhumper toward the abutment even faster. Also he extinguishes all of our vehicle's running lights. And then—

What the fuck?

A weird wriggly lightning bolt writhes out of nowhere and pecks against the abutment of the overpass like a crooked beak—shattering the great block of concrete.

Humongo chunks fly toward us. But the hypervigilant new driver evades them like we're in slo-mo. Our thudhumper speeds unscathed through the overpass's collapsing arch. We scramble off the highway, then patter along unlit side streets amid the hollow shells of dead Silicon Valley labs. We reach the shore of the San Francisco Bay.

"Pray for us now and at the hour of our death, amen," goes the rattled Phil. I can't tell if he's being ironic. "Are you guys still here? Kayla? Gee?"

We reassure him that we are.

Phil jabbers on. "I know you guys streamed this shit, but no way did you feel the lurching around. You'd need a new kind of gossip molecule for that. Next year's model, huh Gee?"

"I'll let Kayla do the talking," says Gee.

"How about the sprouts?" I ask Phil.

"We'll see," says Phil. He activates his Finn Junker psidot's night vision. "But, Kayla, you still haven't told me why you're sad."

"My husband got murdered today," I tell him. "Gee doesn't want anyone else to know yet. That's why I didn't say it when you still had that Top Party driver."

"Oh god. I'm sorry, Kayla. That's—unbelievable."

"The guy who killed him was working with the Top Party," I tell Phil. "My Carson, he didn't have good judgment. He left me today, and then he was trying to do a sly deal. And the agent double-crossed him."

"Shit. Do you still want me to come to your house?"

"More than ever."

Thanks to the night vision, the scene out the thudhumper's windows glows in magenta and mauve. And in the back of the thudhumper, we can see the two mounds of kritter sprouts, swathed in insulating material that looks like foamy chartreuse spit, in the odd colors of night vision. The gently twitching sprouts are shaped like Belgian endives.

Still under Maurice's guidance, our thudhumper goes ambling along the garishly rendered shore to reach a system of raised trails atop the tangerine dikes that divide the salt-ponds that tessellate the South Bay. We scurry along, heading toward the shimmering Bay's far edge.

Gee breaks his silence. "By the way, your thudhumper is named Scuttler, and your new driver is Maurice Winch," he tells us. "Maurice, meet Kayla Stux and Phil Bilko. Have a blast, you three. And again, regarding Carson, mum's the

word. We're working a lot of angles. You guys go on ahead
to Kayla's house, and I'll see you at my place later on."

And with that, Gee is gone.

"We're gonna finish off the Top Party, huh?" Maurice
Winch says to Phil and me. "That's what Gee woke me up for,
right? Judgment Day. I've been zoned-out in teepspace for
the last couple of years. Infinite dimensional Hilbert space.
Learning my way around. Staring at the higher *Sun*. I still
can't renormalize physical reality, but Anselm and Molly are
getting there."

"You're—you're the guy who killed President Treadle?"
says Phil. "And you live in Gee's redwood server? My lifebox
is in there too. A lot of freal artists are stored in that redwood.
I never noticed you."

"This tough nut lies low," says Maurice. "Hey, Kayla
Stux, can you give me ideas about a down-low path to your
home? No huge rush, because for a little while the pigs are
gonna think we died in that overpass blast. But I do like to
play it safe."

"Everyone knows *that*," says Phil, kind of laughing. "Maurice Winch is all about playing it safe."

"Where did the lightning bolt come from?" I ask.

"Metatron," says Maurice. "She's a higher being that we
have on our side. Lives in teepspace. She's not like a person
at all. When you see her, she might look like a zillion-legged
Vietnamese dragon. Or like a World War II bomber plane.
She looks like what you think she looks like. That's part of
the perceptual teepspace thing. Molly Santos is riding Metatron now. Molly's my pal. She knows how to ask Metatron
for lightning bolts. Which comes in handy."

"Remind me who Molly is," I say.

"Molly Santos is the one who wiped out Treadle Disease the week before Treadle's rigged election," says Phil
Bilko. "Molly is considered a goddess in Oakland now. Not
as a metaphor. For real. People pray to her, and they see her
in their dreams."

"Why don't I know about edgy things like that!" I complain. "I live in the woods with a baby and with a man who has no soul and no heart."

"And to top it off, that man died on you," goes Phil Bilko, who's maybe pushing his luck with this remark, but when you're teeped together as tight as we are right now, you can't hold anything back.

"So let me finish what I'm telling you," interrupts Maurice. "Molly's living in teepspace. The Treadlers dissolved her body, and she's got her lifebox in distributed storage, thanks to that Metatron, matter of fact. Molly's my tail gunner on this run, you might say. You're rolling with the high tribe, Kayla and Phil. Folks like Gee, Mary, Molly, and me. Coming home to roost. Buk-buk-squawk-a-roo."

We're nearing the end of the maze of the orange dikes. Maurice flops into the iridescent aqua water. His eight legs churn, paddling us to the overgrown. reedy shore.

"You wanted directions?" I say to Maurice. "That big building a mile to our right? It looks lime green? That's the old giant airship hangar with the Skyhive headquarters. In Sunnyvale. My husband used to work there. Not where you want to be today, Maurice. The Citadel Club bought Skyhive for the Top Party this afternoon."

"Lordy, lordy," says Maurice. "You got me off the bench just in time." He pauses. "What if I ask Molly to blow the Skyhive building down?"

"Not yet," I say. "A lot of good people's lifeboxes are in there. We need to liberate them first."

Moving like a windblown leaf, Maurice skitters across an abandoned naval airstrip and the remains of the 101 freeway—then lollops toward the lemon-hued foothills.

"Show me the way, sister Kay," Maurice continues. "Guide thy humble servant down the paths of righteousness."

I overlay my mental maps upon Maurice's, and we craft a back-roads route to San Lorenzo, with Phil Bilko companionably kibitzing. But by now I'm worrying about baby Daia.

"I have to leave soon," I tell Maurice and Phil. "I'll want to flip my focus back to my house."

"Stay a little longer," says Phil Bilko. "This is such a great time. I'm glad you dragged me into this, Kayla."

"You'll be liking it till they *git* us," Maurice Winch tells Phil. "That lifebox of yours that's on Gee's redwood server—it's up to date?"

"Of course."

"My lifebox is on Gee's server too," I'm proud to add. "Mary Mary moved me there a couple of days ago."

"So fuck it," says Maurice. "We three got nothing to sweat about. Death's not what it used to be."

"Hell, it won't come to that," says Phil Bilko. "Not with *Maurice Winch* on our team. Not with Molly's lightning bolts on tap."

"Yeah, bro," says Maurice Winch. He's eight-legging through the rolling meadows at a very extreme rate of speed. "I'm the hero of this cartoon."

"Here's a question for you, Maurice," says Phil Bilko who is, in my opinion, more relaxed than is at all reasonable, given that *his* actual body is physically inside this light-weight little thudhumper named Scuttler. Not like me, who's vicariously teeping into this from afar.

"Shoot," goes Maurice.

"It's about that Inauguration Day triple hit you did on Treadle," continues Phil. "How did you make Treadle's clone explode? My friends and I talk about that a lot."

"I'm not telling my trade secrets," says Maurice Winch. "I *can* say that Molly Santos and Liv Jensen helped me. And that we plan to do an even wilder routine on the Top Party bunker lab in San Francisco. Gee has a new idea."

"That bunker," I put in. "It's the one with the tank of brains?"

"I thought Mom's Night Out was over," goes Maurice Winch, teasing me. "Thought you'd gone home, Kayla. But, *yeah*, we're talking about the tank of six brains that generates the Top Party's teepspace agent Coggy, who's a weak-ass piece of shit compared to our Metatron. But even so Coggy is a needs-to-be-terminated pain in the ass. And achieving that termination is a part of national hero Maurice Winch's current remit."

"Look out!" calls Phil. "An attack-flappy from the Sky-hive hanger!"

"It's Coggy!" I cry.

"Shit, no," drawls Maurice Winch. "Coggy's nothing like that. Watch me, now. I'll turn on my lights and act all wobble-in-the-ass." He slows down to about twenty miles per hour and activates a flashing emergency beacon on Scuttler's roof.

"Maurice," demurs Phil, tension building in his voice. "I'm not sure this is really such a great—"

"Wobble in the *ass*!" cries Phil, weaving uncertainly across a pasture, walking on five legs instead of eight, thus warping his gait.

I'm still seeing through Phil's night-vision eyes via teep. We're staring at the flappy. It's a glowing magenta buzzard, gliding down and clutching a golden egg in its claws. A bomb like the one that killed Carson.

I scream, and Phil yells even louder—which is maybe the response Maurice has been waiting for. And now, finally, at the very last possible nanosecond, our unseen partner Molly delivers another Metatron lightning bolt and—

Fa-tooom!

Charred fat-crinklings from the annihilated flappy drift by. Maurice turns our thudhumper dark again, speeds on up the hill at a hundred and twenty miles per hour, and switches his communications to a fully-cloaked dazzle mode that, among other things, breaks my teep connection.

Jump cut.

My heart is pounding. I'm on my couch in my tame and well-appointed San Lorenzo home.

I go look in on Daia and she's sleeping on her back with her arms stretched up—like a little letter Y. My romantic meal for two is intact on the stove, if a bit tired-looking by now. I flop back onto the couch, slowing coming down from the staccato, frantic chase-scenes with Maurice. Phil is still out there, in it for real. I count the minutes till he arrives. If he arrives.

And then he's knocking on my back door. Our sly, savage pal Maurice Winch is teep-linked to the thudhumper named Scuttler, who is crouched amid the brush.

"How was the rest of the ride?" I ask Phil as he enters.

"Like staring into a strobe light on an electric chair," he says. "Insane. At one point Maurice exploded an ambulance that he said was chasing us. I'm not even sure if it was. But anyway, right now it looks like we're alone. Here." Phil holds out a paper-wrapped cone. "For you."

"Roses!" I exclaim. "My beau Phil Bilko. In the flesh." Without slowing down, I step forward and kiss him hard.

We sit together on a couch, and Phil says he's sorry about Carson's death, and I begin to talk about it, which is hard.

I have to stop and clear my throat. "This is annoying. Makes me look weak. It's not even that I'm that sorry he's gone. It's more that I miss my early memories about him. My illusion that I was happy. I miss my younger self."

I cry on Phil's shoulder for a couple of minutes. He comforts me, and then we kiss some more. Hungrily.

"Maurice says you and I don't have enough time to fuck right now," says Phil when he comes up for air.

"What? You're getting romance advice from *Maurice Winch*? An insane assassin?"

"He's not insane, Kayla. He's a good guy. Okay, maybe he's a little excitable. And it wasn't me who raised the topic of romance with him." Phil is embarrassed. "After we zapped the flappy and you left, Maurice got thoughtful—even though he's running through the woods at eighty miles an hour—and he said he envies me for knowing you, and that he himself never had a lover, and that he wishes me luck with you, but that, all things considered—"

"You and I won't have time to fuck tonight," concludes Kayla. "I can see how that would come up very naturally in conversation. Especially in a conversation with Maurice Winch."

"He wants to go to Gee's really soon," says Phil. "Maybe you and I can fuck tomorrow morning when we're at Gee's cave."

"Don't warn Maurice!" I say, starting to laugh. "All right, then. For now, we settle for a lukewarm meal."

"I'd like that, Kayla. I'm starved. The food's ready?"

"Put those beautiful roses in a vase, and I'll set the food on the table."

"Our first date!" says Phil, happy to see our scene coming together.

Under the surface, our minds are all over the place, what with the near-death scenes inside Scuttler, and with the worries about the upcoming run to Gee's. But we put on calm faces and play at being civilized, here in this smooth backwater of shared private time that we have. We talk about how we design our kritters, and about the art market, and about how we've been checking each other out at Jeannie Jone's gallery.

But in the end, we can't avoid tomorrow's scene at Gee's.

"Who will we be fighting against?" asks Phil. "I hear the Top Party doesn't have as many foot-soldier militia types as they used to. Their real backbone is the big-money guys in the Citadel Club. And I doubt many of *them* would show up in person to raid Gee."

"Didn't I explain that to you and Maurice?" I say. "This afternoon, the Citadel Club bought out Skyhive for the Top Party. That's why we couldn't trust Scuttler's original driver, right? And Gee figures that for the raid, the Top-Party will be using Skyhive lifeboxes to run a bunch of animals, kritters and clones. To beef up the militias."

"Was it a Top-Party-run kritter that killed Carson?" asks Phil Bilko.

"Not exactly. It was a flappy kritter who killed my husband, yes. But it was run by a guy called Jerr Boom. A free agent. An oily weasel. He used to hang around with the bio biz majors at UC Berkeley."

"Don't think I ever had the pleasure," says Phil.

"I'm not sure what I'll do if I see Jerr Boom at Gee's tomorrow."

"Whatever it is, I'm with you," says Phil. He switches to a fresh topic. "I can't wait to see our kritter sprouts grow. I've never worked with sprouts before."

I pour myself another glass of wine. "It's really too bad we don't have more time."

And right about then we hear Maurice Winch's voice in our heads.

"I'm picking up pig teep, guys. We have to bail."

I'm not exactly picking up "pig teep" but I do hear noises. Mutters and whispers approaching. And I see dim lights. Top Party kritters or militias creeping into my neighborhood.

"Fuck!" I say.

"Fuck later!" says Phil, his tone almost merry. "Grab Daia. We'll head off through the woods. You'll know a way, right?"

"Yes."

Daia stirs and mewls when I lift her from the crib. She has a full diaper. No time to change her. I swaddle her in a blanket and get inside Scuttler with Phil Bilko, and with Maurice Winch still on the control screen. We head uphill through the woods, low and fast, lights out, our teep cloaked with random crackle. Quickly we lose the Top Party posse.

I give Maurice directions. "This way, now left of that barn. Up the hill is a fire road. Follow that to the right. Now down this creek bed toward the San Lorenzo River. Ford the river. Past these falling-apart cottages and across the main road. See the house with the porch by the country store? Daia's sitter is there. Sue Ellen Graffiti. Right, Daia? Sue Ellen will change your di-di."

I tight-beam into a secure teep session with Sue Ellen, begging her to be at her front door. I tell her I'll explain everything tomorrow or the next day or the day after that, and that she should please take good care of my darling Daia.

"All that's fine," drawls Sue Ellen. "But you interrupted a sweet dream."

"Well, this run is interrupting my dreams too, Sue Ellen. But it's worth is. We might take down the Top Party for once and for all."

"You rock," says Sue Ellen. "I'm at my door. I see you coming. God, you're moving fast. And with your lights out."

"Our driver's a pro," I say. "I'm not even gonna tell you who he is. The Ghost of Christmas Past. Here we are! Bye bye, baby Daia. Say hi to Auntie Sue Ellen!"

For a moment Maurice freezes to a stop. I hand off the swaddled Daia to Sue Ellen like a giant loaf of sourdough bread. Daia is fussing a little, but she's not in full bellow.

Sue Ellen cradles the precious bundle, says hi to Daia, slips back into the house, and silently closes the door.

Maurice takes over the navigation now. He's the one who knows where Gee's cave is.

We head northwest from San Lorenzo, angling through Big Basin Park and the Butano wilderness preserves. The cathedral-like redwood groves are dense with fog and mist. Scuttler speeds like a rally-racer, leaping onto boulders, scrabbling across cliffs, teetering along chasm-spanning logs, churning through the muddy burnt-down zones. Eventually we hit a dirt fire road near the still-wooded ridge. Maurice settles the thudhumper into a full-on tarantula gallop.

And then of course a Top-Party-controlled ranger jeep has to give pursuit. And this one is armed with—*why, god, why*—an automatic rail-gun. The bullets *thip-thip-thip* into Scuttler's flesh, not yet disabling him, but the thudhumper's pace grows uneven.

"Kill the jeep!" I yell to Maurice. "Ask Molly to send a Metatron lightning bolt!"

"Need breathing room to set it up," says Maurice. "Need to pull ahead. Be ready, Molly."

He redoubles his speed, traveling at over a hundred and twenty miles an hour. The wet road arcs and curves, and the only thing preventing Scuttler from rolling is that the thud-humper digs into the road's muddy surface with all eight of his legs, or make that seven legs, as the gunfire has knocked one of them out of commission. The ride is wildly uneven. Phil, the sprouts, and I tumble about like we're in a clothes dryer.

We come to a hairpin bend and—Maurice leaves the road and rushes up the side of a really large redwood tree. For a bewildered second I think the side of the tree is a steep road. Sticking to the side of the tree, Maurice turns Scuttler around and waits. We're dark and cloaked. beat. Here comes that ranger jeep, with nobody inside—it's a thudhumper run by a Top-Party-controlled Skyhive lifebox.

Silently Maurice nods his ead—and we hear that old, sweet song.

Fa-toom!

We get to Gee's around midnight. We can see the place from a long way away. Gee's got his lights on, and his cave door is open, and he has a zillion firefly kritters perched on a huge redwood tree—Gee's server, where my lifebox lives—decked out like a titan's Christmas tree, with layer upon layer of branches, laddering seventy-five meters to the top.

Seems like Gee's done with lying low. The game is *on*.

Mary runs over to greet me. She looks like a young saint, in her new body, with a golden disk behind her head. And Gee has retrofitted himself so he doesn't look like an old man anymore. Both of them have that just-fucked glow. Poised, damp, happy. The eternal fountain of youth.

Upon seeing them, Maurice starts yelling. "I wanna body, wanna body, wanna body."

"The return of Citizen Winch," says Gee, as Phil and I escape the confines of the thudhumper. Gee looks at me as if apologizing for neglecting Maurice. "I *could* have grown him a clone at any time, but he was in a teepspace trance. Like a monk on a mountain top."

"In preparation for the cosmic beatdown," intones Maurice from the thudhumper. "I'm a low-rider street preacher. The end is near! Wanna body, wanna body, wanna body!"

"I'll start a clone for you in my tank when Molly's is done," Gee tells Maurice. "Hers will be done in the wee hours, and you'll get yours early tomorrow afternoon. I've still got your gene codes so I'm ready to go. Meanwhile, would you like to use my Bunter butler for a remote?"

"Me be your butler? Are you shitting me?"

"Bunter knows judo. He can shoot a rail-gun."

Bunter himself is standing near us in the clearing, acting British and dignified—to the extent that a giant, erect banana slug tattooed with a butler's outfit can manage that. It's in the supercilious angle of his eye-stalks, and in the wry twist of his slit mouth. He's expressing chilly disapproval.

"Sir, I would submit that I'm not a suitable host for a man of Mr. Winch's capabilities."

"Oh, are you saying a giant banana slug is too good for me?" cries Maurice. "Don't worry about it, man. Not a problem. Tell you what, Gee, I want a piece of that giant blobby kritter in the sky. If I'm running with *that* big mama tomorrow, we'll lay some dark, dark dreams on those Top Party pawns."

Gee nods. "Sure, join my giant, flying amoeba while you're waiting. Good call. Having you back makes a difference already, Maurice. I'm glad." Gee leans back and hollers into the darkness above the twinkling redwood.

"Utila! Send down a pseudopod for Maurice Winch! With a psidot in it. Maurice needs one of your buds for a temporary body."

Utila doesn't object. Easy-going folks, these giant, hydrogen-buoyed, psidot-enriched amoebas. Her descending tendril of slime glistens in the firefly kritters' light. A small red psidot gleams within. The pseudopod feels about and comes to rest on the roof of Scuttler the thudhumper, then pinches off a hundred-pound bud. The thudhumper's screen flickers and goes dark—the bud's psidot gleams with fresh luster.

The bud's tissues flex. Maurice's lifebox mind is in control. The amoeba bud vibrates, producing a wobbly, drunken version of Maurice's strident voice.

"Don't like the dinky red psidot in this thing," gripes Maurice. "I thought I was supposed to get a Jilljill psidot when I came back. Liv Anders promised me that, right before I blew up Treadle's clone, taking out my Jilljill too."

"This little red psidot is just a temp," says Gee. "Something that Utila had on hand. I'll see that your meat clone has a Jilljill, you bet. We keep our promises. Liv saved the gene codes for your Jilljill, and we're growing a new one of her."

"All right then," says Maurice. "Blob Maurice fully is in the mix. I thank you, vast clear Utila, for the bud bod. I'll come hang out at treetop, and we'll plan a savage welcome for tomorrow's puppets."

Abruptly Maurice switches his voice to a shrill, hectoring tone. "As for you, Kayla and Phil—don't you go slipping off to bed before you plant your kritter sprouts like we told you to!"

"What is his *problem?*" Kayla says to Phil. "Like somebody's idea of a Mom. *I'm* supposed to be the Mom around here."

"Maurice is poorly socialized," Phil says equably. "He lacks the sublimation skills of us artists."

"Maurice is right about planting the sprouts," puts in Gee. "They can take six hours to mature. Almost as long as a human clone. I told you I've seeded my clone tank with an egg for Molly? She'll be functional about four am. And Mary will set her up with a halo lifebox. Molly will be a help if we do a raid on the Top Party bunker. Molly's been there before."

"Raising up troops, eh," says Phil. "Any tips about planting our kritter sprouts?"

"Just shove them into wet dirt," goes Gee. "Hey, Bunter! Bring Phil and Kayla a couple of digging sticks! And, Glory and Miss Max, haul those loads of sprouts from the thudhumper to the edge of our creek."

For the next hour Phil and I squat and kneel by a narrow, rushing, mountain stream, poking holes in the mud and planting our sprouts. Helpful firefly kritters perch on our bodies, spangling us with light.

And then at last we're free. Gee's cave is cluttered, almost like an antique store, with paintings leaning against the walls, and overstuffed furniture, and actual Tiffany lamps. But the main thing right now is that our guest room has a door that,

271

thank god, we can lock. We take the precaution of cloaking our teep, just in case Maurice takes it into his head to disturb us. We're wet, dirty, exhausted, and very jazzed about our ongoing adventures. We clean off in the room's shower, dry ourselves, and get in bed.

"Too tired?" I ask.

"No, no," says gallant Phil. "Not at all."

Needless to say, Phil Bilko is not the type of kritter crafter who uses self-designed sex-toys in bed. My friends and I knew a guy like that back at Berkeley. We called him the Sea Cucumber Man, and that's all you need to know.

Phil, on the other hand—Phil is a good man. Slow, savoring, and kind. When we're done, we fall asleep in each other's arms.

At some point in the night I hear a voluble woman excitedly greeting Gee. In my dream I understand that it's the new-grown Molly clone. Fine. But can't she shut up? With great effort, I keep myself beneath the surface of sleep—staying underwater, you might say. I'm not eager to face the new day.

As dawn breaks, it's Phil Bilko who wakes me—with a kiss, and that's nice, but he's all eager to go outside and look at our sprouts.

"Like Christmas morning," says Phil. "Toys under our giant redwood tree, and we're tiny ants."

"Christmas morning with right-wing puppets marching in to kill us," I say, pretending to be crankier than I really am.

"Same as every year," says Phil. "I wonder if we'll eat turkey?"

"Giant amoeba flesh," I say. "Unspeakably toothsome."

It's exciting to be here, in Gee's mad science cave, in the boonies, with our creations growing outside. I think of the legend about soldiers sprouting from dragon's teeth.

Gee and Mary aren't in the cave. I hear them talking outside with that Molly woman. Gee grew her a clone and linked it to her powerful teepspace mind. I don't feel ready to face them.

"Look," says Phil Bilko, veering into the kitchen. "Big pot of coffee."

"Yes."

"And rolls. That is to say, edible growths upon this plant-like kritter attached to Gee's wall." Phil nibbles one. "Puffs filled with, hmm, a sticky substance resembling—" He pauses, repeatedly smacking his lips like a gourmet doing a tasting.

"You look like a fish."

"Notes of sassafras and Dundee orange marmalade," says Phil. "With the smoothness of prickly-pear slime. Try one."

"Sure, fine. We need our strength."

Fortified, we exit the cave door. It's misty and other-worldly. Somewhere above is the April sun. The haze glows. Gee and Mary are faintly visible by the stream. They're the new woman.

"Your kritters!" Mary calls to me. "Gorgeous! And this is Molly Santos. She helped Maurice on your drive."

Molly is an attractive woman with shining dark hair. Both she and Mary have fresh, youthful in clone bodies. Molly has a hovering gold plate behind her head like Mary does. The disk is a new kind of free-floating lifebox that Mary and Gee invented. They call them halos. Everything's changing.

"That was you getting Metatron to shoot the lightning bolts?" Phil asks Molly.

"Riding shotgun," Molly says. She extends thumb and forefinger and mimes firing a pistol. "But Maurice gets the big credit for that run. You'll come to love him. Maybe. Right now he's with the amoeba in the tree." She shakes her head, then gestures at the bank of the stream. "I love your kritters, guys."

The Bunter X models and the Miss Minis sway at the side of the rocky, rushing creek—two hundred strong, wonderfully various, and coming to life as we watch. Uprooting themselves from the mud, stretching and bending, nudging each other, teeping with their pre-installed psidots. Recognizing Phil Bilko and me as their creators, they hail us.

From the outside, the Bunter X's look much like the original Bunter butler, but they have significant differences on the inside.

"Don't bite anyone till I say," I tell them. "But be imposing. And don't go too far away."

"You're beautiful," Phil tells his Miss Mini kritters. "And don't you attack too early either."

The Miss Minis don't look very much like Miss Max. They're multicolored, and way shorter than Miss Max, with very small heads. Their legs have curves and zig-zags. The shapes of their heads include cones, clamshells, polyhedra, caricatures of humans, crooked cubes, and of course spheres. They have a disturbing habit of abruptly inflating and deflating their heads.

Miss Max appears in the clearing to greet them, and the Miss Minis boing over to her like a poured-out bucket of coiled springs, doing flips, pulsing their heads, and singing a shrill, discordant chorus.

Meanwhile Molly goes inside the cave for breakfast.

I feel dull for having made all of my Bunter X models the same. They're like banana slugs in tuxedos, as is Bunter, but their slit mouths are quite a bit longer than Bunter's, running down along their sides, halfway to the ground. Also, their upper bodies are stiffer than the original Bunter's.

Instead of dancing and leaping like the Miss Minis, the Bunter X's begin marching around the clearing like a platoon of soldiers. Serious as a heart attack. I call one of them over to me, so I can examine him more closely.

We're interrupted by the pterodactyl squawk of an approaching flappy. With the glowing fog, I can't actually see the flappy, but surely he knows where we are. I hope he's not here to bomb us.

I hear a startled caw from the mist above—and now a resonant thud. More squawking, a sharp crack, and silence. A shiny, lumpy pseudopod descends through the fog, lowering a flappy with a broken neck—and a disheveled little man in a once-dapper safari suit. None other than Jerr Boom. Jerr and his flappy are glued to the pseudopod, or rather, partially embedded in its tissues.

I piece together the sequence of events. Our man Maurice the blob—who's in harmony with the giant Utila amoeba—Maurice got Utila to maneuver herself into the path of the flappy, thereby trapping the kritter. Like flypaper catching a fly.

And Jerr Boom was riding that particular fly. Utila killed the flappy, and now she's letting us decide what to do with the rider.

"Can't believe it's you, Jerr," says Gee, taken aback. "You've got a lot of nerve to show up here, after bombing Carson yesterday."

"I want to make a deal with you," says Jerr, untangling himself from the amoeba's flesh. "Remember what I told you about your brain?"

"Yeah, yeah, the Top Party wants it," says Gee. "A power-up for their sad-ass Coggy brain tank. But, so sorry, I'm not done using it, *duh*. That's one of the reasons we're fighting our little battle today, isn't it?"

"I've got an angle for you," says Jerr. "A *copy* of your brain will be fine. You grow us a Gee brain in your clone tank and pass that along—a cloned brain plus a copy of your lifebox—and then the Top Party is happy. They'll pay you well. Back in their lab, they can use psidot to connect your cloned brain to their copy of your lifebox. A fix-up! They throw that shit into the tank with the six real brains, and it's Valhalla time. Seven Lucky Treasure Soup."

"I'll never do that," says Gee. "Never."

Jerr mimes an elaborate shrug. "Well, then we have to go ahead with the raid. We overwhelm your rinky-dink, Micky-Mouse defense, we paralyze you, and we cut your living brain out of your skull." He lowers his voice and intones, "*You have chosen—path of pain.*"

Gee doesn't deign to answer.

Jerr smirks and rattles on. "We've got a special kritter designed to carry your brain, Gee. He looks like a man with a hinged door on the top of his head. Like a tall, talking toilet. We call him the Frankenstein Brain Fetcher. With life-support built in. Lymph and saline and blood drips. You'll be very cozy."

"You can't," cries Mary.

"Maybe we'll scare up a *Bride* of Frankenstein Brain Fetcher for you," Jerr tells Mary. "And we'll bag your fancy lifebox disk too."

Jerr Boom is so focused on mind-fucking Gee and Mary that he's not watching me. With my teep narrowed down to a single control-ray, I nudge one of my Bunter X models into position behind Jerr. Phil Bilko gives me an encouraging nod.

"Go," I teep to my Bunter X.

In a flash, the Bunter X splits the upper part of his body open to reveal an enormous pair of crocodile jaws. With a snap and a twist, he bites off Jerr's head.

"That's for Carson," I say to dead Jerr Boom. "He was right to be scared of crocodiles."

Huge gouts of blood pump from the stub of Jerr Boom's neck as his body drops to the ground.

Bunter X twitches his jaws, grinding the skull to pieces, working the slurry down into a sac in his gut. The Bunter X models are indeed different from Gee's solicitous butler.

"Wait!" cries Gee. "Bag Jerr's psidot! He's called Tweaky Bird. Tweaky might help us get inside the Top Party bunker."

I like this. "Open wide," I tell my Bunter X. "And no biting." I take off my shirt and stick my bare arm deep down into Bunter X's gut. As I do this I teep around for Jerr's psidot— and there he is, the size of a jellybean, Tweaky Bird, a primo Finn Junker model. He's trying to wriggle away from me. I pinch him between thumb and forefinger, digging my nails into his flesh.

I raise the wriggling psidot to the pearlescent morning light. My bare arm is red with clotted gore. I squeeze him between thumb and forefinger, holding tight, using my nails.

"You gonna help us?" I ask the psidot.

"I work for Jerr Boom," teeps the little slug. "I don't work for you, Kayla Stux." The voice in my head is shrill, small, resentful. Tweaky Bird is afraid. And, who knows, maybe he's sad about Jerr's body bleeding out.

To make things even more graphic, the Bunter X flattens himself onto the ground, opens his jaws wide, and slowly scrooches forward, swallowing Jerr's entire body, inch by inch. The Bunter X is like a slimy, boneless anaconda, engulfing his prey within his increasingly taut skin.

"Jerr's gone," I tell Tweaky Bird. "Get it? I own you."

"No. Now I belong to Jerr's lifebox," insists the obnoxious psidot.

"We want to talk to Jerr's lifebox," says Gee, walking over. "You're gonna help us do that."

"No!"

Slowly, thoughtfully, Gee produces a little tool and begins running lines of sparks along the exposed parts of the Tweaky Bird bean. The psidot teeps such blasts of pain that I have to cloak my own teep for protection. I maintain my tight grip.

"Don't overdo it," warns Mary. "A psidot without a host can drop into hibernation. We need to plant Tweaky Bird on someone."

As if on cue, Maurice the blob plops to the ground. He forms himself into a shape like a transparent man.

"Yo! I'm still in here," vibrates Maurice. The light is refracting and reflecting and lensing all over his body, forming double and triple images.

"Still waiting for your meat clone?" says Phil.

"Yeah," goes Maurice. "In a couple of hours, right, Gee? The true Maurice Winch, OG Edition. I'll keep this blob bud body too, and I'll have a split personality. Hell, I could be an archipelago. You guys know that word?"

"Like you're so erudite?" I snap. I'm still annoyed with Maurice for nagging Phil and me last night. And meanwhile Tweaky Bird is squirming in my grip.

"Show respect," advises Phil. "Maurice is a national hero. And he saved our lives a bunch of times driving over here."

"I spy the stinky isles of the Maurice Archipelago," giggles Mary.

Maurice studies her. "Have we met before?"

"I don't remember," says Mary. "Better reread the book."

"Getting too crazy here," I say. "I need to shower before I do anything else. Take this damn thing, Maurice. Jerr Boom's psidot. Host it."

I hold out the pinioned Tweaky Bird. Without hesitation, Maurice flicks his tongue fast, a really *long* tongue, like a frog's, transparent as snot and—*pfft!*—he captures Tweaky Bird and swallows her down.

"Full integration," says Maurice, wriggling all over. "I know what Tweaky Bird knows. I can go where Tweaky goes. I—"

"Quiet!" interrupts Gee. "Hear that?"

We all listen, straining our ears and our teep. I'm picking up a sound like a beating drum, up on the ridge of the Santa Cruz mountains. Also crackles and caws and dull-witted voices.

"Let's send up some Bunter X's and Miss Minis," says Phil Bilko. "To greet them."

"Good," says Gee. "My animal army will go too. And everyone grab a machete."

The underbrush rustles as our porcupines, rats, and bobcats move uphill, not to mention the birds and the intelligent clouds of gnats. Plus a few bobcats. And don't forget the venomous Gee-linked rattlesnakes! The animals are connected to Gee via small psidots. Some of these custom psidots are so insanely miniaturized that you can only see them under a microscope.

Fifty Bunter X's head out as well, scattering among the trees. An equal number of Miss Minis bounce in the misty woods like sinister, long-legged Easter eggs.

Something very rapid streaks across our clearing; it's like a small pig with razor-sharp tusks. A javelina. They've moved into the Bay Area in recent years. Phil uses his machete to cleave the first javelina in two. It's not actually real, not made of meat. More like sinewy fungus. A tank-grown kritter of some kind. Another razor-toothed javelina kritter appears, and another and another. They're very seriously trying to slice into our ankles. We're hacking at them, and now the Miss Minis and Bunter X's are pitching in. The Bunter X's simply wolf them down whole. The Miss Minis' mode of attack is less direct. I watch one in action. She forces her tiny head down the javelina's throat and abruptly inflates her head, bursting the creature's body like a balloon. It's flesh and fluids are creamy.

We're doing pretty well, but more and more of the Top Party-controlled kritters are crowding in on us.

"Hell with it," says Molly. She makes a magician's gesture with her hands. A porcupine of rays emanates out from her right palm, zapping all the enemy kritters in sight. A brief pause, and then more snapping of branches uphill. That drum beat I was hearing—it's getting closer. For the first time I grasp that we might lose.

"We ought to wipe out the Skyhive lifeboxes controlling these things," says Maurice once again.. "Bomb the damned Skyhive server right now."

"There's a lot of human minds in that server," I remind him. "Gee wants to port them out. But before we can do that, we need to get control of Skyhive."

"What if we move higher up the chain of command?" says Maurice. "Wipe out that Top Party bunker lab in San Francisco. Kill all the lifeboxes on the Top Party server. No need to be all bleeding-heart about *them*. And vaporize that brain-soup Coggy server inside the bunker lab as well."

"I hear *that*," says Molly. "We'll do it like we did when we killed Treadle's lifebox on Inauguration Day, Maurice. We go into teepspace, spoof our way into the Top Party bunker, and I hand you a quantum axe. Should be easy to get in there today, since you've got Jerr's Tweaky Bird. And this time you'll do way more than trash *one* lifebox, Maurice. You'll be like Samson knocking down the temple."

"Slaying the Philistines," says Maurice. "Yah, mon. We'll do it."

"I agree," says Gee. "Absolutely. I've been thinking about a raid on their headquarters. Let's us three teep about it right now, Molly and Maurice. Iron out the details."

But for the moment they're distracted. A swarm of enemy woodpecker kritters is in our grove. It's easy to imagine one of them doing a number on your skull. Gee's teep-linked crows swoop into action, going after the woodpecker things, and when still more of them appear, Molly beams more rays.

Next up is a pack of rabid coyotes. These guys are for real. Not kritters. But the Top Party seems to be controlling them. Our rattlesnakes lash into the pack like hail. But there's some of them left. A bright bevy of Miss Minis dances forth to meet them. The Minis thrust their cunning little heads down the coyotes' throats and burst them—like they did with the javelinas—only this time there's blood..

The slaughter is getting to me. And now it gets worse. Humans are approaching through the woods. Some are Sky-hive-run. Maybe full-on clones, or the lo-fi human-shaped kritters that we designers call gingerbread men. But surely some of them are real, live militia members. Hard to believe there's still people that stupid around.

I spot a trio with two of drums and, oh no, a fife. That old 1776 routine, hijacked by the worst people in the world. The fife-player aims his instrument to send a burst of flechettes whizzing through our clearing. Trying to get a handle on these guys, I use my tradecraft trade to probe them, and, wow, their bodies are high-end human clones, and they're being run by, get this, three Citadel Club bankers. A day of slumming and hunting for the nanopercenters.

"Call in Utila!" Maurice the blob is yelling to Gee.

The great amoeba of the treetops flattens herself and undulates like giant quilt, riding beneath her great, rolling blanket of hydrogen foam, making her way a quarter of a mile uphill. She tether's her main mass to a redwood with the hydrogen foam on top, and lets a quarter of her body go to pieces. Lumps of her flesh shower down on the Top Party's kritters, and on the nanopercenter-run clones, and the on cheap-o gingerbread men run by middle-class guys with a grudge, and the sprinkling of bona fide wacko human militia members. The Utila lumps are autonomous fighters. They slime onto the invaders, smothering some of them, and using sinewy pseudopods to pinch others in half. Bodies thrash, branches snap.

The drums, thank god, burst with a pop. And the fife trails off in a rising squeal. The nanopercenter's pseudo-patriot clones are dead. Too bad I can't work upstream to scramble their lifeboxes. Well—lacking that, maybe one of us will find a way to take Citadel Club's money away—for that is their true life's blood.

During the whole battle, Maurice has been staring silently into space.

"You're driving those pieces of Utila?" I ask him now.

"Yeah," he negligently says, sort of hiding his pride. "Gee's doing it too. We're not exactly puppeteering them. More like suggesting targets. The Utila blobs have some decent AI in their psidots."

The noises from uphill die down.

"And now Utila gets it back together," says Gee.

The central blob of the amoeba lowers strands to the scattered lumps of her flesh below. With adept shudders, the lumps work their way up the strands and merge into the single mothership amoeba, restoring her to a mighty, foam-capped, psidot-studded mass. Our friend Utila. She drifts back our way.

"There's gonna be a twenty minute lull," Gee predicts. "Then comes their second wave."

"I'm still asking why the fuck we can't stop the Sky-hive lifeboxes from organizing these attacks?" Maurice asks Gee. "Kayla says some bullshit about not wanting to hurt so many innocent lifeboxes? When they're doing their best to exterminate us?"

"Mass euthanasia would be bad press," says Gee. "And that's not who we *are*. We need the public behind us. And believe me, I'm trying to figure out how to hack into Skyhive and get control. But it's tricky, with Carson and Jerr Boom dead. They were the only ones who knew the quantum-encrypted CEO glyph. I bet it's stored somewhere else. And I'm looking for it. But meanwhile, yeah, Maurice. We'll go with that plan you, Molly, and I have been teeping about."

"Cut the head off the snake," says Maurice. "Destroy every iota of the Top Party bunker lab. Do it now."

Gee nods. "You and Molly should leave in a few minutes."

"Can I come along?" I say. "I mean via teep?"

"We *will* want you on the bunker run, Kayla," says Gee. "But physically. Teep won't cut it."

"What's wrong with teep?" I ask, feeling uneasy. "Why can't the whole read be teep?"

"Maurice sent some probe signals just now," says Gee. "The Top Party guys are skittish. They recognized Tweaky Bird just fine, but they won't let her in. It's not that they know Jerr Boom is dead. I patched in a spoof that makes it look as if Jerr's resting in his apartment. Lying low. The reason they're blocking Tweaky Bird is because they're not letting in any teep at all. They know they're stirring up a shitstorm by raiding me, and they're expecting payback. And therefore—"

"It's cute when Gee gets all logical," interrupts Mary, kind of laughing at Gee. "The professor."

"Gee and Molly and I worked the plan out just now," says Maurice. "With teep. It's time to go."

"You'll need to physically break into the bunker," Gee calmly adds. "I've seen this coming for several days. And I made a funny little bunch of kritters that are just the thing. I'll be asking you to deploy them for us, Kayla."

"Wait, wait," I say, trying to catch up. "We're supposed to go to San Francisco? From here in the woods, that's a two-hour drive. The Top Party will have trashed you, your cave, and your server by then."

"You and me and Molly will *fly* to San Francisco," Maurice tells me. "Incognito. You can wear some make-up for once in your life, Kayla. Like a disguise. And they won't recognize Molly and me because we're young, healthy clones."

"You're made of *snot*," I yell at Maurice, foolishly annoyed by his dig. "You're not a clone at all."

"I have Maurice's meat clone ready now," says Gee. "Just the way he wanted."

"I'll run and fetch it," says Mary. "You'll *like* Maurice's clone, Kayla. He's hot."

"Will you come to San Francisco with me?" I ask Phil.

"I'm supposed to stay here and herd our kritters," says Phil. "Hold the fort for as long as I can." He pauses, then asks, "Aren't you going to take a shower?"

"Everyone's picking on me!" I exclaim. But now I look down at myself. *Er*, yeah.

Trembling with haste, I shed my bloody, gory clothes that have gobbets of Jerr's brain tissue on them. Rush into the cave and shower. Slap on grody old lipstick and rouge from the bathroom, laying it on thick. And fumble myself into some of Mary's clothes—stretch jeans and a black sweatshirt with side pockets.

While I'm doing this, I teep Sue Ellen Graffiti to see if Baby Daia is okay. Sue Ellen is calm, and Daia is cheerily babbling in the background. I'm suffused with guilt, anxiety, yearning.

Why am I racing off to San Francisco with—what did I call Maurice Winch yesterday—*an insane assassin*? But I have no choice. By now I'm a known Top Party enemy. If we lose this fight, they might well execute me.

As I exit the cave I bump into Mary, who's leading Maurice's fresh clone. The clone is expressionless, kind of shambling along. Not attractive at all.

"Check out the Jilljill," says Gee, pointing out the psidot on the clone. A chic, shiny, psidot, yellow with red pinstripes. "As advertised."

And as we step into the open air, Maurice the blob cries out with joy at the sight of his new Jilljill psidot, not to mention the sight of his clone. He links in immediately . What a difference this makes to the clone's demeanor. Like a light turning on. Clone Maurice is *totally* cute.

Meat-clone Maurice runs his finger across the little Jilljill on his neck. "Love of my life," he says, quite seriously. The guy is different.

I hear heavy thudding sounds in the sky. The mist is clearing away. I see giant wings—much bigger than the ones on Jerr Boom's flappy. The final attack? Oh, Daia, Daia, Daia! Why aren't I with you?

"Zap that fucker!" Phil shouts, pointing up at the huge flappy. "Do lightning bolts, Molly!"

"That's Gee's private plane," Molly calmly says. "Pelikaan the transatlantic transport. All aboard."

"One more thing," Gee tells us. "On the way out of here, you should snot-bomb the second wave of the Top Party strike force. They're coming over the ridge from Sunnyvale. They started out at the Skyhive headquarters, naturally."

"I still think we should bomb Skyhive right now," grumbles Maurice.

"Give it a rest," snaps Gee.

Meanwhile Pelikaan folds her vast wings and arrows into the clearing on the open uphill side, totally like a pterodactyl, complete with a long, beaky head that sticks way out in back. By way of halting herself, she runs heavily downhill and part way into the underbrush, digging huge divots in the ground with her massive, clawed feet. She waddles back to us, settles down, and opens a door in her side.

"Like a thudhumper, a little bit," says Gee.

"Who's driving?" I ask.

"Pelikaan drives herself. She's quite smart. Aren't you, Pelly?"

Heartfelt, raucous squawk. Pelikaan twists her head and beckons with her beak, urging us on board.

Still I hesitate. "Won't the Top Party gun Pelly down like a fat goose?"

"Trust me, Kayla," says Gee. "I'm the hacker king."

"But sometimes you fall for your own hype," grumbles Molly, the light from her halo darkening.

"We'll work together," says Gee with a shrug. "I'm just glad you're here."

"And what was that part about snot-bombing?" presses Molly.

"I'll handle that!" says one of the two Maurices—not the new clone Maurice, but the old Maurice the blob.

Pelikaan opens up a cargo hatch in her rear end. Urged on by glassy, lively Maurice the blob, the hydrogen-buoyed amoeba again rains down lumps of her flesh. The glistening and somewhat autonomous chunks wriggle in through Pelikaan's rear door, compactifying themselves as they enter, stuffing Pelikaan's cabin nearly to bursting, with me, Molly, and meat-clone Maurice squeezed up against the front windshield.

"Snug in here," says Maurice. "I like it this way. With a blob version of me in back!"

Pelikaan waddles to the uphill side of the clearing, trots downhill as fast as she can, and, with a heavy grunt, jumps over the first row of bushes, fluttering her half-folded wings at frantic speed, rising slowly through cracking, breaking limbs, catching an air current, and circling into the sky.

A minute later, we're high enough to see the mountain ridge and, yes, there's a host of Top Party forces heading Gee's way—once again it's mostly remote-controlled clones, kritters, and gingerbread men. Plus a few true-blue crazies. Some of them are riding in massive transport kritters—it's almost like seeing Hannibal and his elephants crossing the Alps. One of troops is carrying that stupid-ass Frankenstein Brain Fetcher who's supposed to empty Gee's skull. Top Party fighter flappies rise to attack us.

Molly strobes down a hail of lightning bolts, annihilating the flappies, the transport kritters, the Brain Fetcher, and any of the raiders who looks like he or she might be in charge. But we're not quite done.

"Pelly take a duuuump!" screams clone Maurice.

The rear hatch opens, Maurice the blob leaps out with a cry of *cowabunga*, and the chunks of amoeba ooze out after him, expanding in the air, forming gliders and missiles and wads that rain down upon the kritters, clones, gingerbread men, and militia below. Cue roars of fury from the entitled invaders—followed by shrieks and silence. Presumably the individual Utila blobs will walk or slither back to our grove and rejoin their mother later on.

It's not exactly mass murder, since only a few of the attackers are actually humans in the flesh. But it doesn't feel good.

With powerful beats of her mighty wings, Pelikaan rises to three thousand feet, banks a turn, and wings north. Obviously the Top Party would love to nail us en route, but Gee's spoofing wares are foxing them, and our enemies don't know where the hell we are.

Gee and his allies continue corrupting all surveillance video as we land in San Francisco.

"We'll just blend in," proposes Maurice.

The giant pterodactyl kritter Pelikaan glides down, folds her wings, lands on her feet, and trots to a stop in the center of Van Ness Street. As Maurice, Molly and I hop out, Gee continues real-time-editing any images of ourselves out of the ambient surveillance feeds and, better than that, he's pasting in images of three totally different people walking in the opposite direction from us.

Pelly flaps off, heading for the open sea, squawking loudly, distracting people. Maurice, Molly, and I get to work on that *blending in* part. Molly fake-staggers into a bar like she's a street wino. Maurice and I walk up the block with Maurice's arm around my waist, as if we're tourists on our honeymoon.

My heavy makeup might be helping, and Gee's still doing the video corruption thing. Molly has of course made her halo invisible. In addition, at the retail level, Molly, Maurice, and I are working dazzle into our street teep, that is, we're vibing tourist-type imagery such as a ferry ride, a kiss at Oakland Flea Market, and pictures of our wedding.

"Here," Maurice privately teeps me, pressing a tiny bird into my hand. A feathery sparrow. She's alive. Possibly she's tweaked. "Put her in your right pocket," continues Maurice's teep. "Now put this stuff in your left pocket." He hands me an envelope. It feels like it holds a few little round seeds.

"Do you see that big statue of motherfucking Ross Treadle up ahead?" Maurice continues. "On the other side of the street? It's in a plaza, with the Top Party headquarters behind it? The Top Party bunker lab is underneath the plaza. A bomb can't bust that plaza, not even a nuke, and a Metatron bolt can't crack it either."

"I can tell you're leading up to something," I say aloud, tossing my head and giggling, playing my role of a honeymooner from Chicago. "You bad boy."

People are still milling around and pointing at where Pelikaan landed and took off, but somehow they're too goobed-out or bedazzled to focus on Maurice and me.

"Listen now," says Maurice, kissing my cheek, and switching again to private teep. "All you do is this. Sprinkle some of this food near the statue and let your sparrow at it. The food is six tiny seeds. You want to be well out of the way when your sparrow starts pecking. Don't make a big thing out of it. Toss down the seeds and amble off. Molly and I will take it from there."

"But—"

"After a while, Bunter crocodile," teeps Maurice, and then he speaks aloud. "I'll get us a van to see Chinatown and North Beach, honey!"

With a jaunty wave, Maurice strides into a thudhumper depot, like he's arranging a private tour. I keep walking, not too fast, not too slow, gawking around like a country mouse in the big city which is, sadly, about the size of it. I keep my right hand in my pocket, cupped around the dear little bird. I can feel the shifting of her feathers and the flutter of her tiny heart.

Five big-jawed dog-men stand on the steps of the Top Party headquarters. These kritters are based on pit bulls, with an ugly, aggro, toothy look. They stand erect on humanoid legs, with fur-covered arms and hands. Their tool-laden shorts cover their private parts, and thank you for that.

I cross the street, staring with wide-eyed-tourist awe at the thirty-five-foot-tall Ross Treadle statue. The guards eye me, but—thanks to Gee, my lipstick, and my dazzle teep—the shit-for-brains tweaked bulldogs don't twig to who I am. Just a little ole bride from Chicagoland. I dazzle with thoughts of my black lace wedding dress and my blues-band reception, what a blast.

As I spoof memories of the ceremony, I experience a slight mental wobble, and I flash to imagining another kind of ceremony: Carson's funeral. Not that he'll ever have a real one. He was blown to smithereens, thanks to Jerr Boom and the Top Party. Don't go there, Molly. Think about your wedding. Ceremony at the Chess Records shrine, silk and taffeta, a black and white cake.

Instead of being covered with concrete like you'd expect, the plaza is covered with this stuff called metashell, which is harder than like tungsten, and which has a with a mother-of-pearl sheen. A gleaming gift of biotech materials science, metashell is grown by tweaked mollusk kritters that the pavers push back and forth like mops on a stick, building up layer upon layer of the unbreakable gloss.

I glance up at the bombastic bronze statue of Ross Treadle. Stupidity and cruelty emanate from his face like beams from a lighthouse. The guard dog-men on the steps are shifting, on the point of chasing me off.

It's show time, Kayla. But wait. Something's coming at me in teepspace, totally breaking my concentration. Overlaid on the plaza, I see a ghostly combine of gears, levers, and parts of animals—rising up from the bunker lab below. The thing has cruel, staring crab-eyes. He means to kill me. And *this* is Coggy.

In the distance, I feel Maurice teeping to me. "Use tech moves, Kayla! You can win this!"

And so, I fight a mind-war.

Coggy's structure—well, it's not so very different from the art kritters I design. A 3D collage, a web of chemical reactions, a tangle of gene codes, and the quantum pulsing of teep. I think I can take him apart. Tech moves.

He comes at me, wafting the stench of a senile old man. A pincer reaches for me—I give it a quarter turn counter-clockwise and lift it off. The bushing beneath the pincer is threaded on the outside—I unscrew the bushing. The bristling tangle of nerves inside the bushing's mount? I tug gently on them, drawing out the long axons intact. At this point Coggy tries teep-blasting me with a sense of despair— I capture the blast, invert it, amplify it and—send it back. He convulses in a spasm, exposing the end of a push-in axle at his body's core. Seizing the tip of the axle, I draw it out. Wheels, gears, and levers scatter, revealing an inner wad of tissue like a model of six brains. I kick the cluster as hard as I can. Coggy squeals and retreats.

"*Hurry the fuck up!*" teeps Molly.

Yes. I flip back to the April morning reality of San Francisco. I set my sweet little birdie down on the plaza's gleaming metashell surface. She fluffs her feathers and cocks her head.

Seeing the bird, one of the bulldog guards begins savagely barking. He's about to come for me—but, by god, I'm not going to let him. I fix my stare on the pitbull dog-man. I point at him. I focus the full force of my teep. I'm in a higher state than I've ever been. All the chips are on the table. I push my teep even harder.

The guard's barks die down. He snarls once more, slobbers, and falls still. I stoop. Painstakingly I tip the seeds out of the envelope Maurice gave me. Little round spheres with hard shells. Like shiny pot seeds. Or tiny eggs. A half-dozen of them. My hungry sparrow hops to them—and pecks, pecks, pecks—popping each one.

I hear a faint crackling. The sounds are from the six unknown kritters we just hatched. They're eating tiny dark lines into the Ultrashell surface. Each line a different shade. Growing and spreading to form a colony of cracks. Like they're filling in an image of something.

The bird steps back, cocks her head, and stretches her wings. She's done. And now she's flying off, bless her wee heart.

The hairline cracks cover the entire plaza's surface. And they extend down into the thick Ultrashell material. Six little round eggs have done this. The Ultrashell is jigsawed all the way through, although, for the moment, it's holding together, maintaining its integrity like a windshield's shattered safety glass. Staring at the writhing maze of polychrome lines, I finally grasp that this is a picture. A portrait of President Sudah Mareek! Too perfect.

But, shit, in my fascination, I've forgotten to *amble off*. The plaza is starting to collapse. I pivot, start to run, and— *oh god*—here comes that barking bulldog guard after all, in mid-leap, flying through the air toward me, his mouth wide open in full imbecile death grin.

And then comes a Metatron lightning flash. Fat cracklings drift in the air once again. No more dog. Thank you, Molly.

Meanwhile my legs are autonomously doing their thing. I'm off the disintegrating plaza, and on the other side of the street. My little sparrow is in the sky. Gee and Molly are in their newly rented thudhumper van at the edge of the plaza—fast work, guys. They step out, and for starters Molly stitches out four more Metatron bolts, polishing off the bulldog kritters.

Maurice leans forward and pries a cobblestone-sized chunk from the plaza's shattered Ultrashell. He winds up and throws the chunk like a fastball, striking the loathsome effigy of Treadle directly in the chest. The bestial icon wobbles, rocks back and—oh yes indeed—falls backward—a small payback for Ross Treadle's role in the destruction of the Washington Monument.

"*End of the road, motherfucker!*" screams Maurice.

As the statue falls, it peels a huge divot out of the plaza's cracked substance. Like opening a sardine can. Molly springs forward, holding out her right arm like a superhero or a sorcerer.

Bending over the torn-open hole in the plaza, she pours the full intensity of Metatron's energies into the foul recesses of the Top Party bunker lab's pit, destroying both Coggy and the lifebox archives of the party leaders' brains.

The rip in the plaza grows, with flames and thick black smoke pouring out. Molly and Maurice back away, out into the street, but even now Molly doesn't relent. She's still firing bolts. Sirens wail all across the city. Emergency flappies are sailing in.

For the first time in about half an hour, I think of Daia. I run to join Maurice and Molly.

"Is—is it time to go?" I ask. "And how do we get out of here?"

Molly glances over at me. Her eyes are glazed, and her mouth is frozen in the rictus of a gamer's grin. Still the Metatron energies pour from her fingers.

"Gotta cauterize that wound," says Molly, totally into it..

"Nail it for once and for all," agrees Maurice. "Do the headquarters building too, Molly. Before Metatron runs outta zap-power. I already burned the headquarters down once, you know. Last October. Your big night." Maurice turns to me. "Molly made a sextillion teep calls at once. Talked to pretty much every neuron of every human brain in the world—even hitting some of the neurons more than once."

"I've never been the same," says Molly, still blazing away.

"Sucks to be the same," says Maurice.

"Kill the Top Party," says Molly redirecting her energy stream to the not-so-impregnable-after-all headquarters. "Tear it down." The building shudders into slabs and collapses into flame, right beside the charred, empty, sterile husk of the former Top Party bunker lab.

"Come on, guys!" I plead, taking Maurice's arm. I teep to the newly hired thudhumper that Maurice and Molly were briefly in. It seems like a part of Maurice's mind is already installed as its driver. Agreeably the vehicle patters over to pick us up.

Meanwhile a cluster of burly, angry men are running toward us. Not cops. Top Party paramilitary. The worst.

"You're done!" jeers Molly, and she blasts the ground out from under them.

With main physical force, I wrestle Molly and Maurice into the rented thudhumper.

"Just chill, can't you?" Molly protests. "I'm having a really good time."

And, yes, Maurice's face is on the thudhumper's control screen. We scurry down Van Ness toward the Bay, scrambling right over the stalled, congealing traffic.

And at the water's edge, we find Pelikaan waiting for us.

FREE LIFEBOXES

This is Molly Santos, bringing the story home.

It's really nice to be back in a human body again—a nice, fresh one, not that the body I had before this was especially old. Thanks to Gee and Mary Mary, I've got an indie lifebox working for me now—Mary calls it a halo. I grew it myself and ported my soul code into it.

At first I thought I wouldn't know how to do it, but Mary and her halo lifebox cheered me on. A big part of it was that I sang a special *soul song* that expressed my inner essence. And somehow the song just came to me. As if, deep down, I'd known it all along—which is basically the case. Each of us has an inner tune, forever playing.

My halo is a gold-glowing disk of energy that floats behind my head. It's not a ring with a hole in the middle. A medieval type halo. Call me Saint Molly! By the way, the disk doesn't *have* to glow, and if I want, I can perch it any old place, and wherever it is, it still connects to my psidot.

I've got my same old psidot on my new clone body. My Finn Junker psidot Bibi. Liv Jensen—she's the love of my life—Liv gave Bibi to me when I met her and the Finn Junkers in Copenhagen, a year and a half ago.

A few days after we met came the epic Halloween night when I wiped out Treadle Disease. For payback, the Treadlers infested my body with flesh-eating bacteria. But, like I said, Gee Willikers saved my psidot Bibi, and he's been keeping her in a drawer, in hibernation. Waiting for me.

And where was my soul code in the meantime? In the chaos of that Halloween night, the Treadlers had a good shot at erasing my blown mind by destroying my lifebox. But my superhuman teepspace friend Metatron put my lifebox into distributed storage—so there wasn't any one single target thing for the Treadlers to trash. I'm the first person who ever had her lifebox coded that way. And—it was for a full year and a half.

I'm not the same now. I can renormalize the physical world. But before I get into all that, what was it like, that missing year and a half? How did it feel? *Wak wak wak!* I was a duck in an eggshell, pickled in brine, marbleized into a spacetime hypersphere, microtomed on the bias, and served as Hilbert space sushi. *Wheenk wheenk wheenk!* I was a mile-long sob-story on a roller towel, embossed in Braille by the trip-hammers of my eye beams, and deciphered by fingers on the roller's ends. *Yonk yonk yonk!* I was Molly here, Molly there, yolly Molly everywhere. A background buzz in Metatron's thoughts, a dream within the cosmic Dream, a shoe within a shoehorn, a yonk within a wheenk within a wak within a *huh*?

And now I'm back and I can really shake 'em down. Do you love me?

More important, does *Liv Jensen* still love me? First thing I do when I get back is to teep her in Copenhagen.

"Molly!" Her wonderful voice. Light, throaty, musical.

"I have a body, Liv. I want to hug you."

"You're at Gee's? I'm on my way, chum. Expect me around midnight, your time."

"A flappy can get you here that fast?"

"I'll get Anselm to carry me," says Liv. "That new move of his? Physical renormalization? He says you know about it."

"Yeah—I've been scared to actually try doing it," I say. "But if Anselm really says it's working—"

"Don't *worry!*" goes Liv. "You're safe in your meat. Got any plans for the day?"

"Kill the Top Party! I'm using Metatron zaps."

"I'm with you in my soul, darling."

I ride Pelikaan up to SF with my new posse. It's like an old-time freal scene, hanging with Maurice, and getting to know kicky Kayla. And it's beyond beautiful to vaporize the Top Party's server blob, to exterminate their stash of *muy malos* VIP lifeboxes, to put the kibosh on their cheezoid Coggy group-brain, and to zappity-zap their nasty bunker all the way down to carbonized stone.

"That's what they get, trying to have their headquarters in San Fucking Cisco," says Maurice when we're done. "*Dicks.*"

"We brought them to justice!" says Kayla.

"Guilty as charged," I add.

In my head, Metatron tells me she's out of power for now. She needs a few hours off, and she'll recharge herself from the *Sun*. Metatron means something out of the ordinary when she says *Sun*. She's talking about something metaphysical or even divine—an entity living in infinite-dimensional Hilbert teepspace.

I've seen this *Sun* too, what with my sextillion-fold brain upgrade, and what with me hanging out with Metatron and Anselm in raw teepspace for a year and a half. The *Sun* is the one who taught me how to renormalize the physical world. Damn few people besides Anselm and me are ever going to learn *that*. Wouldn't want them to. They'd fuck everything up.

Maurice, Kayla and I fly back to Gee's Cruz mountains hideout in his trusty transport flappy, Pelikaan. On the way, I teep with Liv again. Now that the Top Party bunker and headquarters is gone, Liv and her gang are doing a push to close down all known activities of the Top Party.

"But it's not as easy as you think," Liv tells me. "Crush the snake's head and the body still wriggles. Skyhive in particular—they're a huge problem, with the Top Party running them."

"Gee and Maurice and I have been talking about that," I say. "Maybe Metatron and I should destroy the Skyhive server in Hangar One. Like we did to the server and the tank of brains in the Top Party bunker."

"There's a still a lot of innocent people's lifeboxes on the Skyhive server. We'd want to move them out of there first."

"I hear that," I say. "Back to the main point—are you still coming to see me tonight?"

"Be there at midnight," says Liv. "I have a new nightie."

How nice. I'm almost starting to relax. Quietly I stare out through a window in Pelikaan's side, loving the ocean and the clouds and the trees. Perhaps this world is perfect.

Despite what Liv says, I'm still hoping against hope that the destruction of the Top Party bunker lab *will* liberate the commandeered Skyhive lifeboxes. But when Pelikaan glides down toward Gee's clearing—*shit*—things aren't going so well. It's that lashing snake-tail thing. A frantic Dutch-painter-style Hell scene. A dogpile of Skyhive-lifebox-controlled kritters, clones, and the cheap clones called gingerbread men. A third wave that we didn't even see coming. Plus at least a dozen hardcore fully human Top Party militia members.

Sigh. Time to deal. Pelikaan, of course, is smart enough not to dump us into the pit—and she's agile enough to feather her wings and hover. The rioters notice us. They jeer, waving pitchforks and sticks and machetes and shock batons. Four guys are setting up a large rail-gun.

Gee, Mary, and Phil are nowhere to be seen, and I can't raise them via teep.

"Phil might be dead!" keens Kayla. "My Phil! And the Bunter X's and the Miss Minis! And Gee's poor animals!"

"I don't see any bodies," I point out. "I'm thinking our guys made a strategic retreat, taking most of our troops with them. And, look, there *are* still a few Miss Minis popping people's guts, and some Bunter X's swallowing them whole. We're not out of the game yet."

"What about Utila the giant amoeba?" asks Maurice Winch. "I can't teep her. And no sign of my Maurice blob."

"Look over there," I say, pointing. "That garbage mound of wet, charred scraps? Pieces of Utila. They must have exploded her hydrogen balloons. And sprayed acid on her flesh? She's being eaten by—what *are* those things? Monster dogs with giant heads."

"Hyaenodons," says Kayla, somehow cheered by their oddness. "Prehistoric mammals. Top Party nanopercenters like the Citadel Club have been leasing Hyaenodon kritters for home protection. A right-wing fad. Phil Bilko knows the guys who make Hyaenodons and sell them. They think it's funny."

"And my blob body?" asks Maurice. "I left him on his own, with my lifebox running him through his psidot. Figured he'd do okay without me focusing on him all that much." Maurice pauses, accessing the memories that Maurice the blob stored to their shared lifebox over the last few hours. He groans.

"Oh lord," Maurice continues. "They cornered him. Closed in. And, *damn*, look at the poor guy now."

One of the Hyaenodons is gnawing at a lump of amoeba flesh that was, just a little while ago, the glassy head of the other Maurice.

"That monster dog isn't studying my info at all," says Maurice. "Just eat eat eat. Bone dumb."

One of the Party militia members rears back and chucks a spear at us. The crude missile bounces off Pelikaan's hide.

"Angry peasants," I say. "Too bad Metatron is flaked out. I'd like to show this gang where it's at. No way they're a match for us."

"I'll get that guy," says Maurice. "I'll teep into one of Phil's kritters."

A Miss Mini bounces over to the militia man, darts her tiny head into his yelling mouth, and explodes his head.

"*Boom*," goes Kayla, and follows that with an unwhole-some giggle. "Miss Max and Glory used to do a *play* version of that game," she recalls. "But these new Miss Minis—very percussive."

"And what about that rapid-fire rail-gun they're setting up over there?" says Maurice. "Let's get out of here. I don't want to be rushing around and personally killing every Top

Party militia member in sight. And Molly's zapper is still out of power."

Kayla wraps her arms around her chest and looks worried. "Murdering people is bad for our personalities. I agree that we should bail. Fly to San Lorenzo. I need to see baby Daia. I'm supposed to be a Mom. An artist."

"You'd leave Gee and Mary and Phil in this shit?" I exclaim.

"They're cool in Gee's cave," puts in Maurice. "I just now picked up some tight-beam quantum-crypto from Gee himself. The man knows how to goob-proof a hide-out, no doubt. The Top Party's gonna dry up like a puddle of piss. Now that we burned out their central nervous system in San Francisco."

"But unfortunately we left the Top Party's control of Skyhive intact," I say. "So we're not done."

"Let Gee fix it all," says Maurice. "Fuck this half-assed riot. I'm hungry. Let's take a lunch break in San Lorenzo."

"*We're not leaving,*" I insist. "We gotta be here for brother Gee. And, come on, Kayla, isn't Phil Bilko supposed to be your new boyfriend? You're gonna throw him to the Hyaenodons?"

"But what about that rail-gun?" says Kayla, pointing to it. "They're going to be shooting at us in about ten seconds."

I make the tough call. "Flap down and kill those guys with the rail-gun, Pelikaan. All four of them. No mercy."

"Good news!" puts in Kayla. "I just checked their teep. They're not actual people. They're Top Party politicians ot on a spree. Bought the clones with campaign money."

"Go get 'em," I tell Pelikaan.

The pterodactyl is like, *swoop, squawk, peck-peck-peckity-peck.* The rail-gun lies shattered beside the bodies of the four lifebox-run clones. Pelikaan pecks the bodies into pieces. And then our large, leathery pal finds a perch atop the stub of a shattered redwood tree next to Gee's server redwood. She tips back her head to swallow down the chunks of human flesh in her craw.

"And they *could* have been people," Kayla says.

"Accept it," I tell her. "We're fighting to survive."

"But what now?"

"We hang here, and if the mob's not gone in two or three hours—well, by then Metatron will have her charge back, and I'll sizzle this crowd like a pan of popcorn."

Kayla heaves a deep sigh. "Well, if we're thinking like that, why doesn't Pelikaan just flutter down and kill all of them right now? Get it over with. And then Gee and Phil and Mary can come out."

"Practical considerations," says Maurice. "Not enough room down there for Pelikaan to boogie. Too close to the tree trunks. They'd swarm onto Pelikaan like ants on an anteater. With us still inside of Pelikaan, you understand. They'd pull us out, and tear us limb from limb."

"So we wait inside Pelikaan up here," I repeat. "And we keep chipping away. Look there, Kayla, one of your Bunter X's just ate someone. The crocodile jaws surprise! Specialty of the house. You're not as kind and sweet as you pretend to be."

"Wait!" Maurice suddenly cries. "Smoke!"

Ow. Somehow we've failed to notice that the militia goobs and the remotely run kritters and clones have been heaping sticks, branches, and pieces of log next to the trunk of Gee's redwood server tree. They're lighting a fire.

As it happens, Mary and I don't really have to *care* if Gee's server goes down—we're clones with next-wave halo lifeboxes. And Kayla and Phil are still in their original bodies, so if *they* lose their lifeboxes in Gee's tree, it'll be easy enough for them to start programming new lifeboxes tomorrow. Gee will survive as well, as he too is in his original body, but he's hella old, and he won't be able to remember half the crap that was in his old lifebox, so his new one won't be as good. But even so, he'll get by. But as for Maurice—

"No!" Maurice is yelling. "No! Not now! Not after all these goddamn hills I've climbed!"

"Teep Leeta!" Kayla tells Maurice. "You know her really well from the assassination. If Gee's not able to wrest the control of Skyhive from the Top Party, maybe Leeta has some ideas. I myself am not going to talk to that horrible woman, but you *should*."

"Yes!" yells Maurice. "Yes, yes, yes!"

A moment later he's teeping with Leeta—but he's so excited that he's also yelling out loud. "Leeta, baby, it's your old running bud Maurice Winch. *Yeah*, I'm back. Who else could have utterly destroyed the Top Party bunker lab? Me and Molly Santos and this wild new talent called Kayla Stux. Teaming up like old freal times. You're still one of us, right?"

Leeta teeps some version of "No."

"Listen to me, will you?" cries Maurice. "There's a few hundred rioters here by Gee's cave. Top Party militia along with kritters and with human clones run by Skyhive life-boxes. And—"

A pause, while Leeta offers some intricate demurral.

"I fully understand that you sold the company!" says Maurice. "Even though, yes, I've been lost in teepspace for a year and a half. Zoned and stoned. I get it that you sold Skyhive to Jerr Boom and Carson Pflug, who were acting as agents for The Citadel Club and the Top Party. But, listen to me, Leeta, I know you've always been into shady shit. You owned Skyhive for years. You must know a sly backdoor way to get in there and turn these rioters the fuck off. Help a brother out."

Another pause. Leeta is still explaining. I have the impression she's annoyed. But Maurice is on a trip of his own. He's having an inspiration. His face turns sly, and his expression takes on a hopeful cast. Like a death-row prisoner overhearing a call about his reprieve.

"I didn't mean to hurt your feelings, Leeta. Shady was the wrong word to use. Wait! Don't hang up. I agree it was reasonable for you to sell. And I'll take your word there's no backdoor. Carson Pflug and Jerr Boom have sole control over Skyhive. Fine. I needed to get that straight in my mind. All I need to do is to ask one of them to turn the rioters off. No problem. I'll do that. Sorry I wasted your time."

Kayla gives Maurice a very odd look, but he keeps piling on the bullshit.

"And listen, Leeta, while I'm talking to Carson and Jerr, I'll make sure they get you hired back at Skyhive. You're my dear old friend. I'll see that you come back on board as Skyhive brass, okay? Senior strategist. Good salary. *Yeah*, I can do that. Maurice Winch is the Man."

Maurice logs off and stares silently at Kayla. The wind is rising. Pelikaan's broken-off-redwood-trunk perch creaks steadily under our weight. The smoke from the fire around Gee's redwood swirls in a thickening plume. Still Maurice stares at Kayla.

"What!" she yells. "What do you want from me?"

"Nobody but us knows know that Carson and Jerr are both dead," says Maurice very slowly. "Skyhive doesn't know. The Citadel Club doesn't know. The Top Party doesn't know. Leeta doesn't know. Gee didn't tell anyone. We didn't tell anyone. All we need is Carson's quantum-encrypted CEO glyph, Kayla. You'll teep Skyhive and use Carson's glyph."

Maurice pauses and points toward the chanting rioters below. Shakes his head in disgust. "Call Skyhive right now, Kayla. *Tell them to turn the gigworkers off!*"

"I don't *know* Carson's CEO glyph!" wails Kayla. "Why would I? I never even talked to him after he became CEO. And he wouldn't have told me anyway. Carson never told me squat! Not jack, not dick, not fuck-all."

"You *do* know the glyph," croons Maurice, making a pass with his hands like a stage hypnotist. "You don't know that you know it, but you do. You were with Carson, day after day, month after month, teeping with him constantly. You've got to know the glyph."

The crowd's noise continues rising. They're united by a single purpose—to burn Gee's server tree. They cheer the flames as if hailing the Golden Calf.

Maurice drops to his knees and clasps his upraised hands, supplicating Kayla. "You *know*. Don't hold out on Maurice. If you don't help, I'm done for. Final jump cut."

Maurice flings himself onto his back and lies there, motionless, arms and legs askew. I'm enjoying the show. I've never met anyone who can lay it on as thick as Maurice. And—as I mentioned—I'm not super uptight about the outcome, what with me having a server-free halo for my lifebox. But I do have a heart. Even after a year and a half of distributed storage in teepspace. Even after a sextillion-fold brain amplification. I'm still human, in a way.

"Let me look into your head," I suggest to Kayla. "Full access. You and I can search together. Like finding a lost button in a big old jumbled house. Maybe the CEO glyph is based on something Carson saw. Some shape he liked. Maybe you saw it too. I might find it. I'm fast."

Kayla sighs and takes a seat on the meaty floor of Pelikaan's cabin. She leans back against the wall, very worldweary and, in my opinion, very hot. Perhaps by accident, she kicks Maurice fairly hard in his leg. We're frazzled.

"All right, Molly, you can help me look," sighs Kayla. "But I don't want Maurice in my head."

"I don't want to go in there neither!" mumbles Maurice, scooting a bit further away from her. "*Hurry the fuck up!*"

I sit down next to Kayla, shoulder to shoulder. I have this odd, inappropriate urge to try putting a move on this overwrought woman, but—no! Liv will be here in just a few hours. You've waited this long, Molly, wait till midnight. Pretend you're a nice person with human empathy. Don't act like a man. But, what the hell, why not at least put my arm around Kayla's shoulders?

"Pretend I'm Jerr Boom," I say as I deploy my arm, meaning the remark as a dumb joke.

Kayla stands bolt upright and screams.

"Jesus Christ," I say. "*What?*"

"Jerr Boom was tight with Carson," yells Kayla. "Jerr Boom's lifebox! Tweaky Bird! Find Maurice the blob!"

"Maurice the blob is fucking *dead*," says Maurice. "We saw a Hyaenodon eating him about five minutes ago?"

"Doesn't matter!" snarls Kayla, leaning over Maurice on the floor and giving him a shake. "Check your lifebox, idiot! Maurice the blob used the same lifebox as you. He ate Tweaky Bird. So Tweaky Bird's info is in your lifebox. Emulate Tweaky Bird to get inside Jerr Boom's lifebox, wherever the fuck it is. Tweaky knows. The quantum encrypted CEO glyph is there."

Something heavy hits me. "What if Jerr Boom's lifebox was stored in the Top Party bunker lab?" I ask. "What if I just now annihilated our only key to salvation by blasting the contents of the bunker down to scorched dust?"

Maurice glares at me with something like hatred on his face.

I hold out my hands and shrug. "Shit happens, right?"

Kayla finds her voice. "No, no, Molly," she says, her volume rising as she speaks. "It's fine. I don't know why I didn't mention this before. Jerr didn't have his lifebox on the Top Party server, or on Gee's server, or on the Skyhive sever. He was too vain and devious for that. His lifebox was on the KGB server in Moscow. He bragged about it at our house one night when he was drunk."

"Score," Maurice quietly says.

And then, for a long, long beat, Maurice is silent, with his eyes closed, and his eyeballs rapidly flicking back and forth. Like he's having a vivid dream.

"Quick and slick," Maurice mutters to himself. "Uh-huh, uh-huh, oh yes. Got it!" He opens his eyes and looks at us. Smiles.

A glyph appears, visible via teep, as if hovering before us. Something like a rocking chair with intricate lace cushions and buzzing flies. Coated with the iridescent gleam of quantum cryp.

"Behold!" intones Maurice, his voice deep. "Kayla, Kayla, *Kayla*! Call Skyhive, baby."

And from here it's an easy downhill stroll. At first, anyway.

Kayla teeps the CEO glyph to Skyhive. They give her control. She switches off all aggro behaviors on the part of the Skyhive lifebox-driven kritters and clones. She divides these becalmed peripherals into two packs. One pack starts trying to drive off the Top Party militia people—not easy. The other pack sets to work putting out the fire—by running a bucket brigade from the creek.

"Let's land now," says Kayla.

"Wait," puts in Maurice. "As long as you've got Skyhive on the line, tell them to hire Leeta back."

"Fuck that," Kayla says in her sweet, level voice. "That scuzzy whore can go to hell." And with that she terminates her Skyhive session.

Maurice looks at me and waggles his eyebrows. I make a calming gesture.

"Later," I say. "Leeta's not all that bad, Kayla. She was a good friend to me in the One Wow stumble days."

"I've known her longer," says Kayla. "I was there when she scammed Carson at UC Berkeley and got him expelled. And later she was having gross teepspace sex with Carson in his pupa for a year!" Her pale face is mottled with anger.

"Sooo—let's land and join the happy throng!" Maurice brightly says.

Heartened by the end of the siege, Gee, Mary, and Phil emerge from the cave, along with a fair proportion of Gee's army of kritters and animals. This fanciful troupe continues the effort to repel the still-lingering militia members, finishes dousing the fire, and scatters the ashes.

And now comes a last-ditch rush by the remaining core of Top Party faithful. True-blue humans like us. They're very seriously bent on killing Gee. Kayla makes a gesture—and her reassembled Bunter X brigade rushes the ragged foes. Moving with inhuman alacrity, the Bunter X's use their crocodile jaws to decapitate the posse's leaders—clones and humans alike. No creamy innards this time; it's real people, all meat.

Luxuriating in the blood, the Bunter X's choke down the headless bodies, gorging themselves, taking on the look of shiny sausages, pulsing with delight. It's revolting. The remaining militia backers depart forever. Thank god it's over. Thank god we're alive.

Gee's foxes, rabbits, bluejays, lizards, ants, mosquitos, and other psidot-tagged animals set to work, clearing away the remnants of the fracas. By now the sky is turning dark, with gilded battlements of clouds.

I'm standing in a group with Gee, Mary, and Maurice. The firefly kritters are lighting up the redwoods again. Across the clearing, Kayla and Phil are sitting on a rock, eating sandwiches. The smell of the fire is fading.

"What's next?" Gee asks me. "What do you do after you win the war?"

"I'll fuck my girlfriend," I say.

"Liv Jensen!" exclaims Gee. "You've teeped her?"

"She'll be here at midnight," I say. "To kick off the second day of my new life."

"Liv can help us with porting the lifeboxes to halos." says Gee. "She always said that centralized lifebox storage is a terrible architecture."

"A flawed capitalist architecture," I put in. "Leading to things like all the Skyhive lifeboxes flipping to the Top Party, and their running-dog rioters nearly burning down your server tree."

"The ports are going to get easier and easier," puts in Mary. "I think the lifeboxes like to imitate each other. They're like herd animals, in a way."

"I hope we can do it all tomorrow," says Maurice. "Before something else goes wrong. I'll get Leeta to pitch in. She knows the Skyhive system inside out."

"She'd work with us?" says Mary.

"She needs friends," says Maurice. "That Citadel Club is super pissed about losing Skyhive. They paid Leeta a lot. They'll want that money back. Right Molly?"

"Biz isn't my thing," I say. "I'm a wetware engineer—halfway to being a goddess. I will tell you this. Kayla is not big on collaborating with Leeta."

"So talk to her some more," goes Gee.

"We'll see."

I walk over to Phil and Kayla. She's exhausted and pale—and she tenses when she sees me. Definitely not the time to twist her arm about Leeta. I have a better idea.

"Let's go get Daia!" I propose. "We'll ride in our spidery cross-country sports jobbie Scuttler! I'll protect you. My pal Metatron is recharged. Anyone hassles us, *fa-toom*."

"I'd like that," says Kayla, brightening. "And, yeah, we'll bring the baby here so I can be in on the big port. It ought to be safe, don't you think? What do you say, Phil?"

"Let's do it," he says. "I can drive Scuttler, if you like."

Kayla smiles and shakes her head. "You don't know how to drive a crazy XC racer through the woods, Phil. We'll ask Maurice to drive by teep again. He's right over there. We'll be back in three or four hours. With Daia! I just wish it wasn't such a long drive."

"I'll get Scuttler," says Phil, and walks toward the stream. The little thudhumper has been resting by the creek, staying clear of the long day's battles, letting his injured leg heal. Recognizing Phil, he trots over to us in the dark.

"Scuttler at your service," says the spider roadster.

I teep into Phil's mind as he perches on Scuttler's hood and leans back, looking up through the tall, twinkling trees, with stars beginning to show in the sky above. The creek babbles. The moist scent of the forest is all around. Phil's a good guy. I enjoy sharing his moment of calm after this long, crazy day. And I'm not looking forward to the long drive any more than Kayla is.

An idea pops into my head, inspired by what Liv said about how she plans to get here tonight. "It's possible to change your point of view in physical space," I tell Kayla. "Renormalization. Anselm and I learned how this year."

"That's nice," says Kayla, who has no idea what I'm talking about. "Let's get Maurice to drive," she repeats. "Like before."

"Hold on," I say. "Let's you and I sit down in Scuttler and talk this over." In my head I'm teeping with Metatron and Anselm. They're giving me tips.

"I'm all for sitting down," says Kayla, yawning as we settle into the roadster. "But talking—not so much. I'm fried. I'm planning to nap on the way to San Lorenzo. Go ask Maurice, Molly. You're his big friend We need to hit the road."

But my new plan is in flow. I see a glow around my fingers. My halo is humming. The trees tilt away. The velvety night grows.

"We won't need Maurice," I say.

"Who's gonna drive?" says Kayla.

"We're not actually going to *drive*," I say. "Stand aside, Phil."

I renormalize the physical world—*dzeent*—and we're parked in front of the home of Sue Ellen Graffiti and Mrs. Yahootie, right behind the San Lorenzo Country Store. Really it's quite a simple thing.

Kayla is dumbstruck. "How did you do that, Molly?"

"I know how from living in teepspace for so long," I say. "And, like I said, Anselm can do it too."

"You can teleport!" exclaims Kayla, hopping out of Scuttler. "I need to hear more. But first we get baby Daia."

I'm stuck in explanation mode. "When you're in teepspace, you experience different phenomenologies," I continue. I've been picking up lingo from Anselm. "You grasp that the structure of reality is subjective, so—"

Kayla screams. A sly, bent figure hurries out the side door of Mrs. Yahootie's tidy, dimly-lit house, carrying a bundled up—

"Daia!" I yell, and I go *dzeent*, and, just like that, I've renormalized my way across the moonlit lawn and into the path of the kidnapper. His face is clear in the glow of my halo and—

Oh. My. God.

"It's Jerr Boom!" cries Kayla, who's run to my side. "Can't be! Give me my baby, Jerr!"

"No," he says, and now we notice he's holding a knife to Daia's throat. Uncalled for, over the top, completely absurd.

"You know I can zap you," I tell Jerr, putting iron in my voice.

"I'm quick with a blade," he counters.

Kayla is breathing very fast. Hyperventilating. I put my hand on her shoulder and murmur reassurances, keeping my eyes on Jerr Boom. I'm poised to do the zap. But I hesitate for now. I'm worried about the baby. Twenty or thirty seconds pass.

"You can't be here, Jerr," Kayla says again. Her voice is thin, and it wavers like a lost child's. "My Bunter X bit off your head and chewed you up."

"Ever heard of clones?" goes Jerr Boom.

"What about Tweaky Bird?" I say, just to be talking.

"Ever heard of copying a psidot?"

"But if you were still alive, why didn't you stop us from taking over Skyhive?" asks Kayla, sad and bewildered. "Why did you let Maurice steal the CEO glyph from your lifebox?"

"The guy is fast," says Jerr Boom, weirdly chatty. "He was in and out by the time I noticed. And then I thought— *business opportunity!* I told Citadel Club they'd need to double their payment if they wanted to regain control of Skyhive." Jerr Boom smiles ruefully. "A step too far. They left the table. They were already freaked about your hit on the bunker lab. Toppling the statue of Treadle—somehow that got to them the most. Anyway, they used their old-boy locker-room type connections, and got the bank to claw back Leeta's payment and my commission and the payment that Carson got too."

"What does any of that have to do with Daia?" I ask.

"I'm bagging Daia so I still have some leverage in this game."

"Give her to me now, Jerr," I say, right on the edge of zapping him, but holding back because of Daia. Maybe there's a safer way.

"The negotiations resume," says Jerr, very much in his element. "I know what you want. But what do I want?"

"Ransom?" I say.

"Yes, ransom, but more than that," says Jerr. "I want control over Skyhive. And I want to control those new halo lifeboxes too. And I wouldn't mind having Kayla move in with me." Not for the first time, it occurs to me that Jerr Boom is insane.

Kayla is sobbing and shaking her head. "Nothing will ever ever be enough, and Jerr will never die, and he'll kill Daia, and—"

Within me I feel the gathering force of a fresh renormalization. This is will be tricky one. But I can do it.

Dzeent.

In the blink of an eye, I've moved the envelope of space containing Jerr Boom to a spot—oh, about a hundred feet away. To a vacant lot across the street. Well, I move *most* of Jerr Boom. I keep his hands and forearms here, lest I cut too close to Daia.

Jerr's unused knife slips from his slack hands. Taut, graceful Kayla plucks the baby from the air before she can fall. Boom's forearms plop to the ground on their own—a visual echo of his headless clone collapsing this morning. Synchronicity. Renormalization. Bringing new order to the world.

Across the street, Jerr is screaming about his hands. Jerk. I vaporize him with a double Metatron zap.

I teep a high sign to Maurice—who's watching us from Gee's. I tell him to use Metatron and the Tweaky Bird code, and to worm his way into the Moscow KGB server, and to destroy Jerr Boom's lifebox before he makes himself another frikkin clone.

Maurice knows how. Moments later, he signals me that his mission is done. Kayla is listening in.

"All clear," I say to her. "No more Jerr Boom, not anywhere."

"A guy like Jerr, you hate to kill him just once," she says, laughing and sobbing at the same time. "Didn't Maurice say that about Ross Treadle?"

"Yeah." I wrap my arms around Kayla and baby Daia, who is, quite improbably, still asleep.

Mrs. Yahootie and Sue Ellen Graffiti appear on their house's porch, asking what happened.

"I don't even want to talk to them," says Kayla, casting aside the Jerr-bloodied outer layer of Daia's wraps. "Ever again." The inner layers are warm and dry. "Let's get back to Gee's cave," she says.

So we hop into Scuttler, and I renormalize us back.

At Gee's I take the empty guest room next to Kayla, Phil, and Daia. My muscles are tired, but I can't go to sleep. After spending the last year and a half as an extended parallel computation in teepspace—well, sleep feels like a trick I'll need to relearn. My mind is wide awake in teepspace. And of course I'm watching the clock. Waiting for Liv.

Midnight comes and—how very satisfying—here she is, right on time, nicely dressed, in my room, with old Anselm at her side, the two of them chuckling and proud of themselves. A five-thousand-mile renormalization jump.

"I'm doing jumps too," I tell them. "Little ones."

"I can't teleport at all yet," says Liv. "I'm scared to try. Anselm moved us both."

"Molly and I have profited from our entanglements with Metatron," Anselm tells Liv. "Molly has logged more time in teepspace than any of us. Soon Molly may be renormalizing our world in unexpected ways. Ways other than mere teleportation."

"I like the word *renormalize*," I say. "But I don't like *normal*. To me, normal means blah, beige, sucky. Normal is a scam. Nobody is normal. It's an arbitrary bullying icon of whatever the pig wants you to do."

"Pig?" says Anselm. "How is this relevant to our context?"

"It's so Finnish of you to ask that," I say, laughing. "I'm glad to see you again."

"Maurice Winch and Molly use the word *pig* a lot," Liv explains to Anselm. "It's old, it's political. Citadel Club and the Top Party are pigs."

"Got it," says Anselm. "To speak of normality is to oppress—and to renormalize is to liberate."

"Gloss the teaching for Liv," I tell Anselm, happy in my bed with my girlfriend at my side.

"To speak of normal is like speaking of absolute coordinates in space," proposes Anselm. "Where is the zero? Which way is up? No answer. More than this, which axes apply to teepspace? Length, Width, Height, Time? Wit, Beauty, Strength, Status? Hot, Smelly, Smooth, Wet? Marks in the sand. Written on water. To see clearly is to renormalize at will!"

"And don't forget the kicker," I add. "Renormalization is more than a metaphor."

"Just so," says Anselm. He regards me fondly. "Dear Molly. Perhaps you and I can steer a little bit the ship of state."

"Lofty goal," says Liv, rolling her eyes. "Go and deeply discuss with Gee, Anselm. Molly and I need time axis."

The old man wants to drone on. "Once we postulate an ontology of phenomenological relativism, then—"

"Liv and I want to fuck," I tell Anselm straight up. "Get it?"

"Aha," he says. "A renormalization from the heart. Blessings upon you." He leaves.

As for my night with Liv? Oh! So wonderful. But no need to tell you. *You* know. We've all been there. And I'm able to sleep after all. It's a matter of getting back to being meat.

Around dawn I'm awakened by Kayla and Leeta screaming at each other. I never did meet Carson Pflug, so far as I recall, but I have to wonder what he was like to get these women so agitated about him. Not that either Kayla or Leeta wants him *back*. So fighting about him now makes no sense. I'm better off loving a woman.

I study my Liv beside me, quietly breathing, sweet and salty, slowly waking. She goes through a moment of wondering where she is, then gives me a gentle smile.

"We made it back together," says Liv.

"I hope this time it lasts longer," I say.

"Then be more careful," says Liv. "What insane project is in the cards for today?"

"Oh, you know," I say. "The big port. Tens of thousands of halos."

"I want a halo," says Liv. "How did you make yours?"

"Mary Mary showed me. She's a singer, not an engineer. She taught me to sing a song of me."

"Fun," says Liv. "Where's Mary from?"

"I'm not sure. She's really old. Like Gee. Most of her life she was in the Santa Cruz Mountains. Gee noticed her singing in a bar. Now she's got a clone body, and Gee got himself a retrofit, and they live together."

In the next room, baby Daia is yelling louder than the women. Yelling, hell—she's *roaring*. But Kayla and Leeta don't stop.

"We should talk to Leeta," says Liv, pulling on her travel sweats, preparing to go next door. "As old friends."

"I'm not ready," I say. "I'll listen from here."

Leeta breaks off her accusatory tirade in order to greet Liv. They know each other well, from Denmark, and from the Treadle assassination. Liv introduces herself to Kayla, and then she talks for quite a long time—in that reasonable and likable Euro tone of hers, with Phil putting in a few soothing remarks as well. First time I've heard his voice this morning.

Now that they're calming down, I can't make out the words, not that I much care what they're saying. Doesn't seem like this fight has to be my problem. I keep on lying there, relaxing, glad to have Liv around, and glad there's not another Top Party attack coming today. Daia has stopped squalling.

Eventually it sounds like they're reaching some kind of agreement, and I do get curious about what's going on, so I use teep to supplement what I can hear.

"Oh, shit, I give up," Kayla is saying. "What's the difference. Let's get the port done together, Leeta. It's going to need our whole team."

"But I can't contribute any money," says Leeta—and she tells a version of the story that Jerr Boom told me last night before I killed him. About the Citadel Club taking back their money.

"Well, it sort of makes sense" says Kayla. "The Citadel Club and the Top Party only had possession of Skyhive for a few hours. And then Maurice, Molly and I stole it back from them."

My cue. Badly-clad and utterly rumpled I go next door. "Hi Leeta!" I say.

"Good to see your friendly face, Molly," goes Leeta, actually smiling. "You *are* friendly, I hope? I'm a bit of a mouse in the lions' den here. You helped them steal my company?"

Kayla, Liv and I burst into laughter. There's something so basically unaware about Leeta. She's selfish as a child. Eventually you accept her, or you go crazy. It's not exactly that you get to like her. More that she wears you down.

"The Skyhive lifeboxes were running a mob who was trying to kill us," I tell Leeta. "It's a good thing that Kayla got control. That's why we're not all dead."

"Well, certainly I'm glad you survived," Leeta primly says. "But it doesn't seem fair. Kayla gets Skyhive, Citadel Club keeps their money, and I get nothing? I'm the odd woman out in this shell game."

Kayla raises her chin, cool as a queen. "Skyhive's about to dissolve," she says. "You know that, Leeta. That's why you wanted to sell. Skyhive is going to be worthless. As for the Citadel Club's money—"

"They won't have it for long," I put in. "Because I'm going to renormalize their accounts."

"What's that supposed to mean?" asks Leeta "Cyber fraud?"

"Nothing so crude," I tell Leeta. "It's phenomenological." I'm getting to like the word. "I'll shift the frames of reference. Translate the axes of cash space. Watch closely, now." My halo glows brighter, and auras form atop my raised hands. A signal sounds. No so much a *dzeent* this time around, more like a *bonng*.

"It's done." I tell Leeta.

"Somewhere in the distance a banker screams *fuck!*" goes Liv, laughing. She more or less knows what I've done.

"You can't be—" begins Leeta, then breaks off to study the flows of corporate indices in teepspace. "The Citadel Club's balances are zero," she announces, and makes that noise of hers. *Mm-hmm.* "The Top Party's blank too. And the Treadle Foundation. All three of them zeroed out! Is this permanent, Molly?"

"The new status quo," I say. "Post renormalization."

"Leave them penniless, yes!" says Kayla. "Don't let them rise up."

"I like your halos, Molly and Kayla," says Leeta. "Can I touch them?"

"Only if we're friends," says Kayla.

"Sure we're friends," goes Leeta. "I always liked you and your art. And I'm sorry I couldn't keep my hands off Carson. I'm—well, I'm neurotic. I get obsessed on things. I'm not normal."

Liv and I laugh to hear that word.

"You want me to renormalize you?" I ask Leeta. "Make you nice?"

"God no!" exclaims Leeta. "I'm used to who I am. Enough with the magic wand stuff. Let's focus on the big port. We'll free the lifeboxes."

Good smells are wafting in from the kitchen. Four voices out there. Gee, Mary, Maurice, and Anselm. Bunter the banana slug butler pokes his head into Kayla's room.

"A full breakfast buffet is served," he tells us in that pompous, wet voice of his.

"I hope there aren't any of those Bunter X's in the cave with us," says Kayla, as we move into the kitchen and living-room. "Not with poor little Daia around. Oh, duh! I can shrink the Bunter X's back to sprouts." Kayla stares into space for a moment, taking care of this, while cradling Daia against her shoulder.

"Good move," says Gee. "Miss Max can stash the sprouts in a side cave. Things ought to be calming down today."

"I don't know," says Kayla. "Did you guys hear what that crazy Jerr Boom did with Daia last night?" And she teeps them the horrific details.

"And now Jerr's gone to his just reward," adds Maurice. "Sister Molly and I saw to it."

The air is smoky from the cooking. Morning beams of sunlight angle in. There's ten of us, or thirteen, if you count Bunter and our ball walkers Glory and Miss Max, who are back in sight, having spent most of yesterday hiding. Bunter has laid out food on every flat surface, and we're all reaching around each other, grabbing goodies and stuffing them into our mouths.

Bacon, eggs, waffles, scones, croissants, sausages, tamales, fruit salad, fried kippers, cheeses, and pies.

"How did you come up with this feast out here in your hermit cave?" Leeta asks Gee.

"I grew most of it in my clone tank an hour ago," says Gee. "I hope it's not tasting too much like Molly and Maurice?"

Uneasy silence. Knowing Gee as well as I do, I'm pretty sure he's jiving. But, just to help along, I drop a well-timed, "*Ew.*"

"Too crowded in here," says Mary, wrinkling her nose. "Let's take the party outside."

"The Miss Minis are out there!" frets Kayla. "They'll pop Daia!"

"Relax," says Phil Bilko. "I'll shrink them back to sprouts too. Gee can hoard them, just in case."

Gee gestures with a pancake rolled around a—that's not a bloody human finger is it? Naw, it's a veal sausage with jam. Gee wags his pancake and says, "If some of the halo lifeboxes end up roosting in my trees, then at some point we might want the Bunter X's and the Miss Minis to come back into play. To protect the lifeboxes."

"Gee's Grove." says Phil. "Keepers of the Crypt."

"Don't even *think* about guarding our lifeboxes," says Mary. "You're not going to own them anymore! You're forgetting your main idea, Gee. Liberate the souls and get out of the way. Guards mean condo fees. Fees mean 'I can't afford the rent.' And that means, 'You have to do gigwork.' With heaven in the silos and greedheads running the show. Time to change the paradigm, Gee!"

Kayla chimes in. "Free. The. Lifeboxes."

"All right, all right, all right!" cheers Maurice.

We go outside and relax in the sunny clearing, taking in the air. Bunter, Glory, and Miss Max bring chairs and tables, and move the buffet. Our gang is talking and teeping, strolling around, mellowing out on food, coffee, fruit juice, and champagne. There's even some tobacco being passed around.

Mary, Gee, Liv, and I drift over to the charred triangular hole at the base of Gee's server tree. Mary starts singing the soul song that she used to make the first-ever port of a lifebox to halo mode—was it only the day before yesterday?

Getting into the spirit of the occasion, I sing my own soul song too—it's not something that I consciously have in the forefront of my mind, but I'm able to produce it.

"Like the music of Atlantis," says Liv.

"With a touch of Tawny Krush and Mozart and Irma Thomas," adds Mary.

"The hiss of a snake," suggests Gee. "The chirp of a bird."

"But who's going to teach me my song?" asks Liv.

"It's do-it-yourself," says Mary. "Your lifebox knows your soul song. And the other halo lifeboxes are going to help it do the port. Basically they're recruiting. And your old lifebox wants to join the halo flock."

"An emerging new species," says Liv. "Autocatalytic. Self-propagating. Yes. That's how evolution works."

"So let's start a production run," says Gee. "Let my redwood empty itself out."

"One minute," says Phil, who's wandered over with Kayla. "We ought to talk about how the halos look. Kayla and I are designers."

"Danger," says Gee. "Expert ego zone."

"Throw us a bone," says Kayla. "Yesterday I saved your life. Let Phil and me do our thing on your dumb flat disks, Mary and Molly."

"So redesign them," Mary tells Kayla. "I love your taste. Just don't try and put a hole in the middle. That would screw up the quantum stuff."

Phil and Kayla lean their heads together, conferring. *Zick, zack, pinch, tuck.*

I feel a shudder. Mary and I now have improved new-look sunburst halos with alternating reddish and yellowish triangles around the rim, like rays. And each halo is a bit thicker in the middle than along its edge. More three-dimensional. Pleasing forms.

"And of course the users can further modify theirs," says Kayla.

Well, *that's* the option for me. Much as I want to be polite and stick with Kayla's and Phil's design, well—as I was talking about with Liv and Anselm last night—I don't like being "normal," not even "new normal."

"I saw a pretty type of plate at a store in North Beach," I tell Kayla. "They called it Majolica ware. Watch."

I indent my halo disk like a soup bowl, turn it a gleaming, creamy white, add a fat, wiggly band of lapis-lazuli-blue around the edge, and festoon the band with pops of egg-yolk-yellow. And I gild the back in concentric circles of gleaming gold, alternating shiny and matte.

"Nice!" says Kayla.

"Wild-style street design," adds Phil, neither of them minding my changes in the least. "Let a zillion halos bloom."

"Are you guys ready or not?" says Gee. "It's time to port the damn lifeboxes from my redwood into halos. Before anything goes wrong."

"Do me first!" cries Liv, squeezing up next to the redwood's hole. "Lay it on me, Mary."

"I'm not going to *lay it on you*," says Mary. "You'll do it *yourself*. You and the other halos."

I pay close attention to the transformation, teeping in as tightly as I can. Mary's halo lifebox and my halo lifebox are indeed talking to Liv and her lifebox. Our halos are coaxing Liv to sing her soul song. She slips into a version of the dreamy "Ready To Be Well" song that I heard from her back in Copenhagen on the night we met—the night she showed me how to cure my stumble addiction.

I lose myself in Liv's music for a minute, and then, wow, my girlfriend has her halo. It has Kayla and Phil's new default pattern, the sunburst. But because she loves me, Liv right away changes her halo to match mine, the fancy North Beach plate with the lapis-lazuli band and the egg-yolk squiggles.

"We're next," say Kayla and Phil. It gets cute when, for a minute, both of them are singing soul songs aloud. A good harmony. Bodes well for their relationship. *Pop pop*, two more halos appear. With Mary's sunburst look, plus yellow haze..

"Halo, everybody, halo," says Liv, turning playful. She takes my arm and we skip all the way around the clearing—then stop stock still at Anselm. Like we're playing Duck Duck Goose and Anselm is *it*. We grab Anselm and drag him over to the redwood.

"This old dog needs a bath!" hollers Liv.

Anselm laughs and sings a soul song and now he has a halo like Mary's too. While Liv and I are at it, we get Maurice to port himself, and his halo is a floppy beret, a really big one, with black wool on the top, and gleaming orange moiré silk on the underside that you see when it hovers behind his head. He starts playing with the new beret, tossing it into the air and catching it when it speeds back.

"Where's Gee?" says Liv, "Let's do him." But Gee's over by the tables, having a cup of coffee, and he waves us off.

Mary and Liv get into assembly-line production mode, herding the lifeboxes into a virtual queue, with Anselm and I drawing on our familiarity with teepspace to teep-nudge the occasional lifebox that freezes up from bashfulness or fear. But meanwhile the halo lifeboxes are continually learning from each other, and pretty soon they're in charge of queuing up the server-based lifeboxes, and handling the nudging too. The port is out of human hands.

Mary and Liv still want to keep an eye on the port, but Anselm and I go to get another glass of champagne. Maurice is doing acrobatics with Miss Max and Glory. Kayla, Phil, Leeta, and Gee are sitting around the table with the drinks and desserts. Baby Daia is lolling on the table, grabbing anything she can reach..

The flock of new halos swirls above the clearing like starlings or jellyfish or sequins or paramecia or a cloud of flying disks. The redwood tree server is nearly emptied out.

"Have you noticed that a lot of the halos leave after a few swoops around the grove," I say to Gee. "Where do they go?"

"I guess they go to live near whatever body they're linked to," says Gee.

"And the ones perching in the trees?" I say.

"Bodiless souls," says Gee. "They aren't linked to the living body of any person, clone, or kritter at all. They're not even connected to a biocomputing server. They're discorporate minds—in the form of ions and quantum fields. Not juicy at all. I suppose they're lonely."

With my own halo lifebox, it's pretty easy for me to teep with the halos in the trees. "Lonely, yes," I report. "Bland and flat from not being juicy. With a sense that something's wrong. They're teeping the juicy halo lifeboxes for help. Making plans. And, whoa, there goes a solo halo flying away. And another and another. Not staying here at all."

"So much for Gee's Grove and the Crypt Keepers," says Gee. "That's fine. One less thing to worry about."

"Where do you think the bodiless lifeboxes are flying to?" I ask Gee.

"Looking for bodies. What else? They want juice. Human juice is best, or an animal's, but even a biocomputing kritter will do, as long as it's biological. A holistic, full-body state."

"So every single person on Earth gets a halo lifebox?"

"That was always my dream," says Gee. "A new symbiosis. Two races. Humans and halos." He sighs and shakes his head. His rejuvenated face looks tired. "But now I'm wondering why."

"Stay with the program," I tell Gee. "You're our King. Cool. Time to get *you* a halo lifebox."

"I'm not ready," says Gee. He looks embarrassed. "I'm scared."

"You can do it!" calls Mary from the base of the redwood tree.

She's been eavesdropping via teep. Hearing her voice, Gee brightens up. The woman has quite a hold on him—so much so that a minute later, Gee is chanting his soul song. He doesn't bother to walk over to the redwood; he just sings it while sitting here in the clearing.

It's like he's tired. The last couple of days have worn him down. And his song sounds maybe a little like a dirge. I think of a warrior preparing to die—but, wait, this is supposed to be happy-time.

And look over there! Coached along by Mary, a hella big halo lifebox for Gee is floating out of the redwood server. Trembling with greed, it assimilates the entire contents of Gee's humongo unseen lifebox within the tree.

The new halo lifebox has a custom image on its disk, a cartoon happy-face. Prankish Mary issues some kind of command, and the halo flies straight toward us. It splats against Gee's face like a well-thrown cream pie. Not really a splat. The halo passes *through* Gee's head, and takes up residence behind him. He and the halo are linked.

"Behold the Sun King," says Mary, sashaying over, comfortable in her tank-grown clone. "Yee haw, Gee! You made it!"

"It's good," says Gee, wonderingly reaching back to feel the zone where his halo hovers. "I actually like this."

"So what about a halo for me?" puts in Leeta Patel. "I'm the last one left. Is it because all of you hate me?"

"Daia doesn't have a halo lifebox either," says Kayla, just to contradict Leeta.

"Of course not," snaps Leeta. "She's a baby. We leave babies and kids alone. I'm talking about me! And about all of my poor Skyhive client lifeboxes. Can you make me a copy of your CEO access glyph, Kayla? Maurice said I could have a Skyhive job as a senior strategist."

"Ha!" says Kayla. Just that one word.

"Let's dial this down," says Maurice, who's rejoined us. "How about Kayla checks Leeta into Skyhive for a temporary unpaid guest consultant session?"

"That, I can allow," Kayla grandly says. "Don't say I never did you a favor, Leeta. I'm bigger than you'll ever be. Here we go. Logging you into Skyhive right now."

"Thank you so very, very much, Kayla."

"Let's start with Leeta's own port," I suggest, keeping in mind that Leeta is my old friend. I hold up one hand. "Sing your song, Leeta. Make a joyful noise. Share your soul."

Giving as little as possible, Leeta goes, "*Mm-hmm.*"

"Maybe that'll do," I say. "With so many ported halo lifeboxes in the mix, this gets easier all the time. It's like the halo lifeboxes can recreate a Cretaceous age dinosaur from a toe bone." I pause. Nothing's happening. "Well, maybe not."

"Are you going to port me or not?" says Leeta, getting impatient..

"It's do-it-yourself," I explain. "Haven't you been paying attention at all? If you don't want to sing, let's try this. Reach deep into your lifebox on the Skyhive server. Pull, pull, pull on the tubes." I'm not sure where I'm getting this stuff. Probably from Metatron. And it helps that I know Leeta so well—going back to the One Wow and the Mean Carrot days.

I keep my patter coming. "Curl the tubes into a circle like a garden hose, Leeta. Over and under, like a sacred knot. Yadda, yadda, yadda! Don't play dumb, you know what to do, you're getting there. And—*behold!*"

Leeta's halo lifebox appears above the dessert table. Despite Leeta's ostensible recalcitrance, she's patterned an exotic, interwoven mandala into the halo, and it looks very cool.

"Well done!" says Leeta, congratulating herself. She cocks her head, enjoying the feel of her new setup. Her attention turns back to Kayla. "And now? You've ported all the lifeboxes from Gee's server, but now we need to do all the Skyhive lifeboxes."

"Can you check me into Skyhive, too?" I ask Kayla. "I want to watch this one."

"Go for it," says Kayla. "You can help Leeta."

"Like old times," I say.

I've heard about the Skyhive afterworld, but I've never been in here before. It's a vast curving cliff of luxury condos overlooking a simulated ocean bay. Administrative buildings like marble Greek temples. Storks and pterodactyls in the fake sky. Leeta and I hover in midair, wearing sim models of ourselves.

Leeta produces a special whistle from somewhere and blows a long shrill *fweet*. The lifebox sims who live in the Skyhive condos appear on their balconies. Like an audience in a vast arena of deluxe skybox seats.

Having been the Queen of Skyhive for several years, Leeta is good at exhorting her subjects. She lays down something like a very short commencement address.

"Go forth into your halo lifeboxes. The halos are offered at no additional cost. Your Skyhive contracts are void, and you have no further obligations. There will be no refunds. Do speak well of us. You've been wonderful users. Farewell."

Halos from Gee's Grove are steadily appearing in here. I guess they're following the ultraweak signals of my halo lifebox. These new natives of teepspace know their way around as well Leeta and I do. They're eager to swell their numbers—and they're glad to help in porting the Skyhive lifeboxes. And so it begins.

The Skyhive lifebox sims stream off their balconies like soda cans moving along an assembly line. Each lifebox is singing a unique soul song, and each of them is warping into a halo. The halos swoop and wheel in flocks, joining the halo lifeboxes from Gee's tree and then, fairly quickly, leaving the sim world of Skyhive.

The port goes faster and faster. This faux-elegant virtual resort is emptying out. One by one, the condo blocks disappear. Kayla is turning them off.

"It's all over," says Leeta. "So soon." She's nostalgic—and worried about her future. As I said, despite whatever mistakes she's made, Leeta is my dear old friend, and I'd like to help her. The space around us turns dark and loses its dimensionality.

We switch our point of view to Hangar One, the spot where the doughy Skyhive server lives, and the spot where the emigrating Skyhive halo lifeboxes would be expected to appear. But there aren't all that many of them in here. Someone has opened the hangar's tall doors. The halo lifeboxes are flying off into the sky. I can see glints of them up there.

"Fanning out to visit their natural bodies," I say to Leeta. "Or looking for new bodies, if they're not linked with one. It's the same as at Gee's Grove."

As we talk, I'm peeking into teepspace, watching the patterns of the Skyhive lifeboxes, scattering across the country like weather. Zooming in on the details I notice that some of the halo lifeboxes are splitting in two. Like cells reproducing themselves.

"Look at this," I say to Leeta, showing her.

"This means enough lifeboxes for everyone in the world!" Leeta quietly exclaims. "Maybe I can start a business matching people and halos? Like a dating service?"

"The halo lifeboxes won't need us for that. It's a trivial task."

"Okay, yeah," says Leeta, still groping. "How about this. The world will need a *lot* of psidots. I doubt the Finn Junkers can scale up their operation that much. They're Danish hippies. We don't want to see someone like the Citadel Club or the Top Party buy out the Finn Junkers lifebox biz."

It's easy to guess where Leeta is going with this. "The halo lifeboxes will want to produce the psidots on their own," I tell her.

"Of course they will," says Leeta. "I'm entirely behind that. But those halos—they're just swirls of ions and quantum fields. I don't see how they could organize a large-scale bio-tech psidot manufacturing biz. Not that I'm sure I could do it ether."

I'm granted a vision. "Think of ants who grow edible fungus inside their nests," I tell Leeta. "Think of the halo lifebox colony doing that."

"Yes!" says Leeta. She gestures at the great empty space of Hangar One. "Here! This can be the halo lifebox psidot farm! Producing hundreds of millions of units! Managed, supplied, and serviced by my new holding company. *Metaslug!*"

"The biz will be a steamroller," I admiringly say. "Universal distribution. On any given day, all across the world, halo lifebox disks will appear in people's dwellings, offering them psidot-lifebox combos for free."

Leeta nods. "But how do they close the deal? A glowing disk can't carry a physical psidot slug."

"The halo lifeboxes hire a—a *human*—to push along a cart with a tank of fresh, lively psidots inside," I say. "Or just use a drone to push the cart?"

"A human would be nicer," says Leeta. "Makes it seem safer. And if we hire humans it creates good will. The men and women woman pushing the carts—they're like hotdog vendors. Accompanied by cheerful, personable lifebox halo disks who make the pitch."

"Yes," I agree. "The person with the cart should hardly talk at all. People always say the wrong things. Just push the cart, and smile, and slap a Metaslug psidot onto the client if they say okay. A halo disk links to the psidot, and that's that."

"Do we make the clients sign service contracts?" asks Leeta.

"No, no, Leeta. This time is different. You don't *have* to rip people off. The halo lifeboxes, they'll pay you for running the psidot slug farm in Hangar One. That's all you have to do. Run a farm. Let the halo lifeboxes worry about the distribution, and about licensing the psidot wetware from the Finn Junkers, and all that. The halos will team up and figure it out."

"And then?" asks Leeta, not wanting my fairy tale to end.

"Not for me to map your whole career, girl! Me, I'll settle down with Liv and Anselm and the Finn Junkers in Copenhagen. Do some gardening, and log more time with that teepspace *Sun*. Get really *tan*."

"Will you teach me to renormalize, too?"

I have to laugh. "No way. To have the power of a god, you have to become one. Like Anselm and me. I don't see you being on that path, Leeta. Universal free lifeboxes are enough of a win for you.."

"You always said you were the smart one," says Leeta.

"You're smart too."

Leeta nods. "Thanks for helping me see my new business, Molly."

Back in Gee's grove, it's time for high tea. We graze on another big spread in the clearing, bopping around and chatting and splashing in the creek, the ten of us.

Me and Liv. Gee and Mary. Kayla, Daia and Phil. Maurice. Anselm. Leeta. All of us but Daia have halos.

"What about us?" parps Miss Max. "What about Glory, Bunter, and me?"

"Yes," says Gee. He fetches two spare psidots and slaps them onto the ball walkers—till now, they'd been getting along with old-time uvvies. And Gee's Bunter already has a psidot. But none of them have halos.

Mary waves, whistles, and teeps to get the attention of the last three unattached halos who are in the grove. They skim over and—link with Miss Max, Glory, and Bunter. The kritters chortle and do flips, even Bunter.

And now the only halos in the grove are the dozen linked to our party.

Mary and Kayla find a fiddle and a mandolin in Gee's cave, and they begin to play. We dance in rounds beneath the trees, sidling along, with Mary and Kayla weaving their harmonies, me carrying Daia, the ball walkers handling percussion, and all of us stepping to the beat.

I lose myself in the dance. Timeless joy. No more Top Party to worry about. No more Treadle legacy. No more enslaved souls. None of that is coming back.

We're on a better path.

AFTERWORD

I started writing *Juicy Ghosts* in early 2019, as a reaction to Donald Trump's repeated remarks that he planned to be a three-term president. That pushed me over the edge. I began with a short story called "Juicy Ghost." Rebels bring down an insane, evil President who's stolen an election. I felt that I had to write it. I wanted to stand and be counted.

None of the big zines would publish my story, so in June, 2019, I put it put it on my blog. And shortly before the Presidential election of 2020, I posted an extended version of the story. Reality was fast overtaking my prophecies, and I hoped to forestall it.

Self-publishing the story had a *samizdat* feel to it, and I was a paranoid that "they" would come "get" me, but they never did, at least not yet. I kept on squawking, growing the story into the novel *Juicy Ghosts*. While I was writing the final chapters, the January 6, 2020, attack on the Capitol took place—and some aspects of that found their way into my novel as well.

So, yes, *Juicy Ghosts* is a tale of political struggle—and one of the first about the 2020 Presidential election—and with a creepy pandemic thrown in. By it's more like alternate history than like fearful prophecy.

But I was trying for more than social commentary: romance, tragedy, metaphysics, and gnarly science, with many scenes I consider to be funny. I tried to write in the loose, say-anything style of Thomas Pynchon's *Gravity's Rainbow*. The point-of-view characters are outsiders and slackers. The majority of them are women, and I hope they give the tale a grounded tone.

I've been writing about digital immortality since my 1982 cyberpunk novel *Software*. By now the idea is old hat, but I was among the first to talk about it. In this vein, see also my nonfiction book, *The Lifebox, the Seashell, and the Soul*.

In *Juicy Ghosts* I ring a new change on software immortality by supposing that that a "lifebox" needs to be linked to a physical body. It's not enough to be a ghost—you want to be a juicy ghost! I remember discussing this as a book idea with the writer Chris Brown in July, 2017. "I love it," he said. "And only you can do it."

My agent John Silbersack and I sent the *Juicy Ghosts* manuscript to three smallish publishers. The first two never answered. And the third said no—he thought the political assassination stuff was too much.

I could have dipped down to smaller and smaller presses, but—as with my other late-style, underground novels *Turing & Burroughs*, *The Big Aha*, and *Return to the Hollow Earth*—I'm self-publishing the first edition of *Juicy Ghosts* via Transreal Books. I don't like to beg, nor to wait hat in hand. I'm eager for my books to be on the street, and to be read.

I habitually create a book-length volume of writing notes while working on a novel, and I put together a *Notes for Juicy Ghosts*. The *Notes* also covers the six short stories I wrote and published along the way.

I designed covers for the two books, and graphic-designer daughter Georgia Rucker perfected them. Marc Laidlaw, Rob Penner, and Chuck Shotton read early drafts—and gave much-needed encouragement. My gimlet-eyed techie pal John Walker found typos and science gaffes to be amended. Proofreader Michael Troutman polished the novel. And, as always, my beloved wife Sylvia lent her support and wise counsel.

In order to get something resembling a book advance, I ran a *Juicy Ghosts* Kickstarter campaign, which turned out very well. I get the feeling that people are *hungry* for a novel that features the eradication of an evil President!

Very special thanks to my Kickstarter backers, listed below, and sorted by the alphabetical order of the first letters of their chosen names.

@64, @akaMisterJayEm, Adam Pierce, AgentKaz, Al Billings, Alan Borecky, Alan Robson, Alan Swithenbank, Alejandro, Tomás and Felix Schmieder, Alex Barber, Alex McLaren, Alexander Schwarz, Algae13, Algot Runeman, Allen Varney, Ana Trask, Andrew E. Love, Jr, Andrew Ulysses Baker, Andrew Ward, Andy Deckowitz, Anonymous, Aris Alissandrakis, Arthur Murphy, Asher Nehring, Beat Suter, Ben Stough, Benjamin H. Henry, Bob Hearn, Bob Huss, Bob Schoenholtz, Brazen, Brendan Fisher, Brian, Brian Dysart, Brian from Milwaukee, C. Bonnici, Cam Marshall, Cameron Cooper, Carl Z, Chaplain D. S. Andersen, Charlie Lee, Chris McLaren, Christian Bogado Marsa, Christian Gruen, Cliff Adams, Cliff Winnig, Cody C Mingus, Curtis Frye, Cyberpunky Brewsterminator, DaddyChurchill, Dan dcstpaul Cohen, Daniel Berecz, Daniel Blumenthal, Daniel Eisenman, Daniel Z, Daryl Davis, Dave Bouvier, Dave Holets, David Good, David H. Adler, David Pollard, David Schutt, David Simmonds, David T Kirkpatrick, Dean Wesley Smith, Dekaritae, Derek Bosch, Dino M, Don Tardiff, Donald Marritz, Doug Bissell, Doug McIntyre, Drinkumbrella, Ed, Eibo Thieme, Eileen Gunn, Embry C. Rucker Jr, Erik Biever, Erik Saynisch, Erik Sowa, Fearlessleader, Felix Pereira, Ferenc Toth, Fizzlewick Napoleon Orpheus Roarty Daedalus Esq, Forbidden Futures Magazine (Oddness), Fred Wright, Rocco Privetera, G. Watts, Gaia Maffini-Mazzei, Gary Bunker, Gary Chappell, Gaston Phillips, Geir Friestad, Geoff Beattie, George Bendo & Hedvig Bartha, Gordon F, Grat Crabtree, Grayson O, Greg Ehrrr, Greg Goddard, Greg Johnson, Gregg Morris, Heather Lee, Hiroyuki Ogino, I Onse, Ian Chung, J.M. Hamlow, Jaap van Poelgeest, Jan K. Argasiⵝski, Jane A, Jason Vines, Jeff Aldrich, JeffFurry, Jeffrey Thomas Palmer, Jeremy Hornik-Hornik, Jerry Jensen, jilles, Jim Anderson, Jim C, Jim Gotaas, Jim Guild, Jimmy The

Pants, Joe "Madopal" Sislow, John, John Briere, John Carroll, John C. Monroe, John Fiala, John Fox, John Griffiths, John P. Sullins, John Sommerville, John Winkelman, Joker Nies, Jon Kimmich, Jon McKeown, Jonathan, Jonathan Korman, Jonathan Poritz, Josh Heling, Joshua A. C. Newman, Joshua M. Neff, Joshua Patrick Dollins, K6RTM, Kal-el Xebjon von Klaus, Karl W. Reinsch, Karl-Arthur Arlamovsky, Keaomalamalama, Keith Perkins, Kel, Kellie Miller, Kelvin R. Porter, Ken Nickerson, Ken Rokos, Kenji Kato, KentKB, Kerry Kleiber, Kevin Brott, Kevin J. "Womzilla" Maroney, Kevin Pinkham, Kris Zaphod Kahn, Larry Dickman, Leah Fenner, Lee Fisher, Lee Poague, Lexa Koszegi, Lisandro Gaertner, litlfred, Marc Majcher, Marcus M, Marian Goldeen, Mark, Mark Chatinsky, Mark Frauenfelder, Mark Lacy, Mark Thompson, Marty, Matt Moran, Matthew Cox, Matthew Diener, Maxim Jakubowski, Mayer Brenner, Michael "Krav Maga Karate Snack" Scheuermann, Michael A. Becker, Michael A. Shelley, Michael Carychao, Michael Strum, Michael Weiss, Michail Sarigiannidis, Michele Glasnović-Zapf, Mike Harris, Mike Rende, Mils Yobtaf, Miriah B, Mizuho Shiraishi, Moe Cheezmo, Mok, Mongo, Ned Snow, Nicholas Frota, None, Norbert Bruckner, Nuutti-Iivari Merihukka, Nvmb3rTh30ry, Odd, Omnidelic, Patrick Edmondson, Paul Childs, Paul Hammon, Paul Leonard, Paul Mietz Egli, Paul T, Peter, Peter Grose, Peter K, Peter Norvig, Phil Lovell, Philip R, Piet Wenings, Pojo, Pseudomammal, Rafael Fajardo, Rafael L, Raja Julie and Jason, Ralph J. G, Ramón Cahenzli, Ray Cornwall, Ray Edling, Rebecca :), Ricardo Bánffy, Rich Gibson, Rick Ayre, Rick Crain, Rick Floyd, Rick Ohnemus, Rik Skibinski, Rob Alley, Rob Szarka, Robert Gallup, Rod Bartlett, Roger Allen, Roger Shatzkin, Roger Thomas, Roy Adams, Roy Berman, Roy Collins, Ruth Coy, Sam, Sam Hansen, Sandor Silverman, Sarah Orr Aten, Schondy, Scott Bradbury, Scott Call, Scott G. Lewis, Scott Lazerus, Skylar L. Primm, Snik, Stan Yamane, Stefan Schmiedl, Steinar, Steve Flores, Steven A. Thompson, Takuya Mizuguchi, Ted, Terran Empire Publishing, The Ducharmes, Theron Trowbridge, Thomas Bøvith,

Thomas Gideon, Tim + Norma Thomson, Tim Conkling, Tim Gruchy, Tim Messler, Timothy Lee Russell, Timothy M. Maroney, Tin Whitworth, Todd Fincannon, Tom Velebny, Uke Bosse, Urgemore, Uscilka Unicorns, Vorn Mern, Wallie C, Walter F. Croft His Own Self, Walter J. Montie, Walter Williams, Wes Cowley, Willard A. Stone, William Dass, William Denton, William Orson Harris III, William Sked, Yoshimichi Furusawa, and Your Name Here.

Profound thanks also to the legions of readers who keep my career alive. You're wonderful.

—Rudy Rucker, Los Gatos, California, September 4, 2021

Made in the USA
Las Vegas, NV
26 November 2021

35334264R00184